THE OCCUPATION TRILOGY

THE OCCUPATION TRILOGY

LA PLACE DE L'ÉTOILE · THE NIGHT WATCH · RING ROADS

Patrick Modiano

Translated from the French by Caroline Hillier,
Patricia Wolf, and Frank Wynne

BLOOMSBURY

NEW YORK · LONDON · OXFORD · NEW DELHI · SYDNEY

Bloomsbury USA
An imprint of Bloomsbury Publishing Plc

1385 Broadway
New York
NY 10018
USA

50 Bedford Square
London
WC1B 3DP
UK

www.bloomsbury.com

BLOOMSBURY and the Diana logo are trademarks of Bloomsbury Publishing Plc

This book is supported by the
Institut français (Royaume-Uni) as
part of the Burgess program
(www.frenchbooknews.com)

INSTITUT
FRANÇAIS
ROYAUME-UNI

First published in Great Britain 2015
First U.S. edition published 2015

Preface © William Boyd, 2015

ISBN: TPB: 978-1-63286-372-0
ePub: 978-1-63286-373-7

Library of Congress Cataloging-in-Publication Data has been applied for.

2 4 6 8 10 9 7 5 3

Typeset by Integra Software Services Pvt. Ltd.
Printed and bound in the U.S.A. by Thomson-Shore Inc., Dexter, Michigan

To find out more about our authors and books visit www.bloomsbury.com. Here you will find extracts, author
interviews, details of forthcoming events, and the option to sign up for our newsletters.

Bloomsbury books may be purchased for business or promotional use. For information on bulk purchases
please contact Macmillan Corporate and Premium Sales Department at specialmarkets@macmillan.com.

CONTENTS

INTRODUCTION

As our journey into the future continues – the present moment drifting away, our own biographies lengthening, our pasts receding, inexorably, quietly becoming 'history' in the distance – so certain aspects of those retreating eras seem to come more sharply into focus and claim our attention. The longer view allows us to see these features of the recent past as truly defining characteristics of those decades that we've lived through.

Take 1968, for example, nearly fifty years ago now, the year that the first novella in Patrick Modiano's *Occupation Trilogy* was published. In 1968 I was running my school's film society. I decided to conclude my tenure of the role with a controversial double bill and duly screened Alain Resnais's *Last Year in Marienbad* (1961) and Federico Fellini's *Juliet of the Spirits* (1965). I confess the choice was entirely pretentious, a consequence of pure sixth-form pseudo-intellectual bravado, but, while I was genuinely baffled by *Marienbad*, I was haunted by *Juliet of the Spirits* – for reasons that defy cogent analysis – and the film remains similarly haunting today, after several further viewings over the years. Something about those two films sums up for me the cultural mood of the 1960s – or at least one aspect of the cultural mood of that time: they are wilfully difficult to understand; they play fast and loose with chronology and ratiocination; the surreal seems more pertinent and familiar than the real. But in those days this seemed intensely stimulating and exciting – we were drawn to an art that occupied the mysterious, the vague and the allusive rather than one that conventionally confronted the blunt realities of the here and now.

Patrick Modiano's three short novels – *La Place de l'Étoile*, *The Night Watch* (originally published in English as *Night Rounds*) and *Ring Roads* – resonate with that same knowing liberty and cool audacity and, as a result, Modiano became a modish and cult author at the time. Reading these novels anew for this introduction, I was still struck forcibly by this 1960s free-wheeling, free-form disregard for the well-constructed solidities of the traditional novel. Their tone, their style and their values are very much creatures of the time of their writing.

But Modiano's trio are not just convenient cultural touchstones. There is an element in them, underlying the careful obscurantism and the nonchalant moodiness, that gives a deeper resonance. It's important to remember that Modiano was exceptionally young when they were published: he was twenty-two when *La Place de l'Étoile* appeared in 1968. *The Night Watch* arrived a year later and he was only twenty-six when the last of the trilogy, *Ring Roads*, emerged in 1972. They are bravura, young-man's novels, particularly the first, which announced the advent of a precocious literary talent and star. All three are short, each just over a hundred pages, and they gain their collective title from the connection with *L'Occupation* – France's enduringly bitter and divisive subjugation by Nazi Germany during 1941–44.

La Place d'Étoile is the most frenetic. It's as if the young Modiano had gathered together every controversial and combustible issue of twentieth-century French history and literature – and whatever else took his fancy – and thrown them together in this rambunctious tale of a Jewish collaborator called Raphael

Schlemilovitch. Anti-Semitism, the Gestapo, Dreyfus, Auschwitz, *Action Francaise*, collaboration, betrayal and bad faith all contribute to the neurotic picaresque of this episodic and still startling, shocking novel. If, today, Michel Houellebecq is considered the bad-boy of contemporary French literature then he must have learned a lot from *La Place de l'Étoile*: blatant offence is freely given, taboos are blithely violated and no sacred cow is sacrosanct as we explore the fraught psychic landscape of Raphael Schlemilovitch, Jew turned Nazi sympathiser. He is, of course, the ultimate unreliable narrator. At one stage he fantasises about seducing Eva Braun and talks of his meetings with Hitler. When, at the novel's end, he wakes up – entirely improbably – on the couch in Freud's Vienna consulting rooms, everything we have read before is thrown into stark, sceptical relief.

Both *The Night Watch* and *Ring Roads* also deal with the Occupation. *The Night Watch* is the story of a young French collaborator instructed to break into and betray a resistance cell. In this novel, the narrator is unnamed and the point of view more subjective. There are long passages of unparagraphed internal monologue interspersed with lyrics from popular pre-war songs as Modiano confronts France's guilty ambivalence about the Occupation years. In *La Place de l'Étoile* Schlemilovitch reflects that 'There were many of us who slept with Germany and the memory of it is sweet'. In a significant way this assertion is the bedrock of all of Modiano's fiction since his debut in 1967, a fact highlighted by the Nobel committee when they awarded him the literature prize in 2014.

Modiano was born in 1945 and has written of his own struggles to come to terms with what occurred in France during the years immediately prior to his birth. His father, a Sephardic Jew of Italian origin, seems to have been involved in the wartime black market and some form of petty gangsterism but never told his son anything of his life between 1941 and 1944. Therefore it is not surprising that fathers and father-figures proliferate in all three novels, notably in *Ring Roads*, the most terse and oblique of the three. It concerns a son's quest for his father, a man somehow confined in a strange commune in a village near the forest of Fontainebleau. Modiano has a great facility for topographical description, both evocative and precise, but in *Ring Roads* everything else is deliberately blurred, including the historical period. Only at the end does it become apparent that the central character's search for his missing father is taking place during the war. The encounter is unsatisfactory – the father has no recollection of his son, while the son's abiding memory is of his father's attempt to kill him by pushing him under the wheels of an underground train, some ten years before the events of the novel begin.

There is a change of style in *Ring Roads* – noticeably shorter sentences, a clipped objectivity. Modiano was classified by critics as having joined the ranks of the *nouveau roman* – but, whatever the novel's mannered obliquities, the same historical concerns run beneath the surface. The novel has an epigraph from Rimbaud: 'If only I had a past at some other point in French history. But no, nothing.' This, you might imagine, is Modiano's private plaint: condemned by the date of his birth and the shady wartime career of his father to spend his literary working life exploring the consequence of *L'Occupation*, *Collaboration* and *Résistance* – such as it was. He has often been a brave and solitary voice – what happened between 1941 and 1944 is not a subject that is raised in France with much enthusiasm, even today.

However, perhaps Modiano's most controversial move in airing and confronting the unspoken subject of the widespread passive and active collaboration of the French population in the Second World War occurred just after the publication of *Ring Roads* when, working with the director Louis Malle, he wrote the screenplay of the film *Lacombe, Lucien* (1974). It is effectively the fourth panel of the trilogy, making it a tetralogy, and the light it casts back on the three novels is revealing. *Lacombe, Lucien* is the story of a simple country boy who tries to join the Resistance and is rejected, so guilelessly enlists in the French Gestapo instead. It's a powerful and disturbing film precisely because it makes no moral judgements. Lucien seems an entirely thoughtless collaborator – without conscience or venality or any sense of guilt. It shows just how easy it is – in circumstances such as those of 1941–44 – to become complicit.

In an aside in *La Place de l'Étoile* – a novel steeped in French literature, by the way, for all its modernity – Modiano facetiously lists the clothes to wear and the ambience to arrange in order to read certain classics of the French literary canon there by enhancing the experience. You don't need to put on your beads and flares and listen to Françoise Hardy to relish *The Occupation Trilogy* fully, but curiously and most unusually – usually it's the other way round – your reading of these remarkable and seminal novels will be immeasurably enhanced by a viewing of *Lacombe, Lucien*, before or after.

William Boyd
London, June 2015

La Place de l'Étoile

For Rudy Modiano

In June 1942, a German officer approaches a young man and says, 'Excuse me, monsieur, where is the Place de l'Étoile?'
The young man gestures to the left side of his chest.
(Jewish story)

I

This was back when I was frittering away my Venezuelan inheritance. Some talked of nothing but my beautiful youth and my black curls, others called me every name under the sun. Rereading an article about me written by Léon Rabatête in a special edition of *Ici la France*: ' . . . how long do we have to suffer the antics of Raphäel Schlemilovitch? How long can this Jew brazenly flaunt his neuroses and his paroxysms with impunity from le Touquet to Cap d'Antibes, from le Baule to Aix-les-Bains? Once again, I ask: how long can dagos of his ilk be allowed to insult the sons of France? How long must we go on washing our hands of this Jewish scum . . . ?' Writing about me in the same newspaper, Doctor Bardamu spluttered: ' . . . Schlemilovitch? . . . Ah, the foul-smelling mould of the ghettos! . . . that shithouse lothario! . . . runt of a foreskin! . . . Lebano-ganaque scumbag! . . . rat-a-tat . . . wham! . . . Consider this the Yiddish gigolo . . . this rampant arsefucker of Aryan girls! . . . this brazenly Negroid abortion! . . . frenzied Abyssinian young nabob! . . . Help! . . . La-di-da-di-da! . . . rip his guts out . . . hack his balls off! . . . Preserve the Doctor from this spectacle! . . . in the name of God, crucify him! . . . this foreign trash with his filthy cocktails . . . this Jewboy with his international palaces! . . . his orgies *made in Haifa*! . . . Cannes! . . . Davos! . . . Capri *e tutti quanti*! . . . vast devoutly Hebrew brothels! . . . Preserve us from this circumcised fop! . . . from his salmon-pink Maserati! . . . his Sea of Galilee yachts! . . . his Sinai neckties! . . . may his Aryan slave girls rip off his prick! . . . with their perfect French teeth . . . their delicate little hands . . . gorge out his eyes! . . . death to the Caliph! . . . Revolution in the Christian harem! . . . Quick! . . .

Quick! . . . refuse to lick his balls! . . . to pander to him for his dollars! . . . Free yourselves! . . . stay strong, Madelon! . . . otherwise you'll have the Doctor sobbing! . . . wasting away! . . . oh hideous injustice! . . . It's a plot by the Sanhedrin! . . . They want the Doctor dead! . . . take my word for it! . . . the Israelite Central Consistory! . . . the Rothschild Bank! . . . Cahen d'Anvers! . . . Schlemilovitch! . . . help Doctor Bardamu, my little girls! . . . save me! . . .'

The Doctor never did forgive me for the copy of *Bardamu Unmasked* I sent him from Capri. In the essay, I revealed the sense of wonder I felt when, as a Jewish boy of fourteen, I read *The Journey of Bardamu* and *The Childhood of Louis-Ferdinand* in a single sitting. Nor did I shrug off the author's anti-Semitic pamphlets as good Christian souls do. Concerning them, I wrote: 'Doctor Bardamu devotes considerable space in his work to the Jewish Question. This is hardly surprising: Doctor Bardamu is one of us; he is the greatest Jewish writer of all time. This is why he speaks of his fellow Jews with passion. In his purely fictional works, Dr Bardamu reminds us of our Race brother Charlie Chaplin in his taste for poignant details, his touching, persecuted characters . . . Dr Bardamu's sentences are even more "Jewish" than the rococo prose of Marcel Proust: a plaintive, tearful melody, a little showy, a tad histrionic . . .' I concluded: 'Only the Jews can truly understand one of their own, only a Jew can speak perceptively about Dr Bardamu.' By way of response, the doctor sent me an insulting letter: according to him, with my orgies and my millions I was orchestrating the global Jewish conspiracy. I also sent him my *Psychoanalysis of Dreyfus* in which I categorically affirmed his guilt; a novel idea coming from a Jew. I elaborated the following theory: Alfred Dreyfus passionately loved the France of Saint Louis, of Joan of Arc, of Les Chouans. But France, for her part, wanted nothing to do with the Jew Dreyfus. And so he betrayed her, as a man might avenge himself on a scornful woman with spurs fashioned like fleurs-de-lis. Barrès, Zola and Deroulède knew nothing of such doomed love.

Such an analysis no doubt disconcerted the doctor. I never heard from him again.

The paroxysms of Rabatête and Bardamu were drowned out by the praise heaped upon me by society columnists. Most of them cited Valery Larbaud and Scott Fitzgerald: I was compared to Barnabooth, I was dubbed 'The Young Gatsby'. In magazine photographs, I was invariably shown with my head tilted slightly, gazing towards the horizon. In the columns of the romance magazines, my melancholy was legendary. To the journalist who buttonholed me on the steps of the Carlton, the Normandy or the Miramar, I ceaseless proclaimed my Jewishness. In fact, my actions ran counter to the virtues cultivated by the French: discretion, thrift, work. From my oriental forebears, I inherited my dark eyes, a taste of exhibitionism and luxury, an incurable indolence. I am not a son of France. I never knew a life of grandmothers who made jam, of family portraits and catechism. And yet, I constantly dream of provincial childhoods. My childhood is peopled by English governesses and unfolds on beaches of dubious repute: in Deauville, Miss Evelyn holds my hand. Maman neglects me in favour of polo players. She kisses me goodnight when I am in bed, but sometimes she does not take the trouble. And so, I wait for her, I no longer listen to Miss Evelyn and the adventures of David Copperfield. Every morning, Miss Evelyn takes me to the Pony Club. Here I take my riding lessons. To make maman happy, I will be the most famous polo player in the world. The little French boys know all the football teams. I think only of polo. I whisper to myself the magic words, 'Laversine', 'Cibao-La Pampa', 'Silver Leys', 'Porfirio Rubirosa'. At the Pony Club, I am often photographed with the young princess Laïla, my fiancée. In the afternoons, Miss Evelyn takes us to La Marquise de Sevigné for chocolate umbrellas. Laïla prefers lollipops. The ones at La Marquise de Sevigné are oblong and have a pretty stick.

Sometimes I manage to give Miss Evelyn the slip when she takes me to the beach, but she knows where to find me: with ex-king Firouz or Baron Truffaldine, two grown-ups who are friends of mine. Ex-king Firouz buys me pistachio sorbets and gushes: 'You have a sweet tooth like myself, my little Raphaël!' Baron Truffaldine is always alone and sad at the Bar au Soleil. I walk up to his table and stand in front of him. The old man launches into interminable anecdotes featuring characters called Cléo de Merode, Otéro, Émilienne d'Alencon, Liane de Pougy, Odette de Crécy. Fairies probably, like the ones in the tales of Hans Christian Andersen.

The other props that clutter my childhood include orange beach parasols, the Pré-Catalan, Hattemer Correspondence Courses, *David Copperfield*, the Comtesse de Ségur, my mother's apartment on the quai Conti and three photos taken by Lipnitzki in which I am posed next to a Christmas tree.

Then come the Swiss boarding schools in Lausanne and my first crushes. The Duisenberg given me for my eighteenth birthday by my Venezuelan uncle Vidal glides through the blue evening. I pass through a gate and drive through the park that slopes gently to Lake Leman and leave the car by the steps leading up to a villa twinkling with lights. Girls in pale dresses are waiting for me on the lawn. Scott Fitzgerald has written more elegantly that I ever could about these 'parties' where the twilight is too tender, the laughter and the shimmering lights too harsh to bode well. I therefore recommend you read the author, you will have a precise idea of the parties of my adolescence. Failing that, read *Fermina Marquez* by Larbaud.

If I shared the pleasures of my cosmopolitan classmates in Lausanne, I did not quite resemble them. I often went off to Geneva. In the silence of the Hôtel des Bergues, I would read the Greek bucolic poets and strive to elegantly translate the *Aeneid*. In the course of one such retreat, I made the acquaintance of a young aristocrat from Touraine, Jean-François Des Essarts. We were the same age and I was astounded by the breadth of his knowledge. At our first meeting, he recommended that I read – in no particular order – Maurice Scève's *Délie*, Corneille's comedies, the memoirs of Cardinal de Retz. He initiated me into the grace and the subtleties of French.

In him, I discovered precious qualities: tact, generosity, a great sensitivity, a scathing wit. I remember Des Essarts used to compare our friendship to the one between Robert de Saint-Loup and the narrator of *In Search of Lost Time*. 'You're a Jew, like the narrator,' he would say, 'and I'm related to the Noailles, the Rochechouart-Mortemarts and the La Rochfoucaulds like Robert de Saint-Loup. Don't worry, for a century now the French aristocracy have had a soft spot for Jews. I'll show you a few pages by Drumont in which this upstanding man castigates us for it bitterly.'

I decided never to return to Lausanne and, without the slightest compunction, sacrificed my cosmopolitan friends for Des Essarts.

I turned out my pockets. I had exactly a hundred dollars. Des Essarts did not have a *centime* to his name. Even so, I suggested he give up his job as sports correspondent for La Gazette de Lausanne. I had just remembered that, during a weekend spent in England, some friends had dragged me to a manor near Bournemouth to see a collection of old automobiles. I tracked down the name of the collector, Lord Allahabad, and sold him my Duisenberg for fourteen thousand pounds. On such a sum we could live decently for a year without having to depend on having money wired by my uncle Vidal.

We moved into the Hôtel des Bergues. I still have dazzling memories of this early period of our friendship. In the morning, we would loiter among the antique dealers of old Geneva. Des Essarts passed on to me his passion for bronzes. We bought some twenty pieces which cluttered up our rooms, among them a verdigris allegory representing 'Toil' and a pair of magnificent stags. One afternoon, Des Essarts informed me that he had acquired a bronze footballer:

'Parisian snobs will soon be falling over themselves to pay big money for these things. Take my word for it, my dear Raphäel! If it were up to me, the thirties style would be back in vogue.'

I asked him why he had left France:

'Military service did not suit my delicate constitution,' he explained, 'so I deserted.'

'We shall fix that,' I told him. 'I promise to find you a skilled craftsman here in Geneva to make you false papers: you'll be able to go back to France anytime you like without having to worry.'

The dubious printer we managed to track down produced a Swiss birth certificate and passport in the name Jean-François Lévy, born in Geneva on July 30, 194—.

'Now I'm one of your lot,' said Des Essarts, 'I was bored of being a goy.'

I immediately decided to send an anonymous confession to the left-wing Paris newspapers. I wrote as follows:

'Since November last, I have been guilty of desertion but the French military authorities have decided it is safer to hush up my case. I told them what today I am declaring publicly. I am a JEW and the army that spurned the services of Capitaine Dreyfus can do without mine. I have been condemned for failing to fulfil my military duties. Time was, the same tribunal condemned Alfred Dreyfus because he, a JEW, had dared to choose a career in the army. Until such time as this contradiction can be explained to me, I refuse to serve as a second-class soldier in an army that, to this day, has wanted nothing to do with a Maréchal Dreyfus. I urge all young French Jews to follow my example.'

I signed it: JACOB X.

As I had hoped, the French left feverishly took up the moral dilemma of Jacob X. It was the third Jewish scandal in France after the Dreyfus affair and the Finaly Affair. Des Essarts got in on the game, and together we wrote a dazzling 'Confession of Jacob X' which was serialised in a Parisian weekly: Jacob X had been taken in by a French family whose name he chose not to reveal consisting of a Pétainist colonel, his wife, a former canteen worker, and three sons, the eldest of whom joined the mountain infantry, the second the marines, the youngest had been accepted to the military academy of Saint-Cyr.

The family lived in Paray-le-Monial and Jacob X had grown up in the shadow of the basilica. The living room walls were bedecked with portraits of Gallieni, of Foch and Joffre, with colonel X's military cross and a number of *francisques*. Under the influence of his adoptive family, the young Jacob X came to worship the French army: he, too, would go to Saint-Cyr, he, like Pétain, would be a maréchal. At school, Monsieur C., the history master, discussed the Dreyfus Affair. Before the war, Monsieur C. had held an important post in the PPF. He was well aware that Colonel X had betrayed Jacob X's parents to the Germans and his life had been spared after the liberation only because he had adopted the little Jew. Monsieur C. despised the *pétainisme* of the X family: he revelled in the idea of causing dissension within the family. After the lesson, he called Jacob X over and whispered: 'I'm sure you find the Dreyfus Affair very upsetting. A young Jewish boy like you must feel personally affronted by such injustice.' To his horror, Jacob X discovers he is a Jew. Having identified with Maréchal Foch, with Maréchal Pétain, he suddenly discovers that he is like Capitaine Dreyfus. And yet he does not seek to avenge himself through treason like Dreyfus. He receives his call-up papers and can see no way out but to desert.

The confession divided French Jews. The Zionists advised Jacob X to emigrate to Israel. There he could legitimately aspire to the baton of a maréchal. The assimilated, self-loathing Jews claimed that Jacob X was an agent provocateur in the pay of neo-Nazis. The Left passionately defended the young deserter. Sartre's article, 'Saint Jacob X: Actor and Martyr' sparked the offensive. Everyone will remember the most germane passage: 'Tomorrow, he will think of himself as a Jew, but a Jew in abjection. Beneath the glowering stares of Gallieni, Joffre and Foch whose portraits hang on the walls of the living room, he will become a vulgar deserter, this boy who, since childhood, had worshipped the French army, "La Casquette du père Bugeaud" and Pétain's *francisques*. In short, he will experience the delicious shame of feeling Other, that is to say Evil.'

Various pamphlets circulated demanding that Jacob X return in triumph. A public meeting was held at la Mutualité. Sartre pleaded with Jacob X to forego anonymity, but the obstinate silence of the deserter discouraged even the best intentioned.

We take out meals at le Bergues. In the afternoons, Des Essarts works on a book about pre-revolutionary Russian cinema. As for me, I translate Alexandrian poets. We settle on the hotel bar to work on these trivial tasks. A bald man with eyes like embers regularly comes and sits at the table next to ours. One afternoon, he speaks to us, staring at us intently. Suddenly, from his pockets, he takes an old passport and proffers it. To my astonishment I read the name Maurice Sachs. Alcohol makes him talkative. He tells us of his misadventures since 1945, the date of his supposed death. He was, successively, a Gestapo officer, a GI, a cattle trader in Bavaria, a broker in Anvers, a brothel-keeper in Barcelona, a clown in a Milan circus under the stage name Lola Montès. He finally settled in Geneva where he runs a small bookshop. To celebrate this chance meeting, we drink until three in the morning. From that day forth, we and Maurice are inseparable and we solemnly vow to keep secret the fact that he is alive.

We spend our days sitting behind piles of books in the back office of his bookshop, listening as he brings 1925 to life for us. In a voice made gravelly by alcohol, Maurice talks about Gide, Cocteau, Coco Chanel. The adolescent of the Roaring Twenties is now a fat old man gesticulating wildly at the memory of Hispano-Suiza automobiles and Le Boeuf sur le Toit.

'Since 1945, I've been living on borrowed time,' he confides, 'I should have died when the moment was right, like Drieu la Rochelle. Trouble is: I'm a Jew, I have the survival instincts of a rat.'

I make a note of this comment and, the following day, bring Maurice a copy of my study *Drieu and Sachs: where primrose paths lead*. In the study, I show how two young men in 1925 lost their way because they lack depth of character: Drieu, the grand young man of Sciences-Po, a French petit bourgeois fascinated by convertibles, English neckties and American girls, who passed himself off as a hero of the Great War; Sachs, a young Jew of great charm and dubious morals, the product of a putrid post-war generation. By 1940, tragedy is sweeping Europe. How will our two bright young things react? Drieu remembers that he was born on the Cotentin Peninsula and spends four years singing the 'Horst-Wessel-Lied' in a shrill falsetto. For Sachs, occupied Paris is an Eden where he can lose himself in wild abandon. This is a Paris that offers him pleasures much more intense that the Paris of 1925. Here it is possible to traffic in gold, rent apartments and sell off the furniture, trade ten kilos of butter for a sapphire, convert the sapphire into scrap metal, etc. Night and fog mean there is no need for explanations. But above all, there is the thrill of being able to buy his life on the black market, to purloin each beat of his heart, to feel himself the prey in a hunt! It is difficult to imagine Sachs in the Résistance, fighting alongside French petty bureaucrats for the reinstatement of morality, legality and the light of day. Towards 1943, when he can feel the baying pack and the ratcatchers moving in, he signs up as a volunteer in Germany and, later, becomes an active member of the Gestapo. I have no wish to upset Maurice: I have him die in 1945 and pass over in silence his various incarnations from 1945 to the present day. I conclude thus: 'Who would have thought that, twenty years later, the charming young man of 1925 would be savaged by dogs on the plains of Pomerania?'

Having read my study, Maurice says:
'It's very neat, Schlemilovitch, the parallel between Drieu and myself, but I have to say I would prefer a parallel between Drieu and Brasillach. Compared to them I was a mere prankster. Write something for tomorrow morning and I shall tell you what I think.'

Maurice is delighted to be mentoring a young man. Doubtless he is remembering the first visits he made, his heart pounding, to Gide and Cocteau. He is greatly pleased with my *Drieu and Brasillach*. I attempted to address the following question: what were the motives that prompted Drieu and Brasillach to collaborate?

The first part of this study was entitled: 'Pierre Drieu la Rochelle, or the eternal love affair between the SS and the Jewess.' One subject recurs frequently in the novels of Drieu: the Jewish woman. That noble Viking, Gilles Drieu, had no hesitation about pimping Jewish women, a certain Myriam for example. His attraction to Jewish women can also be explained in the following manner: ever since Walter Scott, it has been understood that Jewish women are meek courtesans who submit to the every whim of their Aryan lords and masters. In the company of Jewish women Drieu had the illusion of being a crusader, a Teutonic knight. Up to this point, there was nothing very original in my analysis, Drieu's commentators have all focussed on the role of the Jewess in his writings. But Drieu as collaborator? This I explain easily: Drieu was fascinated by Doric masculinity. In June 1940, the real Aryans, the true warriors, descend on Paris: Drieu quickly shucks off the Viking costume he hired to violate the young Jewish girls of Passy. He discovers his true nature: beneath the steely blue gaze of the SS officers, he softens, he melts, he suddenly feels an oriental languidness. All too soon, he is swooning into the arms of the conquerors. After their defeat, he immolates himself. Such passivity, such a taste for Nirvana are surprising in a man from Normandy.

The second part of my study was entitled 'Robert Brasillach, or the Maid of Nuremberg.' 'There were many of us who slept with Germany,' he confessed, 'and the memory of it will remain sweet.' His impulsiveness reminds me of the young Viennese girls during the Anschluss. As German soldiers marched along Ringstraße, girls dressed up in their chicest dirndls to shower them with roses. Afterwards they strolled in the Prater with these blonde angels. Then came a magical twilight in the Stadtpark where they kissed an SS Totenkopf while murmuring Schubert lieder in his ear. My God, how handsome the youths were on the far side of the Rhine! How could anyone not fall in love with Hitler Youth Quex? In Nuremberg, Brasillach could scarcely believe his eyes: the bronzed muscles, the pale eyes, the tremulous lips of the Hitlejungend and the cocks you could sense straining in the torrid night, as pure a night as falls over Toledo from Los Cigarrales ... I met Robert Brasillach at the École Normale Supérieure. He affectionately referred to me as his 'dear little Moses', or his 'dear little Jew'. Together, we discovered the Paris of Pierre Corneille and René Clair, dotted with pleasant bistros where we would sip glasses of white wine. Robert would talk maliciously about our teacher André Bellessort and we would plan delightful little pranks. In the afternoons, we would 'coach' dim-witted, pretentious young Jewish numbskulls. At night, we would go to the cinematograph or share with our fellow class-mates a copious *brandade de morue*. Towards midnight, we would drink the iced orangeades Robert so loved because they reminded him of Spain. This, then, was our youth, the deep morning never to be regained. Robert embarked on a brilliant career as a journal-ist – I remember an article he wrote about Julien Benda. We were strolling through the Parc Montsouris and, in his manly voice, our own 'Grand Meaulnes' was denouncing Benda's intellectual-ism, his Jewish obscenity, his Talmudist's senility. 'Excuse me,' he said to me suddenly, 'I've probably offended you. I'd forgotten you were an Israelite.' I blushed to the tips of my fingers. 'No, Robert, I'm an honorary goy! Surely you must know that Jean Lévy, Pierre-Marius Zadoc, Raoul-Charles Leman, Marc Boasson, René Riquieur, Louis Latzarus, René Gross – all Jews like me – were passionate supporters of Maurras? Well, I want to work at *Je suis partout*, Robert! Please, introduce me to your friends! I'll write the anti-Semitic column instead of Lucien Rebatet! Just imagine the scandal: Schlemilovitch calls Blum a yid!' Robert was delighted at the prospect. Soon, I struck up a friendship with P.-A. Cousteau, 'the bronzed and virile Bordeaux boy,' Caporal Ralph Soupault, Robert Adriveau, 'dyed-in-the-wool fascist and sentimental luminary of our dinner parties', the jolly Alain Laubreaux from Toulouse and, lastly, Lucien Rebatet of the mountain infantry ('Now there's a man: he wields a pen the same way he will wield a gun when the day comes'). I immedi-ately gave this peasant from the Dauphiné a few helpful ideas for his anti-Semitic column. From that day on, Rebatet was constantly asking for my advice. I've always thought that goys are like bulls in a china shop when it comes to understanding Jews. Even their anti-Semitism is cack-handed.

We used the same printworks as *l'Action Française*. I was dandled on Maurras' lap, stroked Pujo's beard. Maxime Real del Sarte wasn't bad either. Such delightful old men!

June 1940. I leave the merry band of *Je suis partout*, though I miss our meetings at the Place Denfert-Rochereau. I am weary of journalism and beginning to nurture political ambitions. I resolve to become a Jewish collaborator. Initially, I embark on a little high-society collaborationism: I patronise tea parties with the Propaganda-Staffel, dinners with Jean Luchaire, suppers on the Rue Lauriston, and carefully cultivate Brinon as a friend. I avoid Céline and Drieu la Rochelle, too Jewified for my taste. I quickly make myself indispensable; I am the only Jew, the 'good Jew' of the Collaborationist movement. Luchaire introduces me to Abetz. We arrange to meet. I set out my conditions: I want 1) to replace that vile little Frenchman Darquier de Pellepoix at the General Commissariat for Jewish Affairs, 2) to be given complete freedom of action. It seems to me absurd to eliminate 500,000 French Jews. Abetz seems keenly interested but does not follow up on my proposals. Nonetheless, I remain on excellent terms with him and with Stülpnagel. They advise me to contact Doriot or Déat. I don't much like Doriot because of his communist past and his braces. Déat, I see as something of a radical-socialist schoolmaster. A newcomer impresses me by his beret. I would like to say a word about Jo Darnand. Every anti-Semite has his 'good Jew': Jo Darnand is my idealized image of a good Frenchman 'with his warrior face surveying the plains'. I become his right-hand man and form solid ties with the *Milice*: the boys in navy blue have their good points, take my word for it.

Summer, 1944, after various military raids in the Vercors region, we hole up in Sigmaringen with members of the Franc-Garde. In

December, during the Ardennes Offensive, I am gunned down by a GI named Lévy who looks so like me he could be my brother.

In Maurice's bookshop I found all the back-issues of *Le Gerbe*, of *Pilori* and *Je suis partout* and a few Pétainist pamphlets on the subject of training 'leaders'. Aside from pro-German literature, Maurice possesses the complete works of forgotten writers. While I read the anti-Semites Montandon and Marques-Rivière, Des Essarts becomes enthralled by the novels of Édouard Rod, Marcel Prévost, Estaunié, Boylesve, Abel Hermant. He pens a brief essay: *What Is Literature?* which he dedicates to Jean-Paul Sartre. Des Essarts is an antiquarian at heart, he intends to rehabilitate the reputations of the 1880s novelists he has just discovered. He might just as easily defend the style of Louis-Philippe or Napoleon III. The last section of his essay is entitled 'A Guide to Reading Certain Writers' and is addressed to young persons eager to improve their minds: 'Edouard Estaunié,' he writes, 'should be read in a country house at about five in the afternoon with a glass of Armagnac in hand. When reading O'Rosen or Creed, the reader should wear a formal suit, a club tie and a black silk pocket handkerchief. I recommend reading René Boylesve in summertime, in Cannes or Monte-Carlo at about eight in the evening wearing an alpaca suite. The novels of Abel Herman require sophistication: they should be read aboard a Panamanian yacht while smoking menthol cigarettes . . .'

Maurice, for his part, is writing the third tome of his memoirs: *The Revenant*, a companion volume to *The Sabbath* and *The Hunt*.

As for me, I have decided to be the greatest Jewish–French writer after Montaigne, Marcel Proust and Louis-Ferdinand Céline.

I used to have the passions and the paroxysms of a young man. Today, such naivety makes me smile. I believed that the future of Jewish literature rested on my shoulders. I looked toward the past and denounced the two-faced hypocrites: Capitaine Dreyfus, Maurois, Daniel Halévy. Proust, with his provincial childhood, was too assimilated to my mind. Edmond Fleg too nice, Benda too abstract – why play the pure spirit, Benda? The archangel of geometry? The great ascetic? The invisible Jew?

There were some beautiful lines by Spire:

Oh fervour, oh sadness, oh violence, oh madness,
Indomitable spirits to whom I am pledged,
What am I without you? Come then defend me
Against the cold, hard Reason of this happy earth . . .

And, again:

You would sing of strength, of daring,
You will love only dreamers defenceless against life
You will strive to listen to the joyous songs of peasants,
To soldiers' brutal marches, to the graceful dances of little girls
You shall have ears only for tears . . .

Looking eastward, there are stronger personalities: Heinrich Heine, Franz Kafka . . . I loved Heine's poem 'Doña Clara:' in Spain, the daughter of the Grand Inquisitor falls in love with a handsome knight who looks like Saint George. 'You have nothing in common with the vile Jews,' she tells him. The handsome knight then reveals his identity:

Ich, Señora, eur Geliebter,
Bin der Sohn des vielbelobten,
Großen, schriftgelehrten Rabbi
Israel von Saragossa. *

Much fuss was made of Franz Kafka, the elder brother of Charlie Chaplin. A few Aryan prigs put on their jackboots to trample his work: they promoted Kafka to professor of philosophy. They contrast him with the Prussian Emmanuel Kant, with the Danish genius Søren Kierkegaard, with the southerner Albert Camus, with J.-P. Sartre the half-Alsatian, half-Périgourdine penny-a-liner. I wonder how Kafka, so frail, so timid, could withstand such an onslaught.

Since becoming a naturalised Jew, Des Essarts had unreservedly embraced our cause. Maurice, on the other hand, worried about my increasing racism.

'You keep harping on at old stories,' he would say, 'it's not 1942 anymore, old man! If it were, I would be strongly advising you to follow my example and join the Gestapo, that would change your perspective! People quickly forget their origins, you know! A little flexibility and you can change your skin at will! Change your colour! Long live the chameleon! Just watch, I can become Chinese, Apache, Norwegian, Patagonian, just like that! A quick wave of the magic wand! Abracadabra!'

I am not listening to him. I have just met Tania Arcisewska, a Polish Jew. This young woman is slowly killing herself, with no

---

* 'I, Senora, your beloved, am the son of the learned and glorious Don Isaac Ben Israëç, Rabbi of the synagogue of Saragossa.'

convulsions, no cries, as though it were the most obvious thing in the world. She uses a Pravaz syringe to shoot up.

'Tania exerts a baleful influence over you,' Maurice tells me, 'why don't you find yourself a nice little Aryan girl who can sing you lullabies of the homeland.'

Tania sings me the *Prayer for the Dead of Auschwitz*. She wakes me in the middle of the night and shows me the indelible number tattooed on her shoulder.

'Look what they did to me Raphaël, look!'

She stumbles over to the window. Along the banks of the Rhône, with admirable discipline, black battalions parade and muster outside the hotel.

'Look at all the SS officers, Raphaël! See the three cops in leather coats over there on the left? It's the Gestapo, Raphaël! They're coming to the hotel! They're coming for us! They're going to gather us back to the Fatherland!'

I quickly reassure her. I have friends in high places. I have no truck with the petty pissants of the Paris *Collabo*. I'm on first name terms with Goering; Hess, Goebbels and Heydrich consider me a friend. She's safe with me. The cops won't touch a hair on her head. If they try, I'll show them my medals; I'm the only Jew ever to be awarded the Iron Cross by Hitler himself.

One morning, taking advantage of my absence, Tania slashes her wrists. Though I was careful to hide my razor blades. Even I feel my head spin when I accidentally see those little metal objects: I feel an urge to swallow them.

The following day, an Inspector dispatched especially from Paris interrogates me. Inspecteur La Clayette, if memory serves. This woman, Tania Arcisewska, he tells me, was wanted by the police in France. Possession and trafficking of drugs. You never know what to expect with foreigners. Bloody Jews. Fucking Mittel-European delinquents. Well, anyway, she's dead and it's probably for the best.

I'm surprised by the eagerness of Inspecteur La Clayette and his keen interest in my girlfriend: former member of the Gestapo, probably.

As a memento, I kept Tania's collection of puppets: characters from the *commedia dell'arte*, Karagiozis, Pinocchio, Punchinello, the Wandering Jew, the Sleepwalker. She had placed them around her before killing herself. I think they were her only friends. Of all the puppets, my favourite is the Sleepwalker, with his arms outstretched and his eyes tight shut. Lost in her nightmare of barbed wire and watchtowers, Tania was very like him.

Then Maurice disappeared. He had always dreamed of the Orient. I can imagine him living out his retirement in Macau or Hong Kong. Maybe he's recreating his days in the Forced Labour unit on a kibbutz somewhere. I think that's the most plausible scenario.

For a week, Des Essarts and I were utterly at a loss. We no longer had the strength to concern ourselves with things of the mind and were frightened for the future: we had only sixty Swiss francs to our name. But Des Essarts' grandfather and my Venezuelan uncle Vidal drop dead the same day. Des Essarts assumes the titles of Duke and Lord; I have to make do with a vast fortune in bolivars. I was dumbfounded by my uncle Vidal's will: apparently being dandled on an old man's knee for five years is enough to make you his sole heir.

We decide to go back to France. I reassure Des Essarts: the French police are on the lookout for a Duke and Lord gone AWOL, but not for a certain Jean-François Lévy of Geneva. As soon as we cross the border, we break the bank at the casino Aix-les-Bains. I give my first press conference at the Hôtel Splendide. I'm asked what I plan to do with my bolivars: set up a harem? Build pink marble palaces? Become a patron of arts and literature? Devote myself to philanthropic works? Am I a romantic? A cynic? Will I become playboy of the year? Take the place of Rubirosa, Farouk, Ali Khan?

I will play the youthful billionaire in my own way. Obviously, I have read Larbaud and Scott Fitzgerald, but I am not about to emulate the spiritual torments of A.W. Olson Barnabooth or the puerile romanticism of Gatsby. I want to be loved for my money.

I discover I have tuberculosis and am panic-stricken. I must hide this inopportune illness which will otherwise lead to a surge in my popularity throughout the thatched cottages of Europe. Faced with a rich young man who is handsome and tubercular, little Aryan girls are apt to turn into Sainte Blandine. To discourage any such benevolence, I remind journalists that I am a Jew. Accordingly, I am drawn only to money and pleasure. People consider me photogenic: very well, I'll pull faces, wear orangutan masks, model myself on the archetypal Jew that Aryans came to peer at in the Palais Berlitz in 1941. I evoke memories of Rabatête and Bardamu. Their insulting articles compensate me for my suffering. Sadly, no one reads these authors anymore. Society journals and the romance magazines insist on showering me with praise: I am a youthful heir of great charm and originality. Jew? In the sense that Jesus Christ and Albert Einstein were Jews. So what? As a last resort I buy a yacht, *The Sanhedrin*, which I convert into a high-class brothel. I moor it off Monte Carlo, Cannes, La Baule, Deauville. From each mast, three speakers broadcast texts by doctor Bardamu and Rabatête, my preferred PR people: Yes, through my millions and my orgies, I personally preside over the International Jewish Conspiracy. Yes the Second World War was directly triggered by me. Yes, I am a sort of Bluebeard, a cannibal who feeds on Aryan girls though only after raping them. Yes, I dream of bankrupting the entire French peasantry and Jewifying the region of Cantal.

I quickly grown weary of these posturings. With my friend Des Essarts, I hole up in the Hôtel Trianon in Versailles to read Saint-Simon. My mother worries about my poor health. I promise to write a tragicomedy in which she will have the starring role. After that, tuberculosis can slowly carry me off. Or maybe I'll commit suicide. Thinking about it, I decide not to go out with a flourish. I would only end up being compared to L'Aiglon or Young Werther.

That evening, Des Essarts wanted me to go with him to a masked ball.

'And don't come dressed as Shylock or Süss the Jew like you always do. I've rented you a magnificent costume, you can go as Henri III. I rented a Spahi uniform for myself.'

I declined his invitation on the pretext that I had to finish my play as soon as possible. He took his leave with a sad smile. As the car was driving out the hotel gates, I felt a pang of regret. A little later my friend killed himself on the Autoroute Ouest. An inexplicable accident. He was wearing his Spahi uniform. There was not a scratch on him.

I quickly finished my play. A tragicomedy. A tissue of invective against *goyim*. I felt sure it would rile Parisian audiences; they would never forgive me for flaunting my neuroses and my racism on stage in such a provocative manner. I set much store by the virtuoso finale: in a white-walled room, father and son clash; the son is wearing a threadbare SS uniform and a tattered Gestapo trench coat, the father a skullcap, sidelocks and a rabbi's beard. They parody an interrogation scene, the son playing the role of the torturer, the father the role of the victim. The mother bursts into the room and rushes at them, arms outstretched, eyes wild. She wails the 'Ballad of Marie Sanders, the "Jews Whore".' The son grabs his father by the throat and launches into the 'Horst-Wessel-Lied' but cannot drown out his mother's voice. The father, half choking, mewls the 'Kol Nidrei', the great Prayer of Atonement. Suddenly, a door at the back of the stage is flung open: four nurses circle the protagonists and, with difficulty, overpower them. The curtain falls. No one applauds. People stare at me suspiciously. They had expected better manners from a Jew. I'm an ungrateful wretch. A boor. I have appropriated their clear and limpid language and transformed it into a hysterical cacophony.

They had hoped to discover a new Proust, a rough-hewn Yid polished by contact with their culture, they came expecting sweet music only to be deafened by ominous tom-toms. Now they know where they stand with me. I can die happy.

I was terribly disappointed by the reviews the following morning. They were patronising. I had to face facts. I would meet with no hostility from my peers, excepting the occasional Lady Bountiful and old men who looked like Colonel de la

Rocque. The newspapers spent even more column inches concerned with my state of mind. The French have an overweening affection for whores who write memoirs, pederast poets, Arab pimps, Negro junkies and Jewish provocateurs. Clearly, there was no morality any more. The Jew was a prized commodity, we were overly respected. I could graduate from Saint-Cyr and become Maréchal Schlemilovitch: there would be no repeat of the Dreyfus Affair.

After this fiasco, all that was left was for me to disappear like Maurice Sachs. To leave Paris for good. I bequeathed a part of my inheritance to my mother. I remembered that I had a father in America. I suggested he might like to visit me if he wanted to inherit 350,000 dollars. The answer came by return of post: he arranged to meet me in Paris and the Hôtel Continental. I was keen to pamper my tuberculosis. To become a prudent, polite young man. A real little Aryan. The problem was I didn't like sanatoriums. I preferred to travel. My woppish soul longed for beautiful, exotic locations.

I felt that the French provinces would provide these more effectively than Mexico or the Sunda Islands. And so I turned my back on my cosmopolitan past. I was keen to get to know the land, with paraffin lamps, and the song of the thickets and the forests.

And then I thought about my mother, who frequently toured the provinces. The Karinthy Theatre Company, light comedy guaranteed. Since she spoke French with a Balkan accent, she played Russian princesses, Polish countesses and Hungarian horsewomen. Princess Berezovo in Aurillac. Countess Tomazoff in Béziers. Baronne Gevatchaldy in Saint-Brieuc. The Karinthy Theatre Company tours all over France.

II

My father was wearing an *eau de Nil* suit, a green-striped shirt, a red tie and astrakhan shoes. I had just made his acquaintance in the Ottoman Lounge of the Hôtel Continental. Having signed various papers making over a part of my fortune to him, I said:

'In short, your New York business ventures are a dismal flop? What were you thinking, becoming chairman and managing director of Kaleidoscope Ltd.? You should have noticed that the kaleidoscope market is falling by the day! Children prefer space rockets, electromagnetism, arithmetic! Dreams aren't selling any more, old man. And let me be frank, you're a Jew, which means you have no head for commerce or for business. Leave that honour to the French. If you knew how to read, I would show you the elegant comparison I drew up between Peugeot and Citroën: on the one hand, a provincial man from Montbéliard, miserly, discreet, prosperous; on the other, André Citroën, a tragic Jewish adventurer who gambles for high stakes in casinos. Come, come, you don't have the makings of a captain of industry. This is all an act! You're a tightrope walker, nothing more! There's no point putting on an act, making feverish telephone calls to Madagascar, to Lichtenstein, to Tierra del Fuego! You'll never offload your stock of kaleidoscopes.'

My father wanted to visit Paris, where he had spent his youth. We had a couple of gin fizzes at Fouquet's, at the Relais Plaza, at the bars of Le Meurice, the Saint James Albany, the Élysée-Park, the Georges V, the Lancaster. This was his version of the provinces. While he puffed on a Partagas cigar, I was thinking about Touraine and the forest of Brocéliande. Where would I choose to live out my exile? Tours? Nevers? Poitiers? Aurillac?

Pézenas? La Souterraine? Everything I knew of the French provinces I had learned from the pages of the Guide Michelin and various authors such as François Mauriac.

I had been particularly moved by a text by this writer from the Landes: *Bordeaux, of Adolescence*. I remember Mauriac's surprise when I passionately recited his beautiful prose: 'That town in which we were born, in which we were a child, an adolescent, is the only one we must forbear to judge. It is part of us, it is ourselves, we carry it within us. The history of Bordeaux is the history of my body and my soul.' Did my old friend understand that I envied him his adolescence, the Marianist Brothers school, the Place des Quinconces, the scents of balmy heather, of warm sand, of resin? What adolescence could I, Raphäel Schlemilovitch, recount other than that of miserable little stateless Jew? I would not be Gérard de Nerval, nor François Mauriac, nor even Marcel Proust. I had no Valois to stir my soul, no Guyenne, no Combray. I had no Tante Léonie. Doomed to Fouquet's, to the Relais Plaza, to the Élysée Park where I drink disgusting English liqueurs in the company of a fat New York Jew: my father. Alcohol fosters a need in him to confide, as it had Maurice Sachs on the day we first met. Their fates are the same with one small difference: Sachs read Saint-Simon, while my father read Maurice Dekobra. Born in Caracas to a Sephardic Jewish family, he hurriedly fled the Americas to escape the police of the dictator of the Galapagos islands whose daughter he had seduced. In France, he became secretary to Stavinsky. In those days, he looked very dapper: somewhere between Valentino and Novarro with a touch of Douglas Fairbanks, enough to turn the heads of pretty Aryan girls. Ten years later his photograph was among those at the anti-Jewish exhibition at the Palais Berlitz, accompanied by the caption: 'Devious Jew. He could pass for a South American.'

My father was not without a certain sense of humour: one afternoon, he went to the Palais Berlitz and offered to act as a guide for several visitors to the exhibition. When they came to the photo, he cried: 'Peek-a-boo! Here I am!'. The Jewish penchant for showing off cannot be overstated. In fact, my father had a certain sympathy for the Germans since they patronised his favourite haunts: the Continental, the Majestic, Le Meurice. He lost no opportunity to rub shoulders with them in Maxim's, Philippe, Gaffner, Lola Tosch and other nightclubs thanks to false papers in the name Jean Cassis de Coudray-Macouard.

He lived in a tiny garret room on the Rue des Saussaies directly opposite the Gestapo. Late into the night he would sit up reading *Bagatelles pour un massacre*, which he found very funny. To my stupefaction, he could recite whole pages from the book. He had bought it because of the title, thinking it was a crime novel.

In July 1944, he managed to sell Fontainebleau forest to the Germans using a Baltic baron as a middleman. With the profits of this delicate operation, he immigrated to the United States where he set up the company Kaleidoscope Ltd.

'What about you?' he asked, blowing a cloud of Partagas smoke into my face, 'Tell me about your life.'

'Haven't you been reading the papers?' I said wearily, 'I thought *Confidential* magazine in New York devoted a special issue to me? Basically, I've decided to give up this shallow, decadent cosmopolitan life. I'm retiring to the provinces, the French countryside, back to the land. I've just settled on Bordeaux, the Guyenne, as a rest cure for my nerves. It's also a little homage to an old friend, François Mauriac. I'm guessing the name means nothing to you?'

We had one for the road in the bar at the Ritz.

'May I accompany you to this city you mentioned earlier?' he asked out of the blue, 'you're my son, we should at least take a trip together. And besides, thanks to you, I'm now the fourth-richest man in America!'

'By all means come along if you like. After that, you can go back to New York.'

He kissed me on the forehead and I felt tears come to my eyes. This fat man with his motley clothes was genuinely moving.

Arm in arm, we crossed the Place Vendôme. My father sang snatches of *Bagatelles pour un massacre* in a fine bass voice. I was thinking about the terrible things I had read during my childhood. Particularly the series *How to kill your father* by André Breton and Jean-Paul Sartre (the 'Read Me' series for boys). Breton advised boys to station themselves at the window of their house on the Avenue Foch and slaughter the first passing pedestrian. This man necessarily being their father, a *préfet de police* or a textile manufacturer. Sartre temporarily forsook the well-heeled *arrondissements* for the Communist-controlled suburbs of the *banlieue rouge*: here, middle-class boys were urged to approach the brawniest labourers, apologise for being bourgeois brats, drag them back to the Avenue Foch where they would smash the Sèvres china, kill the father, at which point the young man would politely ask to be raped. This latter method, while exhibiting greater perversity, the rape following the murder, was also more grandiose: the proletariat of all countries were being called upon to settle a family spat. It was recommended that young men insult their father before killing him. Some who made a name for themselves in such literature developed charming expressions. For example: 'Families, I despise you' (the son of a French pastor). 'I'll fight the next war in a German uniform.' 'I shit upon the French army' (the son of a French *préfet de police*). 'You are a BASTARD' (the son of a French naval officer). I gripped my father's arm more tightly. There was nothing to distinguish between us. Isn't that right, my podgy papa? How could I kill you? I love you.

We caught the Paris–Bordeaux train. From the window of the compartment, France looked particularly splendid. Orléans, Beaugency, Vendôme, Tours, Poitiers, Angoulême. My father was no longer wearing a pale green suit, a pink buckskin tie, a tartan shirt, a platinum signet ring and the shoes with the astrakhan spats. I was no longer called Raphäel Schlemilovitch. I was the eldest son of a notary from Libourne and we were heading back to our home in the country. While a certain Raphäel Schlemilovitch was squandering his youth in Cap Ferrat, in Monte Carlo and in Paris, my obdurate neck was bowed over Latin translations. Over and over, I repeated to myself 'Rue d'Ulm! Rue d'Ulm!' feeling my cheeks flush. In June I would pass the entrance exam to the École Normale Supérieure. I would definitively 'go up' to Paris. On the Rue d'Ulm, I would share rooms with a young provincial lad like myself. An unshakeable friendship would develop between us. We would be Jallez and Jephanion. One night, we would climb the steps of the Butte Montmartre. We would see Paris laid out at our feet. In a soft, resolute voice we would say: 'Now, Paris, it's just you and me!' We would write beautiful letters to our families: 'Maman, I love you, your little man.' At night, in the silence of our rooms, we would talk about our future mistresses: the Jewish baronesses, the daughters of captains of industry, actresses, courtesans. They would admire our brilliance and our expertise. One afternoon, hearts pounding, we would knock on the door of Gaston Gallimard: 'we're students at the École Normale

Supérieure, monsieur, and we wanted to show you our first essays.'
Later, the Collège de France, a career in politics, a panoply of
honours. We would be part of our country's elite. Our brains would
be in Paris but our hearts would ever remain in the provinces. In the
maelstrom of the capital, we would think fondly of our native
Cantal, our native Gironde. Every year, we would go back to clear
out our lungs and visit out parents somewhere near Saint-Flour or
Libourne. We would leave again weighted down with cheeses and
bottles of Saint-Émilion. Our mamans would have knitted us thick
cardigans: the winters in Paris are cold. Our sisters would marry
pharmacists from Aurillac and insurance brokers from Bordeaux.
We would serve as examples to our nephews.

G are Saint-Jean, night is waiting for us. We have seen nothing of Bordeaux. In the taxi to the Hôtel Splendid, I whisper
to my father:

'The driver is definitely a member of the French Gestapo, my
plump papa.'

'You think so?', my father says, playing along, 'that could
prove awkward. I forgot to bring the fake papers in the name
Coudray-Macouard.'

'I suspect he's taking us to the Rue Lauriston to visit his friends
Bonny and Lafont.'

'I think you're wrong: I think he's heading for the Gestapo
headquarters on Avenue Foch.'

'Maybe Rue des Saussaies for an identity check?'

'The first red light we come to, we make a run for it.'

'Impossible, the doors are locked.'

'What then?'

'Wait it out. Keep your chin up.'

'We could probably pass for Jewish collaborators. Sell them Fontainebleau forest at a bargain price. I'll tell them I worked at *Je suis partout* before the war. A quick phone call to Brasillach or Laubreux or Rebatet and we're home free . . .'

'You think they'll let us make a phone call?'

'It doesn't matter. We'll sign up to join the LVF or the *Milice*, show a little goodwill. In a green uniform and an alpine beret we can make it to the Spanish border. After that . . .'

'Freedom . . .'

'Shh! He's listening . . .'

'He looks like Darnand, don't you think?'

'If it is him, we've really got problems. The *Milice* are bound to give us a tough time.'

'I don't like to say, but I think I was right . . . we're taking the motorway heading west . . . the headquarters of the *Milice* is in Versailles . . . We're really in the shit!'

At the hotel bar, we sat drinking Irish coffee, my father was smoking his Upmann cigar. How did the Splendid differ from the Claridge, from the George V, and every other caravanserai in Paris and Europe? How much longer can grand hotels and Pullman cars protect me from France? When all is said and done, these goldfish bowls made me sick. But the resolutions I had made gave me a little hope. I would sign up to study *lettres supérieures* at the Lycée de Bordeaux. When I passed my entrance exam, I would be careful not to sign Rastignac, from the heights of the Butte Montmartre. I had nothing in common with this gallant little Frenchman. 'Now, Paris, it's just you and me!' Only paymasters from Saint-Flour or Libourne could be so starry-eyed. No, Paris was too much like me.

An artificial flower in the middle of France. I was counting on Bordeaux to teach me true values, to put me in touch with the land. After I graduated, I would apply for a post as a provincial schoolteacher. I would divide my days between a dusty classroom and the Café du Commerce. I would play cards with colonels. On Sunday afternoons, I would listen to old mazurkas from the bandstand in the town square. I would fall in love with the mayor's wife, we'd meet on Thursdays in a *hôtel de passe* in the next town. It would all depend on the nearest country town. I would serve France by educating her children. I would belong to the battalion of the 'black hussars' of truth, to quote Péguy, whom I could count among my colleagues. Gradually I would forget my shameful origins, the dishonourable name Schlemilovitch, Torquemada, Himmler and so many other things.

Rue Sainte-Catherine, people turned as we passed. Probably because of my father's purple suit, his Kentucky green shirt and the same old shoes with the astrakhan spats. I fondly wished a policeman would stop us. I would have justified myself once and for all to the French, tirelessly explaining that for twenty years we had been corrupted by one of their own, a man from Alsace. He insisted that the Jew would not exist if goys did not condescend to notice him. And so we are forced to attract *their* attention by wearing garish clothes. For us, as Jews, it is a matter of life and death.

The headmaster of the lycée invited us into his office. He seemed to doubt whether the son of this dago could genuinely want to study *lettres supérieures*. His own son – *Monsieur le proviseur* was proud of his son – had spent the holidays tirelessly swotting up on his *Maquet-et-Roger**. I felt like telling the head-master that, alas, I was a Jew. Hence: always top of the class.

The headmaster handed me an anthology of Greek orators and told me to open the book at random. I had to gloss a passage by Aeschines. I acquitted myself brilliantly. I went so far as to trans-late the text into Latin.

The headmaster was dumbfounded. Was he really ignorant of the keenness, the intelligence of Jews? Had he really forgotten the great writers we had given France: Montaigne, Racine, Saint-Simon, Sartre, Henry Bordeaux, René Bazin, Proust, Louis-Ferdinand Céline . . . On the spot, he suggested I skip the first year and enrolled me straight into the second year – *khâgne*.

'Congratulations, Schlemilovitch,' he said, his voice quavering with emotion.

After we had left the lycée, I rebuked my father for his obse-quiousness, his Turkish Delight unctuousness in dealing with the *proviseur*.

'What are you thinking, playing Mata Hari in the office of a French bureaucrat? I could excuse your doe eyes and your obsequi-ousness if it was an SS executioner you were trying to charm! But doing your belly dance in front of that good man! He was hardly going to eat you, for Christ's sake! Here, I'll make you suffer!'

I broke into a run. He followed me as far as Tourny, he did not even ask me to stop. When he was out of breath, he probably thought I would take advantage of his tiredness and give him the slip forever. He said:

'A bracing little run is good for the heart . . . It'll give us an appetite . . .'

---

* Latin grammar

He didn't even stand up for himself. He was trying to outwit his sadness, trying to tame it. Something he learned in the pogroms, probably. My father mopped his forehead with his pink buckskin tie. How could he think I would desert him, leave him alone, helpless in this city of distinguished tradition, in this illustrious night that smelled of vintage wine and English tobacco? I took him by the arm. He was a whipped cur.

Midnight. I open the bedroom window a crack. The summer air, 'Stranger on the shore', drifts up to us. My father says:

'There must be a nightclub around here somewhere.'

'I didn't come to Bordeaux to play the lothario. And anyway, you can expect meagre pickings: two or three degenerate kids from the Bordeaux bourgeoisie, a couple of English tourists . . .'

He slips on a sky-blue dinner jacket. I knot a tie from Sulka in front of the mirror. We plunge into the warm sickly waters, a South American band plays rumbas. We sit at a table, my father orders a bottle of Pommery, lights an Upmann cigar. I buy a drink for an English girl with dark hair and green eyes. Her face reminds me of something. She smells deliciously of cognac. I hold her to me. Suddenly, slimy hotel names come tumbling from her lips: Eden Rock, Rampoldi, Balmoral, Hôtel de Paris: we had met in Monte Carlo. I glance over the English girl's shoulder at my father. He smiles and makes conspiratorial gestures. He's touching, he probably wants me to marry some Slavo-Argentinian heiress, but ever since I arrived in Bordeaux, I have been in love with the Blessed Virgin, with Joan of Arc and Eleanor of Aquitaine. I try to explain this until three in the morning but he chain-smokes his cigars and does not listen. We have had too much to drink.

We fell asleep at dawn. The streets of Bordeaux were teeming with cars mounted with loudspeakers: 'Operation rat extermination campaign, operation rat extermination campaign. For you, free rat poison, just ask at this car. Citizens of Bordeaux, operation rat extermination . . . operation rat extermination . . .'

We walk through the streets of the city, my father and I. Cars appear from all sides, hurtling straight for us, their sirens wailing. We hide in doorways. We were huge American rats.

In the end we had to part ways. On the evening before term started, I tossed my clothes in a heap in the middle of the room: ties from Sulka and the Via Condotti, cashmere sweaters, Doucet scarves, suits from Creed, Canette, Bruce O'lofson, O'Rosen, pyjamas from Lanvin, handkerchiefs from Henri à la Pensée, belts by Gucci, shoes by Dowie & Marshall . . .

'Here,' I said to my father, 'you can take all this back to New York — a souvenir of your son. From now on the *khâgne* scholar's beret and the ash-grey smock will protect me from myself. I'm giving up smoking Craven and Khédive. From now on it's shag tobacco. I've become a naturalised Frenchman. I'm definitely assimilated. Will I join the category of military Jews, like Dreyfus and Stroheim? We'll see. But right now, I am studying to apply to the *École Normale Supérieure* like Blum, Fleg and Henri Franck. It would have been tactless to apply to the military academy at Saint-Cyr straightaway.'

We had a last gin-fizz at the bar of the Splendid. My father was wearing his travelling outfit: a crimson fur cap, an astrakhan coat and blue crocodile-skin shoes. A Partagas cigar dangled from his lips. Dark glasses concealed his eyes. He was crying, I realised, from the quaver in his voice. He was so overcome he forgot the language of this country and mumbled a few words in English.

'You'll come and visit me in New York?' he asked.

'I don't think so, old man. I'm going to die before very long. I've just got time to pass the entrance exam to the *École Normale*

Supérieure, the first stage of assimilation. I promise you your grandson will be a Maréchal de France. Oh, yes, I am planning to try and reproduce.'

On the station platform, I said:

'Don't forget to send me a postcard from New York or Acapulco.'

He hugged me. As the train pulled out, my Guyenne plans seemed suddenly laughable. Why had I not followed this unhoped-for partner in crime? Together, we would have outshone the Marx Brothers. We ad-lib grotesque maudlin gags for the public. Schlemilovitch *père* is a tubby man dressed in garish multi-coloured suits. The children are thrilled by these two clowns. Especially when Schlemilovitch junior trips Schlemilovitch *père* who falls head-first into a vat of tar. Or when Schlemilovitch *fils* rips away a ladder and sends Schlemilovitch *père* tumbling. Or when Schlemilovitch *fils* surreptitiously sets fire to Schlemilovitch *père*, etc.

They are currently performing at the Cirque Médrano, following a sell-out tour of Germany. Schlemilovitch *père* and Schlemilovitch *fils* are true Parisian stars, though they shun elite audiences in favour of local cinemas and provincial circuses.

I bitterly regretted my father's departure. For me, adulthood had begun. There was only one boxer left in the ring. He was punching himself. Soon he would black out. In the meantime, would I have the chance – if only for a minute – to catch the public's attention?

It was raining, as it does every Sunday before term starts. The cafés were glittering more brightly than usual. On the way to the lycée, I felt terribly presumptuous: a frivolous young Jew cannot suddenly aspire to the dogged tenacity conferred upon scholarship students by their patrician ancestry. I remembered what my old friend Seingalt had written in chapter II of volume III of his memoirs: 'A new career was opening before me. Fortune was still my friend, and I had all the necessary qualities to second the efforts of the blind goddess on my behalf save one – perseverance.' Could I really become a *normalien*?

Fleg, Blum and Henri Franck must have had a drop of Breton blood.

I went up to the dormitory. I had had no experience of secular schooling since Hattemer (the Swiss boarding schools in which my mother enrolled me were run by Jesuits). I was shocked, therefore, to find there were no prayers. I conveyed my concerns to the other boarders. They burst out laughing, mocked the Blessed Virgin and then suggested I shine their shoes on the pretext that they had been there longer than I.

My objection was twofold:

1) I could not understand why they had no respect for the Blessed Virgin.

2) I had no doubt that they had been here 'before me', since Jewish immigration to the Bordeaux area did not begin until the fifteenth century. I was a Jew. They were Gauls. They were persecuting me.

Two boys stepped forward to arbitrate. A Christian Democrat and a Bordeaux Jew. The former whispered to me that he didn't want too much talk of the Blessed Virgin because he was hoping to forge ties with students on the extreme left. The latter accused me of being an 'agent provocateur'. Besides, the Jew didn't really exist, he was an Aryan invention, etc., etc.

I explained to the former that the Blessed Virgin was surely worthy of a falling out with anyone and everyone. I informed him of how strongly Saint John of the Cross and Pascal would have condemned his toadying Catholicism. I added that, moreover, as a Jew it was not my place to give him catechism lessons.

The comments of the latter filled me with a profound sadness: the goys had done a fine job of brainwashing.

I had been warned; thereafter they completely ostracised me.

Adrien Debigorre, who taught us French literature and language, had an imposing beard, a black frockcoat, and a club foot that elicited mocking comments from the students. This curious character had been a friend of Maurras, of Paul Chack and Monsignor Mayol de Lupé; French radio listeners will probably remember the 'Fireside chats' Debigorre gave on Radio-Vichy.

In 1942, Debigorre is part of the inner circle of Abel Bonheur, the Ministre de l'Éducation nationale. He is indignant when Bonheur, dressed as Anne de Bretagne, declares in a soft tremulous tone: 'If we had a princess in France, we should push her into the arms of Hitler', or when the minister praised the 'manly charms' of the SS. Eventually he fell out with Bonheur, nicknaming him *la Gestapette*, something Pétain found hilarious. Retiring to the Minquier islands, Debigorre tried to organise commandos of local fishermen to mount a resistance against the British. His Anglophobia rivalled that of Henri Béraud. As a child he had solemnly promised his father, a naval lieutenant from Saint-Malo, that he would never forget the 'TRICK' of Trafalgar. During the attack on Mers-el-Kébir, he is said to have thundered: 'They will pay for this!' During the war, he kept up a voluminous correspondence with Paul Chack and would read us passages from their letters. My classmates missed no opportunity to humiliate him. At the beginning of class, he would stand up and sing 'Maréchal, nous voilà'! The blackboard was covered with *francisques* and photographs of Pétain. Debigorre would talk but no one paid him any heed. Sometimes, he would bury his head in his hands and sob. One student, a colonel's son named Gerbier, would shout 'Adrien's blubbing!' The whole class would roar with laughter. Except me, of course. I decided to be the poor man's bodyguard. Despite my recent bout of tuberculosis, I stood six foot six and weighed nearly 200 pounds, and as luck would have it, I had been born in a country of short-arsed bastards.

I began by splitting Gerbie's eyebrow. A lawyer's son, a boy named Val-Suzon, called me a 'Nazi'. I broke three of his vertebrae in memory of SS officer Schlemilovitch who died on the Russian front during the Ardennes Offensive. All that remained was to bring a few little Gauls to heel: Chatel-Gérard, Saint-Thibault, La Rochepot. Thereafter it was I and not Debigorre who read Maurras, Chack or Béraud at the beginning of class. Terrified of my vicious streak, you could hear a pin drop, this was the reign of Jewish terror and our old schoolmaster soon found his smile again.

After all, why did classmates make such a show of seeming disgusted?

Surely Maurras, Chack and Béraud were just like their grandfathers.

Here I was taking the trouble to introduce them to the healthiest, the purest of their compatriots and the ungrateful bastards called me a 'Nazi' . . .

'Let's have them study the *Romanciers du terroir*,' I suggested to Debigorre. 'These little degenerates need to study the rural novels celebrating their fathers' glories. It'll make a change from

Trotsky, Kafka and the rest of that gypsy rabble. Besides, it's not like they even understand them. It takes two thousand years of pogroms, my dear Debigorre, to be able to tackle such books. If I were called Val-Suzon, I wouldn't be so presumptuous. I'd settle for exploring the provinces, quenching my thirst from French springs! Listen, for the first term, we'll teach them about your friend Béraud. A good solid writer from Lyons seems entirely appropriate. A few comments on novels like *Les Lurons de Sabolas* . . . We can follow up with Eugène le Roy: *Jacquou le Croquant* and *Mademoiselle de la Ralphie* will teach them the beauties of the Périgord. A little detour through Quercy courtesy of Léon Cladel. A trip to Bretagne under the aegis of Charles Le Goffic. Roupnel can take us on a tour of Bourgogne. The Bourbonnais will hold no secrets for us after reading Guillaumin's *La Vie d'un simple*. Through Alphonse Daudet and Paul Arène we will smell the scents of Provence. We can discuss Maurras and Mistral! In the second term, we can revel in the Touraine autumn with René Boylesve. Have you read *L'Enfant à la balustrade*? It's remarkable! The third term will be devoted to the psychological novels of the Dijon author Édouard Estaunié. In short, a sentimental tour of France! What do you think of my syllabus?'

Debigorre was smiling and clasping my hands in his. He said to me:

'Schlemilovitch, you are a scholar and patriot! If only the native French lads were like you!'

D ebigorre often invites me to his home. He lives in a room cluttered with books and papers. On the walls hang yellowing photographs of various oddballs: Bichelonne, Hérold-Paquis and admirals Esteva, Darlan and Platón. His elderly housekeeper serves us tea. At about 11 p.m. we have an aperitif on the terrace of the Café de Bordeaux. On my first visit, I surprise him hugely by talking about the Maurras' mannerisms and Pujo's beard. 'But you weren't even born, Raphäel!' Debigorre thinks it is a case of transmigration of souls, that in some former life I was a fierce supporter of Maurras, a pureblood Frenchman, an unrepentant Gaulois and a Jewish collaborator to boot: 'Ah, Raphäel, how I wish you had been in Bordeaux in June 1940! Picture the outrageous scenes! Gentlemen with beards and black frockcoats! University students! Ministers of the RÉ-PU-BLI-QUE are chattering away! Making grand gestures! Réda Caire and Maurice Chevalier are singing songs! Suddenly – BANG! – blond bare-chested youths burst into the Café du Commerce! They start a wholesale massacre! The gentlemen in frockcoats are thrown against the ceiling. They slam into the walls, crash into the rows of bottles. They splash about in puddles of Pernod, heads slashed by broken glass! The manageress, a woman named Marianne, is running this way and that. She gives little cries. The woman's an old whore! THE SLUT! Her skirt falls off. She's gunned down in a hail of machine gunfire. Caire and Chevalier suddenly fall silent. What a sight, Raphäel, for enlightened minds like ours! What vengeance! . . . '

Eventually, I tire of my role as martinet. Since my classmates refuse to accept that Maurras, Chack and Béraud are their people, since they look down on Charles Le Goffic and Paul Arène, Debigorre and I will talk to them about some more universal aspects of 'French genius': vividness and ribaldry, the beauties of classicism, the pertinence of moralists, the irony of Voltaire, the subtleties of psychological novels, the heroic tradition from Corneille to Georges Bernanos. Debigorre bridles at the mention of Voltaire. I am equally repulsed by that bourgeois 'rebel' and anti-Semite, but if we don't mention him in our *Panorama of French genius*, we will be accused of bias. 'Let's be reasonable,' I say to Debigorre, 'you know perfectly well that I personally prefer Joseph de Maistre. Let's make a little effort to include Voltaire.'

Once again, Saint-Thibault disrupts one of our lectures. An inopportune remark by Debigorre, 'The utterly French grace of the exquisite Mme de La Fayette', has my classmate leaping from his seat in indignation.

'When are you going to stop talking about "French genius", about how something is "quintessentially French", about "the French tradition"?' bellows the young Gaulois. My mentor Trotsky says that the Revolution knows no country . . .

'My dear Saint-Thibault,' I said, 'you're starting to get on my nerves. You are too jowly and your blood too thick for the name Trotsky from your lips to be anything other than blasphemy. My dear Saint-Thibault, your great-great-uncle Charles Maurras wrote that it is impossible to understand Mme de La Fayette or Chamfort unless one has tilled the soil of France for a thousand years! Now it is my turn to tell you something, my dear Saint-Thibault: it takes a thousand years of pogroms, of auto-da-fés and ghettos to understand even a paragraph of Marx or Bronstein . . . BRONSTEIN, my dear Saint-Thibault, and not Trotsky as you so elegantly call him! Now shut your trap, my dear Saint-Thibault, or I shall . . .'

The parents' association were up in arms, the headmaster summoned me to his office.

'Schlemilovitch,' he told me, 'Messieurs Gerbier, Val-Suzon and La Rochepot have filed a complaint charging you with assault and battery of their sons. Defending your schoolmaster is all very commendable but you have been behaving like a lout. Do you realise that Val-Suzon has been hospitalised? That Gerbier and La Rochepot have suffered audio-visual disturbances? These are elite *khâgne* students! You could go to prison, Schlemilovitch, to prison! But for now you will leave this school, this very evening!'

'If these gentlemen want to press charges,' I said, 'I am prepared to defend myself once and for all. I'll get a lot of publicity. Paris is not Bordeaux, you know. In Paris, they always side with the poor little Jew, not with the brutish Aryans! I'll play the persecuted martyr to perfection. The Left will organise rallies and demonstrations and, believe me, it will be the done thing to sign a petition in support of Raphäel Schlemilovitch. All in all, the scandal will do considerable damage to your prospects for promotion. Remember Capitaine Dreyfus and, much more recently, all the fuss about Jacob X, the young Jewish deserter . . . Parisians are crazy about us. They always side with us. Forgive us anything. Wipe the slate clean. What do you expect? Moral standards have gone to hell since the last war – what am I saying? Since the Middle Ages! Remember the wonderful French custom where every Easter the Comte de Toulouse would ceremoniously slap the head of the Jewish community, while the man begged 'Again, *monsieur le comte*! One more, with the pommel of your sword! Batter me! Rip out my guts! Trample my corpse!' A blessed age. How could my forebear from Toulouse ever imagine that one day I would break Val-Suzon's vertebrae? Put out the eye of a Gerbier or a La Rochepot? Every dog has his day, headmaster. Revenge is a dish best served cold. And don't think even for a minute that I feel remorse. You can tell the young men's parents that I'm sorry I didn't slaughter them. Just imagine the trial. A young Jew, pale and passionate, declaring that he sought only to avenge the beatings regularly meted out to his ancestors by the Comte de Toulouse! Sartre would defend me, it would take centuries off him! I'd be carried in triumph from the Place de l'Étoile to the Bastille! I'd be a fucking prince to the young people of France!'

'You are loathsome, Schlemilovitch, LOATHSOME! I refuse to listen to you a moment longer.'

'That's right, *monsieur le proviseur*, loathsome!'

'I am calling the police this instant!'

'Oh, surely not the police, *monsieur le proviseur*, call the Gestapo, please.'

I left the lycée for good. Debigorre was upset to lose his finest pupil. We met up two or three times at the Café de Bordeaux. One Sunday evening, he did not appear. His housekeeper told me he had been taken to a mental home in Arcachon. I was strictly forbidden from seeing him. Only monthly visits from family members were permitted.

I knew that every night my former teacher was calling out to me for help because apparently Léon Blum was hounding him with implacable hatred. Via his housekeeper, he sent me a hastily scrawled message: 'Save me, Raphäel. Blum and the others are trying to kill me. I'm sure of it. They slip into my room like reptiles in the night. They taunt me. They threaten me with butcher's knives. Blum, Mandel, Zay, Salengro, Dreyfus and the rest of them. They want to hack me to pieces. I'm begging you, Raphäel, save me.'

That was the last I heard of him.

Old men, it would seem, play a crucial role in my life.

Two weeks after leaving the lycée, I was spending my last few francs at the Restaurant Dubern when a man sat down at the table next to mine. My attention was immediately drawn to his monocle and his long jade cigarette holder. He was completely bald, which gave him a rather unsettling appearance. As he ate, he never took his eyes off me. He beckoned the head waiter with an insolent flick of the finger: his index seemed to trace an arabesque in the air. I saw him write a few words on a visiting card. He pointed to me and the head waiter brought over the little white rectangle on which I read:

VICOMTE CHARLES LÉVY-VENDÔME
Master of Ceremonies, would like the pleasure of your acquaintance

He takes a seat opposite me.

'Excuse my rather cavalier manner, but I invariably force an entry into other people's lives. A face, an expression, can be enough to win my friendship. I was most impressed by your resemblance to Gregory Peck. Aside from that, what do you do for a living?'

He had a beautiful, deep voice.

'You can tell me your life story somewhere more dusky. What do you say to the Morocco?'

At the Morocco, the dance floor was utterly deserted despite Noro Morales' wild *guarachas* blasting from the loudspeakers. Latin America was decidedly the vogue in Bordeaux that autumn.

'I've just been expelled from school,' I explained, 'aggravated assault. I'm a young hoodlum, and Jewish to boot. My name is Raphäel Schlemilovitch.'

'Schlemilovitch? Well, well! All the more reason that we should be friends. I myself belong to a long-established Jewish family from the Loiret. My ancestors were jesters to the dukes of Pithiviers for generations. Your life story does not interest me. I wish to know whether or not you are looking for work.'

'I am looking, *monsieur le vicomte.*'

'Very well then. I am a host. I host . . . I conceive, I develop, I devise . . . I have need of your help. You are a young man of impeccable pedigree. Good presence, come-hither eyes, American smile. Let us speak man to man. What do you think of French girls?'

'Pretty.'

'And?'

'They would make first-class whores!'

'Admirable! I like your turn of phrase! Now, cards on table, Schlemilovitch! I work in the white slave trade! As it happens, the French girl is particularly prized in the market. You will supply the merchandise. I am too old to take on such work. In 1925, it required no effort; these days, if I wish to be attractive to women, I have them smoke opium beforehand. Who would have thought the sultry young Lévy-Vendôme would turn into a satyr when he turned fifty? Now, you Schlemilovitch, you have many years ahead of you; make the most of them! Use your natural talents to debauch your Aryan girls. Later, you can write your memoir. It will be called *The Rootless*: *the story of seven French girls who could not resist the charms of Schlemilovitch the Jew only to find themselves, one fine day, working in brothels in the Orient or in South America.* The moral of the story: they should not have trusted this Jewish lothario, they should have stayed on the cool mountain slopes, in the verdant groves. You will dedicate your memoir to Maurice Barrès.'

'As your wish, *monsieur le vicomte.*'

'Now, to work, my boy. You leave immediately for the Haute-Savoie. I have just received an order from Rio de Janeiro: "Young French mountain girl. Brunette. Husky." From there, you will move on to Normandy. This time the order is from Beirut: "Elegant French girl whose ancestors fought in the crusades.

Good provincial landed gentry." The client is clearly a lecher after our own hearts! An emir who wants to avenge himself for Charles Martel . . .'

'Or the sack of Constantinople by the crusaders . . .'

'If you prefer. In short, I have found what he requires. In the Calvados region . . . A young woman . . . descended from a venerable aristocratic family! Seventeenth-century château! Cross and Lance heads with fleurs-de-lis on a field Azure. Hunting parties! The ball is in your court, Schlemilovitch. There is not a moment to lose. We have our work cut out for us! The abductions must involve no bloodshed. Come, have one last drink at my place, then I will accompany you to the station.'

Lévy-Vendôme's apartment is furnished in the Napoleon III style. The vicomte ushers me into his library.

'Have you ever seen such exquisite bindings?' he says, 'I am a bibliophile, it is my secret vice. See, if I take down a volume at random: a treatise on aphrodisiacs by René Descartes. Apocrypha, nothing but apocrypha . . . I have single-handedly reinvented the whole history of French literature. Here we have the love letters of Pascal to Mlle de La Vallière. A bawdy saga by Boussuet. An erotic tale by Mme de La Fayette. Not content with debauching the women of this country, I wanted to prostitute French literature in its entirety. To transform the heroines of Racine and Marivaux into whores. Junia willingly copulating with Nero as a horrified Britannicus looks on. Andromache throwing herself into the arms of Pyrrhus at their first meeting. Marivaux's countesses donning their maids' uniforms and "borrowing" their lovers for the night. As you can see, Schlemilovitch, being involved in the white slave trade does not preclude being a man of culture. I have spent forty years writing apocrypha, devoting myself to dishonouring the most illustrious writers of France. Take a leaf out of my book, Schlemilovitch! Vengeance, Schlemilovitch, vengeance!'

Later, he introduces me to his henchmen, Mouloud and Mustapha.

'They are at your disposal,' he says, 'I shall send them to you the moment you ask. One never can tell with Aryan women. Sometimes one has to make a show of brute force. Mouloud and Mustapha are peerless when it comes to taming even the most unruly spirits – they're former Waffen SS from the Légion nord-africaine. I met them at Bonny and Laffont's place on Rue Lauriston back when I was secretary to Joanovici. Marvellous fellows. You'll see!'

Mouloud and Mustapha are so alike they could be twins. The same scarred face, the same broken nose, the same disturbing rictus. They immediately show me the greatest kindness.

Lévy-Vendôme accompanies me to the gare Saint-Jean. On the station platform, he hands me three bundles of banknotes.

'For personal expenses. Telephone to keep me up to date. Vengeance, Schlemilovitch! Vengeance! Be ruthless, Schlemilovitch! Vengeance! Ven . . .'

'As you say, *monsieur le vicomte.*'

III

Lake Annecy is romantic, but a young man working in the white slave trade must put such thoughts from his mind.

I catch the first bus for T., a market town I have chosen at random on the Michelin map. The road rises steeply, the hairpin bends make me nauseous. I feel ready to abandon my fine plans. But before long, my taste for the exotic and the desire to air my lungs in the Savoie win out over my despondency. Behind me, a few soldiers start singing 'Les montagnards sont là,' and I immediately join in. Then I stroke my wide-rib corduroy trousers, stare down at my clumpy shoes and the alpenstock bought second-hand in a little shop in old Annecy. The tactic I propose to adopt is as follows: in T., I will pass myself off as a young, inexperienced climber who knows of the mountains only from the novels of Frison-Roche. With a little skill, I should quickly ingratiate myself. I can introduce myself to the locals and furtively scout out a young girl worth shipping off to Brazil. For greater security, I have decided to take on the unassailably French identity of my friend Des Essarts. The name Schlemilovitch sounds dubious. The local savages doubtless heard about Jews back when the *Milice* were overrunning the area. The most important thing is not to arouse their suspicions. Suppress my Lévi-Straussian ethnological curiosity. Refrain from staring at their daughter like a horse trader, otherwise they will sniff out my oriental ancestry.

The bus pulls up in front of the church. I sling my rucksack over my shoulder, make my alpenstock ring against the cobbles and stride confidently to the Hôtel des Trois Glaciers. I am immediately captivated by the copper bedstead and the wallpaper in room 13. I telephone Bordeaux to inform Lévy-Vendôme of my arrival and whistle a minuet.

At first, I noticed an unease among the natives. They were unsettled by my tall stature. I knew from experience that one day this would work to my advantage. The first time I crossed the threshold of the Café Municipal, alpenstock in hand, crampons on my shoes, I felt all eyes turn to size me up. Six foot four, five, six, seven? The bets were on. M. Gruffaz, the baker, guessed correctly and scooped the pot and immediately struck up a keen friendship with me. Did M. Gruffaz have a daughter? I would find out soon enough. He introduced me to his friends, the lawyer Forclaz-Manigot and the pharmacist Petit-Savarin. The three men offered me an apple brandy that had me coughing and spluttering. They told me they were waiting for their friend Aravis, a retired colonel, for a game of belote. I asked permission to join them, feeling grateful that Lévy-Vendôme had taught me belote just before I left. I remembered his pertinent remark: 'I should warn you now that working in the white slave trade is not exactly exciting, especially when one is trading in young French girls from the provinces. You must cultivate the interests of a commercial traveller: belote, billiards and aperitifs are the best means of infiltrating these groups.' The three men asked the reason for my stay in T. I explained, as planned, that I was a young French aristocrat with a keen interest in mountaineering.

'Colonel Aravis will like you,' Forclaz-Manigot confided. 'Stout fellow, Aravis, used to be a mountain infantryman. Loves the peaks. Obsessed with climbers. He'll advise you.'

Colonel Aravis arrives and looks me up and down, considering my future as an alpine chasseur. I give him a hearty handshake and click my heels.

'Jean-François Des Essarts! Pleased to meet you, sir!'

'Strapping lad!' he says to the others, 'perfect for the force!'

He becomes paternal:

'I fear, young man, that we don't have time to put you through the rock-climbing exercise that would have given me a better sense of your talents. Never mind, another time. But I guarantee I'll make a seasoned climber out of you. You seem hale and willing and that's the important part!'

My four new friends settle down to playing cards. Outside, it is snowing. I engross myself in reading *L'Écho-Liberté*, the local newspaper. I discover there is a Marx Brothers film playing at the cinema in T. There are six of us, then, six brothers exiled in the Savoie. I feel a little less alone.

On reflection I found the Savoie as charming as I had Guyenne. Was this not the homeland of Henry Bordeaux? When I was about sixteen, I read *Les Roquevillard*, *La Chartreuse du reposoir* and *Le Calvaire du Cimiez* with devotion. A stateless Jew, I hungrily drank in the rustic redolence of these master-pieces. I cannot understand why Henry Bordeaux has fallen from favour in recent years. He had a decisive influence on me and I will be forever loyal to him.

Luckily, I discovered my new-found friends had tastes identical to mine. Aravis read the works of Capitaine Danrit, Petit-Savarin had a weakness for René Bazin and Gruffaz, the baker, set great store by Édouard Estaunié. He had nothing to teach me about the virtues of that particular writer. In *What is literature?*, Des Essarts described the author as follows: 'I consider Édouard Estaunié to be the most deviant author I have ever read. At first glance, Estaunié's characters seem reassuring: paymasters, postmistresses, provincial seminarians, but do not be deceived by appearances: the paymaster has the soul of an anarchist bomber, the postmistress works as a prostitute after her shift at the PTT, the young seminarian is as bloodthirsty as Gilles de Rais . . . Estaunié chose to camouflage vice beneath black frockcoats, mantillas, even soutanes: he is de Sade as petty clerk, he is Genet dragged up as Saint Bernadette of Lourdes.' I read this passage to Forclaz-Manigot, telling him that I had written it. He congratulated me and invited me to dinner. During the meal,

I surreptitiously studied his wife. She seemed a little mature, but, if I found nothing better, I decided I would not be choosy. And so, we were living out a novel by Estaunié: the young French aristocrat, so keen on mountaineering, was really a Jew working in the white slave trade; the lawyer's wife, so reserved, so provincial, would all too soon find herself in a Brazilian brothel if I so decided.

Beloved Savoie! To my dying day I will have fond memories of Colonel Aravis. Every little French boy has a grandfather just like him somewhere in the depths of the provinces. He is ashamed of him. Our friend Sartre would like to forget his great uncle Doctor Schweitzer. When I visit Gide in his ancestral home at Cuverville, he mutters over and over, 'Families, I despise you! Families, I despise you!' Only Aragon, my childhood friend, has not spurned his origins. I am grateful to him for that. When Stalin was alive, he would proudly tell me, 'The Aragons have been cops, father and son, for generations!' One point in his favour. The other two are nothing more than wayward children.

I, Raphäel Schlemilovitch, listened respectfully to my grandfather, Colonel Aravis, as once I had listened to my great-uncle Adrien Debigorre.

'Become a mountain infantryman, Des Essarts, goddammit! You'll be a heartthrob with the ladies. A strapping fellow like you! In uniform, you would turn heads.'

Unfortunately, the uniform of the *chasseurs alpins* reminded me of the *Milice* uniform I had died in twenty years earlier.

'My love of uniforms has never brought me luck,' I explained to the colonel. 'Back in 1894, it got me a notorious trial and several years imprisoned on Devil's Island. The Schlemilovitch Affair, remember?'

The colonel was not listening. He stared me straight in the eye and bellowed:

'Head up, dear boy, please! A strong handshake. Above all don't snigger. We have had enough of seeing the French race denigrated. What we want now is purity.'

I felt very moved. This was just the sort of advice Jo Darnand used to give me when we were battling the Résistance.

Every night, I report back to Lévy-Vendôme. I talk to him about Mme Forclaz-Manigot, the lawyer's wife. He tells me his client in Rio is not interested in mature women. This left me doomed to spending quite some time in the lonely heights of T. I am champing at the bit. Colonel Aravis will be no help, he lives alone. Neither Petit-Savarin nor Gruffaz has daughters. On the other hand, Lévy-Vendôme has specifically forbidden me from meeting young village girls other than through their parents or their husbands: a reputation for being a skirt-chaser would close all doors to me.

IN WHICH THE ABBÉ PERRACHE
GETS ME OUT OF A SCRAPE

I run into this clergyman while in the course of a leisurely stroll around T. Leaning against a tree, he is studying nature, a typical Savoyard parish priest. I am struck by the goodness etched into his face. We strike up a conversation. He talks to me about the Jew Jesus Christ. I talk to him about another Jew named Judas of whom Jesus Christ said 'Good were it for that man if he had never been born!' Our theological discussion continues all the way to the village square. Father Perrache is saddened by my preoccupation with Judas. 'You are a desperate soul,' he tells me gravely, 'despair is the worst sin of all.' I tell this saintly man that my family have sent me to T. to get some fresh air into my lungs and some order into my thoughts. I tell him about my all-too-brief time studying in Bordeaux, explaining that I hated the radical socialist atmosphere of the lycée. He rebukes me for my intransigence. 'Think of Péguy,' he says, 'he divided his time between Chartres cathedral and the *Ligue des insituteurs*. He did his best to teach Jean Jaurès about the glories of Saint Louis and Joan of Arc. One tries not to be too elitist, my son! I tell him I prefer Monsignor Mayol de Lupé: a Catholic should take Christ's interests seriously, even if it means enlisting in the LVF. A Catholic should wield a sword, should declare, like Simon de Montfort, 'God will know His own!' In fact, the Inquisition, in my opinion, was a public health measure. I think it was compassionate of Torquemada and Ximénes to want to cure these people who complacently wallowed in their sickness, in their Jewry; it was kind-hearted of them to offer them a surgical solution rather than leaving them to die of their consumption.' After that, I sing the praises of Joseph de Maistre and Édouard Drumont and inform him that God has no time for the mealy-mouthed.

'Neither for the mealy-mouthed nor for the proud,' he tells me, 'and you are committing the sin of Pride, which is just as grave as the sin of Despair. Here, let me set you a little task. You can consider it a penance, an act of contrition. The bishop of this diocese will be visiting the school here in T. a week from now: you will write a welcoming speech which I will pass on to the headmaster. It will be read to His Grace by a young pupil on behalf of the whole community. In it, you will show level-headedness, compassion and humility. Let us pray this exercise brings you back to the path of righteousness! I know you are a lost sheep who wants only to return to the flock. Each man in his darkness goes towards his Light! I have faith in you.' (Sighs.)

A young blonde girl in the garden of the presbytery. She stares at me curiously: Fr. Perrache introduces me to his niece Loïtia. She is wearing the navy blue uniform of a boarding school girl.

Loïtia lights a paraffin lamp. The Savoyard furniture smells of wax polish. I like the chromolithograph on the left-hand wall. The priest gently lays a hand on my shoulder:

'Schlemilovitch, you can write and tell your family that you are now in good hands. I shall see to your spiritual health. The mountain air will do the rest. And now, my boy, you are going to write the welcoming speech for the bishop. Loïtia, could you please bring us tea and some brioches? This man needs to build up his strength.'

I look at Loïtia's pretty face. The nuns at Notre-Dame-des-Fleurs insist that she wear her blonde hair in plaits but, thanks to me, soon she will let it tumble over her shoulders. Having decided to introduce her to the wonders of Brazil, I step into her uncle's study and pen a welcoming speech for His Grace Nuits-Saint-Georges:

'Your Grace,

'In every parish of the noble diocese that it has pleased Providence to entrust to him, the Bishop Nuit-Saint-Georges is welcome, bringing as he does the comfort of his presence and the precious blessings of his ministry.

'But he is particularly welcome here in the picturesque valley of T., renowned for its many-hued mantle of meadows and forests . . .

'This same valley which a historian of recent memory called "a land of priests fondly attached to their spiritual leaders". Here in this school built through magnanimous, sometimes heroic gestures . . . Your Grace is at home here . . . and an eddy of joyous impetuousness, stirring our little universe, has anticipated and solemnized your arrival.

'Your Grace, you bring the comfort of your support and the light of your counsel to the teachers, your devoted collaborators whose task is a particularly thankless one; you bestow upon the pupils, the benevolence of your fatherly smile and an interest of which they strive to be deserving . . . We joyfully commend you as an informed educator, a friend to youth, a zealous promoter of all things that foster the influence of Christian Schools – a living reality and the promise of a bright future of our country.

'For you, Your Grace, the well-tended lawns that flank the gates are freshly coiffed and a scattering of flowers – despite the bleakness of the season – sing their symphony of colours; for you, our House, ordinarily a buzzing, boisterous hive, is filled with contemplation and with silence; for you, the somewhat humdrum rhythm of classes and courses has interrupted its flow . . . This is a great and holy day, a day of serene joy and of good resolutions!

'We wish to participate, Your Grace, in the great work of renewal and reconstruction on the building sites excavated in this new era by the Church and by France. Honoured by your visit and mindful of such counsel as you choose to offer, with joyful hearts we offer Your Grace the traditional filial salute:

'Blessed be Bishop Nuits-Saint-Georges,

'*Heil* to His Grace our Bishop!'

I hope my work pleases Father Perrache and allows me to cultivate our precious friendship: my career in the white slave trade depends on it.

Fortunately, he dissolves into tears as he reads from the first lines and lavishes me with praise. He will personally share the delights of my prose with the headmaster.

Loïtia is sitting by the fire. Her head is tilted to one side, she has the pensive look of a girl in a Botticelli painting. She will be a big hit in the brothels of Rio next summer.

Canon Saint-Gervais, the school principal, was very satisfied with my speech. At our first meeting, he suggested I might replace the history teacher, Fr. Ivan Canigou, who had disappeared without leaving a forwarding address. According to Saint-Gervais, Fr. Canigou, a handsome man, had been unable to resist his vocation as a missionary and planned to convert the Gentiles of Xinjiang; he would not be seen again in T. Through Fr. Perrache, the Canon knew of my studies for the *École Normale Supèrieure* and had no doubts as to my talents as a historian.

'You would take over from Fr. Canigou until we can find a new history teacher. It will give you something to keep you occupied. What do you say?'

I raced to break the good news to Fr. Perrache.

'I personally implored the Canon to find something to occupy your free time. Idleness is not good for you. To work, my child! You are back on the right path! Take care not to stray again!'

I asked his permission to play belote which he readily gave. At the Café Municipal, Colonel Aravis, Forclaz-Manigot and Petit-Savarin greeted me warmly. I told them of my new post and we drank plum brandy from the Meuse and clapped each other on the back.

At this particular point in my biography, I think it best to consult the newspapers. Did I enter a seminary as Perrache advised me? Henry Bordeaux's article 'Fr. Raphäel Schlemilovitch: a new "Curé d'Ars"' (*Action française*, October 23, 19—) would seem to suggest as much: the novelist compliments me for the apostolic zeal I show in the tiny Savoie village of T.

Meanwhile, I take long walks in the company of Loïtia. Her delightful uniform and her hair colour my Saturdays navy blue and blonde. We bump into Colonel Aravis, who gives us a knowing smile. Forclaz-Manigot and Petit-Savarin have even offered to stand witness at our wedding. Gradually, I forget the reasons why I came to Savoie and the sardonic smirk of Lévy-Vendôme. No, I will never deliver the innocent Loïtia into the hands of Brazilian pimps. I will settle permanently in T. Peacefully and humbly, I will go to work as a schoolteacher. By my side, I shall have a loving wife, an old priest, a kindly colonel, a genial lawyer and a pharmacist . . . Rain claws at the windows, the fire in the hearth gives off a gentle glow, *monsieur l'abbé* is speaking to me softly, Loïtia is bent over her needlework. From time to time our eyes meet. Fr. Perrache asks me to recite a poem . . .

My heart, smile towards the future now . . .
The bitter words I have allayed
And darkling dreams have sent away.

And then:

. . . The fireside, the lamplight's slender beam . . .

At night, in my cramped hotel room, I write the first part of my memoir to be rid of my turbulent youth. I gaze confidently at the mountains and the forests, the Café Municipal and the church. The Jewish contortions are over. I hate the lies that caused me so much pain. The earth, the earth does not lie.

Chest proudly puffed with fine resolutions, I took wing and set off to teach the history of France. Before my pupils, I indulged in a wild courtship of Joan of Arc. I set off on all the Crusades, I fought at Bouvines, at Rocroi, on the bridge at Arcola. I quickly realised, alas, that I lacked the *furia francese*. The blonde chevaliers outpaced me as we marched and the banners with their fleurs-de-lis fell from my hands. A Yiddish woman's lament spoke to me of a death that wore no spurs, no plumes, no white gloves.

In the end, when I could bear it no longer, I pointed my forefinger at Cran-Gevrier, my best pupil:

'It was a Jew who broke the vase of Soissons! A Jew, d'you hear me! Write out a hundred times "It was a Jew who broke the vase of Soissons!" Learn your lessons, Cran-Gevrier! No marks, Cran-Gevrier! You will stay back after class!'

Cran-Gevrier started to sob. So did I.

I stalked out of the classroom and sent a telegram to Lévy-Vendôme to tell him I would deliver Loïtia the following Saturday. I suggested Geneva as a possible rendezvous for the handover. Then, I stayed up until three o'clock in the morning writing a critique of myself, 'A Jew in the Countryside', in which I derided my weakness for the French provinces. I did not mince words: 'Having been a collaborationist Jew like Joanovici-Sachs, Raphaël Schlemilovitch is now playing out a "Back to the land" shtick of a Barrès-Pétain. How long before we get the squalid farce of the militarist Jew like Capitaine Dreyfus-Stroheim? The self-loathing Jew like Simone Weil-Céline? The eminent Jew in the mould of Proust-Daniel Halévy-Maurois? We would like Raphäel Schlemilovitch simply to be a Jew . . .'

This act of contrition done, the world once again took on the colours that I love. Spotlights raked the village square, boots pounded the cobbled streets. Colonel Aravis was rudely awakened, as were Forclaz-Manigot, Gruffaz, Petit-Savarin, Fr. Perrache, my best pupil Cran-Gevrier and my fiancée Loïtia. They were interrogated about me. A Jew hiding out in the Haute-Savoie. A dangerous Jew. Public enemy number one. There was a price on my head. When had they last seen me? My friends would unquestionably turn me in. The *Milice* were already on their way to the Hôtel des Trois Glaciers. They broke down the door to my room. And there, sprawled on my bed, I waited, yes, I waited and whistled a minuet.

I drink my last plum brandy at the Café Municipal. Colonel Aravis, the lawyer Forclaz-Manigot, the pharmacist Petit-Savarin and Gruffaz the baker wish me a safe journey.

'I'll be back tomorrow night for our game of belote,' I promise, 'I'll bring you some Swiss chocolate.'

I tell Fr. Perrache that my father is staying in a hotel in Geneva and would like to spend the evening with me. He makes a little something for me to eat and tells me not to dawdle on the way back.

I get off the bus at Veyrier-du-Lac and take up my position outside Notre-Dame-des-Fleurs. Soon afterwards, Loïtia comes through the wrought iron gates. After that, everything goes as I had planned. Her eyes shine as I talk to her of love, of empty promises, of abductions, of adventures, of swashbucklers. I lead her to Annecy coach station. From there we take a bus to Geneva. Cruseilles, Annemasse, Saint-Julien, Geneva, Rio de Janeiro.

Giraudoux's girls love to travel. This one, however, seems a little anxious. She reminds me she doesn't have a suitcase. Don't worry. We'll buy everything we need when we get there. I'll introduce her to my father, Vicomte Lévy-Vendôme, who will shower her with gifts. He's very sweet, you'll see. Bald. He has a monocle and a long jade cigarette-holder. Don't be scared. This gentlemen means well. We cross the border. Quickly. We drink fruit juice at the bar of the Hôtel des Bergues while we wait for the vicomte. He strides up to us, flanked by his henchmen Mouloud and Mustapha. Quickly. He puffs nervously on his jade cigarette-holder. He adjusts his monocle and hands me an envelope stuffed with dollars.

'Your wages! I'll take care of the young lady! You have no time to lose! From Savoie you go to Normandy! Call me on my Bordeaux number as soon as you arrive!'

Loïtia gives me a panicked glance. I tell her I will be right back.

That night, I walked along the banks of the Rhône thinking of Jean Giraudoux, of Colette, Marivaux, Verlaine, Charles d'Orléans, Maurice Scève, Rémy Belleau and Corneille. I am coarse and crude compared to such people. I am unworthy. I ask their forgiveness for being born in the Île-de-France rather than Vilnius, Lithuania. I scarcely dare write in French: such a delicate language putrefies beneath my pen . . .

I scrawl another fifty pages. After that, I shall give up literature. I swear it.

In Normandy, I will put the finishing touches to my sentimental education. Fougeire-Jusquiames, a little town in Calvados, set off by a seventeenth-century château. As in T., I take a hotel room. This time, I pass myself off as a sales representative for exotic foods. I offer the manageress of Les Trois-Vikings some Turkish delight and question her about the lady of the manor, Véronique de Fougeire-Jusquiames. She tells me everything she knows: *madame la marquise* lives alone, the villagers see her only at high mass on Sundays. Every year, she organises a hunt. Tourists are allowed to visit the château on Saturday afternoons for three hundred francs a head. Gérard, the Marquise's chauffeur, acts as guide.

That same evening, I telephone Lévy-Vendôme to tell him I have arrived in Normandy. He implores me to carry out my mission as quickly as possible: our client, the Emir of Samandal, has been daily sending impatient telegrams threatening to cancel the contract if the merchandise is not delivered within the week. Clearly, Lévy-Vendôme does not understand the difficulties I face. How can I, Raphäel Schlemilovitch, make the acquaintance of a marquise overnight? Especially since I am not in Paris, but in Fougeire-Jusquiames, in the heart of rural France. Around here, no Jew, however handsome, would be allowed anywhere near the château except on Saturdays with all the other paying guests.

I spend all night studying a dossier compiled by Lévy-Vendôme on the lineage of the marquise. Her pedigree is excellent. The *Directory of French Nobility*, founded in 1843 by Baron Samuel Bloch-Morel, offers the following summary: 'FOUGEIRE-JUSQUIAMES: Seat: Normandie-Poitou. Lineage: Jourdain de Jusquiames, a natural son of Eleanor of Aquitaine. Motto: "Jusquiames, do or damn, Fougère ne'er despair." The House of Jusquiames supplants the earlier comtes de Fougeire in 1385. Title: duc de Jusquiames (hereditary duchy) under letters patent of 20 September 1603; made hereditary member of the *Chambre des pairs* by the decree of 30 August 1817. Hereditary Duke-Peer (duc de Jusquiame) Cadet branch: *baron romain*, papal brief of 19 June 1819, ratified by the decree of 7 September 1822; prince with right of transmission to all descendants by decree of the King of Bavaria of 6 March 1846. Advanced to the dignity of hereditary Count-Peer, by the edict of June 10, 1817. Arms: Gules on a field Azure, Fleurs-De-Lis sautéed with Stars per Saltire.'

In their chronicles of the Fourth Crusade, Robert de Clary, Villehardouin and Henri de Valenciennes offer testaments to the good conduct of the Seigneurs de Fougeire, Froissard, Commynes and Montluc and heap praise upon the valiant Capitaine de Jusquiames. In chapter X of his history of Saint Louis, Joinville recalls a good deed by a knight of the de Fougiere family: 'Then did this right worthy man raise up his sword and smite the Jew 'twixt the eyes dashing him to the ground. And lo! the Jews did turn and flee taking with them their wounded master.'

On Sunday morning, he posted himself at the entrance to the church. Shortly before eleven o'clock, a black limousine pulled into the square; his heart was pounding. A blonde woman was walking towards him but he dared not look at her. He followed her into the church, struggling to master his emotions. How pure her profile was! Above her, a stained glass window depicted the entrance of Eleanor of Aquitaine into Jerusalem. She looked just like the Marquise de Fougeire-Jusquiames. The same blonde hair, the same tilt of the head, the same slender, delicate neck. His eyes moved from marquise to queen and he thought: 'How beautiful she is! What nobleness! I see before me a proud Jusquiames, a descendent of Eleanor of Aquitaine.' Or 'The glories of the Jusquiames precede the reign of Charlemagne, they held the power of life and death over their vassals. The Marquise de Jusquiames is descended in direct line from Eleanor of Aquitaine. She neither knows nor would she deign to know any of the people gathered here.' Certainly not Schlemilovitch. He decided to abandon his efforts: Lévy-Vendôme would surely understand that they had been presumptuous. To transform Eleanor of Aquitaine into the denizen of a brothel. The prospect was repugnant. One may be called Schlemilovitch and yet nurture a flicker of sensitivity in one's heart. The organ and the hymns awakened his nobler disposition. Never would he give up this princess, this fairy, this saint of the Saracens. He would strive to be her hireling, a Jewish pageboy, granted, but mores have changed since the twelfth century and the Marquise de Fougeire-Jusquiames would not take offence at his origins. He would take on the identity of his friend Des Essarts so he might more readily introduce himself. He would talk to her about his own forebears, about Foulques Des Essarts who gutted two hundred Jews before setting off for the Crusades. Foulques was right to do so, these Jews boiled the Host, their slaughter was too kind a punishment, for the bodies of even a thousand Jews are not the equivalent of the sacred Body of Our Lord.

As she left the mass, the Marquise glanced distantly at her congregation. Was it some illusion? Her eyes of periwinkle blue seemed to fix on him. Did she sense the devotion he had vowed to her not an hour since?

He raced across the church square. When the black limousine was only twenty metres away, he collapsed in the middle of the road, pretending a fainting fit. He heard the brakes squeal. A mellifluous voice murmured:

'Gérard, help that poor young man into the car! A sudden malaise no doubt! His face is so pale! We will prepare a hot toddy for him at the château.'

He was careful not to open his eyes. The back seat on which the chauffeur laid him smelled of Russian leather but he had only to repeat to himself the sweet name of Jusquiames for a scent of violets and brushwood to caress his nose. He was dreaming of the blonde tresses of Princess Eleanor, of the château towards which he was gliding. Not for a moment did it occur to him that, having been a collaborationist Jew, a bookish Jew, a bucolic Jewish, he was now in danger, in this limousine emblazoned with the Marquise's coat of arms (Gules on a field Azure, Fleurs-De-Lis sautéed with Stars per Saltire), of becoming a snobbish Jew.

The Marquise asked him no questions as though she found his presence entirely natural. They strolled together through the grounds of the château, she showed him the flowers and the beautiful spring waters. Then, they went up to the house. He admired the portrait of Cardinal de Fougeire-Jusquiames. He found the Marquise enchanting. The inflections of her voice were pierced by the jagged contours of the land itself. Subjugated, he murmured to himself: 'The energy and charm of a cruel little girl of one of the noble families of France who from her childhood had been brought up in the saddle, had tortured cats, gouged out the eyes of rabbits . . .'

After a candlelit dinner served by Gérard, they sat and chatted by the monumental fireplace in the drawing room. The Marquise talked to him about herself, about her grandparents, her uncles and cousins . . . Soon, nothing of the Fougeire-Jusquiames family was unknown to him.

I stroke a Claude Lorrain hanging on the left-hand wall of my bedroom: *The Embarkation of Eleanor of Aquitaine for the Orient*. Then I study Watteau's *Sad Harlequin*. I step around the Savonnerie carpet, fearful of soiling it. I do not deserve such a prestigious room. Nor the *epée de page* – the little sword upon the mantel. Nor the Philippe de Champaigne that hangs next to my bed, a bed in which Louis XIV slept with Mlle de La Vallière. From my window, I see a woman on horseback galloping through the grounds. For the Marquise goes every morning at five o'clock to ride Bayard, her favourite horse. At a fork in the path, she disappears. Nothing now disturbs the silence. And so I decide to embark upon a sort of biographical novel. I have memorised every detail the Marquise graciously gave me on the subject of her family. I shall use them to write the first volume of the work, which will be called *The Fougeire-Jusquiames Way, or the Memoirs of Saint-Simon as revised by Scheherazade and a handful of Talmudic Scholars*. In my childhood days, on the quai Conti in Paris, Miss Evelyn would read me the *Thousand and One Nights* and the *Memoirs* of Saint-Simon. Then she would turn out the light. She would leave the door to my room ajar so that I might hear, before I fell asleep, Mozart's *Serenade in G major*. Taking advantage of my drowsy state, Scheherazade and the Duc de Saint-Simon would cast shadows with a magic lantern. I would see the Princesse des Ursins step into the caves of Ali Baba, watch the marriage of Aladdin and Mlle de la Vallière, the abduction of Mme Soubise by the caliph Harun al-Rashid. The splendours of the Orient mingling with those of Versailles created a magical world which I will try to recreate in my novel.

Night falls, the Marquise de Fougeire-Jusquiames passes beneath my window on horseback. She is the faerie Mélusine, she is *La Belle aux cheveux d'or*. Nothing has changed since those days when my English governess read to me. Miss Evelyn would often take me to the Louvre. We had only to cross the Seine. Claude Lorrain, Philippe de Champaigne, Watteau, Delacroix, Corot coloured my childhood. Mozart and Haydn lulled it. Scheherazade and Saint-Simon brightened it. An exceptional childhood, a magical childhood I should tell you about. Immediately, I begin *The Fougeire-Jusquiames Way*. On a sheet of vellum bearing the arms of the Marquise, in a nervous hand, I write: 'It was, this "Fougeire-Jusquiames," like the setting of a novel, an imaginary landscape which I could with difficulty picture to myself and longed all the more to discover, set in the midst of real lands and roads which all of a sudden would become alive with heraldic details . . .'

This evening, they did not converse in front of the hearth as usual. The Marquise ushered him into a large boudoir papered in blue and adjoining her chamber. A candelabra cast a flickering glow. The floor was strewn with crimson cushions. On the walls hung bawdy prints by Moreau le Jeune, Girard and Binet, a painting in an austere style that might have been the work of Hyacinthe Rigaud depicted Eleanor of Aquitaine about to give herself to Saladin, the leader of the Saracens.

The door opened. The Marquise was dressed in a gauze dress that left her breasts free.

'You name is Schlemilovitch, isn't it?' she asked in a coarse accent he had never heard her use. 'Born in Boulogne-Billancourt? I read it on your identity card! A Jew? I love it! My great-great-uncle Palamède de Jusquiames said nasty things about Jews but he admired Marcel Proust! The Fougeire-Jusquiames, or at least the women in the family, are not prejudiced against Orientals. My ancestor, Eleanor, took advantage of the Second Crusade to cavort with Saracens while the miserable Louis VII was sacking Damascus! In 1720, another of my ancestors, the Marquise de Jusquiames, found the Turkish ambassador's son very much to her taste! On that subject, I notice you have compiled a whole Fougeire-Jusquiames dossier! I am flattered by the interest you take in our family! I even read the charming little passage, no doubt inspired by your stay at the château: 'It was, this "Fougeire-Jusquiames", like the setting of a novel, an imaginary landscape . . .' Do you take yourself for Marcel Proust, Schlemilovitch? That seems ominous! Surely you're not going to waste your youth copying out *In Search of Lost Time*? I warn you now, I'm not some fairy from your childhood! Sleeping Beauty! The Duchesse de Guermantes! *La femme-fleur*. You're wasting your time! Treat me like some whore from the Rue des Lombards, stop drooling over my aristocratic titles! My field Azure with fleurs-de-lis. Villehardouin, Froissart, Saint-Simon and all that lot! Snobbish little Jewish socialite! Enough of the quavering, the bowing and scraping! I find those gigolo good looks of yours devilishly arousing! Electrifying! Handsome thug! Charming pimp! Pretty boy! Catamite! Do you really think Fougeire-Jusquiames is "like the setting of a novel, an imaginary landscape"? It's a brothel, don't you see? The château has always been a high-class brothel. Very popular during the German occupation. My late father, Charles de Fougeire-Jusquiames, pimped for French intellectual collaborators. Statues by Arno Breker, young Luftwaffe pilots, SS Officers, Hitlerjugend, everything was arranged for the pleasure of these gentlemen! My father understood that sex often determines one's political fortunes. Now, let's talk about you, Schlemilovitch! Let's not waste time! You're a Jew? I suppose you'd like to rape a queen of France. I have various costumes up in the attic. Would you like me to dress as Anne of Austria, my angel? Blanche de Navarre? Marie Leszczyńska? Or would you rather fuck Adélaïde de Savoie? Marguerite de Provence? Jeanne d'Albret? Choose! I'll dress up a thousand different ways. Tonight, all the queens of France will be your whores . . .'

The week that ensued was truly idyllic: the Marquise constantly changed her costume to rekindle his desires. Together with the queens of France, he ravished Mme de Chevreuse, the Duchesse de Berry, the Chevalier d'Éon, Bossuet, Saint Louis, Bayard, Du Guesclin, Joan of Arc, the Comte de Toulouse and Général Boulanger.

He spent the rest of his time getting better acquainted with Gérard.

'My chauffeur enjoys an excellent reputation in the underworld,' confided Véronique. 'The gangsters call him The Undertaker or Gérard the Gestapo. Gérard was one of the Rue Lauriston gang. He was my late father's secretary, his henchman . . .'

His own father had also encountered Gérard the Gestapo. He had mentioned him during their time in Bordeaux. On 16 July 1942 Gérard had bundled Schlemilovitch *père* into a black truck: 'What do you say to an identity check at the Rue Lauriston and a little spell in Drancy?' Schlemilovitch *fils* no longer remembered by what miracle Schlemilovitch *père* escaped the clutches of this good man.

One night, leaving the Marquise, you surprised Gérard leaning on the balustrade of the veranda.

'You like the moonlight? The still pale moonlight, sad and fair? A romantic, Gérard?'

He did not have time to answer you. You grabbed his throat. The cervical vertebrae cracked slightly. You have a distasteful penchant for desecrating corpses. With the blade of a Gillette Extra-Blue, you slice away the ears. Then the eyelids. Then you gouge the eyes from their sockets. All that remained was to smash the teeth. Three heel kicks were enough.

Before burying Gérard, you considered having him stuffed and sent to your poor father, but you could no longer remember the address of Schlemilovitch Ltd., New York.

All loves are short-lived. The Marquise, dressed as Eleanor of Aquitaine, will succumb, but the sound of a car will interrupt our frolics. The brakes will shriek. I will be surprised to hear a gypsy melody. The drawing room door will be suddenly flung open. A man in a red turban will appear. Despite his fakir outfit, I will recognise the vicomte Charles Lévy-Vendôme.

Three fiddle players will appear behind him and launch into a second *czardas*. Mouloud and Mustapha will bring up the rear.

'What is going on, Schlemilovitch?' the vicomte will ask. 'We have had no news from you in days!'

He will wave to Mouloud and Mustapha.

'Take this woman to the Buick and keep a close eye on her. My apologies, madame, for bursting in unannounced, but we have no time to lose! You see, you were expected in Beirut a week ago!'

A few power slaps from Mouloud will snuff out any vague inclination to resist. Mustapha will gag and bind my companion.

'It's in the bag!' Lévy-Vendôme will quip as his henchmen drag Véronique away.

The vicomte will adjust his monocle.

'You mission has been a fiasco. I expected you to deliver the Marquise to Paris, instead of which I was personally forced to come to Fougeire-Jusquiames. You are fired, Schlemilovitch! Now, let us talk of something else. Enough melodrama for one evening. I propose we take a tour of this magnificent house in the company of our musicians. We are the new lords of Fougeire-Jusquiames. The Marquise is about to bequeath us all her worldly goods. Whether she wishes to or not!'

I can still picture that curious character with his turban and his monocle exploring the château, candelabra in hand, while the violinists played gypsy airs. He spent some time studying the portrait of cardinal de Fougeire-Jusquiames, stroked a suit of armour that had belonged to an ancestor, Jourdain, a natural son of Eleanor of Aquitaine. I showed him my bedrooms, the Watteau, the Claude Lorrain, the Philippe de Champaigne and the bed in which Louis XIV and Mlle de La Vallière had slept. He read the short passage I had written on the emblazoned paper: 'It was, this "Fougeire-Jusquiames" . . .' etc. He gave me a spiteful look. At that moment, the musicians were playing *Wiezenleid*, a Yiddish lullaby.

'Decidedly, Schlemilovitch, your time here at Fougeire-Jusquiames did not do you much good! The scents of old France have quite turned your head. When is the christening? Planning to be a 100 per cent pureblood Frenchman? I have to put a stop to your ridiculous daydreams. Read the Talmud instead of poring over histories of the Crusades. Stop slavering over the heraldic almanacs . . . Take my word for it, the star of David is worth more than all these "chevrons à sinoples" or "Gules, two lion passants", or "Azure, three fleurs-de-lis d'or". You don't imagine you're Charles Swann, do you? You're not planning to apply for membership of the Jockey Club? To join the social whirl of the Faubourg Saint-Germain. You may remember that Charles Swann himself, that idol of duchesses, arbiter of elegance, darling of the Guermantes, remembered his origins when he grew old. If I might be permitted, Schlemilovitch?'

The vicomte gestured to the violinists to interrupt their playing and, in a stentorian voice, declaimed:

'Perhaps too, in these last days, the physical type that characterises his race was becoming more pronounced in him, at the same time as a sense of moral solidarity with the rest of the Jews, a solidarity which Swann seemed to have forgotten throughout his life, and which, one after another, his mortal illness, the Dreyfus case and the anti-Semitic propaganda had revived . . .'

'We always return to our own people, Schlemilovitch! Even after long years of straying!'

In a monotone he recited:

'The Jew is the substance of God; non-Jews are but cattle seed; non-Jews are created to serve Jews. We order that every Jew, three times each day, should curse the Christian peoples and call upon God to exterminate them with their kings and princes. The Jew who rapes or despoils a non-Jewish woman or even kills her must be absolved in justice for he has wronged only a mare.'

He removed his turban and put on a false, preposterously hooked nose.

'You've never seen me play the role of Süss the Jew? Picture it, Schlemilovitch! I have just killed the Marquise, I have drunk her blood like a self-respecting vampire. The blood of Eleanor of Aquitaine and her valiant knights! Now I unfold my vulture's wings. I grimace. I contort myself. Musicians, please, play your wildest *czardas*. See my hands, Schlemilovitch! The nails like talons! Louder, musicians, louder! I cast a venomous glance at the Watteau, the Philippe de Champaigne, I will rip up the Savonnerie carpet with my claws! Slash the old master paintings! In a short while, I will run about the château howling in a terrifying manner. I will overturn the crusaders' suits of armour! When I have sated my rage, I will sell this ancestral home. Preferably to a South American magnate. The king of *guano*, for example. With the money I shall buy sixty pairs of crocodile-skin moccasins, emerald green alpaca suits, panther-skin coats, ribbed shirts with orange stripes. I shall have thirty mistresses, Yemenites, Ethiopians, Circassians. What do you think, Schlemilovitch? Don't be afraid, my boy, all this hides a deep sentimental streak.'

There was a moment of silence. Lévy-Vendôme gestured for me to follow him. Outside on the steps of the château, he whispered.

'Let me be alone, please. Leave immediately. Travel forms the young mind. Go east, Schlemilovitch, go east! A pilgrimage to the source: Vienna, Constantinople, the banks of the Jordan. I am almost tempted to go with you. Leave France as soon as possible! Go! This country has wronged you. You have taken root here. Never forget that we are the international association of fakirs and prophets. Have no fear, you will see me again. I am needed in Constantinople to engineer the gradual halt to the cycle. Gradually the seasons will change, first the spring, then the summer. Astronomers and meteorologists know nothing, take my word for this, Schlemilovitch. I shall disappear from Europe towards the end of the century and go the Himalayas. I will rest. I will reappear here eighty-five years to the day from now, sporting the sidelocks and beard of a rabbi. Goodbye for now. I love you.'

IV

Vienna. The last tramways glided into the night. On Mariahilfer Straße, we felt fear overcoming us. A few more steps and we would find ourselves on the Place de la Concorde. Take the métro, count off the reassuring rosary: Tuileries, Palais-Royal, Louvre, Châtelet. Our mother would be waiting for us, Quai Conti. We would drink lime-blossom and mint *tisane* and watch the shadows cast on the walls of our bedroom by the passing river boats. Never had we loved Paris more, nor France. A winter's night, a Jewish painter, our cousin, staggering around Montparnasse, muttering as he died '*Cara, cara Italia*'. By chance he had been born in Livorno, he might have been born in Paris, in London, in Warsaw, anywhere. We were born in Boulogne-sur-Seine, Île-de-France. Far from here, Tuileries. Palais-Royal, Châtelet. The exquisite Mme de La Fayette. Choderlos de Laclos. Benjamin Constant, dear old Stendhal. Fate had played us a cruel trick. We would not see our country again. Die on Mariahilfer Straße like stray dogs. No one could protect us. Our mother was dead or mad. We did not know our father's New York address. Nor that of Maurice Sachs. Or Adrien Debigorre. As for Charles Lévy-Vendôme, there was no point calling on him. Tania Arcisewska was dead because she had taken our advice. Des Essarts was dead. Loïtia was probably slowly becoming accustomed used to far-flung brothels. We made no effort to clasp them to us, these faces that passed through our lives, to cling to them, to love them. Incapable of the slightest act.

We arrived at the Burggarten and sat on one of the benches. Suddenly we heard the sound of a wooden leg striking the ground. A man was walking towards us, a monstrous cripple . . . His eyes were luminous, his sweeping fringe and his stubby moustache glistened in the darkness. His lips were set in a rictus that made our hearts pound. His left arm, which he extended, tapered to a hook. We had expected to run into him in Vienna. Inevitably. He was wearing the uniform of an Austrian corporal the better to terrify us. He threatened us, bellowing: '*Sechs Millionen Juden! Sechs Millionen Juden!*' Shrapnel from his booming laugh pierced our chests. He tried to gouge our eyes out with his hook. We ran away. He followed us, shrieking: '*Sechs Millionen Juden! Sechs Millionen Juden!*' For a long time we ran through the dead city, this drowned city washed up on the shore. Hofburg, Palais Kinsky, Palais Lobkowitz, Palais Pallavicini, Palais Porcia, Palais Wilczek . . . Behind us, in a rasping voice Captain Hook sang 'Hitlerleute', thumping the pavement with his wooden leg. It seemed to us we were the only people in the city. After killing us, our enemy would wander these empty streets like a ghost until the end of time.

The streetlights along the Graben help me see things more clearly. Three American tourists persuade me that Hitler is long since dead. I follow them, trailing a few metres behind. They turn onto Dorotheergasse and go into the nearest café. I take a table at the back. I don't have a *schilling* and I tell the waiter I am waiting for someone. With a smile, he brings me a newspaper. I discover that last night, at midnight, Albert Speer and Baldur von Schirach left Spandau prison in a big black Mercedes. At a press conference in the Hilton Hotel in Berlin, Schirach declared: 'Sorry to have kept you waiting so long.' In the photo, he is wearing a turtleneck sweater. Cashmere, probably. *Made in Scotland*. Gentleman. Former Gauleiter of Vienna. Fifty thousand Jews.

A young, dark-haired woman, chin resting on her open palm. I wonder what she is doing here, alone, so forlorn among the beer drinkers. Surely she belongs to that race of humans I have chosen above all other: their features are harsh and yet delicate, in their faces you can see their enduring loyalty to grief. Anyone but Raphäel Schlemilovitch would take these anaemics by the hand and beg them to make their peace with life. As for me, those I love, I kill. And so I choose those who are weak, defenceless. To take an example, I killed my mother with grief. She demonstrated exceptional meekness. She would beg me to have my tuberculosis treated. I would gruffly snap: 'You don't treat tuberculosis, you nurture it, you cherish it like a dancehall girl.' My mother would hang her head. Later, Tania asks me to protect her. I hand her a razor blade, a Gillette Extra-Blue. In the end, I anticipated her wishes: she would have been bored living with a fat man. Slyly suicided while he was singing the praises of nature in springtime. As for Des Essarts, my brother, my only friend, was it not I who tampered with the brakes of the car so he could safely shatter his skull?

The young woman looks at me with astonished eyes. I remember something Lévy-Vendôme said: force an entry into other people's lives. I take a seat at her table. She gives a faint smile of a melancholy I find ravishing. I immediately decide to trust her. And besides, she is dark. Blond hair, pink complexions, porcelain eyes get on my nerves. Everything that radiates health and happiness turns my stomach. Racist after my fashion. Such prejudices are forgivable in a young consumptive Jew.

'Are you coming?' she says.

There is such gentleness in her voice that I resolve to write a beautiful novel and dedicate it to her: '*Schlemilovitch in the Land of Women.*' In it, I will show how a little Jew seeks refuge among women in moments of distress. Without women, the world would be unbearable. Men are too serious. Too absorbed in their elegant abstractions, their vocations: politics, art, the textile business. They have to respect you before they will help you. Incapable of an unselfish action. Sensible. Dismal. Miserly. Pretentious. Men would leave me to starve to death.

We leave the Dorotheergasse. After this point, my memories are hazy. We walk back along the Graben and turn left. We go into a café much larger than the first. I drink, I eat, I recover my health while Hilda – that is her name – gazes at me fondly. Around us, every table is occupied by several woman. Whores. Hilda is a whore. In the person of Raphäel Schlemilovitch, she has just found her pimp. In future, I will call her Marizibill: when Apollinaire wrote about the 'Jewish pimp, red-haired and ruddy-faced' he was thinking of me. I own this place: the waiter who brings me my *alcools* looks like Lévy-Vendôme. German soldiers come to my establishment to console themselves before setting off for the Eastern Front. Heydrich himself sometimes visits. He has a soft spot for Tania, Loïtia and Hilda, my prettiest whores. He feels no revulsion when he straddles Tania, the Jewess. Besides, Heydrich himself is a *Mischling*. Given his lieutenant's zeal, Hitler turned a blind eye. I have similarly been spared, Raphäel Schlemilovitch, the biggest pimp of the Third Reich. My girls have been my shield. Thanks to them I will not know Auschwitz. If, by chance, the Gauleiter of Vienna should change his mind about me, in a day Tania, Loïtia and Hilda could collect the money for my ransom. I imagine five hundred thousand Reichsmarks would suffice, given that a Jew is not worth the rope required to hang him. The Gestapo will look the other way and let me disappear to South America. No point dwelling on such things: thanks to Tania, Loïtia and Hilda I have considerable influence over Heydrich. From him, they can get a document countersigned by Himmler certifying that I am an honorary citizen of the Third Reich. The Indispensable Jew. When you have women to protect you, everything falls into place. Since 1935, I have been the lover of Eva Braun. Chancellor Hitler was always leaving her alone at the Berchtesgaden. I immediately begin to think how I might turn this situation to my advantage.

I am skulking around the Berghof when I meet Eva for the first time. The instant attraction is mutual. Hitler comes to Obersalzberg once a month. We get along very well. He gracefully accepts my role as escort to Eva. Such things seem to him so futile . . . In the evenings, he tells us about his plans. We listen, like two children. He has given me the honorary title of SS Brigadenführer. I should dig out the photo on which Eva wrote *'Für mein kleiner Jude, mein gelibter Schlemilovitch – Seine Eva.'*

Hilda gently lays a hand on my shoulder. It is late, the customers have left the café. The waiter is reading *Der Stern* by the bar. Hilda gets up and slips a coin into the jukebox. Instantly, the voice of Zarah Leander lulls me like a gentle, husky river. She sings 'Ich stehe im Regen' – 'I am standing in the rain'. She sings 'Mit roten Rosen fängt die Liebe meistens an' – 'Love always begins with red roses'. It often ends with Gillette Extra-Blue razor blades. The waiter asks us to leave the café. We walk along a desolate avenue. Where am I? Vienna? Geneva? Paris? And this woman clutching my arm, is she Tania, Loïtia, Hilda, Eva Braun? Later, we find ourselves standing in the middle of an esplanade in front of an illuminated basilica. The Sacré-Cœur? I slump onto the seat of a hydraulic lift. A door is opened. A vast white-walled bedroom. A four-poster bed. I fall asleep.

The following day, I got to know Hilda, my new friend. Despite her dark hair and her delicate face, she was a little Aryan girl, half-German, half-Austrian. From her wallet, she took several photographs of her father and her mother. Both dead. The former in Berlin during the bombings, the latter disembowelled by Cossacks. I was sorry I had never known Herr Murzzuschlag, a stiff SS officer and perhaps my future father-in-law. I was much taken by their wedding photograph: Murzzuschlag and his young bride in Bruxelles, intriguing passers-by with his immaculate uniform and the contemptuous jut of his chin. This was not just anybody: a friend of Rudolph Hess and Goebbels, on first name terms with Himmler. Hitler himself, when awarding him the Cross of Merit, said 'Skorzeny and Murzzuschlag never let me down.'

Why had I not met Hilda in the thirties? Frau Murzzuschlag makes *kneidel* for me, her husband fondly pats my cheeks and says:

'You're a Jew? We'll sort that out, my boy! Marry my daughter! I'll take care of the rest! *Der treue Heinrich** will understand.'

I thank him, but I do not need his help: lover of Eva Braun, confidant of Hitler, I have long been the official Jew of the Third Reich. To the end, I spend my weekends in Obersalzberg and the Nazi bigwigs show me the utmost respect.

Hilda's bedroom was on the top floor of a grand old townhouse on Backerstraße. The room was remarkable for its spaciousness, its high ceilings, a four poster bed, a picture window. In the middle, a cage with a Jewish nightingale. In one corner, a wooden horse. Here and there, a number of kaleidoscopes. Each stamped 'Schlemilovitch Ltd., New York'.

'Probably a Jew,' Hilda confided, 'but he makes beautiful kaleidoscopes. I adore kaleidoscopes. Look in this one, Raphäel! A human face made up of a thousand brilliant facets constantly shifting . . .'

I want to confess to her that my father was responsible for these miniature works of art, but she constantly kvetches to me about the Jews. They demand compensation on the pretext that their families were exterminated in the camps, they are bleeding Germany white. They drove around in Mercedes drinking champagne while the poor Germans were working to rebuild their country and living hand-to-mouth. Oh, the bastards! First they corrupted Germany, now they were pimping it.

The Jews had won the war, had killed her father, raped her mother, her position was unshakeable. Better to wait a few days

---

* Himmler

before showing her my family tree. Until then, I would be the epitome of Gallic charm: the Grey Musketeers, the insolence, the elegance, the *made in Paris* spirit. Had not Hilda complimented me on the mellifluent way I spoke French?

'Never,' she would say, 'never have I heard a Frenchman speak his mother tongue as beautifully as you.'

'I'm from Touraine,' I explained. 'We pride ourselves on speaking the purest French. My name is Raphäel de Château-Chinon, but don't tell anyone. I swallowed my passport so I could remain incognito. One more thing: as a good Frenchman, I find Austrian food DIS-GUS-TING! When I think of the *canards à l'orange*, the nuits-saint-georges, the sauternes and the *poularde de Bresse*! Hilda, I will take you to France, knock some of the rough edges off you. *Vive la France*, Hilda! You people are savages!'

She tried to make me forget Austro-German uncouthness, talking to me about Mozart, Schubert. Hugo von Hofmannsthal.

'Hofmannsthal?' I said, 'A Jew, my little Hilda! Austria is a Jewish colony. Freud, Zweig, Schnitzler, Hofmannsthal, it's a ghetto! I defy you to name me a great Tyrolean poet! In France, we don't allow ourselves to be overrun like that. The likes of Montaigne and Proust and Louis-Ferdinand Céline have never succeeded in Jewifying our country. Ronsard and Du Bellay are there, keeping an eye open for any trouble! In fact, my little Hilda, we French make no distinction between Germans, Austrians, Czechs, Hungarians and all the other Jews. And don't talk to me about your papa, SS Murzzuschlag, or the Nazis. All Jews, *meine kleine* Hilda, the Nazis are the shock troops of the Jews! Think about Hitler, the little runt of a corporal wandering the streets of Vienna, beaten, numb with cold, starving to death! Long live Hitler!'

She listened to me, her eyes wide. Soon I would tell her more brutal truths. I would reveal my identity. I would choose the perfect moment and whisper into her ear the confession the nameless knight made to the Inquisitor's daughter:

Ich, Señora, eur Geliebter,
Bin der Sohn des vielbelobten,
Großen, schriftgelehrten Rabbi
Israel von Saragossa.

Hilda had obviously never read Heine's poem.

In the evenings, we would often go to the Prater. I love funfairs. 'The thing is, Hilda,' I explained, 'funfairs are terribly sad. The "enchanted river", for example, you get into a boat with your friends, you are carried along by the current and when you come to the end you get a bullet in the back of the head. Then there's the House of Mirrors, the rollercoaster, the merry-go-rounds, the shooting galleries. You stand in front of the distorting mirrors and your emaciated face, your skeletal chest terrify you. The cars on the rollercoaster systematically derail and you break your back. The merry-go-rounds are surrounded by archers who shoot little poisoned darts into your spine. The merry-go-round never stops, victims fall from the wooden horses. From time to time, the machinery seizes up, clogged with piles of corpses and the archers clear the area for the newcomers. Passers-by are encouraged to stand in little groups inside the shooting galleries. The archers are told to aim between the eyes, but sometimes an arrow goes wide and hits an ear, an eye, a gaping mouth. When they hit their mark, the archers are awarded five points. When the arrow goes astray, five points are deducted. The archer with the highest score wins a young blonde Pomeranian girl, an ornament made of silver paper and a chocolate skull. I forgot to mention the lucky bags at the sweet stalls: every bag sold contains a few amethyst blue crystals of cyanide, with instructions for use: "*Na, friss schon!*"* Bags of cyanide for everyone. Six million of them! We're happy here in Theresienstadt...'

Next to the Prater is a large park where lovers stroll; in the gathering dark I led Hilda under the leafy boughs, next to the banks of flowers, the blue-tinged lawns. I slapped her three times. It gave me pleasure to watch blood trickle from the corners of her mouth. Great pleasure. A German girl. Who once had loved an SS Totenkopf. I know how to bear an old grudge.

Now, I let myself slip down the slope of confession. I look nothing like Gregory Peck as I claimed earlier. I have neither the energy nor the *keep smiling* spirit of the American. I look like my cousin, the Jewish painter Modigliani. They called him 'The Tuscan Christ'. I forbid the use of this moniker to refer to my handsome tubercular face.

But actually, no, I look no more like Modigliani than I do like Gregory Peck. I'm the spitting image of Groucho Marx: the same eyes, the same nose, the same moustache. Worse still, I'm a dead ringer for Süss the Jew. Hilda had to notice at all costs. For a week now, she had not been firm enough with me.

L ying around her room were recordings of the 'Horst-Wessel-Lied' and the 'Hitlerleute' which she kept in memory of her father. The vultures of Stalingrad and the phosphorus of Hamburg will eat away at the vocal cords of these warriors. Everyone's

---

* 'Go on, eat up!'

turn comes eventually. I bought two record-players. To compose my *Judeo-Nazi Requiem*, I simultaneously played the 'Horst-Wessel-Lied' and the 'Einheitsfrontlied' of the International Brigades. Next I blended the 'Hitlerleute' with the anthem of the Thälmann-Kolonne, the last cry of Jews and German communists. And then, at the end of the *Requiem*, Wagner's *Götterdämmerung* conjured Berlin in flames, the tragic destiny of the German people, while the litany for the dead of Auschwitz evoked the pounds into which six million dogs were hurled.

Hilda does not work. I inquire about the source of her income. She explains that she sold some Biedermeier furniture belonging to a dead aunt for twenty thousand *schillings*. Barely a quarter of that sum is left.

I tell her my concerns.

'Don't worry, Raphäel,' she says.

Every night she goes to the Blaue Bar at the Hotel Sacher. She seeks out the most well-heeled guests and sells them her charms. After three weeks, we have fifteen hundred dollars. Hilda develops a taste for the profession. It offers her a discipline and a stability she has not had until now.

She artlessly makes the acquaintance of Yasmine. This young woman also haunts the Hotel Sacher offering her dark eyes, her bronzed skin, her oriental languor to Americans passing through.

At first, they compare notes on their profession, and quickly become the best of friends. Yasmine moves in to Backerstraße, the four-poster bed is big enough for three.

Of the two women in your harem, these two charming whores, Yasmine quickly became your favourite. She talks to you of Istanbul, where she was born, of the Galata Bridge, the Valide Mosque. You feel a sudden urge to reach the Bosphorus. In Vienna, winter is drawing in and you will not make it out alive. When the first snows began to fall, you clung more tightly to your Turkish friend. You left Vienna and visited cousins who manufactured playing cards in Trieste. From there, a brief detour to Budapest. No cousins left in Budapest. Exterminated. In Salonika, the birthplace of your family, you discovered the same desolation, the Jewish community of this city had been of particular interest to the Germans. In Istanbul, your cousins Sarah, Rachel, Dinah and Blanca celebrated the return of the prodigal son. You rediscovered your taste for life and for *lokum*. Already, your cousins in Cairo were waiting impatiently for you to visit. They asked for news of your exiled cousins in London, in Paris, in Caracas.

You spent some time in Egypt. Since you did not have a penny to your name, you organised a funfair in Port Said with all your old friends as exhibits. For twenty dinars a head, passers-by could watch Hitler in a cage declaiming Hamlet's soliloquy, Göring and Rudolph Hess on the trapeze, Himmler and his performing dogs, Goebbels the snake charmer, von Schirach the sword swallower, Julius Streicher the wandering Jew. Some distance away, the 'Collabo's Beauties' were performing an improvised 'Oriental' revue: there was Robert Brasillach dressed as a sultan, Drieu la Rochelle as the *bayadère*, Albert Bonnard as the guardian of the seraglio, Bonny and Lafton the bloodthirsty viziers and the missionary Mayo de Lupé. The 'Vichy Follies' singers were performing an operetta extravaganza: among the troupe were a Maréchal, admirals Esteva, Bard and Platón, a few bishops, brigadier Darnand and the traitorous Prince Laval. Even so, the most visited stall in the fairground was the one where people stripped your former mistress Eva Braun. She was still a handsome woman. For a hundred dinars each, aficionados could find out for themselves.

After a week, you abandoned your cherished ghosts and left with the takings. You crossed the Red Sea, reached Palestine and died of exhaustion. And there you were, you had made it all the way from Paris to Jerusalem.

Between them, my two girlfriends earned three thousand *schillings* a night. Prostitution and pandering suddenly seemed to me to be ill-paid professions unless practised on the scale of a Lucky Luciano. Unfortunately, I was not cast from the same mould as that captain of industry.

Yasmine introduced me to a number of dubious individuals: Jean-Farouk de Mérode, Paulo Hayakawa, the ageing Baroness Lydia Stahl, Sophie Knout, Rachid von Rosenheim, M. Igor, T.W.A. Levy, Otto da Silva and others whose names I've forgotten. With these shady characters, I trafficked gold, laundered counterfeit zlotys and sold wild grasses like hashish and marijuana to anyone who wished to graze on them. Eventually I enlisted in the French Gestapo. Badge number S. 1113. Working from the Rue Lauriston.

I had been bitterly disappointed by the *Milice*. There, the only people I had met were boy scouts just like the brave lads in the Résistance. Darnand was an out-and-out idealist.

I felt more comfortable around Pierre Bonny, Henri Chamberlin-Lafont and their acolytes. What's more, on the Rue Lauriston I met up with my old ethics teacher, Joseph Joanovici.

To the killers in the Gestapo, Joano and I were the two in-house Jews. The third was in Hamburg. His name was Maurice Sachs.

One tires of everything. In the end I left my two girlfriends and the merry little band of crooks who jeopardized my health. I followed an avenue as far as the Danube. It was dark, snow was falling benignly. Would I throw myself into the river or not? Franz-Josefs-Kai was deserted, from somewhere I could hear snatches of a song, 'Weisse Weihnacht', ah yes, people were celebrating Christmas. Miss Evelyn used to read me Dickens and Andersen. What joy the next morning to find thousands of toys at the foot of the tree. All this happened in the house on the Quai Conti, on the banks of the Seine. An exceptional childhood, a magical childhood I no longer have time to tell you about. An elegant swan dive into the Danube on Christmas Eve? I was sorry I had not left a farewell note for Hilda and Yasmine. For example: 'I will not be home tonight, for the night will be black and white.' No matter. I consoled myself with the thought that these two whores had probably never read Gérard de Nerval. Thankfully, in Paris, no one would fail to see the link between Nerval and Schlemilovitch, the two winter suicides. I was incorrigible. I was prepared to appropriate another man's death just as I had appropriated the pens of Proust and Céline, the paintbrushes of Modigliani and Soutine, the gurning faces of Groucho Marx and Chaplin. My tuberculosis? Had I not stolen it from Franz Kafka? I could still change my mind and die like him in the Kierling sanatorium not far from here. Nerval or Kafka? Suicide or sanatorium? No, suicide did not suit me, a Jew has no right to commit suicide. Such luxury should be left to Werther. What then? Turn up at Kierling sanatorium? Could I be sure that I would die there, like Kafka?

I did not hear him approach. He brusquely shoves a badge into my face on which I read POLIZEI. He asks for my papers. I've forgotten them. He takes me by the arm. I ask him why he does not use his handcuffs. He gives a reassuring little laugh.

'Now, now, sir, you've had too much to drink. The Christmas spirit, probably. Come on now, I'll take you home. Where do you live?'

I obstinately refuse to give him my address.

'Well, in that case I have no choice but to take you to the station.'

The apparent kindness of the policeman is getting on my nerves. I've already worked out that he belongs to the Gestapo. Why not just tell me straight out? Maybe he thinks I will put up a fight, scream like a stuck pig? Not at all. Kierling sanatorium is no match for the clinic where this good man plans to take me. First, there will be the customary formalities: I will be asked for my surname, my first name, my date of birth. They will ensure I am genuinely ill, force me to take some sinister test. Next, the operating theatre. Lying on the table, I will wait impatiently for my surgeons Torquemada and Ximénes. They will hand me an x-ray of my lungs which I will see are nothing but a mass of hideous tumours like the tentacles of an octopus.

'Do you wish us to operate or not?' Dr Torquemada will ask me calmly.

'All we need do is transplant two stainless steel lungs,' Dr Ximénes will gently explain.

'We have a superior professional conscientiousness,' Dr Torquemada will say.

'Together with an acute interest in your health,' said Dr Ximénes.

'Unfortunately, most of our patients love their illness with a fierce passion and consequently see us not as surgeons . . .'

'. . . but as torturers.'

'Patients are often unjust towards their doctors,' Dr Ximénes will add.

'We are forced to treat them against their will,' Dr Torquemada will say.

'A thankless task,' Dr Ximénes will add.

'Do you know that some patients in our clinic have formed a union?' Dr Torquemada will ask me. 'They have decided to strike, to refuse to allow us to treat them . . .'

'A serious threat to the medical profession,' Dr Ximénes will add. 'Especially since the unionist fever is infecting all sectors of the clinic . . .'

'We have tasked a very scrupulous practitioner, Dr Himmler, to crush this rebellion. He is systematically performing euthanasia on all the union members.'

'So what do you decide . . .' Dr Torquemada will ask me, 'the operation or euthanasia?'

'There are no other possible alternatives.'

Events did not unfold as I had expected. The policeman was still holding my arm, telling me he was walking me to the nearest police station for a simple identity check. When I stepped into his office, the Kommisar, a cultured SS officer intimately familiar with the French poets, asked:

'Say, what have you done, you who come here, with your youth?'

I explained to him how I had wasted it. And then I talked to him about my impatience: at an age when others were planning their future, I could think only of ending things. Take the gare de Lyon, for example, under the German occupation. I was supposed to catch a train that would carry me far away from misfortune and fear. Travellers were queuing at the ticket desks. I had only to wait half an hour to get my ticket. But no, I got into a first class carriage without a ticket like an imposter. At Chalon-sur-Saône, when the German ticket inspectors checked the compartment, they caught me. I held out my hands. I told them that despite the false papers in the name Jean Cassis de Coudray Macouard, I was a JEW. The relief!

'Then they brought me to you, Herr Kommissar. You decide my fate. I promise I will be utterly docile.'

The Komissar smiles gently, pats my cheek and asks whether I really have tuberculosis.

'It doesn't surprise me,' he says. 'At your age, everyone is consumptive. It needs to be treated, otherwise you end up spitting blood and dragging yourself along all your life. This is what I've decided: if you'd been born earlier, I would have sent you to Auschwitz to have your tuberculosis treated, but we live in more civilised times. Here, this is a ticket for Israel. Apparently, over there, the Jews . . .'

The sea was inky blue and Tel Aviv was white, so white. As the boat came alongside, the steady beat of his heart made him feel he had returned to his ancestral land after two thousand years away. He had embarked at Marseille, with the Israeli national shipping line. All through the crossing, he tried to calm his rising panic by anaesthetising himself with alcohol and morphine. Now, with Tel Aviv spread out before him, he could die, his heart at peace.

The voice of Admiral Levy roused him from his thoughts.

'Good crossing, young man? First time in Israel? You'll love our country. A terrific country, you'll see. Lads of your age are swept up by the extraordinary energy that, from Haifa to Eilat, from Tel Aviv to the Dead Sea . . .'

'I'm sure you're right, Admiral.'

'Are you French? We have a great love of France, the liberal traditions, the warmth of Anjou and Touraine, the scents of Provence. And your national anthem, it's beautiful! *"Allons enfants de la patrie!"* Capital, capital!'

'I'm not entirely French, Admiral, I am a French JEW. A French JEW.'

Admiral Levy gave him a hostile glare. Admiral Levy looks like the twin brother of Admiral Dönitz. After a moment Admiral Levy says curtly:

'Follow me, please.'

He ushers the young man into a sealed cabin.

'I advise you to be sensible. We will deal with you in due course.'

The admiral switches off the electricity and double locks the door.

He sat in total darkness for almost three hours. Only the faint glow of his wristwatch still connected him to the world. The door was flung open and his eyes were dazzled by the bare bulb dangling from the ceiling. Three men in green oilskins strode towards him. One of them held out a card.

'Elias Bloch, Secret State Police. You're a French Jew? Excellent! Put him in handcuffs!'

A fourth stooge, wearing an identical trench coat, stepped into the cabin.

'A very productive search. In the gentleman's luggage we found several books by Proust and Kafka, reproductions of Modigliani and Soutine, some photos of Charlie Chaplin, Erich von Stroheim and Groucho Marx.'

93

'Your case is looking more and more serious,' says the man named Elias Bloch. 'Take him away!'

The men bundle him out of the cabin. The handcuffs chafe his wrists. On the quayside, he tripped and fell down. One of the officers takes the opportunity to give him a few swift kicks in the ribs then, grabbing the chain linking the handcuffs, dragged him to his feet. They crossed the deserted docks. A police van exactly like the ones used by the French police in the roundup on 16 July 1942 was parked on the street corner. Elias Bloch slid into the seat next to the driver. The young man climbed into the back followed by three officers.

The police van sets off up the Champs-Élysées. People are queuing outside the cinemas. On the terrace of Fouquet's, women are wearing pale dresses. It was clearly a Saturday evening in spring.

They stopped at the Place de l'Étoile. A few GIs were photographing the Arc de Triomphe, but he felt no need to call to them for help. Bloch grabbed his arm and marched him across the *place*. The four officers followed a few paces behind.

'So, you're a French Jew?' Bloch asked, his face looming close.

He suddenly looked like Henri Chamberlin-Lafont of the French Gestapo Française.

He was bundled into a black Citroën parked on the Avenue Kléber.

'You're for it now,' said the officer on his right

'For a beating, right, Saul?' said the officer on his left.

'Yes, Isaac, he's in for a beating,' said the officer driving.

'I'll do it.'

'No, let me! I need the exercise,' said the officer on his right.

'No, Isaac! It's my turn. You got to beat the shit out of the English Jew last night. This one's mine.'

'Apparently this one's a French Jew.'

'That's weird. Why don't we call him Marcel Proust?'

Isaac gave him a brutal punch in the stomach.

'On your knees, Marcel! On your knees!'

Meekly he complied. The back seat made it difficult. Isaac slapped him six times.

'You're bleeding, Marcel: that means you're still alive.'

Saul whipped out a leather belt.

'Catch, Marcel Proust,' he said.

The belt hit him on the left cheek and he almost passed out.

'Poor little brat,' said Isaiah. 'Poor little French Jew.'

He passed the Hôtel Majestic. All the windows of the great façade were dark. To reassure himself, he decided that Otto Abetz flanked by all the jolly fellows of the Collaboration were in the lobby for him, the guest of honour at a Franco-German dinner. After all, was he not the official Jew to the Third Reich?

'We're taking you on a little tour of the area,' said Isaiah.

'There are a lot of historical monuments around here,' said Saul.

'We'll stop at each one so you have a chance to appreciate them.'

They showed him the buildings requisitioned by the Gestapo: Nos. 31 *bis* and 72 Avenue Foch. 57 Boulevard Lannes. 48 Rue de Villejust. 101 Avenue Henri-Martin. Nos. 3 and 5 Rue Mallet-Stevens. Nos. 21 and 23 Square de Bois-de-Boulogne. 25 Rue d'Astorg. 6 Rue Adolphe-Yvon. 64 Boulevard Suchet. 49 Rue de la Faisanderie. 180 Rue de la Pompe.

Having finished the sightseeing tour, they headed back to the Kléber-Boissière sector.

'So what did you make of the 16th *arrondissement*?' Isaiah asked him.

'It's the most notorious district in Paris,' said Saul.

'And now, driver, take us to 93 Rue Lauriston, please,' said Isaac.

He felt reassured. His friends Bonny and Chamberlin-Lafont would soon put an end to this tasteless joke. They would drink champagne together as they did every night. René Launay, head of the Gestapo on the Avenue Foch, 'Rudy' Martin from the Gestapo in Neuilly, Georges Delfanne from the Avenue Henri-Martin and Odicharia from the 'Georgia Gestapo' would join them. Order would be restored.

Isaac rang the bell at 93 Rue Lauriston. The building looked deserted.

'The boss is probably waiting for us at 3 *bis* Place des États-Unis for the beating,' said Isaiah.

Bloch paced up and down the pavement. He opened the door to number 3 *bis* and dragged the young man inside.

He knew this *hôtel particulier* well. His friends Bonny and Chamberlin-Lafont has remodelled the property to create eight holding cells and two torture chambers, since the premises at 93 Rue Lauriston served as the administrative headquarters.

They went up to the fourth floor. Bloch opened a window.

'The Place des États-Unis is quiet this evening,' he said. 'See how the streetlights cast a soft glow over the leaves, my young friend. A beautiful May evening. And to think, we have to torture you. The bathtub torture, as it happens. How sad. A little glass of curaçao for Dutch courage? A Craven? Or would you prefer a little music? In a while, we'll play you a little song by Charles Trenet. It will drown out your screams. The neighbours are sensitive. They prefer the voice of Trenet to the sound of you being tortured.'

Saul, Isaac and Isaiah entered. They had not taken off their green trench coats. He immediately noticed the bathtub in the middle of the room.

'It once belonged to Émilienne d'Alençon,' Bloch said with a sad smile. 'Admire the quality of the enamelling, my friend, the floral motifs, the platinum taps.'

Isaac wrenched his hands behind his back while Isaiah put on the handcuffs. Saul turned on the phonograph. Raphäel immediately recognised the voice of Charles Trenet:

Formidable,
J'entends le vent sur la mer.
Formidable
Je vois la pluie, les éclairs.
Formidable
Je sens bientôt qu'il va faire,
qu'il va faire
Un orage
Formidable . . .

Sitting on the window ledge, Bloch beat time.

They plunged my head into the freezing water. My lungs felt as though they might explode at any minute. The faces I had loved flashed past. The faces of my mother and my father. My old French teacher Adrien Debigorre. The face of Fr. Perrache. The face of Colonel Aravis. And then the faces of all my wonderful fiancées – I had one in every province. Bretagne, Normandy, Poitou. Corrèze. Lozère. Savoie . . . Even one in Limousin. In Bellac. If these thugs spared my life, I would write a wonderful novel: *Schlemilovitch and the Limousin*, in which I would show that I am a perfectly assimilated Jew.

They yanked me by the hair. I heard Charles Trenet again:

> . . . *Formidable.*
> *On se croirait au ciné-*
> *Matographe*
> *Où l'on voit tant de belles choses,*
> *Tant de trucs, de métamorphoses,*
> *Quand une rose*
> *est assassinée . . .*

'The second dunking will last longer,' Bloch explains wiping away a tear.

This time, two hands press down on my neck, two more on the back of my head. Before I drown, it occurs to me I have not always been kind to maman.

But they drag me back into the fresh air.

> *Et puis*
> *et puis*
> *sur les quais,*
> *la pluie*
> *la pluie*
> *n'a pas compliqué*
> *la vie*

qui rigole
et qui se mire dans les flaques des rigoles.

'Now let's get down to business,' says Bloch, stifling a sob.

They lay me on the floor. Isaac takes a Swiss penknife from his pocket and makes deep slashes in the soles of my feet. Then he orders me to walk across a heap of salt. Next, Saul conscientiously rips out three of my fingernails. Then, Isaiah files down my teeth. At that point Trenet was singing:

Quel temps
pour les p'tits poissons.
Quel temps
pour les grands garçons.
Quel temps
pour les tendrons.
Mesdemoiselles nous vous attendrons . . .

'I think that's enough for tonight,' said Elias Bloch, shooting me a tender look.

He stroked my chin.

'This is the prison for the foreign Jews,' he said, 'we'll take you to the cell for French Jews. You're the only one at the moment. But there will be more along soon. Don't you worry.'

'The little shits can sit around talking about Marcel Proust,' said Isaiah.

'When I hear the word culture, I reach for my truncheon,' said Saul.

'I get to deliver the *coup de grâce*!' said Isaac.

'Come now, don't frighten the young man,' Bloch said imploringly.

He turned to me.

'Tomorrow, you will be advised about the progress of your case.'

Isaac and Saul pushed me into a little room. Isaiah came in and handed me a pair of striped pyjamas. Sewn onto the pyjama jacket was a yellow star of David on which I read *Französisch Jude*. As he closed the reinforced door, Isaac tripped me and I fell flat on my face.

The cell was illuminated by a nightlight. It did not take me long to notice the floor was strewn with Gillette Extra-Blue blades. How had the police known about my vice, my uncontrollable urge to swallow razor blades? I was sorry now that they had not chained me to the wall. All night, I had to tense myself, to bite my hand so as not to give in to the urge. One false move and I was in danger of gulping down the blades one by one. Gorging myself on Gillette Extra-Blues. It was truly the torment of Tantalus.

In the morning, Isaiah and Isaac came to fetch me. We walked down an endless corridor. Isaiah gestured to a door and told me to go in. Isaac thumped me on the back of the head by way of goodbye.

He was sitting at a large mahogany desk. Apparently, he was expecting me. He was wearing a black uniform and I noticed two Stars of David on the lapel of his jacket. He was smoking a pipe, which gave him a more pronounced jawline. Had he been wearing a beret, he might have passed for Joseph Darnand.

'You are Raphäel Schlemilovitch?' he asked in a clipped, military tone.

'Yes.'

'French Jew?'

'Yes.'

'You were arrested last night by Admiral Levy aboard the ship *Zion*?'

'Yes.'

'And handed over to the police authorities, to Commandant Elias Bloch to be specific?'

'Yes.'

'And these seditious pamphlets were found in your luggage?'

He passed me a volume of Proust, Franz Kafka's *Diary*, the photographs of Chaplin, von Stroheim and Groucho Marx, the reproductions of Modigliani and Soutine.

'Very well, allow me to introduce myself: General Tobie Cohen, Commissioner for Youth and Raising Morale. Now, let's get straight to the point. Why did you come to Israel?'

'I'm a romantic by nature. I didn't want to die without having seen the land of my forefathers.'

'And you are intending to RETURN to Europe, are you not? To go back to this playacting, this farce of yours? Don't bother to answer, I've heard it all before: Jewish angst, Jewish misery, Jewish fear, Jewish despair . . . People wallow in their misfortunes, they ask for more, they want to go back to the comfortable world of the ghettos, the delights of the pogroms. There are two possibilities, Schlemilovitch: either you listen to me and you follow my instructions, in that case, everything will be fine. Or you continue to play the rebel, the wandering Jew, the martyr, in which case I hand you over to Commandant Elias Bloch. You know what Elias Bloch will do with you?'

'Yes, sir!'

'I warn you, we have all the means necessary to subdue little masochists like you,' he said, wiping away a tear. 'Last week, an English Jew tried to outsmart us. He turned up from Europe with the same old hard-luck stories: Diaspora, persecution, the tragic destiny of the Jewish people! . . . He dug his heels in, determined to play the tormented soul! He refused to listen! Right now, Bloch and his lieutenants are dealing with him! I can assure you, he will get to experience real suffering. Far beyond his wildest expectations. He is finally about to experience the tragic destiny of the Jewish people! He asked for Torquemada, demanded Himmler himself! Bloch is taking care of him! He's worth more than all the Grand Inquisitors and Gestapo officers combined. Do you really want to end up in his hands, Schlemilovitch?'

'No, sir.'

'Well then, listen to me: you have just arrived in a young, vigorous, dynamic country. From Tel Aviv to the Dead Sea, from Haifa to Eilat, no one is interested in hearing about the angst, the malaise, the tears, the HARD LUCK STORY of the Jews. No one! We don't want to hear another word about the Jewish critical thinking, Jewish intelligence, Jewish scepticism, Jewish contortions and humiliations, Jewish tragedy . . . (his face was bathed in tears.) We leave all that to callow European aesthetes like you. We are forceful people, square-jawed, pioneers, not a bunch of Yiddish *chanteuses* like Proust and Kafka and Chaplin. Let me tell you, we recently organised an auto-da-fé on Tel Aviv main square: the works of Proust, Kafka and their ilk, reproductions of Soutine, Modigliani and other invertebrates, were burned by our young people, fine boys and girls who would have been the envy of the *Hitlerjugend*: blond, blue-eyed, broad-shouldered, with a confident swagger and a taste for action and for fighting! (He groaned.) While you were off cultivating your neuroses, they were building their muscles. While you were kvetching, they were working in kibbutzim! Aren't you ashamed, Schlemilovitch?'

'Yes, sir! General, sir!'

'Good! Now promise me that you will never again read Proust, Kafka and the like or drool over reproductions of Modigliani and

Soutine, or think about Chaplin or von Stroheim or the Marx Brothers, promise me you will forget Doctor Louis-Ferdinand Céline, the most insidious Jew of all time!'

'You have my word, sir.'

'I will introduce you to fine books. I have a great quantity in French! Have you read *The Art of Leadership* by Courtois? Sauvage's *The Restoration of the Family and National Revolution*? *The Greatest Game of my Life* by Guy de Larigaudie? *The Father's Handbook* by Rear-Admiral Penfentenyo? You will learn them by heart, I plan to develop your moral muscle! For the same reason, I am sending you to a disciplinary kibbutz immediately. Don't worry, you will only be there for three months. Just enough time to build up the biceps you sorely lack and cleanse you of the germs of the cosmopolitan Jew. Is that clear?'

'Yes, sir.'

'You may go, Schlemilovitch. I'll have my orderly bring you the books I mentioned. Read them while you're waiting to go and swing a pickaxe in the Negev. Shake my hand, Schlemilovitch. Harder, man, for God's sake! Eyes front! Chin up! We'll make a sabra of you yet!' (He burst into tears.)

'Thank you, general.'

Saul led me back to my cell. He threw a few punches but my warder seemed to have mellowed considerably since the previous night. I suspected him of eavesdropping. He had doubt-less been impressed by the meekness I had shown with General Cohen.

That night, Isaac and Isaiah bundled me into an army truck with a number of other young men, foreign Jews like me. They were all wearing striped pyjamas.

'No talking about Kafka, Proust and that lot,' said Isaiah.

'When we hear the word culture, we reach for our truncheons,' said Isaac.

'We're not too keen on intelligence,' said Isaiah.

'Especially when it's Jewish,' said Isaac.

'And I don't want any of you playing the martyr,' said Isaiah, 'it's gone beyond a joke. It's all very well you pulling long faces for the goyim back in Europe. But here there's just us, so don't waste your time.'

'Understood?' said Isaac. 'You will sing until we reach our destination. A few patriotic songs will do you good. Repeat after me . . .'

At about four in the afternoon, we arrived at the penal kibbutz. A huge concrete building surrounded by barbed wire. All around, the desert stretched as far as the eye could see. Isaiah and Isaac lined us up by the gates and took a roll call. There were eight of us: three English Jews, an Italian Jew, two German Jews, an Austrian Jew and me, a French Jew. The camp commandant appeared and stared at each of us in turn. The sight of this blond colossus in his black uniform did not fill me with confidence. And yet two Stars of David glittered on the lapel of his jacket.

'A bunch of intellectuals, obviously,' he roared at us furiously. 'How can I be expected to create shock troops out of this human detritus? A fine reputation you lot have made for us in Europe with your whining and your critical thinking. Well, gentlemen, here there'll be less bitching and more body building. There'll be no criticism and lots of construction! Reveille tomorrow morning at 06.00 hours. Now, up to your dormitory. Come on! Move it! Hup Two! Hup Two!'

Once we were in bed, the camp commandant strode into the dormitory followed by three young men as tall and blond as himself.

'These are your supervisors,' he said in a soft voice, 'Siegfried Levy, Günther Cohen, Herman Rappoport. These archangels will knock you into shape! The slightest insubordination is punishable by death! Isn't that so, my darlings? Don't hesitate to shoot them if they annoy you . . . A bullet in the temple, no discussions! Understood, my angels?'

He gently stroked their cheeks.

'I don't want these European Jews undermining your moral fibre . . .'

At 06:00 hours, Siegfried, Günther and Hermann dragged us from our beds, punching us as they did so. We pulled on our striped pyjamas. They led us to the administrative office of the kibbutz. We rattled off our surnames, first names, dates of birth to a dark-haired young woman wearing the regulation army khaki shirt and grey-blue trousers. Siegfried, Günther and Hermann stood behind the office door. One after another, my companions left the room after answering the young woman's questions. My turn came. The young woman raised her head and stared me straight in the eye. She looked like the twin sister of Tania Arcisewska. She said:

'My name is Rebecca and I love you.'

I did not know how to answer.

'Listen,' she said, 'they're going to kill you. You have to leave tonight. I'll take care of everything. I'm an officer in the Israeli army so I don't have to answer to the camp commandant. I'll borrow a truck on the pretext that I have to go to Tel Aviv to attend a meeting of the chiefs of staff. You'll come with me. I'll steal Siegfried Levy's papers and give them to you. That way you won't have to worry about the police for the time being. Later, we'll see what we can do. We could take the first boat to Europe and get married. I love you, I love you! I'll have you brought to my office at eight o'clock tonight. Fall out!'

We broke rocks in the blazing sun until 5 p.m. I had never handled a pickaxe before and my pale hands were bleeding horribly. Siegfried, Günther and Hermann smoked Lucky Strikes and stood guard. At no point during the day did they utter a single word and I assumed they were mute. Siegfried raised a hand to let us know our work was finished. Hermann walked over to the three English Jews, took out his revolver and shot them, his eyes utterly expressionless. He lit a Lucky Strike and puffed on it, staring up at the sky. After summarily burying the English Jews, our three guards led us back to the kibbutz. We were left to stare out through the barbed wire at the desert. At eight o'clock, Hermann Rappoport came to fetch me and escorted me to the administrative office.

'I feel like having a little fun, Hermann!' Rebecca said, 'Leave this little Jew with me, I'll take him to Tel Aviv, rape him and kill him, promise!'

Hermann nodded.

'Well then, it's just the two of us!' she said ominously.

As soon as Rappoport left the room, she squeezed my hand affectionately.

'Follow me, we don't have a moment to lose!'

We went out through the gates and climbed into a military truck. She got behind the steering wheel.

'Freedom is ours!' she said, 'We'll stop in a little while. You can slip on Siegfried's uniform, I've just stolen it. His papers are in the inside pocket.'

We reached our destination at 11 p.m.

'I love you and I want to go back to Europe,' she told me. 'Here there's nothing but thugs, soldiers, boy scouts and *nudniks*. In Europe we'll be happy. We'll be able to read Kafka to our children.'

'Yes, my darling Rebecca. We'll dance all night and tomorrow morning we'll catch the first boat for Marseille!'

The soldiers we encountered in the street snapped to attention as Rebecca passed.

'I'm a lieutenant,' she said, smiling. 'But I can't wait to throw this uniform away and go back to Europe.'

Rebecca knew a clandestine nightclub in Tel Aviv where we danced to the songs of Zarah Leander and Marlene Dietrich. It was a very popular club among young women in the army. To gain admittance, their companions had to wear a Luftwaffe officer's uniform. The dim lighting was conducive to intimacy. Their first dance was a tango, 'Der Wind hat mir ein Lied erzählt', sung by Zarah Leander in a smouldering voice. He murmured into Rebecca's ear 'Du bist der Lenz nachdem ich verlangte.' During their second dance, 'Schön war die Zeit', he held her shoulders and kissed her passionately on the lips. The voice of Lala Andersen quickly snuffed out that of Zarah Leander. At the first words of 'Lili Marlene', they heard the police sirens. There was a great commotion but no one could get out: Commandant Elias Bloch, Saul, Isaac and Isaiah had burst into the club, waving their revolvers.

'Round up all these fools,' roared Bloch, 'but first, do a quick identity check.'

When his turn came, Bloch recognised him in spite of the Luftwaffe uniform.

'Schlemilovitch? What are you doing here? I thought you had been sent to a disciplinary kibbutz! And wearing a Luftwaffe uniform! Clearly European Jews are irredeemable.'

'Your fiancée?' He gestured to Rebecca. 'A French Jew I'm guessing? Dressed as an Israeli army officer! This just gets better and better! Look, here come my friends. Well, I'm a generous man, let's crack open a bottle of champagne!'

They were quickly surrounded by a group of revellers who clapped them on the shoulder. He recognised the Marquise de Fougeire-Jusquiames, Vicomte Lévy-Vendôme, Paulo Hayakawa, Sophie Knout, Jean-Farouk de Mérode, Otto da Silva, M. Igor, the ageing Baroness Lydia Stahl, the princess Chericheff-Deborazoff, Louis-Ferdinand Céline and Jean-Jacques Rousseau.

'I've just sold fifty thousand pairs of socks to the Wehrmacht,' announced Jean-Farouk de Mérode as they sat down.

'And I've sold ten thousand tins of paint to the Kreigsmarine,' said Otto da Silva.

'Did you know those boy scouts on Radio Londres have condemned me to death?' said Paulo Hayakawa. 'They call me the "Nazi brandy bootlegger"!'

'Don't worry,' said Lévy-Vendôme, 'we'll buy up the French *Résistants* and the Anglo-Americans the same way we bought the Germans! Always keep in mind this maxim by our master Joanovici: "I did not sell myself to the Germans. It is I, Joseph Joanovici, Jew, who BUYS Germans."'

'I've been working for the French Gestapo in Neuilly for almost a week,' said M. Igor.

'I'm the best informant is Paris,' said Sophie Knout. 'They call me Miss Abwehr.'

'I just love the Gestapo,' said the Marquise de Fougeire-Jusquiames, 'they're so much more manly than everyone else.'

'You're so right,' said Princess Chericheff-Deborazoff, 'all those killers make me so *hot*.'

'There's a lot of good to be said for the German occupation,' said Jean-Farouk de Mérode, flashing a purple crocodile-skin wallet stuffed with banknotes.

'Paris is a lot calmer,' said Otto da Silva.

'The trees are blonder,' said Paulo Hayakawa.

'And you can hear the church bells,' said Lévy-Vendôme.

'I hope Germany is victorious!' said M. Igor.

'Would you care for a Lucky Strike?' asked the Marquise de Fougeire-Jusquiames, proffering a cigarette case of emerald-studded platinum. 'I get them regularly from Spain.'

'No, some champagne! Let's drink to the health of the Abwehr!' said Sophie Knout.

'And the Gestapo!' said Princess Chericheff-Deborazoff.

'A little stroll in the Bois de Boulogne?' suggested Commandant Bloch, turning toward him, 'I feel like a breath of fresh air! Your fiancée can join us. We'll meet up with our little gang on the Place de l'Étoile at midnight for a last drink!'

They found themselves outside on the Rue Pigalle. Commandant Bloch gestured to the three white Delahayes and the black Citroën parked outside the club.

'These all belong to our little gang,' he explained. 'We use the back Citroën for the round-ups. So let's take one of the Delahayes, if you don't mind. It will be more cheery.'

Saul got behind the wheel, he and Bloch sat in the front, with Isaiah, Rebecca and Isaac in the back.

'What were you doing at the Grand-Duc?' Commandant Bloch asked him. 'Don't you know the nightclub is reserved for French Gestapo officers and black market traffickers?'

As they approached the Place de l'Opéra, he noticed a large banner that read 'KOMMANDANTUR PLATZ'.

'How glorious to be riding in a Delahaye,' said Bloch, 'especially in Paris in May 1943. Don't you agree, Schlemilovitch?'

He stared at him intently. His eyes were kindly and compassionate.

'Let's make quite sure we understand one another, Schlemilovitch, I have no wish to thwart your vocation. Thanks to me, you will almost certainly be awarded the Martyr's Palm you've aspired to since the day you were born. Oh yes, a little later, I plan to personally give you the greatest gift you could wish for: a bullet in the back of the neck! Beforehand, we will eliminate your fiancée. Happy?'

To ward off his fear, he gritted his teeth and summoned his memories. His love affairs with Eva Braun and Hilda Murzzuschlag. His first strolls through Paris, summer 1940, in his SS Brigadenführer uniform: this was the dawn of a new era, they were going to cleanse the world, cure it forever of the Jewish plague. They had clear heads and blond hair. Later, his Panzer crushes the meadows of the Ukraine. Later still, here he is with Field Marshal Rommel striding through the desert sands. He is wounded in Stalingrad. The phosphorus bombs in Hamburg will do the rest. He followed the Führer to the last. Is he going to let himself be intimidated by Elias Bloch?

'A burst of lead in the back of the head! What do you say, Schlemilovitch?'

The eyes of commandant Bloch are on him again.

'You're one of the ones who takes his beating with a sad smile! A true Jew, the genuine, hundred per cent, *made in Europa* Jews.'

They turned into the Bois de Boulogne.

He remembers afternoons spent at the Pré-Catelan and the Grande Cascade under the watchful eye of Miss Evelyn but he will not bore you with his childhood. Read Proust, that would be best.

Saul stopped the Delahaye in the middle of the Allée des Acacias. He and Isaac dragged Rebecca out and raped her in front of my very eyes. Commandant Bloch had already handcuffed me and the car doors were locked. It hardly mattered, I would not have lifted a finger to protect my fiancée.

We drove towards the château de Bagatelle. Isaiah, more sophisticated than his two companions, gripped Rebecca by the throat and forced his penis into my fiancée's mouth. Commandant Bloch gently stabbed me in the thighs with a dagger and before long my immaculate SS uniform was drenched with blood.

Then the Delahaye stopped at the junction near Les Cascades. Isaiah and Isaac dragged Rebecca from the car again. Isaac grabbed her hair and tugged her head back. Rebecca started to laugh. The laugh grew louder, echoing around the woods, grew louder still until it reached a dizzying height and splintered into sobs.

'Your fiancée has been liquidated,' whispers Commandant Bloch, 'don't be sad. We have to get back to our friends!'

And indeed the whole gang is waiting for us on the Place de l'Étoile.

'It's after curfew,' says Jean-Farouk de Mérode, 'but we have specially-issued *Ausweise*.'

'Why don't we go to the One-Two-Two,' suggests Paulo Hayakawa. 'They have sensational girls there. No need to pay. I just have to flash my French Gestapo card.'

'Why don't we conduct a few impromptu searches of the bigwigs in the neighbourhood?' says M. Igor.

'I'd rather loot a jeweller's,' says Otto da Silva.

'Or an antiques shop,' says Lévy-Vendôme, 'I've promised Göring three *Directoire* desks.'

'What do you say to a raid?' asks Commandant Bloch, 'I know a hideout of *Résistants* on the Rue Lepic.'

'Wonderful idea!' cries Princess Chericheff-Deborazoff. 'We can torture them in my *hôtel particulier* on the Place d'Iéna.'

'We are the kings of Paris,' says Paulo Hayakawa.

'Thanks to our German friends,' says M. Igor.

'Let's have fun!' says Sophie Knout, 'we're protected by the Abwehr and the Gestapo.'

'*Après nous le déluge!*' says the Marquise de Fougeire-Jusquiames.

'Why not come down to the Rue Lauriston,' says Bloch, 'I've just had three cases of whisky delivered. Let's end the evening with a flourish.'

'You're right, commandant,' says Paulo Hayakawa, 'after all, they don't call us the Rue Lauriston Gang for nothing.'

'RUE LAURISTON! RUE LAURISTON!' chant the Marquise de Fougeire-Jusquiames and the Princess Chericheff-Deborazoff.

'No point taking the cars,' says Jean-Farouk de Mérode, 'we can walk there.'

Up to this point, they have been kind to me, but no sooner do we turn into the Rue Lauriston than they turn and glare at me in a manner that is unbearable.

'Who are you?' demands Paulo Hayakawa.

'An agent with the Intelligence Service,' says Sophie Knout.

'Explain yourself,' says Otto da Silva.

'I don't much care for that ugly mug of yours,' declares the elderly Baroness Lydia Stahl.

'Why are you dressed as an SS officer?' Jean-Farouk de Mérode asks me.

'Show me your papers,' orders M. Igor.

'Are you a Jew?' asks Lévy-Vendôme. 'Come on, confess!'

'Who do you think you are, you little thug, Marcel Proust?' inquires the Marquise de Fougeire-Jusquiames.

'He'll tell us what we want to know in the end,' declares Princess Chericheff-Devorazoff, '*tongues are loosened at Rue Lauriston.*'

Bloch puts the handcuffs on me again. The others question me with renewed vigour. I feel a sudden urge to vomit. I lean against a doorway.

'We don't have time to waste,' says Isaac, 'March!'

'Make an effort,' says Commandant Bloch, 'we'll soon be there. It's at number 93.'

I stumble and collapse on the pavement. They encircle me. Jean-Farouk de Mérode, Paulo Hayakawa, M. Igor, Otto da Silva and Lévy-Vendôme are all wearing striking pink evening suits and fedoras. Bloch, Isaiah, Isaac, and Saul are more austere in their green trench coats. The Marquise de Fougeire-Jusquiames, Princess Chericheff-Devorazoff, Sophie Knout and the elderly Baroness Lydia Stahl are each wearing a white mink and a diamond rivière.

Paulo Hayakawa is smoking a cigar and casually flicking the ash in my face, Princess Chericheff-Devorazoff is playfully jabbing my cheeks with her stiletto heels.

'Aren't you going to get up, Marcel Proust?' asks the Marquise de Fougeire-Jusquiames.

'Come on, Schlemilovitch,' Commandant Bloch implores me, 'We only have to cross the street. Look, there's number 93 . . .'

'He is an obstinate young man,' says Jean-Farouk de Mérode. 'If you'll excuse me, I'm going to drink a whisky. I can't bear to be parched.'

He crosses the road, followed by Paulo Hayakawa, Otto da Silva and M. Igor. The door to number 93 closes behind them.

Sophie Knout, the elderly Baroness Lydia Stahl, Princess Chericheff-Devorazoff, and the Marquise de Fougeire-Jusquiames quickly join them. The Marquise de Fougeire-Jusquiames wraps her mink coats around me, whispering in my ear:

'This will be your shroud. Adieu, my angel.'

This leaves Bloch, Isaac, Saul, Isaiah and Lévy-Vendôme. Isaac tries to haul me to my feet, tugging on the chain connecting the handcuffs.

'Leave him,' says Commandant Bloch, 'he's better lying down.'

Saul, Isaac, Isaiah and Lévy-Vendôme go and sit on the steps outside number 93. They stare at me and weep.

'I'll join the others a little later,' Commandant Bloch says to me in a sad voice. '*The whisky and champagne will flow as usual on Rue Lauriston.*'

He brings his face close to mine. He really is the spitting image of my old friend Henri Chamberlin-Lafont.

'You are going to die in an SS uniform,' he says. 'You are touching, Schlemilovitch, very touching.'

From the windows of number 93, I hear a burst of laughter and the chorus of a song:

Moi, j'aime le music-hall
Ses jongleurs
Ses danseuses légères . . .

'Hear that?' asks Bloch, his eyes misted with tears. 'In France, everything ends with a song, Schlemilovitch! So keep your spirits up!'

From the right-hand pocket of his trench coat, he takes a revolver. I struggle to my feet and stagger back. Commandant Bloch does not take his eyes off me. Sitting on the steps opposite, Isaiah, Saul, Isaac and Lévy-Vendôme are still sobbing. I consider the façade of number 93 for a moment. From the windows Jean-Farouk de Mérode, Paulo Hayakawa, M. Igor, Otto da Silva, Sophie Knout, the elderly Baroness Lydia Stahl, the Marquise de Fougeire-Jusquiames, Princess Chericheff-Devorazoff, Inspector Bonny pull faces and thumb their noses at me. A sort of cheerful sadness washes over me, one I know only too well. Rebecca was right to laugh a while ago. I summon my last ounce of strength. A nervous, feeble laugh. Gradually it swells until it shakes my whole body, doubling me over. It hardly matters that Commandant Bloch is slowly coming towards me, I feel utterly at ease. He waves his revolver and roars:

'You're laughing? YOU'RE LAUGHING? Well, take that you little Jew, take that!'

My head explodes, but I do not know whether from the bullets or from my delirious joy.

The blue walls of the room and the window. By my bed sits Sigmund Freud. To make sure I'm not dreaming, I reach out my right hand and stroke his bald pate.

' . . . my nurses picked you up on the Franz-Josefs-Kai tonight and brought you to my clinic here in Pötzleinsdorf. A course of psychoanalysis will clarify things in my mind. You'll soon be a healthy, optimistic, sporty young man, I promise. Here, I want you to read this insightful essay by your compatriot Jean-Paul Schweitzer de la Sarthe: *Anti-Semite and Jew*. There is one thing you must understand at all costs. THE JEW DOES NOT EXIST, as

Schweitzer de la Sarthe so aptly puts it. YOU ARE NOT A JEW, you are a man among other men, that is all. You are not a Jew, as I have just said, you are suffering from delusions, hallucinations, fantasies, nothing more, a slight touch of paranoia . . . No one wishes you harm, my boy, all people want is to be kind to you. We are living in a world at peace. Himmler is dead, how can you remember all these things? You were not even born, come now, be reasonable, I beg you, I implore you, I . . .'

I am no longer listening to Dr Freud. And yet he goes down on his knees, arms outstretched, he pleads with me, takes his head in his hands, rolls on the floor in despair, crawls on all fours, barks, begs me again to let go of my 'hallucinatory delusions', my 'Jewish neuroses', my 'Yiddish paranoia'. I am astonished to see him in such a state: does he find my presence so disturbing?

'Stop the gesticulating.' I say, 'The only doctor I will allow to treat me is Dr Bardamu, Louis-Ferdinand Bardamu . . . A Jew like me . . . Bardamu. Louis-Ferdinand Bardamu . . .'

I got up and walked with some difficulty to the window. The psychoanalyst lay sobbing in a corner. Outside, the Pötzleinsdorfer Park was glittering with snow and sunlight. A red tram was coming down the avenue. I thought about the future being offered me: a swift cure thanks to the tender mercies of Dr Freud, men and women waiting for me at the entrance to the clinic, their expressions warm and friendly. The world, full of amazing ventures, a hive of activity.

The beautiful Pötzleinsdorfer Park, there, close by, the green-ness and the sunlit pathways.

Furtively, I slip behind the psychoanalyst and pat his head.

'I'm so tired,' I tell him, 'so tired . . .'

The Night Watch

for Rudy Modiano

for Mother

'Why was I identified with the very objects of my horror and compassion?'

Scott Fitzgerald

A burst of laughter in the darkness. The Khedive looked up.
'So you played mah-jongg while you waited for us?'
And he scatters the ivory tiles across the desk.

'Alone?' asks Monsieur Philibert.

'Have you been waiting for us long, my boy?'

Their voices are punctuated by whispers and grave inflections.
Monsieur Philibert smiles and gives a vague wave of his hand.
The Khedive tilts his head to the left and stands, his cheek almost
touching his shoulder. Like a stork.

In the middle of the living room, a grand piano. Purple wallpaper and drapes. Large vases filled with dahlias and orchids. The
light from the chandeliers is hazy, as in a bad dream.

'How about some music to relax us?' suggests Monsieur
Philibert.

'Sweet music, we need sweet music,' announces Lionel de
Zieff.

'"Zwischen heute und morgen?"' offers Count Baruzzi. 'It's a
fox trot.'

'I'd rather have a tango,' says Frau Sultana.

'Oh, yes, yes, please,' pleads Baroness Lydia Stahl.

'"Du, du gehst an mir vorbei",' Violette Morris murmurs
plaintively.

The Khedive cuts it short: 'Make it "Zwischen heute und
morgen".'

The women have too much make-up. The men are dressed in
garish colours. Lionel de Zieff is wearing an orange suit and an
ochre-striped shirt. Pols de Helder a yellow jacket and sky-blue

trousers, Count Baruzzi a dusty-green tuxedo. Several couples start to dance. Costachesco with Jean-Farouk de Méthode, Gaetan de Lussatz with Odicharvi, Simone Bouquereau with Irène de Tranze . . . Monsieur Philibert stands off to one side, leaning against the window on the left. He shrugs when one of the Chapochnikoff brothers asks him to dance. Sitting at the desk, the Khedive whistles softly and beats time.

'Not dancing, *mon petit?*' he asks. 'Nervous? Don't worry, you have all the time in the world. All the time in the world.'

'You know,' says Monsieur Philibert, 'police work is just endless patience.' He goes over to the console table and picks up the pale-green leather-bound book lying there: *Anthology of Traitors from Alcibiades to Captain Dreyfus*. He leafs through it, and lays whatever he finds between the pages – letters, telegrams, calling cards, pressed flowers – on the desk. The Khedive seems intently interested in this investigation.

'Your bedside reading, *mon petit?*'

Monsieur Philibert hands him a photograph. The Khedive stares at it for a long moment. Monsieur Philibert has moved behind him. 'His mother,' the Khedive murmurs, gesturing to the photograph. 'Isn't that right, my boy? Madame your mother?' The boy echoes: 'Madame your mother . . .' and two tears trickle down his cheeks, trickle to the corners of his mouth. Monsieur Philibert has taken off his glasses. His eyes are wide. He, too, is crying.

Just then, the first bars of 'Bei zärtlicher Musik' ring out. A tango, and there is not enough room for the dancers to move about. They jostle each other, some stumble and slip on the parquet floor. 'Don't you want to dance?' inquires Baroness Lydia Stahl. 'Go on, save me the next rumba.' 'Leave him alone,' mutters the Khedive. 'The boy doesn't feel like dancing.' 'One rumba, just one rumba,' pleads the Baroness. 'One rumba, one rumba!' shrieks Violette Morris. Beneath the glow of the chandeliers, they flush, turning blue in the face, flushing to deep purple. Beads of perspiration trickle down their temples, their eyes grow wide. Pols de Helder's face grows black as if it were burning up. Count Baruzzi's cheeks are sunken, the bags under Rachid von Rosenheim's eyes puff bloated. Lionel de Zieff brings one hand to his heart. Costachesco and Odicharvi seem stupefied. The women's make-up begins to crack, their hair turning ever more garish colours. They are all putrefying and will surely rot right where they stand. Do they stink already?

'Let's make it brief and to the point, *mon petit*,' whispers the Khedive. 'Have you contacted the man they call "La Princesse de Lamballe"? Who is he? Where is he?'

'Do you understand?' murmurs Monsieur Philibert. 'Henri wants information about the man they call "La Princesse de Lamballe".'

The record has stopped. They flop down on sofas, on pouffes, into wing chairs. Méthode uncorks a bottle of cognac. The Chapochnikoff brothers leave the room and reappear with trays of glasses. Lussatz fills them to the brim. 'A toast, my friends,' suggests Hayakawa. 'To the health of the Khedive!' cries Costachesco. 'To the health of Inspector Philibert,' says Mickey de Voisins. 'To Madame de Pompadour,' shrills Baroness Lydia Stahl. Their glasses chink. They drain them in one gulp.

'Lamballe's address,' murmurs the Khedive. 'Be a good fellow, *mon petit*. Let's have Lamballe's address.'

'You know we have the whip hand,' whispers Monsieur Philibert.

The others are conferring in low voices. The light from the chandeliers dims, wavering between blue and deep purple. Faces are blurred. 'The Hotel Blitz is getting more difficult every day.' 'Don't worry, as long as I'm around you'll have the full backing of the embassy.' 'One word from Count Grafkreuz, my dear, and the Blitz's eyes are closed for good.' 'I'll ask Otto to help.' 'I'm a close personal friend of Dr Best. Would you like me to speak to him?' 'A call to Delfanne will settle everything.' 'We have to be firm with our agents, otherwise they take advantage.' 'No quarter!' 'Especially since we're covering for them!' 'They should be grateful.' 'We're the ones who'll have to do the explaining, not they!' 'They'll get away scot free, you'll see! As for us . . .!' 'They haven't heard the last of us.' 'The news from the front is excellent. EXCELLENT!'

'Henri wants Lamballe's address,' Monsieur Philibert repeats. 'Make a real effort, *mon petit*.'

'I understand your reticence,' says the Khedive. 'So this is what I propose: to start with, you tell us where we can find and arrest every member of the ring tonight.'

'Just a little warm up,' Monsieur Philibert adds. 'Then you'll find it easier to cough up Lamballe's address.'

'The raid is set for tonight,' whispers the Khedive. 'We're waiting, *mon petit*.'

A yellow notebook bought on the Rue Réaumur. Are you a student? the sales girl asked. (Everyone is interested in young people. The future is theirs; everyone wants to know their plans, bombards them with questions.) You would need a flashlight to find the page. He cannot see a thing in this light. Thumbs through the notebook, nose all but grazing the pages. The first address is in capital letters: the address of the Lieutenant, the ring-leader.

Try to forget his blue-black eyes, the warmth in his voice as he says: 'Everything OK, *mon petit?*' You wish the Lieutenant were rotten to the core, wish he were petty, pretentious, two-faced. It would make things easier. But there is not a single flaw in that rough diamond. As a last resort, he thinks of the Lieutenant's ears. Just thinking about this piece of cartilage is enough to make him want to vomit. How can human beings possess such monstrous excrescences? He imagines the Lieutenant's ears, there, on the desk, larger than life, scarlet and criss-crossed with veins. And suddenly, in a rushed voice, he tells them where the Lieutenant will be tonight: Place du Châtelet. After that, it comes easily. He reels off a dozen names and addresses without even opening the notebook. He speaks in the earnest voice of a good little schoolboy from a fable by La Fontaine.

'Sounds like a good haul,' comments the Khedive. He lights a cigarette, jerks his nose towards the ceiling, and blows smoke rings. Monsieur Philibert has sat down at the desk and is flicking through the notebook. Probably checking the addresses.

The others go on talking among themselves. 'Let's dance some more. I have pins and needles in my legs.' 'Sweet music, that's what we need, sweet music.' 'Let everyone say what they want to hear, all of you! a rumba!' '"Serenata ritmica".' '"So stell ich mir die Liebe vor".' '"Coco Seco".' '"Whatever Lola wants".' '"Guapo Fantoma".' '"No me dejes de querer".' 'Why don't we play hide-and-seek?' A burst of applause. 'Great! Let's play hide-and-seek!' They burst out laughing in the dark. Making it tremble.

Some hours earlier. La Grande Cascade in the Bois de Boulogne. The orchestra was mangling a Creole waltz. Two people came into the restaurant and sat down at the table next to ours. An elderly man with a pearl-gray moustache and a white fedora, an elderly lady in a dark blue dress. The breeze swayed the paper lanterns hanging from the trees. Coco Lacour was smoking his cigar. Esmeralda was placidly sipped a grenadine. They were not speaking. This is why I love them. I would like to describe them in meticulous detail. Coco Lacour: a red-headed giant, a blind man's eyes sometimes aglow with an infinite sadness. He often hides them behind dark glasses, and his heavy, faltering step makes him look like a sleepwalker. How old is Esmeralda? She is a tiny little slip of a girl. I could recount so many touching details about them but, exhausted, I give up. Coco Lacour and Esmeralda, their names are enough, just as their silent presence next to me is enough. Esmeralda was gazing in wide-eyed wonder at the brutes in the dance band. Coco Lacour was smiling. I am their guardian angel. We will come to the Bois de Boulogne every night to savour the soft summer. We will enter this mysterious principality of lakes, wooded paths, with tea-houses hidden amid the dense foliage. Nothing here has changed since we were children. Remember? You would bowl your hoop along the paths in the Pré Catelan. The breeze would caress Esmeralda's hair. Her piano teacher told me she was making progress. She was learning musical theory through the work of Josef Bayer and would soon be playing short pieces by Wolfgang Amadeus Mozart. Coco Lacour would shyly light a cigar, shyly, as through apologising. I love them. There is not a trace of mawkishness in that love. I think to myself: if I were not here, people would trample them. Poor, weak creatures. Always silent. A word, a gesture is all it would take to break them. With me around, they have nothing to fear. Sometimes I feel the urge to abandon them. I would choose a perfect moment. This evening, for example. I would get to my feet and say, softly: 'Wait here, I'll be back in a minute.' Coco Lacour would nod. Esmeralda would smile weakly. I would have to take the first ten paces without turning back. After that, it would be easy. I would run to my car and take off like a shot. The hardest part: not to loosen your grip in the few seconds just before suffocation. But nothing compares to the infinite relief you feel as the body goes limp and slowly sinks. This is as true of water torture as it is of the kind of betrayal that involves abandoning someone in the night when you have promised to return. Esmeralda was toying with her straw. She blew into it, foaming her grenadine. Coco Lacour was puffing on his cigar. Whenever I get that dizzying urge to leave them, I study each of them closely, watching their every movement, studying their expressions the way a man might cling to the low wall on a bridge. If I abandon them, I will return to the solitude I knew in the beginning. It's summertime, I told myself, reassuringly. Everyone will be back next month. And indeed it was summer, but it seemed it dragged on in a strange way. There was not a single car in Paris. Not a single person on the streets. Sometimes a tolling clock would break the silence. At a corner on a sun-drenched boulevard, I thought that this was a bad dream. Everyone had left Paris in July. In the evenings, they would gather one last time on the café terraces along the Champs-Élysées and in the Bois de Boulogne. Never did I feel the sadness of summer more keenly than in those moments. July is the fireworks season. A whole world, on the brink of extinction, was sending up one last flurry of sparks beneath the foliage and the paper lanterns. People jostled each other, they spoke in loud voices, laughed, pinched each other nervously. You could hear glasses breaking, car doors slamming. The exodus was beginning. During the day, I wander through this city adrift. Smoke rises from the chimneys: people are burning their old papers before absconding. They don't want to be weighed down by useless baggage. Rivers of cars stream toward the gates of Paris, and I, I sit on a bench. I would like to join them in this flight, but I have nothing to save. When they're gone, the shadows will suddenly loom up and form a circle around me. I will recognise a few faces. The women are heavily made up, the men have the elegance of Negroes: alligator shoes, brash suits, platinum rings. Some even have a row of gold teeth on permanent display. Here I am, left for the tender mercies of dubious individuals: the rats that take over a city after the plague has wiped out the populace. They give me a warrant card, a gun licence and tell me to infiltrate a 'ring' and destroy it. Since childhood, my life has been littered with so many broken promises, so many appointments I did not keep, that becoming a model traitor seemed like child's play. 'Wait there, I'll be right back . . .' All those faces seen for one last time before darkness engulfs them . . . Some could not believe I would desert them. Others eyed me with an empty stare: 'Are you really coming back?' I remember, too, that peculiar twinge of regret whenever I looked at my watch: they've been waiting for me for five minutes, ten, twenty. Maybe they have not yet given up hope. I would feel the urge to rush off to meet them; my head would spin, on average, for an hour. Grassing people up is much quicker. A few brief seconds, just the time it takes to reel off names and addresses. An informer. I'll even become a killer if they want. I'll gun down my victims with a silencer. Afterwards, I will consider the spectacles, key rings, handkerchiefs, ties – pitiful objects that are insignificant to anyone but their owner and yet move me more deeply than the faces of the dead. Before I kill them, I will stare fixedly at one of the lowliest parts of their person: their shoes. It would be wrong to think that only a flutter of hands, an expression, a look or a tone of voice can move you at the first sight. The most moving thing, for me, are shoes. And when I feel remorse for killing them, it is not their smiles or their virtues I will remember, but their shoes. Anyway, doing dirty work for corrupt cops pays well these days. I've got money spilling out of my pockets. My money helps keep Coco Lacour and Esmeralda safe. Without them I would truly be alone. Sometimes I think that they do not exist. That I am the red-headed blind man, that tiny defenceless girl. A perfect excuse to feel sorry for myself. Give me a minute. The tears will come. I'll finally know the pleasures of 'self-pity' – as the English Jews call it. Esmeralda was smiling at me, Coco Lacour was sucking on his cigar. The old man and the elderly lady in the dark-blue dress. All around us, empty tables. Paper lanterns someone forgot to hang out. I was afraid, every second, of hearing their cars pull up on the gravel driveway. Car doors would slam, they would slowly lumber towards us. Esmeralda was blowing soap bubbles, watching them float away, her face set in a frown. One bubble burst against the elderly lady's cheek. The trees shuddered. The band struck up the first bars of a *czardas*, then a fox trot, then a march. Soon it will be impossible to tell what they're playing. The instruments hiss and hiccup, and once again I see the face of the man they dragged into the living room, his hands bound with a belt. Playing for time, at first he pulled pleasant faces as through trying to distract them. When he could no longer control his fear, he tried to arouse them: made eyes at them, bared his right shoulder with rapid, twitching jerks, started to belly-dance, his whole body trembling. We mustn't stay here a minute longer. The music will die after one last spasm. The chandeliers will gutter out.

'A game of blind man's buff?' 'What a good idea!' 'We won't even need blindfolds!' 'It's dark enough.' 'You're it, Odicharvi!' 'Scatter, everyone!'

They creep around the room. You can hear the closet door open. They're probably plannning to hide there. It sounds as if they're crawling around the desk. The floor is creaking. Someone bumps into a piece of furniture. A face is silhouetted against the window. Gales of laughter. Sighs. Frantic gestures. They run around in all directions. 'Caught you, Baruzzi!' 'Hard luck, I'm Helder.' 'Who's that?' 'Guess!' 'Rosenheim?' 'No.' 'Costachesco?' 'No.' 'Give up?'

'We'll arrest them tonight,' says the Khedive. 'The Lieutenant and all the members of the ring, EVERY LAST ONE. These people are sabotaging our work.'

'You still haven't given us Lamballe's address,' murmurs Monsieur Philibert. 'When are you going to make up your mind, *mon petit*? Come on now . . .'

'Give him a chance, Pierrot.'

Suddenly the chandeliers flicker on again. They blink into the light. There they are around the desk. 'I'm parched.' 'Let's have a drink, friends, a drink!' 'A song, Baruzzi, a song!' '"Il était un petit navire".' 'Go on, Baruzzi, go on!' '"*Qui n'avait ja-ja-ja-ja-mais navigué . . .*"'

'You want to see my tattoos?' asks Frau Sultana. She rips open her blouse. On each breast is a ship's anchor. Baroness Lydia Stahl and Violette Morris wrestle her to the ground and strip her. She wriggles and struggles free of the clutches, giggling and squealing, egging them on. Violette Morris chases her across the living room to the corner where Zieff is sucking on a chicken wing. 'Nothing like a tasty morsel now rationing is here to stay.

Do you know what I did just now? I stood in front of the mirror and smeared my face with foie gras! Foie gras worth fifteen thousand francs a medallion!' (He bursts out laughing.) 'Another cognac?' offers Pols de Helder. 'You can't get it any more. A half-bottle sells for a hundred thousand francs. English cigarettes? I have them flown in direct from Lisbon. Twenty thousand francs a pack.'

'One of these days they'll address me as *Monsieur le Préfet de police*,' the Khedive announces crisply. He stares off into the middle distance.

'To the health of the *Préfet*!' shouts Lionel de Zieff. He staggers and collapses onto the piano. The glass has slipped from his hands. Monsieur Philibert thumbs through a dossier along with Paulo Hayakawa and Baruzzi. The Chapochnikoff brothers busy themselves at the Victrola. Simone Bouquereau gazes at herself in the mirror.

Die Nacht
Die Musik
Und dein Mund

hums Baroness Lydia, doing a quick dance.

'Anyone for a session of sexuo-divine paneurhythmy?' Ivanoff the Oracle whinnies, his voice like a stallion.

The Khedive eyes them mournfully. 'They'll address me as *Monsieur le Préfet*.' He raises his voice: '*Monsieur le Préfet de police!*' He bangs his fist on the desk. The others pay no attention to this outburst. He gets up and opens the left-hand window a little. 'Come sit here, *mon petit*, I have need of your presence, such a sensitive boy, so receptive . . . you soothe my nerves.'

131

Zieff is snoring on the piano. The Chapochnikoff brothers have stopped playing the Victrola. They are examining the vases of flowers one by one, straightening an orchid, caressing the petals of a dahlia. Now and then they turn and dart frightened glances at the Khedive. Simone Bouquereau seems fascinated by her face in the mirror. Her indigo eyes widen, her complexion slowly pales to ashen. Violette Morris has taken a seat on the velvet sofa next to Frau Sultana. Both women have extended the palms of their white hands to Ivanoff's gaze.

'The price of tungsten has gone up,' Baruzzi announces. 'I can get you a good deal. I've got a little sideline with Guy Max in the purchasing office on Rue Villejust.'

'I thought he only dealt in textiles,' says Monsieur Philibert.

'He's changed his line,' says Hayakawa. 'Sold all of his stock to Macias-Reoyo.'

'Maybe you'd rather raw hides?' asks Baruzzi. 'The price of box calf has gone up a hundred francs.'

'Odicharvi mentioned three tons of worsted he wants to get rid of. I thought of you, Philibert.'

'I can have thirty-six thousand decks of cards delivered to you by morning . . . You'll get the top price for them. Now's the time. They launched their *Schwerpunkt Aktion* at the beginning of the month.'

Ivanoff is intent on the palm of the Marquise.

'Quiet!' shouts Violette Morris. 'The Oracle is predicting her future. Quiet!'

'What do you think of that, *mon petit*?' the Khedive asks me. 'Ivanoff rules women with his rod. Though his fame is not exactly iron! They can't do without him. Mystics, *mon cher*. And he plays it to the hilt! The old fool!' He rests his elbows on the edge of the balcony. Below is a peaceful square of the kind you only find in the 16th *arrondissement*. The street lights cast a strange blue glow on the foliage and the bandstand. 'Did you know, *mon fils*, that before the war this grand house we're in belonged to M. de Bel-Respiro?' (His voice is increasingly subdued.) 'In a cabinet, I found some letters that he wrote to his wife and children. A real family man. Look, that's him there.' He gestures to a full-length portrait hanging between the two windows. 'M. de Bel-Respiro in the flesh wearing his Spahi officer's uniform. Look at all those medals! There's a model Frenchman for you!'

'A square mile of rayon?' offers Baruzzi. 'I'll sell it to you dirt cheap. Five tons of biscuits? The freight cars have been impounded at the Spanish border. You'll have no problem getting them released. All I ask is a small commission, Philibert.'

The Chapochnikoff brothers prowl around the Khedive, not daring to speak to him. Zieff is sleeping with his mouth open. Frau Sultana and Violette Morris are hanging on Ivanoff's every word: astral flux . . . sacred pentagram . . . grains of sustenance from the nourishing earth . . . great cosmic waves . . . incantatory paneurhythmy . . . Betelgeuse . . . But Simone Bouquereau presses her forehead up against the mirror.

'I'm not interested in any of these financial schemes,' interrupts Monsieur Philibert.

Disappointed, Baruzzi and Hayakawa tango across the room to the chair where Lionel de Zieff is sleeping and shake his shoulder to wake him. Monsieur Philibert thumbs through a dossier, pencil in hand.

'You see, *mon petit*,' the Khedive resumes (he looks as though he is about to burst into tears), 'I never had any education. After my father died, I was alone and I spent the night sleeping on his grave. It was bitter cold, that night. At fourteen, the reformatory in Eysses . . . penal military unit . . . Fresnes Prison. . . . The only people I met were louts like myself . . . Life . . .'

'Wake up, Lionel!' shrieks Hayakawa.

'We've got something important to tell you,' adds Baruzzi.

'We'll get you fifteen thousand trucks and two tons of nickel for a 15 per cent commission.' Zieff blinks and mops his forehead with a light-blue handkerchief. 'Whatever you like, as long we can eat until we're stuffed fit to burst. I've filled out nicely these last two months, don't you think? It feels good, now that rationing is here to stay.' He lumbers over to the sofa and slips his hand into Frau Sultana's blouse. She squirms and slaps him as hard as she can. Ivanoff gives a faint snicker. 'Anything you say, boys,' Zieff repeats in a grating voice. 'Anything you say.' 'Is everything arranged for tomorrow morning, Lionel?' asks Hayakawa. 'Can I confirm it with Schiedlausky? We'll throw in a truckload of rubber.'

Sitting at the piano, Monsieur Philibert pensively fingers a few notes.

'And yet, *mon petit*,' the Khedive resumes his tale, 'I've always longed for respectability. Please don't confuse me with the characters you see here . . .'

Simone Bouquereau is in front of the mirror, putting on her make-up. Violette Morris and Frau Sultana have their eyes closed. The Oracle, it would appear, is calling upon the celestial bodies. The Chapochnikoff brothers hover around the piano. One of them is winding up the metronome, the other hands Monsieur Philibert a book of sheet music.

'Take Lionel de Zieff for example,' hisses the Khedive. 'The stories I could tell you about that shark! And about Baruzzi! Or

Hayakawa! Every last one of them! Ivanoff? A sleazy blackmailer! And Baroness Lydia Stahl is nothing but a whore!'

Monsieur Philibert riffles through the sheet music. From time to time he drums out the rhythm. The Chapochnikoff brothers glance at him fearfully.

'So you see, *mon petit*,' the Khedive continues, 'the rats have made the most of recent "events" to come out into the open. Indeed, I myself . . . But that's another story. Appearances can be deceptive. Before long, I will be welcoming the most respectable people in Paris. They will address me as Monsieur le Préfet! MONSIEUR LE PRÉFET DE POLICE, do you understand?' He turns around and points to the full-length portrait. 'Me! In my Spahi officer's uniform! Look at those decorations! The *Légion d'honneur*. The Order of the Holy Sepulchre, the Order of Saint George from Russia, the Order of Prince Danilo from Montenegro, the Order of the Tower and Sword from Portugal. Why should I envy Monsieur de Bel-Respiro? I could give him a run for his money!'

He clicks his heels.

Suddenly, silence.

Monsieur Philibert is playing a waltz. The cascade of notes hesitates, unfolds, then breaks like a wave over the dahlias and the orchids. He sits ramrod straight. His eyes are closed.

'Hear that, *mon petit*?' asks the Khedive. 'Just look at his hands! Pierre can play for hours. He never gets cramp. The man is an artist!'

Frau Sultana is nodding gently. The opening chords roused her from her torpor. Violette Morris gets to her feet and all alone she waltzes the length of the living room. Paulo Hayakawa and Baruzzi have fallen silent. The Chapochnikoff brothers listen, mouths agape. Even Zieff seems mesmerized by Monsieur Philibert's hands as they flutter feverishly over the keyboard.

Ivanoff juts his chin, stares at the ceiling. Only Simone Bouquereau carries on as if nothing has happened, putting the finishing touches to her make-up in the Venetian mirror.

Hunched low over the keys, his eyes squeezed shut, Monsieur Philibert pounds the chords with all of his strength. His playing becomes more and more impassioned.

'Like it, *mon petit?*' asks the Khedive.

Monsieur Philibert has slammed the lid of the piano shut. He gets to his feet, rubbing his hands, and strides over to the Khedive. After a pause:

'We just brought someone in, Henri. Distributing leaflets. We caught him red-handed. Breton and Reocreux are in the cellar giving him a good going over.'

The others are still dazed from the waltz. Silent, motionless, they stand precisely where the music left them.

'I was just telling the boy about you, Pierre,' murmurs the Khedive. 'Telling him what a sensitive boy you are, a terpsichorean, a virtuoso, an artist . . .'

'Thank you, Henri. It's all true, but you know how I despise big words. You should have told this young man that I am a policeman, no more, no less.'

'The finest flatfoot in France! And I'm quoting a cabinet minister!'

'That was a long time ago, Henri.'

'In those days, Pierre, I would have been afraid of you. Inspector Philibert! Fearsome! When they make me *préfet de police*, I'll appoint you *commissaire*, my darling.'

'Shut up!'

'But you love me all the same?'

A scream. Then two. Then three. Loud and shrill. Monsieur Philibert glances at his watch. 'Three quarters of an hour already.

He's bound to crack soon. I'll go and check.' The Chapochnikoff brothers follow close on his heels. The others – it would appear – heard nothing.

'You are truly divine,' Paulo Hayakawa tells Baroness Lydia, proffering a glass of champagne. 'Really?' Frau Sultana and Ivanoff are gazing into each other's eyes. Baruzzi is creeping wolfishly towards Simone Bouquereau, but Zieff trips him up. Baruzzi upsets a vase of dahlias as he falls. 'So you've decided to play the ladies' man? Ignoring your beloved Lionel?' He bursts out laughing and fans himself with his light-blue handkerchief.

'It's the guy they arrested,' murmurs the Khedive, 'the one handing out pamphlets. They're working him over. He's bound to crack soon, *mon petit*. Would you like to watch?' 'A toast to the Khedive!' roars Lionel de Zieff. 'To Inspector Philibert!' adds Paulo Hayakawa, idly caressing the Baroness' neck. A scream. Then two. A lingering sob.

'Talk or die!' bellows the Khedive.

The others pay no attention. Excepting Simone Bouquereau, still touching up her make-up in the mirror. She turns, her great violet eyes devouring her face. A streak of lipstick across her chin.

We could still make out the music for a few minutes more. It faded as we reached the junction at Cascades. I was driving. Coco Lacour and Esmeralda were huddled together in the passenger seat. We glided along the Route des Lacs. Hell begins as we leave the Bois de Boulogne: Boulevard Lannes, Boulevard Flandrin, Avenue Henri-Martin. This is the most fearsome residential section in the whole of Paris. The silence that once upon a time reigned here after eight o'clock, was almost reassuring. A bourgeois silence of plush velvet and propriety. One could almost see the families gathered in the drawing room after dinner. These days, there's no knowing what goes on behind the high dark walls. Once in a while, a car passed, its headlights out. I was afraid it might stop and block our way.

We took the Avenue Henri-Martin. Esmeralda was half-asleep. After eleven o'clock, little girls have a hard time keeping their eyes open. Coco Lacour was toying with the dashboard, turning the radio dial. Neither of them had any idea just how fragile was their happiness. I was the only one who worried about it. We were three children making our way through ominous shadows in a huge automobile. And if there happened to be a light at any window, I wouldn't rely on it. I know the district well. The Khedive used to have me raid private houses and confiscate objects of art: Second Empire *hôtels particuliers*, eighteenth-century 'follies', turn-of-the-century buildings with stained-glass windows, faux-châteaux in the gothic style. These days, their sole occupant was a terrified caretaker, overlooked by the owner in his flight. I'd ring the door-bell, flash my warrant card and search the premises. I remember long walks: Ranelagh-La Muette-Auteuil, this was my route. I'd sit on a bench in the shade of the chestnut trees. Not a soul on the streets. I could enter any house in the area. The city was mine.

Place du Trocadéro. Coco Lacour and Esmeralda at my side, those two staunch companions. Maman used to tell me: 'You get the friends you deserve.' To which I'd always reply that men are much too garrulous for my taste, that I can't stand the babble of blowflies that stream out of their mouths. It gives me a headache. Takes my breath away – and I'm short enough of breath already. The Lieutenant, for example, could talk the hind legs off a donkey. Every time I step into his office, he gets to his feet and with an

'Ah, my young friend,' or 'Ah, *mon petit*' he starts his spiel. After that, words come tumbling in a torrent so swift he scarcely has time to articulate them. The verbal torrent briefly abates, only to wash over me again a minute later. His voice grows increasingly shrill. Before long he's chirping, the words choking in his throat. He taps his foot, waves his arms, twitches, hiccups, then suddenly becomes morose and lapses back into a monotone. He invariably concludes with: 'Balls, my boy!' uttered in an exhausted whisper.

The first time we met, he said: 'I need you. We've got serious work to do. I work in the shadows alongside my men. Your mission is to infiltrate the enemy and to report back – as discreetly as possible – about what the bastards are up to.' He made a clear distinction between us: he and his senior officers reaped the honour and the glory. The spying and the double-dealing fell to me. That night, re-reading the *Anthology of Traitors from Alcibiades to Captain Dreyfus*, it occurred to me that my particular disposition was well-suited to double-dealing and – why not? – to treason. Not enough moral fibre to be a hero. Too dispassionate and distracted to be a real villain. On the other hand, I was malleable, I had a fondness for action, and I was plainly good-natured.

We were driving along Avenue Kléber. Coco Lacour was yawning. Esmeralda had nodded off, her little head lolling against my shoulder. It's high time they were in bed. Avenue Kléber. That other night we had taken the same route after leaving L'Heure Mauve, a cabaret club on the Champs-Élysées. A rather languid crowd were grouped together in red velvet booths or perched on bar stools: Lionel de Zieff, Costachesco, Lussatz, Méthode, Frau Sultana, Odicharvi, Lydia Stahl, Otto da Silva, the Chapochnikoff brothers . . . Hot, muggy twilight. The trailing scent of Egyptian perfumes. Yes, there were still a few small islands in Paris where people tried to ignore 'the disaster lately occurred', where a pre-war hedonism and frivolity festered. Contemplating all those faces, I repeated to myself a phrase I had read somewhere: 'Brash vulgarity that reeks of betrayal and murder . . .'

Close to the bar a Victrola was playing:

Bonsoir
Jolie Madame
Je suis venu
Vous dire bonsoir . . .

The Khedive and Monsieur Philibert led me outside. A white Bentley was parked at the foot of Rue Marbeuf. They sat next to the chauffeur while I sat in the back. The street lights spewed a soft bluish glow.

'Don't worry,' the Khedive said, nodding at the driver. 'Eddy has eyes like a cat.'

'Just now,' Monsieur Philibert said to me, taking me by the arm, 'there are all sorts of opportunities just waiting for a young man. You just need to make the best of the situation, and I'm ready to help you, my boy. These are dangerous times we live in. Your hands are pale and slender, and you have a delicate sensibility. Be careful. I have only one piece of advice to offer: don't play the hero. Keep your head down. Work with us. It's either that, or martyrdom or the sanatorium.' 'A little casual double-crossing, for example – might that be of interest?' the Khedive asked. 'Very handsomely rewarded,' added Monsieur Philibert. '. . . and absolutely legal. We'll supply you with a warrant card and a gun licence.' 'All you need do is infiltrate an underground network so we can break it up. You would keep us informed about the activities of the gentlemen in question.' 'As long as you're careful, they won't suspect you.' 'I think you inspire confidence.' 'You look as though butter wouldn't melt in your mouth.' 'And you have a pretty smile.' 'And beautiful eyes, my boy!' 'Traitors always have honest eyes.' The torrent of words was flowing faster. By the end I had the feeling that they were talking at once. Swarms of blue butterflies fluttering from their mouths . . . They could have anything they asked for – informer, hired killer, anything – if they would only shut up once in a while and let me sleep. Spy, turncoat, killer, butterflies . . .

'We're taking you to our new headquarters,' Monsieur Philibert decided. 'An *hôtel particulier* at 3 *bis* Cimarosa Square.' 'We're having a little housewarming,' added the Khedive. 'With all our friends.' '"Home, Sweet Home",' hummed Monsieur Philibert.

As I stepped into the living room, the ominous phrase came back to me: 'A brash vulgarity reeks of betrayal and murder . . .' The gang were all there. With each passing moment, new faces appeared: Danos, Codébo, Reocreux, Vital-Léca, Robert le Pâle . . . The Chapochnikoff brothers poured champagne for everyone. 'Shall we have a little tête-à-tête?' the Khedive whispered to me. 'So, what do you think? You're white as a ghost. Would you care for a drink?' He handed me a champagne glass filled to the brim with some pink liquid. 'You see . . .' he said, throwing open the French doors and leading me on to the balcony, ' . . . from today I am master of an empire. We are no longer talking about acting as a reserve police force. This is going to be big business! Five hundred pimps and touts in our employ! Philibert will help me with the administrative side. I have made the most of the extraordinary events we have endured these past few months.' The air was so muggy it fogged the living-room windows. Someone brought me another glass of pink liquid, which I drank, stifling an urge to retch. 'And what is more . . .' – he stroked my cheek with the back of his hand – 'you can advise me, guide me once in a while. I've had no education.' (His voice had dropped to a whisper.) 'At fourteen, the reformatory in Eysses . . . the penal military unit overseas . . . obscurity . . . But I crave respectability, don't you see?' His eyes blazed. Viciously: 'One day soon I shall be *préfet de police*. They'll address me as MONSIEUR LE PRÉFET!' He hammers both fists on the balcony railing: 'MONSIEUR LE PRÉFET . . . MONSIEUR LE PRÉ-FET!' and immediately his eyes glazed and he stared into the middle distance.

On the square below, the trees gave off a delicate haze. I wanted to leave, but already it was probably too late. He'd grab my wrist, and even if I managed to break his grip I'd have to cross the living room, elbow my way through those dense groups, face an assaulting horde of buzzing wasps. I felt dizzy. Bright circles whirled around me, faster and faster, and my heart pounded fit to burst.

'Feeling a little unwell?' The Khedive takes me by the arm and leads me over to the sofa. The Chapochnikoff brothers – how many of them were there? – were scurrying around. Count Baruzzi took a wad of banknotes from a black briefcase to show to Frau Sultana. Farther off, Rachid von Rosenheim, Paulo Hayakawa, and Odicharvi were talking excitedly. There were others I couldn't quite make out. As I watched, all these people seemed to be crumbling under the weight of their raucous chatter, their jerky movements, their heavy perfumes. Monsieur Philibert was holding out a green card slashed with a red stripe. 'You are now a member of the Service; I've signed you up under the name "Swing Troubadour".' They all gathered around me, flourishing champagne flutes. 'To Swing Troubadour!' Lionel de Zieff roared and laughed until his face turned purple. 'To Swing Troubadour!' squealed Baroness Lydia.

It was at that moment – if I remember correctly – that I felt a sudden urge to cough. Once again I saw maman's face. She was bending over me as she used to do every night before turning out the light, and whispering in my ear: 'You'll end up on the gallows!' 'A toast to Swing Troubadour!' murmured one of the Chapochnikoff brothers, and he touched my shoulder shyly. The others pressed around, clinging to me like flies.

Avenue Kléber. Esmeralda is talking in her sleep. Coco Lacour is rubbing his eyes. It's time they were in bed. Neither of them had any idea just how fragile is their happiness. Of the three of us, only I am worried.

'I'm sorry you had to hear those screams, my child,' says the Khedive. 'Like you, I have a horror of violence, but this man was handing out leaflets. It's a serious offence.'

Simone Bouquereau is gazing at herself in the mirror again, touching up her make-up. The others, relaxed now, lapse into a kind of easy conviviality wholly in keeping with their surroundings. We are in a bourgeois living room, dinner has just ended and the time has come to offer the liqueurs.

'Perhaps a little drink would perk you up, *mon petit*?' suggests the Khedive.

'This "murky chapter" of history we are living through,' remarks Ivanoff the Oracle, 'is like an aphrodisiac to women.'

'People have probably forgotten the heady scent of cognac, what with the rationing these days,' sneers Lionel de Zieff. 'Their tough luck!' 'What do you expect?' murmurs Ivanoff. 'After all, the whole world is going to the dogs . . . But that's not to say I'm exploiting the situation, *cher ami*. Purity is what matters to me.'

'Box caulk . . .' begins Pols de Helder.

'A wagonload of tungsten . . .' Baruzzi joins in.

'And a 25 per cent commission,' Jean-Farouk de Méthode adds pointedly.

Solemn-faced, Monsieur Philibert has reappeared in the living room and is walking over to the Khedive.

'We're leaving in fifteen minutes, Henri. Our first target: the Lieutenant, Place du Châtelet. Then the other members of the network at their various addresses. A fine haul! The young man will come with us, won't you Swing Troubadour? Get ready! Fifteen minutes!' 'A tot of cognac to steady your nerves, Troubadour?' suggests the Khedive. 'And don't forget to come up with Lamballe's address,' adds Monsieur Philibert. 'Understood?'

One of the Chapochnikoff brothers – how many of them are there, anyway? – stands in the centre of the room, a violin resting under his chin. He clears his throat and, in a magnificent bass, begins to sing:

Nur
Nicht
Aus Liebe weinen . . .

The others clap their hands, beating time. Slowly, the bow scrapes across the strings, moves faster, then faster still . . . The music picks up speed.

Aus Liebe . . .

Bright rings ripple out as from a pebble cast on water. They began circling the violinist's feet and now have reached the walls of the *salon*.

Es gibt auf Erden . . .

The singer gasps for breath, it sounds as though another note might choke him. The bow skitters ever faster across the strings. How long will they be able to beat time with their clapping?

Auf dieser Welt . . .

The whole room is spinning now; the violinist is the one still point.

nicht nur den Einen . . .

As a child, you were always frightened of the fairground whirligigs French children call 'caterpillars'. Remember . . .

Es gibt so viele . . .

You shrieked and shrieked, but it was useless. The whirligig spun faster.

Es gibt so viele . . .

And yet you were the one who insisted on riding the whirligigs. Why?

Ich lüge auch . . .

They stand up, clapping . . . The room is spinning, spinning. The floor seems almost to tilt. They will lose their balance, the vases of flowers will crash to the floor. The violinist sings, the words a headlong rush.

Ich lüge auch

You shrieked and shrieked, but it was useless. No one could hear you above the fairground roar.

Es muß ja Lüge sein . . .

The face of the Lieutenant. Ten, twenty other faces it's impossible to make out. The living room is spinning too fast, just like the whirligig 'Sirocco' long ago in Luna Park.

der mir gefällt . . .

After five minutes it was spinning so fast you couldn't recognize the blur of faces of the people below, watching.

heute Dir gehören . . .

And yet, as you whirled past, you could recognise a nose, a hand, a laugh, a flash of teeth, a pair of staring eyes. The blue-black eyes of the Lieutenant. Ten, perhaps twenty other faces. The faces of those whose addresses you spat out, those who will be arrested tonight. Thankfully, they stream past quickly, in time with the music, and you don't have a chance to piece together their features.

und Liebe schwören . . .

The tenor's voice sings faster, faster, he is clinging to the violin with the desperate look of a castaway . . .

Ich liebe jeden . . .

The others clap, clap, clap their hands, their cheeks are puffy, their eyes wild, they will all surely die of apoplexy . . .

Ich lüge auch . . .

The face of the Lieutenant. Ten, perhaps twenty other faces, their features recognisable now. They who will soon be rounded up. They seem to blame you. For a brief moment you have no regrets about giving up their addresses. Faced with the frank stare of these heroes, you are almost tempted to shout out loud just what you are: an informer. But, inch by inch, the glaze on their faces chips away, their arrogance pales, and the conviction that glistened in their eyes vanishes like the flame of a snuffed-out candle. A tear makes its way down the cheek of one of them. Another lowers his head and glances at you sadly. Still another stares at you dazedly, as if he didn't expect that from you . . .

Als ihr bleicher Leib im Wasser . . . (As her pale corpse in the water)

Very slowly their faces turn, turn. They whisper faint reproaches as they pass. Then, as they turn, their features tense, they are no longer focussed on you, their eyes, their mouths are warped with terrible fear. They must be thinking of the fate that lies in store for them. Suddenly, they are like children crying for their mothers in the dark . . .

Von den Bächen in die grösseren Flüsse . . .

You remember all the favours they did you. One of them used to read his girlfriend's letters to you.

Als ihr bleicher Leib im Wasser . . .

Another wore black leather shoes. A third knew the names of every star. REMORSE. These faces will never stop turning and you will never sleep soundly again. But something the Lieutenant said comes back to you: 'The men in my outfit are raring to go. They'll die if they have to, but you won't wring a word from them.' So much the better. The faces are now harder still. The blue-black eyes of the Lieutenant. Ten, perhaps twenty other faces filled with contempt. Since they're determined to go out with a flourish, let them die!

in Flüssen mit vielem Aas . . .

He falls silent. He has set his violin on the mantelpiece. The others gradually become calm. Enveloped by a kind of languor. They slump onto the sofa, into wing chairs. 'You're pale as a sheet, *mon petit*,' murmurs the Khedive. 'Don't worry. Our little raid

148

will be done by the book.' It is nice to be out on a balcony in the fresh air and, for a moment, to forget that room where the heady scent of flowers, the prattle of voices, and the music left you light-headed. A summer night, so soft, so still, you think you're in love.

'Obviously, I realise that we have all the hallmarks of thugs. The men in my employ, our brutal tactics, the fact that we offered you, with your charming innocent face like the baby Jesus, a job as an informant; none of these things augurs well, alas . . .'

The trees and the kiosk in the square below are bathed in a reddish glow. 'And the curious souls who are drawn to what I call our little "HQ": con-artists, women of ill repute, disgraced police officers, morphine addicts, nightclub owners, indeed all these marquises, counts, barons, and princesses that you won't find in any almanac of high society . . .'

Below, along the curb, a line of cars. Their cars. Inkblots in the darkness.

'I'm only too aware that all this might seem rather distasteful to a well-bred young man. But . . .' – his voice takes on a savage tone – 'the fact that you find yourself among such disreputable souls tonight means that, despite that choirboy face of yours,' (Very tenderly) 'we belong to the same world, Monsieur.'

The glare from the chandeliers burns them, eating away at their faces like acid. Their cheeks become gaunt, their skin wizened, their heads will soon be as shrunken as those prized by the Jivaro Indians. A scent of flowers and withered flesh. Soon, all that will remain of this gathering will be tiny bubbles popping on the surface of a pond. Already they are wading through a pinkish mud that has risen to their knees. They do not have long to live.

'This is getting tedious,' declares Lionel de Zieff.

'It's time to go,' says Monsieur Philibert. 'First target: Place du Châtelet. The Lieutenant!'

'Are you coming, *mon petit*?' asks the Khedive. Outside, the black-out, as usual. They pile into the cars. 'Place du Châtelet!' 'Place du Châtelet!' Doors slam. They take off in a screech of tyres. 'No overtaking, Eddy!' orders the Khedive. 'The sight of all these brave boys cheers me up.'

'And to think that we are responsible for this low life scum!' sighs Monsieur Philibert. 'Be charitable, Pierre. We're in business with these people. They are our partners. For better or worse.'

Avenue Kléber. They honk their horns, their arms hang out of the car windows, waving, flapping. They lurch and skid, bumpers pranging. Eager to see who will take the biggest risks, make the loudest noise in the blackout. Champs-Élysées. Concorde. Rue de Rivoli. 'We're headed for a district I know well,' says the Khedive. 'Les Halles – where I spent my youth unloading vegetable carts.'

The others have disappeared. The Khedive smiles and lights a cigarette with his solid gold lighter. Rue de Castiglione. On the left, the column on the Place Vendôme is faintly visible. Place des Pyramides. The car slows gradually, as if approaching a border. On the far side of the Rue du Louvre, the city suddenly seems to crumple.

'We are now entering the "belly of Paris",' remarks the Khedive. The stench, at first unbearable, then gradually more bearable, catches in their throats despite the fact the car windows are closed. Les Halles seems to have been converted into a knacker's yard.

'The belly of Paris,' repeats the Khedive.

The car glides along greasy pavements. Spatters fleck the bonnet. Mud? Blood? Whatever it is, it is warm.

We cross Boulevard de Sébastopol and emerge on to a vast patch of waste ground. The surrounding houses have all been razed; all that remain are fragments of walls and scraps of wallpaper. From what is left, it is possible to work out the location of the stairs, the fireplaces, the wardrobes. And the size of the rooms. The place where the bed stood. There was a boiler here, a sink there. Some favoured wallpapers with patterned flowers, others prints in the style of *toiles de Jouy*. I even thought I saw a coloured print still hanging on the wall.

Place du Châtelet. Zelly's Café, where the Lieutenant and Saint-Georges are supposed to meet me at midnight. What expression should I affect when I see them striding towards me? The others are already seated at tables by the time we enter, the Khedive, Philibert, and I. They gather round, eager to be the first to shake our hands. They clasp us, hug us, shake us. Some smother our faces with kisses, some stroke our necks, others playfully tug at our lapels. I recognize Jean-Farouk de Méthode, Violette Morris, and Frau Sultana. 'How are you?' Costachesco asks me. We elbow our way through the assembled crowd. Baroness Lydia drags me to a table occupied by Rachid von Rosenheim, Pols de Helder, Count Baruzzi, and Lionel de Zieff. 'Care for a little cognac?' offers Pols de Helder. 'It's impossible to get the stuff these days in Paris, it sells for a hundred thousand francs a half-bottle. Drink up!' He pushes the neck of the bottle between my teeth. Then von Rosenheim shoves a cigarette between my lips and takes out a platinum lighter set with emeralds. The light dims, their gestures and their voices fade into the soft half-light, then suddenly, with vivid clarity, I see the face of the Princesse de Lamballe, brought by a unit of the 'Garde Nationale' from La Force Prison: 'Rise, Madam, it is time to go to the Abbey.' I can see their pikes, their leering faces. Why didn't she simply shout 'VIVE LA NATION!' as she was asked to do? If someone should prick my forehead with a pike-staff (Zieff? Hayakawa? Rosenheim? Philibert? the Khedive?), one drop of blood is all it would take to bring the sharks circling. Don't move a muscle. 'VIVE LA NATION!' I would shout it as often as they want. Strip naked if I have to. Anything they ask! Just one more minute, Monsieur Executioner. No matter the price. Rosenheim shoves another cigarette into my mouth. The condemned man's last? Apparently the execution is not set for tonight. Costachesco, Zieff, Helder, and Baruzzi are being extremely solicitous. They're worried about my health. Do I have enough money? Of course I do. The act of giving up the Lieutenant and all the members of his network will earn me about a hundred thousand francs, which I will use to buy a few scarves at Charvet and a Vicuña coat for winter. Unless of course they kill me first. Cowards, apparently, always die a shameful death. The doctor used to tell me that when he is about to die, a man becomes a music box playing the melody that best describes his life, his character, his aspirations. For some, it's a popular waltz; for others, a military march. Still another mews a gypsy air that trails off in a sob or a cry of panic. When your turn comes, *mon petit*, it will be the clang of a can clattering in the darkness across a patch of waste ground. A while ago, as we crossed the patch of waste ground on the far side of the Boulevard de Sébastopol, I was thinking: 'This is where your story will end.' I remembered the slippery slope that brought me to the spot, one of the most desolate in Paris. It all began in the Bois de Boulogne. Remember? You were bowling your hoop on the lawn in the Pré Catelan. Years pass, you move along the Avenue

Henri-Martin and find yourself on the Place du Trocadéro. Next comes the Place de l'Étoile. Before you is an avenue lined with glittering street lights. Like a vision of the future, you think: full of promise – as the saying goes. You're breathless with exhilaration on the threshold of this vast thoroughfare, but it's only the Champs-Élysées with its cosmopolitan bars, its call girls and Claridge, a caravanserai haunted by the spectre of Stavisky. The bleak sadness of the Lido. The tawdry stopovers at Le Fouquet and Le Colisée. From the beginning, everything was rigged. Place de la Concorde, you're wearing alligator shoes, a polka-dot tie, and a gigolo's smirk. After a brief detour through the Madeleine-Opera district, just as sleazy as the Champs-Élysées, you continue your tour and what the doctor calls your MOR-AL DIS-IN-TE-GRA-TION under the arcades of the Rue de Rivoli. Le Continental, Le Meurice, the Saint-James et d'Albany, where I work as a hotel thief. Occasionally wealthy female guests invite me to their rooms. Before dawn, I have rifled their handbags and lifted a few pieces of jewellery. Farther along. Rumpelmayer, with its stench of withered flesh. The mincing queers you beat up at night in the Tuileries gardens just to steal their braces and their wallets. But suddenly the vision becomes clearer: I'm here in the warm, in the belly of Paris. Where exactly is the border? You need only cross the Rue du Louvre or the Place du Palais Royal to find yourself in the narrow, fetid streets of Les Halles. The belly of Paris is a jungle streaked with multi-coloured neon. All around, upturned vegetable carts and shadows hauling huge haunches of meat. A gaggle of pale, outrageously painted faces appear for an instant only to vanish into the darkness. From now on, anything is possible. You'll be called upon to do the dirtiest jobs before they finally kill you off. And if, by some desperate ruse, some last-ditch act of cowardice, you manage to escape this horde of fishwives and butchers lurking in the shadows, you'll die a little farther down the street, on the other side of the Boulevard Sébastopol, there on that patch of waste ground. That wasteland. The doctor said as much. You have come to the end of your journey, there's no turning back. Too late. The trains are no longer running. Our Sunday walks along the Petite Ceinture, the disused railway line that took us in full circle around Paris. Porte de Clignancourt. Boulevard Pereire. Porte Dauphine. Farther out, Javel . . . The stations along the track had been converted into warehouses or bars. Some had been left intact, and I could almost picture a train arriving any minute, but the hands of the station clock had not moved for fifty years. I've always had a special feeling for the Gare d'Orsay. Even now, I still wait there for the pale blue Pullmans that speed you to the Promised Land. And when they do not come, I cross the Pont Solférino whistling a little waltz. From my wallet, I take a photograph of Dr Marcel Petiot in the dock looking pensive and, behind him, the vast pile of suitcases filled with hopes and unrealised dreams, while, pointing to them, the judge asks me: 'What have you done with your youth?' and my lawyer (my mother, as it happened, since no one else would agree to defend me) attempts to persuade the judge and jury that I was 'a promising young man', 'an ambitious boy', destined for a 'brilliant career', so everyone said. 'The proof, Your Honour, is that the suitcases piled behind him are in impeccable condition. Russian leather, Your Honour.' 'Why should I care about those suitcases, Madame, since they never went anywhere?' And every voice condemns me to death. Tonight, you need to go to bed early. Tomorrow is a busy day at the brothel. Don't forget your make-up and lipstick. Practise in front of the mirror: flutter your eyelashes with velvet softness. You'll meet a lot of degenerates who'll ask you to do incredible things. Those perverts frighten me. If I don't please them, they'll kill me. Why didn't she shout: 'VIVE LA NATION'? When my turns comes, I'll shout it as often as they want. I'm a very obliging whore. 'Come on, drink up,' Zieff pleads with me. 'A little music?' suggests Violette Morris. The Khedive comes over to me, smiling: 'The Lieutenant will be here in ten minutes. All you have to do is say hello to him as if nothing were up.' 'Something romantic,' Frau Sultana requests. 'RO-MAN-TIC,' screeches Baroness Lydia. 'Then try to persuade him to go outside.' '"Negra Noche", please,' asks Frau Sultana. 'So we can arrest him more easily. Then we'll pick up the others at their homes.' '"Five Feet Two",' simpers Frau Sultana. 'That's my favourite song.' 'Looks like it's going to be a nice little haul. We're very grateful for the information, *mon petit.*' 'No, no,' says Violette Morris. 'I want to hear "Swing Troubadour"!' One of the Chapochnikoff brothers winds the Victrola. The record is scratched. The singer sounds as if his voice is about to crack. Violette Morris beats time, whispering the words:

Mais ton amie est en voyage
Pauvre Swing Troubadour . . .

The Lieutenant. Was it a hallucination brought on by exhaustion? There were days when I could remember him calling me by my first name, talking to me like a close friend. His arrogance had disappeared, his face was gaunt. All I could see before me was an old lady gazing at me tenderly.

En cueillant des roses printanières
Tristement elle fit un bouquet . . .

He would be overcome by a weariness, a helplessness as through suddenly realising that he could do nothing. He kept repeating: 'You have the heart of a starry-eyed girl . . .' By which, I suppose, he meant that I wasn't a 'bad sort' (one of his expressions). At such times, I would have liked to thank him for his kindness to me, he who was usually so abrupt, so overbearing, but I could not find the words. After a moment I would manage to stammer: 'I left my heart back at Batignolles,' hoping that this phrase would expose my true self: a rough and ready boy, emotional – no – restless underneath and pretty decent on the whole.

Pauvre Swing Troubadour
Pauvre Swing Troubadour . . .

The record stops. 'Dry martini, young man?' Lionel de Zieff inquires. The others gather round me. 'Feeling queasy again?' Count Baruzzi asks. 'You look terribly pale.' 'Suppose we get him some fresh air?' suggests Rosenheim. I hadn't noticed the large photo of Pola Négri behind the bar. Her lips are unmoving, her features smooth and serene. She contemplates what is happening with studied indifference. The yellowed print makes her seem even more distant. Pola Négri cannot help me.

The Lieutenant. He stepped into Zelly's café followed by Saint-Georges around midnight, as arranged. Everything happened quickly. I wave to them. I cannot bring myself to meet their eyes. I lead them back outside. The Khedive, Gouari, and Vital-Leca immediately surround them, revolvers drawn. Only then do I look them square in the eye. They stare at me, first in amazement and then with a kind of triumphant scorn. Just as Vital-Leca is about to slip the cuffs on them they make a break for it and run towards the boulevard. The Khedive fires three shots. They crumple at the corner of Avenue Victoria and the square. Arrested during the next hour are:

Corvisart:	2 Avenue Bosquet
Pernety:	172 Rue de Vaugirard
Jasmin:	83 Boulevard Pasteur
Obligado:	5 Rue Duroc
Picpus:	17 Avenue Félix-Faure
Marbeuf and Pelleport: 28 Avenue de Breteuil	

Each time, I rang the doorbell and, to win their trust, I gave my name.

They're sleeping now. Coco Lacour has the largest room in the house. I've put Esmeralda in the blue room that probably once belonged to the owners' daughter. The owners fled Paris in June 'owing to circumstances'. They'll come back when order has been restored – next year maybe, who knows? – and throw us out of their house. In court, I'll admit that I entered their home illegally. The Khedive, Philibert, and the others will be there in the dock with me. The world will wear its customary colours again. Paris will once more be the City of Light, and the general public in the gallery will pick their noses while they listen to the litany of our crimes: denouncements, beatings, theft, murder, trafficking of every description – things that, as I write these lines, are commonplace. Who will be willing to give evidence for me?

The Fort de Montrouge on a bleak December morning. The firing squad. And all the horrors Madeleine Jacob will write about me. (Don't read them, maman.) But it hardly matters, my partners in crime will kill me long before Morality, Justice, and Humanity return to confound me. I would like to leave a few memories, if nothing else, to leave to posterity the names of Coco Lacour and Esmeralda. Tonight I can watch over them, but for how much longer? What will become of them without me? They were my only companions. Gentle and silent as gazelles. Defenceless. I remember clipping a picture of a cat that had just been saved from drowning from a magazine. Its fur was soaked and dripping with mud. Around its neck, a noose weighted at one end with a stone. Never have I seen an expression that radiated such goodness. Coco Lacour and Esmeralda are like that cat. Don't misunderstand me: I don't belong to the Animal Protection Society or the League of Human Rights. What do I do? I wander through this desolate city. At night, at about nine o'clock, when the blackout has plunged it into the darkness, the Khedive, Philibert and the others gather around me. The days are white and fevered. I need to find an oasis or I shall die: my love for Coco Lacour and Esmeralda. I suppose even Hitler himself felt the need to relax when he petted his dog. I PROTECT THEM. Anyone who tries to harm them will have to answer to me. I fondle the silencer the Khedive gave me. My pockets are stuffed with cash. I have one of the most enviable names in France (I stole it, but in times like these, such things don't matter). I weigh 90kg on an empty stomach. I have velvety eyes. A 'promising' young man. But what exactly was my promise? The Good Fairies gathered around my cradle. They must have been drinking. You're dealing with a formidable opponent. So KEEP YOUR HANDS OFF THEM! I first saw them on the platform at Grenelle métro station and realised that it would take only a word, a gesture to break them. I wonder how they came to be there, still alive. I remembered the cat saved from drowning. The blind red-headed giant's name was Coco Lacour. The little girl – or the little old lady – was Esmeralda. Faced with these two people, I felt pity. I felt a bitter, violent wave break over me. As the tide ebbed, I felt my head spin: push them onto the tracks. I had to dig my nails into my palms, hold my whole body taut. The wave broke over me again, a tide so gentle that I closed my eyes and surrendered to it.

Every night I half-open the door to their rooms as quietly as I can, and watch them sleep. I feel my head spinning just as it did that first time: slip the silencer out of my pocket and kill them. I'll break my last moorings adrift and drift towards the North Pole where there are no tears to temper loneliness. They freeze on the tips of eyelashes. And arid sorrow. Two eyes staring at parched wasteland. If I hesitate at the thought of killing the blind man and the little girl – or the little old lady – how then can I betray the Lieutenant? What counts against him is his courage, his composure, the elegance that imbues his every gesture. His steady blue eyes exasperate me. He belongs to that ungainly breed of heroes. Yet still, I can't help seeing him as a kindly elderly lady. I don't take men seriously. One day I'll find myself looking at them – and at myself – the way I do at Coco Lacour and Esmeralda. The toughest, the proudest ones will seem like frail creatures who need to be protected.

They played mah-jongg in the living room before going to bed. The lamp casts a soft glow on the bookshelves and the full-length portrait of Monsieur de Bel-Respiro. They moved the pieces slowly. Esmeralda tilted her head while Coco Lacour gnawed on his forefinger. All around us, silence. I close the shutters. Coco Lacour quickly nods off. Esmeralda is afraid of the dark, so I always leave her door ajar and the light on in the hallway. I usually read to her for half an hour from a book I found in the nightstand of this room when I appropriated this house: *How to Raise Our Daughters*, by Madame Léon Daudet. 'It is in the linen closet, more than anywhere else, that a young girl begins to sense the seriousness of domestic responsibilities. For is not the linen closet the most enduring symbol of family security and stability? Behind its massive doors lie orderly piles of cool sheets, damask tablecloths, neatly folded napkins; to my mind, there is nothing quite so gratifying to the eye as a well-appointed linen closet . . .' Esmeralda has fallen asleep. I pick out a few notes on the living room piano. I lean up against the window. A peaceful square of the kind you only find in the 16th *arrondissement*. The leaves of the trees brush against the windowpane. I would like to think of this house as mine. I've grown attached to the bookshelves, to the lamps with their rosy shades, to the piano. I'd like to cultivate the virtues of domesticity, as outlined by Madame Léon Daudet, but I will not have the time.

Sooner or later the owners will come back. What saddens me most is that they'll evict Coco Lacour and Esmeralda. I don't feel sorry for myself. The only feelings I have are Panic (which causes me to commit endless acts of cowardice) and Pity for my fellow men; although their twisted faces frighten me, still I find them moving. Will I spend the winter among these maniacs? I look awful. My constant comings and goings between the Lieutenant and the Khedive, the Khedive and the Lieutenant, are beginning to wear me down. I want to appease them both (so they'll spare my life), and this double-dealing demands a physical stamina I don't have. Suddenly I feel the urge to cry. My indifference gives way to what English Jews call *a nervous breakdown*. I wander through a maze of thoughts and come to the conclusion that all these people, in their opposing camps, have secretly banded together to destroy me. The Khedive and the Lieutenant are but a single person, and I am simply a panicked moth flitting one lamp to the next, each time singeing its wings a little more.

Esmeralda is crying. I'll go and comfort her. Her nightmares are short-lived, she'll go back to sleep right away. I'll play mah-jongg while I wait for the Khedive, Philibert, and the others. I'll assess the situation one last time. On one side, the heroes 'skulking in the shadows': the Lieutenant and his plucky little team of graduates from Saint-Cyr Military Academy. On the other, the Khedive and his thugs in the night watch. Tossed about between the two and I and my pitifully modest ambitions: BARMAN at some *auberge* outside Paris. A wrought-iron gate, a gravel driveway. Lush gardens and a bounding wall. On a clear day, from the third-floor windows, you might catch a glimpse of the searchlight on the Eiffel Tower sweeping the horizon.

Bartender. You can get used to such things. Though it can be painful sometimes. Especially after twenty years of believing a brilliant future beckoned. Not for me. What does it entail? Making cocktails. On Saturday nights the orders start to pour in. Gin Fizz, Brandy Alexander, Pink Lady, Irish coffee. A twist of lemon. Two rum punches. The customers, in swelling numbers, throng the bar where I stand mixing the rainbow-coloured concoctions. Careful not to keep them waiting for fear they'll lunge at me if there's a moment's delay. By quickly filling their glasses I try to keep them at bay. I'm not especially fond of human contact. Porto Flip? Whatever they want. I'm serving up cocktails. It's as good a way as any to protect yourself from your fellow man and – why not? – to be rid of them. Curaçao? Marie-Brizard? Their faces flush. They reel and lurch, before long they will collapse dead drunk. Leaning on the bar, I will watch them as they sleep. They cannot harm me anymore. Silence, at last. My breath still coming short.

Behind me, photos of Henri Garat, Fred Bretonnel, and a few other pre-war stars whose smiles have faded over the years. Within easy reach, an issue of *L'Illustration* devoted to the Normandie: The grill room, the chairs along the afterdeck. The nursery. The smoking lounge. The ballroom. The sailors' charity ball on 25 May under the patronage of Madame Flandin. All swallowed up. I know how it feels. I was aboard the Titanic when she sank. Midnight. I'm listening to old songs by Charles Trenet:

. . . Bonsoir
Jolie madame . . .

The record is scratched, but I never tire of listening to it. Sometimes I put another record on the gramophone:

Tout est fini, plus de prom'nades
Plus de printemps, Swing Troubadour . . .

The inn, like a bathyscaphe, comes aground in a sunken city. Atlantis? Drowned men glide along the Boulevard Haussmann.

. . . Ton destin
Swing Troubadour . . .

At Fouquet, they linger at their tables. Most of them have lost all semblance of humanity. One can almost see their entrails beneath their gaudy rags. In the waiting hall at Saint-Lazare, corpses drift in serried groups; I see a few escaping through the windows of commuter trains. On the Rue d'Amsterdam, the patrons streaming out of Le Monseigneur have a sickly green pallor but seem better preserved than the ones before. I continue my night rounds. Élysée-Montmartre. Magic City. Luna Park. Rialto-Dancing. Ten thousand, a hundred thousand drowned souls moving slowly, languidly, like the cast of a film projected in slow motion. Silence. Now and then they brush up against the bathyscaphe, their faces – glassy-eyed, open-mouthed – pressed against the porthole.

. . . Swing Troubadour . . .

I can never go back up to the surface. The air is growing thin, the lights in the bar begin to flicker, and I find myself back at Austerlitz station in summer. Everyone is leaving for the Southern Zone. They jostle each other to get to the ticket windows and board trains bound for Hendaye. They will cross the Spanish border. They will never be seen again. There are still one or two strolling along the station platforms but they too will fade any second now. Hold them back? I head west through Paris. Châtelet. Palais-Royal. Place de la Concorde. The sky is too blue, the leaves are much too delicate. The gardens along the Champs-Élysées look like a thermal spa.

Avenue Kléber. I turn left. Place Cimarosa. *A peaceful square of the kind you only find in the 16th* arrondissement. The bandstand is deserted now, the statue of Toussaint L'Ouverture is eaten away by greyish lichen. The house at 3 *bis* once belonged to Monsieur and Madame de Bel-Respiro. On 13 May, 1897, they held a masked ball on the theme of the Arabian Nights; Monsieur de Bel-Respiro's son greeted guests dressed as a rajah. The young man died the next day in a fire at the Bazar de la Charité. Madame de Bel-Respiro loved music, especially Isidore Lara's 'Le Rondel de l'adieu'. Monsieur de Bel-Respiro liked to paint in his spare time. I feel the need to mention such details because everyone has forgotten them.

August in Paris brings forth a flood of memories. The sunshine, the deserted avenues, the rustle of chestnut trees . . . I sit on a bench and look up at the façade of brick and stone. The shutters now have long since been boarded up. Coco Lacour's and Esmeralda's rooms were on the third floor. I had the attic room at the left. In the living room, a full-length self-portrait of Monsieur de Bel-Respiro in his Spahi officer's uniform. I would spend long moments staring at his face, at the medals that bedecked his chest. *Légion d'honneur*. The Order of the Holy Sepulchre, the Order of Saint George from Russia, the Order of Prince Danilo from Montenegro, the Order of the Tower and Sword from Portugal. I had exploited this man's absence to commandeer his house. The nightmare would end, I told myself, Monsieur de Bel-Respiro would come back and turn us out, I told myself, while they were torturing that poor devil downstairs and he was staining the Savonnerie carpet with his blood. Strange things went on at 3 *bis* while I lived there. Some nights I would be wakened by screams of pain, footsteps scurrying to and fro on the main floor. The Khedive's voice. Or Philibert's. I would look out of the window. Two or three shadowy forms were being bundled into the cars parked outside the house. Doors slammed. The roar of the engines would grow fainter and fainter. Silence. Impossible to get back to sleep. I was thinking about Monsieur de Bel-Respiro's son, about his tragic death. It was not something he had been raised to consider. Even the Princess de Lamballe would have been astonished if she had learned of her own execution a few years beforehand. And me? Who would have guessed that I would be a henchman to a gang of torturers? But all I had to do was light the lamp and go down to the living room, and the familiar order was immediately restored. Monsieur de Bel-Respiro's self-portrait still hung on the wall. The wallpaper was still impregnated with the Arabian perfume of Madame de Bel-Respiro's that made my head spin. The mistress of the house was smiling at me. I was her son, Lieutenant Commander Maxime de Bel-Respiro, home on leave to attend one of the masked balls that brought artists and politicians flocking to No. 3 *bis*: Ida Rubinstein, Gaston Calmette, Federico de Madrazzo, Louis Barthou, Gauthier-Villars, Armande Cassive, Bouffe de Saint-Blaise, Frank Le Harivel, José de Strada, Mery Laurent, Mile Mylo d'Arcille. My mother was playing the 'Le Rondel de l'adieu' on the piano. Suddenly I spotted small bloodstains on the Savonnerie carpet. One of the Louis XV armchairs had been overturned: the man who had been screaming a little while earlier had clearly put up a struggle while they were torturing him. Under the console table, a shoe, a tie, a pen. In the circumstances, it is pointless to carry on describing the guests at No. 3 *bis*. Madame de Bel-Respiro had left the room. I tried to keep the guests from leaving. José de Strada, who was giving a reading from his *Abeilles d'or*, trailed off, petrified. Madame Mylo d'Arcille had fainted. They were going to murder Barthou. Calmette too. Bouffe de Saint-Blaise and Gauthier-Villars had vanished. Frank Le Harivel and Madrazzo were no more than frantic moths. Ida Rubinstein,

Armande Cassive, and Mery Laurent were becoming transparent. I found myself alone in front of the self-portrait of Monsieur de Bel-Respiro. I was twenty years old.

Outside, the blackout. What if the Khedive and Philibert came back with their cars? Decidedly I was not made to live in such troubled times. To ease my mind, I spent the hours until sunrise going through every closet in the house. Monsieur de Bel-Respiro had left behind a red notebook in which he jotted down his thoughts. I read and re-read it many times during those sleepless nights. 'Frank le Harivel lived at 8 Rue Lincoln. This exemplary gentleman, once a familiar sight to people strolling along the Allée des Acacias, is now forgotten . . .' 'Madame Mylo d'Arcille, an utterly charming young woman who is perhaps remembered by devotees of the music halls of yesteryear . . .' 'Was José de Strada – *the hermit of La Muette* – an unsung genius? No one cares to wonder nowadays.' 'Armande Cassive died here, alone and penniless . . .' Monsieur de Bel-Respiro certainly had a sense for the transience of things. 'Does anyone still remember Alec Carter, the legendary jockey? Or Rital del Erido?' Life is unfair.

In the drawers, two or three yellowing photographs, some old letters. A withered bouquet on Madame de Bel-Respiro's desk. In a trunk she left behind, several dresses from Worth. One night I slipped on the most beautiful among them: a *peau-de-soie* with imitation tulle and garlands of pink convolvulus. I have never been tempted by transvestism, but in that moment my situation seemed so hopeless and my loneliness so great that I determined to cheer myself up by putting on some nonsensical act. Standing in front of the Venetian mirror in the living room (I was wearing a Lambelle hat adorned with flowers, plumes, and lace), I really felt like laughing. Murderers were making the most of the blackout. Play along, the Lieutenant had told me, but he knew perfectly well that one day I would join their ranks. Then why did he abandon me? You don't leave a child alone in the dark. At first he is frightened; then he grows used to it, eventually he shuns the daylight altogether. Paris would never again be known as the City of Light. I was wearing a dress and hat that would have made Emilienne d'Alençon green with envy, and brooding on the aimlessness and superficiality of my existence. Surely Goodness, Justice, Happiness, Freedom, and Progress required more effort and greater vision than I possessed? As I was thinking this, I began to make up my face. I used Madame de Bel-Respiro's cosmetics: kohl and *serkis*, the rouge it is said that gave sultanas their youthful, velvety complexion. I conscientiously even dotted my face with beauty spots in the shapes of hearts, and moons and comets. And then, to kill time, I waited for dawn and for the apocalypse.

Five in the afternoon. Sunlight, great curtains of silence falling over the square. I thought I saw a shadow at the only window where the shutters were not closed. Who is living at No. 3 *bis* now? I ring the bell. I hear someone on the stairs. The door opens a crack. An elderly woman. She asks what I want. To visit the house. Out of the question, she snaps back, the owners are away. Then shuts the door. Now she is watching me, her face pressed against the windowpane.

Avenue Henri-Martin. The pathways snaking through the Bois de Boulogne. Let's go as far as the Lower Lake. I would often go out to the island with Coco Lacour and Esmeralda. Ever since I pursued my ideal: studying people from a distance – the farthest possible distance – their frenetic activity, their ruthless scheming. With its lawns and its Chinese pavilion, the island seemed a suitable place. A few more steps. The Pré Catelan. We came here on the night I informed on the Lieutenant's ring. Or were we at La Grande Cascade? The orchestra was playing a Creole waltz. An old gentleman and an elderly lady sat at the table next to ours ... Esmeralda was sipping a grenadine, Coco Lacour was smoking his cigar ... All too soon the Khedive and Philibert would be plaguing me with questions. A ring of figures whirling around me, faster and faster, louder and louder, until finally I capitulate so they will leave me in peace. In the meantime, I didn't waste those precious moments of reprieve. He was smiling. She was blowing bubbles through her straw ... I see them in silhouette, framed against the light. Time has passed. If I had not set down the names – Coco Lacour, Esmeralda – there would be no trace left of their time on this earth.

Farther to the west, La Grande Cascade. We never went that far: there were sentries guarding the Pont de Suresnes. It must have been a bad dream. Everything is so calm now on the path around the lake. Someone on a barge waved to me ... I remember my sadness when we ventured this far. It was impossible to cross the Seine. We had to go back into the Bois. I knew that we were being hunted, that eventually the hounds would flush us out. The trains weren't running. A pity. I would have liked to throw them off the scent once and for all. Get to Lausanne, to neutral territory. Coco Lacour, Esmeralda, and I on the shores of Lake Geneva. In Lausanne, we would have nothing more to fear. The late summer afternoon is drawing to a close, as it is today. Boulevard de la Seine. Avenue de Neuilly. Porte Maillot. Leaving the Bois de Boulogne we would sometimes stop at Luna Park. Coco Lacour liked the coconut shy and the hall of mirrors. We would climb aboard the 'Sirocco', the whirligig spun faster and faster. Laughter, music. One of the stands bore the words in bright letters: 'THE ASSASSINATION OF THE PRINCESS DE LAMBALLE.' On the podium lay a woman and above her bed was a red target which marksmen would try to shoot. Each time they hit the bull's-eye, the bed teetered and out fell the shrieking woman. There were other gruesome attractions. Being the wrong age for such things, we would panic, like three children abandoned at the height of some infernal fairground. What remains of all that frenzy, the tumult, and the violence? A patch of waste ground next to the Boulevard Gouvion-Saint-Cyr. I know the area. I used to live there. Place des Acacias. A *chambre de bonne* on the sixth floor. Back then, everything was perfectly fine: I was eighteen, and – thanks to some forged papers – drawing a Navy pension. No one seemed to wish me ill. I had little human contact: my mother, a few dogs, two or three old men, and Lili Marlene. Afternoons spent reading or walking. The energy of boys my age astounded me. They ran to meet life head on. Their eyes blazed. I thought it was better to keep a low profile. A painful shyness. Suits in neutral colours. That's what I thought. Place Pereire. On warm evenings I would sit on the terrace of the Royal-Villiers cafe. Someone at the next table would smile at me. Cigarette? He proffered a pack of Khédives and we got to talking. He and a friend ran a private detective agency. They suggested I might like to work with them. My innocent looks and my impeccable manners appealed to them. My job was tailing people. After that, they put me to work in earnest: investigations, information-gathering of all sorts, confidential missions. I had my own office at the agency's headquarters, 177 Avenue Niel. My bosses were utterly disreputable: Henri Normand, known as 'the Khedive' (because of the cigarettes he smoked), was a former convict;

Pierre Philibert, a senior police inspector, had been drummed out of the force. I realised that they were giving me 'morally dubious' jobs. But it never occurred to me to leave. In my office on the Avenue Niel, I assessed my responsibilities: first and foremost, I had to provide for maman, who had little enough to live on. I felt bad that until now I had neglected my role as the main wage-earner in the family, but now that I was working and bringing in a regular salary, I would be a model son.

Avenue de Wagram. Place des Ternes. On my left, the Brasserie Lorraine, where I had arranged to meet him. He was being black-mailed and was counting on our agency to get him off the hook. Myopic eyes. His hands shook. Stammering, he asked me whether I had 'the papers'. Yes, I replied, very softly, but first he would have to give me twenty thousand francs. In cash. Afterwards, we'd see. We met again the next day at the same place. He handed me an envelope. The money was all there. Then, instead of hand-ing over 'the papers', I got up and hightailed it. At first I was reluctant to use such tactics but in time you become inured. My bosses gave me a 10 per cent commission on this type of business. In the evening I'd bring maman cartloads of orchids. My sudden wealth worried her. Perhaps she guessed that I was squandering my youth for a handful of cash. She never questioned me about it.

> *Le temps passe très vite,*
> *et les années vous quittent.*
> *Un jour, on est un grand garçon . . .*

I would had preferred to do something more worthwhile than work for this so-called detective agency. Medicine appealed to me, but the sight of wounds and blood make me sick. Moral unpleasantness, on the other hand, doesn't faze me. Being innately suspicious, I'm liable to focus on the worst in people and things so as not to be disappointed. I was in my element at the Avenue Niel, where there was talk of nothing but blackmail, confidence tricks, robbery, fraud, and corruption of all sorts, and where we dealt with clients of the sleaziest morality. (In this, my employers were every bit their equals.) There was only one positive: I was earning – as I've mentioned – a huge salary. This was important to me. It was in the pawnshop on the Rue Pierre Charron (my mother would often go there, but they always refused to take her paste jewellery) that I decided once and for all that poverty was a pain in the arse. You might think I have no principles. I started out a pure and innocent soul. But innocence gets lost along the way. Place de l'Étoile. 9 p.m. The lights along the Champs-Élysées are twinkling as they always do. They haven't kept their promise. This avenue, which seems majestic from afar, is one of the vilest sections of Paris. Claridge, Fouquet, Hungaria, Lido, Embassy, Butterfly . . . at every stop I met new faces: Costachesco, the Baron de Lussatz, Odicharvi, Hayakawa, Lionel de Zieff, Pols de Helder . . . Flashy foreigners, abortionists, swindlers, hack journalists, shyster lawyers and crooked accountants who orbited the Khedive and Monsieur Philibert. Added to their number was a whole battalion of women of easy virtue, erotic dancers, morphine addicts . . . Frau Sultana, Simone Bouquereau, Baroness Lydia Stahl, Violette Morris, Magda d'Andurian . . . My bosses introduced me to this underworld. Champs-Élysées – the Elysian Fields – the name given to the final resting place of the righteous and heroic dead. So I cannot help but wonder how the avenue where I stand came by the name. There are ghosts here, but only those of Monsieur Philibert, the Khedive, and their acolytes.

Stepping out of Claridge, arm in arm, come Joanovici and the Count de Cagliostro. They are wearing white suits and platinum signet rings. The shy young man crossing the Rue Lord-Byron is Eugene Weidmann. Standing frozen in front of Pam-Pam is Thérèse de Païva, the most beautiful whore of the Second Empire. From the corner of the Rue Marbeuf, Dr Petiot smiles at me. On the terrace of Le Colisée: a group of black marketeers are cracking open the champagne. Among them are Count Baruzzi, the Chapochnikoff brothers, Rachid von Rosenheim, Jean-Farouk de Méthode, Otto da Silva, and a host of others . . . If I can make it to the Rond-Point, I might be able to lose these ghosts. Hurry. The gardens of the Champs-Élysées, silent, green. I often used to stop off here. After spending the afternoon in bars along the avenue (at 'business' appointments with the aforementioned), I would stroll over the park for a breath of fresh air. I'd sit on a bench. Breathless. Pockets stuffed of cash. Twenty thousand, sometimes a hundred thousand francs. Our agency was, if not sanctioned, at least toler-ated by the Préfecture de police: we supplied any information they requested. On the other hand, we were running a protection racket involving those I mentioned above, who could truly believe they were paying for our silence, our protection, since Monsieur Philibert still had close ties with senior colleagues on the force, *Inspecteurs* Rothe, David, Jalby, Jurgens, Santoni, Permilleux, Sadowsky, Francois, and Detmar. As for me, one of my jobs was to collect the protection money. Twenty thousand. Sometimes a hundred thousand francs. It had been a rough day. Endless argu-ments. I pictured their sallow, oily faces again: the usual suspects from a police line-up. Some, as usual, had tried to hold out and – though shy and softhearted by nature – I found myself compelled to raise my voice, to tell them I would go straight to the Quai des

Orfèvres if they didn't pay up. I told them about the files my bosses had with their names and their *curricula vitae*. Not exactly glowing reports, those files. They would dig out their wallets, and call me a 'traitor'. The word stung.

I would find myself alone on the bench. Some places encourage reflection. Public gardens, for instance, the lost kingdoms in Paris, those ailing oases amid the roar and the cruelty of men. The Tuileries. The Jardins de Luxembourg. The Bois de Boulogne. But never did I do so much thinking as in the Jardins des Champs-Élysées. What precisely was my job? Blackmailer? Police informant? I would count the cash, take my 10 per cent and go over to Lachaume to order a thicket of red roses. Pick out two or three rings at Van Cleef & Arpels. Then buy fifty dresses at Piguet, Lelong & Molyneux. All for maman – blackmailer, thug, informant, grass, even hired killer I might be, but I was a model son. It was my sole consolation. It was getting dark. The children were leaving the park after one last ride on the merry-go-round. The street lights along the Champs-Élysées flickered on suddenly. I would have been better off, I thought, staying close to the Place des Acacias. Steer clear of junctions and the boulevards to avoid the noise and the unsavoury encounters. How strange it was to be sitting on the terrace of the Royal-Villiers on the Place Pereire, for someone who was so discreet, so cautious, so eager to pass unnoticed. But in life you have to start out somewhere. There's no getting away from it. In the end it sends round to you its recruiting officers: in my case, the Khedive and Monsieur Philibert. On a different night, I might have made more admirable acquaintances who could have encouraged me to go into the rag trade or become a writer. Having no particular bent for any profession, I waited for my elders to decide what I would do. Up to them to figure out what they'd like me to be. I left it in their lap.

Boy scout? Florist? Tennis player? No: Employee of a phony detective agency. Blackmailer, informant, extortionist. I found it quite surprising. I did not have the talents required for such work: the cruelty, the lack of scruples, a taste for sleazy company. Even so, I bravely stuck at it, the way another man might study for a boilermaker's license. The strange thing about guys like me is that they can just as easily end up in the Panthéon as in Thiais cemetery, the potter's field for spies. They become heroes. Or bastards. No one realises they get dragged into this dirty business against their will. That all they wanted, all they cared about was their stamp collection, and being left in peace on the Place des Acacias, where they could breathe in careful little breaths.

In the meantime, I was getting into bad ways. My passivity and my lack of enthusiasm made me all the more vulnerable to the malign influence of the Khedive and Monsieur Philibert. I remembered the words of a doctor who lived across the landing in our apartment block on the Place des Acacias. 'After you reach twenty,' he told me, 'you start to decay. Fewer and fewer nerve cells, my boy.' I jotted this remark down in a notebook, because it's important to heed the experience of our elders. I now realised that he was right. My shady dealings and the unsavoury characters I rub shoulders with would cost me my innocence. The future? A race, with the finish line on a patch of waste ground. Being dragged to a guillotine with no chance to catch my breath. Someone whispered in my ear: you have gained nothing in this life but the whirlwind you let yourself be caught up in . . . gypsy music, played faster and faster to drown out my screams. This evening the air is decidedly balmy. As they always have, the donkeys trudge down the path heading back to the stables having spent the day giving rides to children. They disappear around the corner of the Avenue Gabriel. We will never know how they suffer. Their reticence impressed me. As they trotted past, I once again felt calm, indifferent. I tried to gather my thoughts. They were few and far between, and utterly banal. I have no taste for thinking. Too emotional. Too lazy. After a moment's effort, I invariably arrived at the same conclusion: I was bound to die some day. Fewer and fewer nerve cells. A long slow process of decay. The doctor had warned me. I should add that my profession inclined me toward dwelling on the morose: being an informant and a blackmailer at twenty rather narrows one's sights. A curious smell of old furniture and musty wallpaper permeated 177 Avenue Niel. The light was constantly flickering. Behind my desk was a set of wooden drawers where I kept the files on our 'clients'. I catalogued them by names of poisonous plants: Black Ink Cap, Belladonna, Devil's bolete, Henbane, Livid Agaric . . . Their very touch made me decalcify. My clothes were suffused with the stifling stench of the office on Avenue Niel. I had allowed myself to be contaminated. The disease? An accelerated aging process, a physical and moral decay in keeping with the doctor's prognosis. And yet I am not predisposed towards the morbid.

Un petit village
Un vieux clocher

A little village, and old church tower, these described my fondest hopes. Unfortunately, I lived in a city not unlike a vast Luna Park where the Khedive and Monsieur Philibert were driving me from shooting galleries to rollercoasters, from Punch and Judy shows to 'Sirocco' whirligigs. Finally I lay down on a bench. I wasn't meant for such a life. I never asked anyone for anything. They had come to me.

A little farther along. On the left, the théâtre des Ambassadeurs. They're performing *The Nightwatch*, a long-forgotten operetta. There can't be much of an audience. An elderly lady, an elderly gentleman, a few English tourists. I walk across a lawn, past the last hedge. Place de la Concorde. The street lights hurt my eyes. I stood stock still, gasping for breath. Above my head, the Marly Horses reared and strained with all their might, desperate to escape from their grooms. They seemed about to bolt across the square. A magnificent space, the only place in Paris where you feel the exhilaration you experience in the mountains. A landscape of marble and twinkling lights. Over past the Tuileries, the ocean. I was on the quarter-deck of a liner heading northwest, taking with it the Madeleine, the Opéra, the Berlitz Palace, the church of La Trinité. It might founder at any minute. Tomorrow we would be on the ocean floor, three thousand fathoms down. I no longer feared my shipmates. The rictus grin of the Baron de Lussatz; Odicharvi's cruel eyes; the treacherous Chapochnikoff brothers; Frau Sultana twisting a tourniquet around her upper arm and patting a vein preparing to inject herself with heroin; Zieff with his vulgarity, his solid gold watch, his chubby fingers bedecked in rings; Ivanoff and his sessions of sexuo-divine paneurhythmy; Costachesco, Jean-Farouk de Méthode, and Rachid von Rosenheim discussing their fraudulent bankruptcies; and the Khedive's gang of thugs: Armand le Fou, Jo Reocreux, Tony Breton, Vital-Léca, Robert le Pâle, Gouari, Danos, Codébo . . . Before long, those shadowy figures would be meat for octopuses, sharks, and moray eels. I would share their fate. Of my own free will. This was something I realised quite suddenly one night as I crossed the Place de la Concorde, my arms outstretched, casting a shadow all the way to the Rue Royale, my left hand extended to the Champs-Élysées gardens, my right towards the Rue Saint-Florentin. I might have been thinking of Jesus; in fact I was thinking of Judas Iscariot. A much misunderstood man. It had taken great humility and courage to take upon himself mankind's disgrace. To die of it. Alone. Like a big boy. Judas, my elder brother. Both of us suspicious by nature. We expected little of our fellow man, of ourselves or of any saviour. Will I have the strength to follow you to the bitter end? It is a difficult path. Night was drawing in, but my job as informant and blackmailer has accustomed me to darkness. I put from my mind my uncharitable thoughts about my shipmates and their crimes. After a few weeks' hard work at the Avenue Niel, nothing surprised me anymore. Though they could come up with new poses, it would make no difference. I watched them as they bustled along the promenade deck, down the gangways, carefully noting their ruses and their tricks. A pointless task given that water was already pouring into the hold. Next would come the Grand Salon and the ballroom would be next. With the ship about to sink, I felt pity for even the most savage passengers. Any moment now, Hitler himself would come rushing into my arms, sobbing like a child. The arcades along the Rue de Rivoli. Something serious was happening. I had noticed the endless stream of cars along the outer boulevards. People were fleeing Paris. The war, probably. Some unexpected disaster. Coming out of Hilditch & Key, where I'd just picked out a tie, I studied this strip of fabric men tighten around their throats. A blue-and-white striped tie. That afternoon, I was also wearing a fawn suit and crêpe-soled shoes. In my wallet, a photograph of maman and an out-of date métro ticket. I had just had my hair cut. Such details were of no interest to anyone. People were thinking only about saving their skins. Every man for himself. Before long there was not a soul nor a car in the streets. Even maman had left. I wished that I could cry, but the tears wouldn't come. This silence, this deserted city, was in keeping with my state of mind. I checked my tie and shoes again. The weather was sunny. The words of a song came back to me:

> *Seul*
> *Depuis toujours . . .*

The fate of the world? I didn't even bother to read the headlines. Besides, soon there would be no more newspapers. No more trains. In fact, maman had just managed to catch the last Paris-Lausanne express.

> *Seul il a souffert chaque jour*
> *Il pleure avec le ciel de Paris . . .*

The sort of sad, sweet song I liked. Unfortunately, this was no time for romance. We were living – it seemed to me – through a tragic era. You don't go around humming pre-war tunes when everything around you is dying. It was the height of bad manners. Was it my fault? I never had much of a taste for anything. Excepting the circus, operettas and the music hall.

By the time I reached the Rue de Castiglione, it was dark. Someone was following close behind. A tap on the shoulder. The Khedive. I had been expecting this meeting. At that very moment, on that very spot. A nightmare where I knew every twist and turn in advance. He grabs my arm. We get into a car. We drive through the Place Vendôme. Street lights cast a strange bluish glow. A single window in the Hôtel Continental is lit. Blackout. Better to get used to it, *mon petit*. The Khedive laughs and turns the dial on the radio.

Un doux parfum qu'on respire
c'est
Fleur bleue . . .

A dark mass looms in front of us. The Opéra? The church of La Trinité? On the left, a neon sign reads FLORESCO'S. We are on the Rue Pigalle. He floors the accelerator.

Un regard qui vous attire
c'est
Fleur bleue . . .

Darkness once more. A huge red lantern outside L'Européen on the Place Clichy. We must be on the Boulevard des Batignolles. Suddenly the headlights pick out railings and dense foliage. The Parc Monceau?

Un rendez-vous en automne
c'est
Fleur bleue . . .

He whistles along to the chorus, nodding his head in time. We are driving at breakneck speed. 'Guess where we are, *mon petit?*' He swerves. My shoulder bumps against his. The brakes screech. The light in the stairwell is not working. I grope my way, clutching the banister. He strikes a match, and I just have time to read the marble plaque on the door: 'Normand-Philibert Agency'. We go in. The stench — more nauseating than ever — catches in my throat. Monsieur Philibert is standing in the doorway, waiting. A cigarette dangling from the corner of his lips. He winks at me and, despite my weariness, I manage a smile: maman would have reached Lausanne by now, I think. There, she'd have nothing to fear. Monsieur Philibert shows us into his office. He complains about the fluctuations in electricity. The quavering glow from the brass light overhead does not seem unusual. It had always been like that at 177 Avenue Niel. The Khedive proposes champagne and produces a bottle from his left jacket pocket. As of today, our 'agency' — it appears — is about to expand considerably. 'Recent events' have worked to our advantage. The office is moving to an *hôtel particulier* at 3 *bis* Square Cimarosa. No more small-time work. We're in line for some important work. It's even possible that the Khedive will be named *préfet de police*. In these troubled times, there are positions to be filled. Our job: to carry out investigations, searches, interrogations, and arrests. The 'Cimarosa Square Bureau' will operate on two levels: as an unofficial wing of the police and as a 'purchase office' stocking goods and raw materials that will shortly be unobtainable. The Khedive has already hand-picked some fifty people to work with us. Old acquaintances. All of them, along with their identification photos, are on file at 177 Avenue Niel. Having said this, Monsieur Philibert hands us a glass of champagne. We toast our success. We will be — it seems — kings of Paris. The Khedive pats my cheek and slips a roll of bills into my inside pocket. The two men talk amongst themselves, review the files and the appointment books, make a few calls. Now and then I hear a burst of voices. Impossible to tell what is being said. I go into the adjoining room, which we use as our 'clients'' waiting room. Here they would sit in the battered leather chairs. On the walls, a few colour prints of grape picking. A sideboard and assorted pine furniture. Beyond the far door, another room with an en-suite bathroom. I would regularly stay back at night to put the files in order. I worked in the waiting room. No one would ever guess that this apartment housed a detective agency. It was previously occupied by a retired couple. I drew the curtains. Silence. Flickering light. A smell of withered things. 'Dreaming, *mon petit*?' The Khedive laughs and adjusts his hat in the mirror. We go through the waiting room. In the hall, Monsieur Philibert snaps on a flashlight. We are having a house-warming tonight at 3 *bis* Cimarosa Square. The owners have fled. We have taken over their house. A cause for celebration. Hurry. Our friends are waiting for us at L'Heure Mauve, a cabaret club on the Champs-Élysées . . .

The following week the Khedive orders me to gather information for the 'agency' on the activities of a certain Lieutenant Dominique. We received a memorandum on him with his address, a photo, and the comment: 'Keep under surveillance'. I have to find some way of introducing myself to the man. I go to his house at 5 Rue Boisrobert, in the 15th *arrondissement*. A modest little building. The Lieutenant himself answers the door. I ask for Mr Henri Normand. He tells me I've made a mistake. Then I blurt out my whole story: I'm an escaped POW. A friend said that if I ever managed to escape, I should get in touch with Monsieur Normand, 5 Rue Boisrobert. He would keep me safe. My comrade had clearly given me the wrong address. I don't know a soul in Paris. I have no money. I don't know where to turn. He studies me thoughtfully. I squeeze out a couple of tears to convince him. Next thing I know I'm in his office. In a deep, clear voice he tells me that a boy my age should not let himself be discouraged by the catastrophe that has beset our country. He is still weighing me up. Then, suddenly, he asks: 'Do you want to work with us?' He is head of a group of 'tremendous' guys. Many of them escaped prisoners like myself. Boys from Saint-Cyr Military Academy. Regular officers. A handful of civilians. All raring to go. The best of the best. We are waging a covert war against the powers of evil that have temporarily triumphed. A daunting task, but to brave hearts nothing is impossible. Goodness, Freedom, and Moral Standards will soon be re-established. Lieutenant Dominique swears as much. I don't share his optimism. I'm thinking about the report I'll need to turn in to the Khedive this evening at Square Cimarosa. The Lieutenant gives me a few other facts: he refers to the group as CKS, the Company of the Knights of the Shadows. There is no way they can fight out in the open. This is a subterranean war. We will constantly be hunted. All the members of the group have taken the name of a métro station as a code name. He will introduce them to me shortly: Saint-Georges. Obligado. Corvisart. Pernety. There are more. As for me, I will be known as the 'Princesse de Lamballe'. Why 'Princesse de Lamballe'? A whim of the Lieutenant. 'Are you prepared to join our network? Honour demands it. You should not hesitate for a moment. So — what's your answer?' I reply: 'Yes,' in a hesitant voice. 'Don't ever waver, lad. I know that these are sad times. Thugs and gangsters are running the show. There's a stench of decay in the air. But it won't last. Have a little fortitude, Lamballe.' He suggests I stay with him at the Rue Boisrobert, but I quickly invent an elderly uncle in the suburbs who will put me up. We agree to meet tomorrow afternoon at the Place des Pyramides in front of the statue of Joan of Arc. 'Farewell, Lamballe.' He gives me a piercing look, his eyes narrow, and I can't bear the glint of them. He repeats: 'Farewell, LAM-BALLE,' emphasizing each syllable in a strange way: LAM-BALLE. He shuts the door. Night was drawing in. I wandered aimlessly through these unfamiliar streets. They would be waiting for me at Square Cimarosa. What should I tell them? To put it bluntly, Lieutenant Dominique was a hero. As was every member of his group . . . But I still need to make a report to the Khedive and Monsieur Philibert. The existence of the CKS came as a surprise to them. They were not expecting such an extensive operation. 'You will need to infiltrate the group. Try to get their names and addresses. It could make for a fine haul.' For the first time in my life, I had what people call a pang of conscience. A fleeting pang, as it turned out. I was given an advance of one hundred thousand francs against the information I was to obtain.

Place des Pyramides. You try to forget the past, but your footsteps invariably lead you back to difficult crossroads. The Lieutenant was pacing up and down in front of the statue of Joan of Arc. He introduced me to a tall lad with close cropped blond hair and periwinkle eyes: Saint-Georges, a Saint-Cyr graduate. We went into the Tuileries gardens and sat down at a kiosk near the merry-go-round. It was a familiar setting of my childhood. We ordered three bottles of fruit juice. When he brought them, the waiter told us this was the last of their pre-war supply. Soon there would be no more fruit juice. 'We'll manage without,' said Saint-Georges with a smile. The young man seemed very determined. 'So you're an escaped prisoner?' he said. 'Which regiment?' 'Fifth Infantry,' I replied in a toneless voice, 'but I'd rather not think about that anymore.' With a supreme effort, I added: 'I want only one thing, to carry on the struggle to the end.'

This profession of faith seemed to convince him. He gave me a handshake. 'I've rounded up a few members of the network to introduce to you,' the Lieutenant told me. 'They're waiting for us at the Rue Boisrobert.' Corvisart, Obligado, Pernety, and Jasmin are there. The Lieutenant talks about me enthusiastically: about my distress after our defeat. My determination to fight on. The honour and the solace I felt that I was now a member of the CKS. 'All right, Lamballe, we are going to assign you a mission.' A number of individuals, he explains, have been exploiting recent events to indulge their worst instincts. Hardly surprising given the troubling and unsettling times we are experiencing. These thugs have been afforded complete impunity: they have been issued with warrant cards and gun licences. They are engaged in an odious repression of patriots and honest folk and have committed all manner of crimes. They recently commandeered an *hôtel particulier* at 3 *bis* Cimarosa Square in the 16th *arrondissement*. Their office is publicly listed as the '*Inter-commercial Company Paris-Berlin-Monte Carlo*'. These are all the facts I have. Our duty is to neutralize them as quickly as possible. 'I'm counting on you, Lamballe. You're going to have to infiltrate this group. Keep us informed about plans and their activities. It's up to you, Lamballe'. Pernety hands me a cognac. Jasmin, Obligado, Saint-Georges, and Corvisart give me a smile. Later, we are walking back along the Boulevard Pasteur. The Lieutenant had insisted on going with me as far as the Sèvres-Lecourbe métro. As we say goodnight, he looks me straight in the eye: 'A delicate mission, Lamballe. A kind of double-cross. Keep me informed. Good luck, Lamballe.' What if I told him the truth? Too late. I thought of maman. At least I knew she was safe. I had bought her a villa in Lausanne with the money I had made at Avenue Niel. I could have gone to

Switzerland with her but, out of apathy or indifference, I stayed here. As I have already said, I didn't worry much about the fate of the world. Nor was I particularly concerned about my own fate. I just drifted with the current. Swept along like a wisp of straw. That evening I tell the Khedive about my meeting with Corvisart, Obligado, Jasmin, Pernety, and Saint-Georges. I don't yet know their addresses, but it should not take long to get them. I promise to deliver the information on these men as quickly as possible. And on the others to whom the Lieutenant will doubtless introduce me. The way things are going, we should reel in 'a fine haul'. He repeats this, rubbing his hands. 'I knew you'd win them over with those choirboy good looks.' Suddenly my head starts spinning. Suddenly I inform him that the ringleader is not, as I had thought, the Lieutenant. 'Who then?' I'm teetering on the brink of an abyss; a few steps are all it would take to step back. 'WHO?' But no, I haven't got the strength. 'WHO?' 'A man named LAM-BALLE. LAM-BALLE.' 'Well, we'll get hold of him, don't worry. Find out as much as you can about him.' Things were getting complicated. Was it my fault? Each camp had set me up as a double agent. I didn't want to let anyone down – not the Khedive and Philibert any more than the Lieutenant and lads from Saint-Cyr. You have to choose, I told myself. A squire in the 'Company of the Knights of the Shadows' or a hired agent for a dubious agency on Cimarosa Square? Hero or traitor? Neither one nor the other. A number of books provided me with a cleared perspective: *Anthology of Traitors from Alcibiades to Captain Dreyfus*; *The Real Joanovici*; *The Mysteries of the Chevalier d'Eon*; *Fregoli, the Man from Nowhere*. I felt a kinship with all those men. I am no charlatan. I too have experienced what people call 'deep emotion'. Profound. Compelling. There is only one emotion of which I have first hand knowledge, one powerful enough to make me move mountains: FEAR. Paris was sinking deeper into silence and the blackout. When I talk about this period, I feel as though I'm talking to a deaf man, that somehow my voice isn't loud enough, I WAS SHIT SCARED. The métro slowed as it approached the Pont de Passy. Sèvres-Lecourbe – Cambronne – La Motte-Picquet – Dupleix – Grenelle – Passy. In the morning, I would take the opposite route, from Passy to Sèvres-Lecourbe. From Cimarosa Square in the 16th *arrondissement* to Rue Boisrobert in the 15th. From the Lieutenant to the Khedive. From the Khedive to the Lieutenant. The swinging pendulum of a double agent. Exhausting. Breathless. 'Try to get the names and addresses. Looks like this could be a fine haul. I'm counting on you, Lamballe. You'll get us information on those gangsters.' I would have liked to take sides, but I had no more loyalty to the 'Company of the Knights of the Shadows' than I had to the '*Inter-commercial Company Paris-Berlin-Monte Carlo*'. Two groups of lunatics were pressuring me to do contradictory things, they would run me down until I dropped dead from exhaustion. I was a scapegoat for these madmen. I was the runt of the litter. I didn't stand a chance. The times we were living through required exceptional qualities for heroism or crime. And here I was, a misfit. A weathervane. A puppet. I close my eyes and summon up the smells, the songs of those days. Yes, there was a whiff of decay in the air. Especially at dusk. But I confess, never was twilight more beautiful. Summer lingered, refusing to die. The deserted boulevards. Paris vacant. The sound of a clock tolling. And that smell that clung to the facades of the buildings, to the leaves of the chestnut trees. As for the songs, they were: 'Swing Troubadour', 'Étoile Rio', Je n'en Connais pas la Fin', 'Réginella' . . . Remember. The lavender glow of the lights in the métro carriage making it hard to distinguish the other passengers. On my right, close at hand, the searchlight atop the Eiffel Tower. I was on my way back from the Rue Boisrobert. The métro came to a shuddering halt on the Pont de Passy. I was hoping it would never move again, that no one would come to rescue me from this no man's land between the two banks. Not a flicker. Not a sound. Peace at last. Fade into the half-light. Already I was forgetting the sharp tone of their voices, the way they thumped me on the back, the way they pulled me in opposite directions, tied me in knots. Fear gave way to a kind of numbness. My eyes followed the path of the searchlight. It circled and circled like a nightwatch on his rounds. Wearily. The bright beam faded as it turned. Soon, there would only be a faint, almost imperceptible shaft of light. And I, too, after my endless rounds, my countless comings and goings, would finally melt into the shadows. Without ever knowing what it was all about. Sèvres-Lecourbe to Passy. Passy to Sèvres-Lecourbe. At 10 a.m. every morning, I would report to headquarters on the Rue Boisrobert. Warm welcoming handshakes. Smiles and confident glances from those brave boys. 'What's new, Lamballe?' the Lieutenant would ask. I was giving him increasingly detailed information on the '*Inter-commercial Company, Paris-Berlin-Monte Carlo*'. Yes, it was a police unit entrusted with doing 'dirty jobs'. The two directors, Henri Normand and Georges Philibert, hired thugs from the underworld. Burglars, pimps, criminals scheduled to be deported. Two or three had been sentenced to death. All of them had been issued with warrant cards and gun licences. A shady underworld operated out of Cimarosa Square. The hucksters, heroin addicts, charlatans, whores who invariably come to the surface in 'troubled times'. Knowing they were protected by officers in high places, these people committed terrible acts of violence. It even appeared that their chief, Henri Normand, had influence with the *préfecture de police* and the public prosecutor office, if such bodies still existed. As I went on with my story, I watched dismay and disgust spread over their faces. Only the Lieutenant remained inscrutable. 'Good work, Lamballe! Keep at it. And write up a complete list of the members of the agency.'

Then one morning, everyone seemed to be in a particularly sombre mood. The Lieutenant cleared his throat: 'Lamballe, we need you to carry out an assassination.' I took this statement calmly as though I'd been expecting it for some time. 'We're counting on you, Lamballe, to take down Normand and Philibert. Choose the right moment.' There was a pause during which Saint-Georges, Pernety, Jasmin, and the others stared at me with tears in their eyes. The Lieutenant sat motionless at his desk. Corvisart handed me a cognac. The last drink of the condemned man, I thought. I could clearly see a scaffold in the middle of the room. The Lieutenant played the role of executioner. His recruits would watch the execution, smiling mournfully at me. 'Well, Lamballe? What do you think?' 'Sounds like a good idea,' I replied. I wanted to burst into tears, to confess my tenuous position as double agent. But there are some things you have to keep to yourself. I've always been a man of few words. Not the talkative type. But the others were always eager to pour out their feelings to me. I remember spending long afternoons with the boys of the CKS. We would wander through the streets around the Rue Boisrobert, near Vaugirard. I would listen to their rambling. Pernety dreamed of a just world. His cheeks would flush bright red. From his wallet, he would take out pictures of Robespierre and André Breton. I pretended to admire these two men. Pernety kept talking about 'Revolution', about 'Moral awakening', about 'Our role as intellectuals' in a clipped voice I found extremely irritating. He smoked a pipe and wore black leather shoes – these details still move me. Corvisart agonised about being born into a bourgeois family. He wanted desperately to forget the Parc Monceau, the tennis courts at Aix-les-Bains, the sugarplums from Plouvier's he ate every week at his cousins' house. He asked whether I thought it was possible to be a Socialist and a Christian. As for Jasmin, he wanted to see France fight harder. He had the highest esteem for Henri de Bournazel and knew the names of every star in the sky. Obligado published a 'political journal'. 'We must bear witness,' he explained. 'It's our duty. I cannot stay silent.' But silence is easily learned: a couple of kicks in the teeth will do the trick. Picpus showed me his fiancée's letters. Have a little more patience: according to him, the night-mare would soon be over. We would be living in a peaceful world. We'd tell our children about the ordeals we had suffered. Saint-Georges, Marbeuf, and Pelleport graduated from the academy of Saint-Cyr with a thirst for battle and the firm resolve to meet death singing. As for myself, I thought of Cimarosa Square, where I'd have to turn in my daily report. They were lucky, these boys, to be able to daydream. The Vaugirard district encouraged such things. Tranquil, inviolate, like some remote hamlet. The very name 'Vaugirard' spoke of greenery, ivy, a little stream with mossy banks. In such a haven they could give free reign to their heroic imaginations. They had nothing to lose. I was the one they sent out to battle with the real world, and I was flailing against the current. The sublime, apparently, did not suit me. In the late afternoon, before boarding the métro, I would sit on a bench in the Place Adolphe Cherioux and, for a few last moments, soak up the peace of this village. A little house with a garden. A convent or maybe an old folks' home? I could hear the trees whispering. A cat padded past the church. From nowhere, I heard a gently voice: Fred Gouin singing 'Envoi de fleurs'. And I would forget I had no future. My life would take a different course. With a little patience, as Picpus used to say, I could come through this nightmare alive. I'd get a job as bartender in an *auberge* outside Paris, BARMAN. Here was something that seemed to suit my inclinations and my talents. You stand behind the bar. It protects you from the public. Nor are they hostile, they simply want to order drinks. You mix the drinks and serve them quickly. The most aggressive ones thank you. BARMAN was a much nobler profession than was generally accepted, the only one that deserved comparison with police work or medicine. What did it involve? Mixing cocktails. Mixing dreams, in a sense. Antidotes for pain. At the bar they beg you for it. Curaçao? Marie Brizard? Ether? Whatever they want. After two or three drinks they become maudlin, they reel, they roll their eyes and launch into the long litany of their sufferings and their crimes, plead with you to console them. Hitler, between hiccups, begs your forgiveness. 'What are you thinking about, Lamballe?' 'About flies, Lieutenant.' Once in a while he would invite me into his office for a little tête-à-tête. 'I know you'll carry out the assassination. I trust you, Lamballe.' He took a commanding tone, staring at me with his blue-black eyes. Tell him the truth? But which truth? Double agent? Triple agent? By this time even I no longer knew who I was. Excuse me, Lieutenant, I DO NOT EXIST. I've never had an identity card. He would consider such frivolity unpardonable at a time when men were expected to steel themselves and display great strength of character. One evening I was alone with him. My weariness, like a rat, gnawed at everything around. The walls suddenly seemed swathed in dark velvet, a mist enveloped the room, blurring the outlines of the furniture: the desk, the chairs, the wardrobe. 'What's new, Lamballe?' he asked in a faraway voice that surprised me. The Lieutenant stared at me as he always did, but his eyes had lost their metallic gleam. He sat at the desk, head tilted to the right, his cheek almost resting on his shoulder, in the pensive and forlorn posture of Florentine angels. 'What's new, Lamballe?' he asked again, in the same tone he might have said: 'It really doesn't matter.' His eyes were filled with such gentleness, such sadness that I thought for a moment Lieutenant Dominique had understood everything and had forgiven everything: my role as a double (or triple) agent, my helplessness at being a straw in the wind and whatever wrongs I had committed through cowardice or inadvertence. For the first time, someone was taking an interest in me. I found this compassion terribly moving. In vain, I tried to say some words of thanks. The Lieutenant's eyes grew more and more compassionate, his craggy features softened. His chest sagged. Soon, all that remained of this brimming arrogance and vitality was a kindly, feeble old grandmother. The crashing waves of the outside world broke against the velvet walls. We were sunk down into darkness, into depths where our sleep would be undisturbed. Paris, too, was sinking. From the cabin I could see the searchlight on the Eiffel Tower: a lighthouse guiding us to shore. We would never come ashore. It no longer mattered. 'Time for sleep, son,' the Lieutenant murmured, 'SLEEP.' His eyes shot a parting gleam into the shadows, SLEEP. He glanced one last time into the shadows. 'What are you thinking about, Lamballe?' He shakes my shoulder. In a soldierly voice: 'Prepare yourself for the assassination. The fate of the network is in your hands. Never surrender.' He paces the room nervously. The hard edges of objects had returned. 'Guts, Lamballe. I'm counting on you.' The métro moves off again. Cambronne – La Motte-Picquet – Dupleix – Grenelle – Passy. 9 p.m. On the corner of the Rue Franklin and Rue Vineuse, the white Bentley the Khedive had lent me in return for my services was waiting. The boys of the CKS would not have been impressed. Driving around in an expensive car these days implied activities of questionable morality. Only black marketeers and highly-paid informants could afford such luxuries. I didn't care. Exhaustion dispelled the last of my scruples. I drove slowly across the Place du Trocadéro. A hushed engine. Russian leather seats. I liked the Bentley. The Khedive had found it in a garage in Neuilly. I opened the glove compartment: the owner's registration papers were still there. It was clearly a stolen car. One day or another we would have to account for this. What would I plead in court when they read the charge sheet of the many crimes committed by the 'Inter-commercial Company Paris-Berlin-Monte Carlo'? A gang of thugs, the judge would say. Profiting from other people's suffering and confusion. 'Monsters,' Madeleine Jacob would write. I turned on the radio.

Je suis seul
ce soir
avec ma peine . . .

Avenue Kléber, my heart began to beat a little faster. The front of the Baltimore Hotel. Cimarosa Square. Codébo and Robert le Pâle were standing guard in front of No. 3 *bis*. Codébo gave me a smile, flashing his gold teeth. I walked up one flight and opened the living-room door. The Khedive, in a dusty-pink brocade dressing gown, motioned to me. Monsieur Philibert was checking file cards: 'How's the CKS doing, Swing Troubadour?' The Khedive gave me a sharp rap on the shoulder and handed me a cognac: 'Very scarce. Three hundred thousand francs a bottle. Don't worry. There is no rationing at Cimarosa Square. And the CKS? What's new there?' No, I still hadn't obtained the addresses of the 'Knights of the Shadows'. By the end of the week, for sure. 'Supposing we organise the raid on the Rue Boisrobert for some afternoon when members of the CKS are there? What do you say to that, Troubadour?' I discouraged this plan. Better to arrest them individually. 'We've no time to lose, Troubadour.' I calmed their impatience, promising yet again to come up with more detailed information. Sooner or later they would press me so hard that I would have to keep my promises to get them off my back. The 'round-up' would take place. I would finally earn the title of informant – *donneuse* – the one that made my heart skip, my head spin every time I heard it. DONNEUSE. Still, I tried to postpone the inevitable, assuring my two bosses that the boys in the CKS were innocuous. Dreamers. Full of fanciful ideals, nothing more. Why not let the benighted idiots be? They were afflicted from a common illness, youth, one from which they would quickly recover. In a few months they'd be much more tractable. Even the Lieutenant would give up the battle. And besides, what battle was there, besides a heated exchange of words like Justice, Progress, Truth, Democracy, Freedom, Revolution, Honour, and Patriotism? The whole thing struck me as completely harmless. As I saw it, the only dangerous man was LAM-BALLE, whom I had not yet identified. Invisible. Elusive. The true brains behind the CKS. He would strike, and strike viciously. The mere mention of his name at the Rue Boisrobert provoked whispers of awe and admiration, LAM-BALLE! Who was he? When I asked the Lieutenant, he was evasive. 'LAMBALLE will not spare the thugs and traitors who currently have the upper hand. LAMBALLE strikes hard and fast. We will obey LAMBALLE without question, LAMBALLE is never wrong, LAMBALLE is a great guy, LAMBALLE is our only hope . . .' I could not get any more definite information. With a little patience we would flush out this mysterious character. I kept telling the Khedive and Philibert that capturing Lamballe ought to be our prime target, LAM-BALLE! The others did not matter. They were deluded, they were all talk. I asked that they be spared. 'We'll see. First get us details on this Lamballe. Understood?' The Khedive's lips curled into a menacing leer. Philibert, pensively stroked his moustache and murmured: 'LAM-BALLE, LAM-BALLE.' 'I'll deal with this LAMBALLE once and for all,' the Khedive concluded, 'and neither London, Vichy, nor the Americans will save him. Cognac? Craven A? Help yourself, *mon petit*.' 'We've just made a deal for the Sebastiano del Piombo,' announced Philibert. 'Here's your 10 per cent commission.' He handed me a pale-green envelope. 'Get me some Asian bronzes for tomorrow. We've got a client.' I rather enjoyed this sideline work of looting works of art and bringing them to Cimarosa Square. In the morning, I would inveigle my way into the homes of wealthy people who had fled Paris in the wake of the 'events'. All I needed to do was pick a lock or flash my warrant card to get a key from the concierge. I searched these deserted abandoned houses carefully. The owners, in their flight, often left numerous small items behind: pastels, vases, tapestries, books, manuscripts. That wasn't enough. I searched storerooms, vaults, those places where valuable collections might be hidden in times of uncertainty. An attic in the suburbs rewarded me with Gobelin tapestries and Persian carpets, a musty garage at Porte Champferret was filled with old masters. In a cellar in Auteuil, I found a suitcase full of jewels from antiquity and the Renaissance. I went about this looting cheerfully and even with a sense of pleasure that I would – later – regret in court. We were living through extraordinary times. Theft and trafficking were commonplace these days, and the Khedive, having keenly assessed my talents, used me to track down works of art rather than precious objects of base metal. I was grateful. I experienced great aesthetic pleasures. As when I stood in front of a Goya depicting the Assassination of the Princesse de Lamballe. The owner had tried to save it, stowing it in the vaults at the Franco-Serbian Bank at 3 Rue Helder. All I had to do was show my warrant card and they turned the master-piece over. We sold on the looted property. These were curious times. They made me into a 'rather unsavoury' character. Informant, looter, assassin, perhaps. But no worse than the next man. I followed the crowd, nothing more. I'm not particularly entranced by evil. One day I met an old gentleman covered with rings and laces. In a quavering voice, he told me that he cut pictures of criminals out of *Détective*, finding they had a 'savage', a 'malevolent' beauty. He admired their 'unshakeable, lofty' solitude. He talked to me about one of them, Eugene Weidmann, whom he called 'the angel of the shadows'. This old fellow was a man of letters. I told him that on the day of his execution, Weidmann had worn crepe-soled shoes. His mother had bought them for him in Frankfurt. That if you truly cared for people, it was crucial to discover minor details of this kind. The rest was unimportant. Poor Weidmann! Even as I'm speak, Hitler is sleeping and suck-ing his thumb, I give him a pitying glance. He yaps, like a dreaming dog. He curls up, steadily growing smaller until he fits in the palm of my hand. 'What are you thinking about, Swing Troubadour?' 'About our Führer, Monsieur Philibert.' 'We're going to sell the Frans Hals shortly. You'll get a 15 per cent commission for your trouble. And if you help us capture Lamballe, I'll give you a five hundred thousand franc bonus. Enough to set you up for life. A little cognac?' My head is spinning. It must be the scent of the flowers. The living room was almost buried beneath dahlias and orchids. A huge rosebush between the windows partly hid the self-portrait of Monsieur de Bel-Respiro. 10 p.m. One after another they filed into the room. The Khedive greeted them in a plum-coloured tuxedo flecked with green. Monsieur Philibert gave a curt nod and returned to his files. Now and then he would walk up to one of them, exchange a few words, make some notes. The Khedive was passing around drinks, cigarettes, and *petits fours*. Monsieur and Madame de Bel-Respiro would have been amazed to find such a gathering in their living room: here were the 'Marquis' Lionel de Zieff, convicted of larceny, fraud, receiving stolen property and illegally wearing military decorations; Costachesco, a Romanian banker, stock market speculation and fraudulent bankruptcies; 'Baron' Gaétan de Lussatz, professional ballroom dancer holding dual French and Monegasque nationalities; Pols de Helder, gentleman-thief; Rachid von Rosenheim, voted Mr Germany 1938, professional swindler; Jean-Farouk de Méthode, owner of Cirque d'Automne and L'Heure Mauve, pimp, *persona non grata* throughout the British Commonwealth; Ferdinand Poupet, alias 'Paulo Hayakawa', insurance broker, previously convicted of forgery and use of forgeries; Otto da Silva, '*El Rico Plantador*', cut-rate spy; 'Count' Baruzzi, art expert and heroin addict; Darquier, aka 'de Pellepoix', shyster lawyer; Ivanoff 'the Oracle', a Bulgarian charlatan, 'official tattooist to the Coptic Church'; Odicharvi, police informant in White Russian circles; Mickey de Voisins, '*la soubrette*', homosexual prostitute; Costantini, former air force commandant; Jean Le Houleux, journalist, former treasurer of the Club du Pavois, blackmailer; the Chapochnikoff brothers, whose precise number, their crimes and their professions, I never discovered. A number of women: Lucie Onstein, alias 'Frau Sultana', exotic dancer at *Rigolett's*; Magda d'Andurian, manager of a 'refined, discreet hotel' in Palmyra, Syria; Violette Morris, weightlifting champion, invariably wore men's suits; Emprosine Marousi, Byzantine princess, drug addict and lesbian; Simone Bouquereau and Irène de Tranze, former residents of the One-Two-Two Club; 'Baroness' Lydia Stahl, who loved champagne and fresh flowers. All of these people regularly frequented No. 3 *bis*. They appeared out of the blackout, out of an era of despair and misery, through a phenomenon not unlike spontaneous generation. Most of them held key roles with the 'Inter-commercial Company Paris-Berlin-Monte Carlo'. Zieff, Méthode, and Helder were in charge of the leather department. Thanks to their skilled agents, they could obtain wagon loads of box caulk which was resold through the ICPBMC at twelve times the market price. Costachesco, Hayakawa, and Rosenheim specialized in metals, fats, and mineral oils. Ex-Commandant Costantini operated in a narrower but profitable sector: glassware, perfumes, chamois leathers, biscuits, nuts and bolts. The others were singled out by the Khedive for the more sensitive jobs. Lussatz was entrusted with the funds that arrived at Cimarosa Square in great quantity each morning. Da Silva and Odicharvi tracked down gold and foreign currency. Mickey de Voisins, Baruzzi, and 'Baroness' Lydia Stahl catalogued the contents of private houses where there might be works of art for me to confiscate. Hayakawa and Jean Le Houleux took care of the office accounts. Darquier served as legal counsel. As for the Chapochnikoff brothers, they had no definite function but simply fluttered around. Simone Bouquereau and Irène de Tranze were the Khedive's official 'secretaries'. Princess Marousi facilitated useful connections in social and banking circles. Frau Sultana and Violette Morris made a great deal of money as informers. Magda d'Andurian, an aggressive, hard-headed woman, scoured the North of France and would come up with quantities of tarpaulin and woollens. And finally, let us not forget the members of staff who confined themselves solely to police work: Tony Breton, fop, NCO in the French Foreign Legion, and veteran extortionist; Jo Reocreux, a brothel owner; Vital-Leca, known as 'the Golden Throat', hired assassin; Armand le Fou: 'I'll kill them all, every last one of them'; Codébo and Robert le Pâle, both scheduled for deportation, worked as porters and bodyguards; Danos 'the Mammoth', also known as 'Big Bill'; Gouari, 'the American', freelance armed robber. The Khedive ruled over this cheerful little community which legal chroniclers would later refer to as 'the Cimarosa Square Gang'. In the meantime, business was going well. Zieff was toying with plans to take over various film studios – the Victorine, the Eldorado, and the Folies-Wagram; Helder was organizing a 'general holdings company' to run every hotel on the Riviera; Costachesco was buying up real estate; Rosenheim had announced that 'the whole of France will soon be ours for the asking, to sell to the highest bidder.' I watched and listened to these lunatics. Under the glow of the chandeliers, their faces were dripping sweat. Their voices became more staccato. Rebates, brokerage fees, commissions, supplies on hand, wagon-loads, profit margins. Chapochnikoff brothers, in ever-growing numbers, tirelessly refilled the champagne glasses. Frau Sultana cranked the Victrola. Johnny Hess:

Mettez-vous
dans l'ambiance
oubliez
vos soucis . . .

She unbuttoned her blouse, broke into a jazz step. The others followed suit. Codébo, Danos, and Robert le Pâle entered the living room. They elbowed a path through the dancers, reached Monsieur Philibert, and whispered a few words in his ear. I was staring out of the window. A car with its headlights off was parked in front of No. 3 *bis*. Vital-Léca was holding a flashlight, Reocreux opened the car door. A man, in handcuffs. Gouari brutally pushed him toward the steps up to the house. I thought of the Lieutenant, the boys in Vaugirard. One night I would see them all in chains like this man. Breton would give them the shock treatment. What then . . . Will I be able to live with the guilt? Pernety and his black leather shoes. Picpus and his fiancée's letters. The periwinkle-blue eyes of Saint-Georges. Their dreams, all their wonderful fantasies would come to an end on the blood-spattered walls of the cellar at No. 3 *bis*. And it will be all my fault. That said, don't think I casually use the terms 'shock treatment', 'blackout', 'informant', 'hired killer'. I am reporting what I've seen, what I've lived. With no embellishments. I have invented nothing. All the people I have mentioned really existed. I have gone so far as to use their real names. As for my own tastes, they tend towards hollyhocks, a garden in the moonlight and the tango of happier days. The heart of a star-struck girl . . . I've been unlucky. You could hear their groans rising from the basement, stifled at last by the music. Johnny Hess:

Puisque je suis là
le rythme
est là
Sur son aile il vous
emportera . . .

Frau Sultana was goading them on with high-pitched squeals. Ivanoff was waving his 'lighter-than-iron rod'. They jostled, gasped for breath, their dancing grew spasmodic, upended a vase of dahlias and went back to their wild gesticulating.

La musique
c'est
le philtre magique . . .

The double-doors were flung open. Codébo and Danos propped the man up. He was still in handcuffs. His face was dripping blood. He stumbled and collapsed in the middle of the living room. Everyone froze, waiting. Only the Chapochnikoff brothers moved about, as if nothing was happening, picking up the shards of the broken vase, straightening the flowers. One of them crept towards Baroness Lydia proffering an orchid.

'If we ran into this type of wise guy every day it would be pretty rough for us,' declared Monsieur Philibert. 'Take it easy, Pierre. He'll end up talking.' 'I don't think so, Henri.' 'Then we'll make a martyr of him. Martyrs, it would appear, are necessary.' 'Martyrs are sheer nonsense,' declared Lionel de Zieff in a thick voice. 'You refuse to talk?' Monsieur Philibert asked him. 'We won't trouble you for very long,' whispered the Khedive. 'If you don't answer it means you don't know anything.' 'But if you know something,' said Monsieur Philibert, 'you had better tell us now.'

He raised his head. A bloodstain on the Savonnerie carpet, where his head had rested. An ironic twinkle in his periwinkle-blue eyes (the same colour as Saint-Georges'). Or perhaps contempt. People have been known to die for their beliefs. The Khedive hit him three times. He never looked away. Violette Morris threw a glass of champagne in his face. 'Excuse me, Monsieur,' murmured Ivanoff the Oracle, 'could you hold out your left hand?' People die for their beliefs. The Lieutenant often said: 'All of us are ready to die for our beliefs. Are you, Lamballe?' I didn't dare confess that if I were to die it could only be from disease, fear, or despair. 'Catch!' roared Zieff, and the cognac bottle hit him squarely in the face. 'Your hand, your left hand,' Ivanoff the Oracle implored. 'He'll talk,' sighed Frau Sultana, 'I know he will,' and she bared her shoulders with a wheedling smile. 'All that blood . . .' muttered Baroness Lydia Stahl. The man's head rested on the Savonnerie carpet once more. Danos lifted him up and dragged him from the living room. Moments later, Tony Breton reappeared and in a toneless voice, announced: 'He's dead, he died without talking.' Frau Sultana turned her back with a shrug. Ivanoff stared off into space, his eyes scanning the ceiling. 'You have to admit there are still a few fearless guys around,' commented Pols de Helder.

'Stubborn, you mean,' retorted 'Count' Baruzzi. 'I almost admire him,' declared Monsieur Philibert. 'He's the first I've seen put up such resistance.' The Khedive: 'People like that, Pierre, they SABOTAGE our work.' Midnight. A kind of torpor gripped them. They slumped onto sofas, onto pouffes, into armchairs. Simone Bouquereau stood at the Venetian mirror perfecting her make-up. Ivanoff stared intently at Baroness Lydia Stahl's left hand. The others launched into trivial chatter. About that time the Khedive took me over to the window to talk of his appointment as *préfet de police*, which he felt certain was imminent. He thought about it constantly. At fourteen, the reformatory in Eysses . . . penal military unit in Africa and Fresnes prison. Pointing to the portrait of M. de Bel-Respiro, he named every medal on the man's chest. 'Just substitute my face for his. Find me a talented artist. From now on, my name is Henri de Bel-Respiro.' He repeated, marvelling: 'Henri de Bel-Respiro, *Préfet De Police*.' Such a craving for respectability astonished me, for I had seen it once before in my father, Alexander Stavisky. I still keep the letter he wrote my mother before he took his life: 'What I ask above all is that you bring up our son to value honour and integrity; and, when he has reached the awkward age of fifteen, that you supervise his activities and associations so he may get a healthy start in life and become an honest man.' I believe he would have liked to end his days in a small provincial town. To find some peace and tranquillity after so many years of turmoil, anxiety, delusions and chaos. My poor father! 'You'll see, when I'm *préfet de police* everything will be fine.' The others were chatting in low voices. One of the Chapochnikoff brothers brought in a tray of orangeade. Were it not for the bloodstain in the middle of the carpet and the gaudy costumes, one might think you were in the company of respectable people. Monsieur Philibert rearranged his files, then sat down at the piano. He dusted the keyboard with his handker-chief and opened a piece of music. He played the Adagio from the Moonlight Sonata. 'A terpsichorean, a virtuoso,' whispered the Khedive. 'An artist to his fingertips. I sometimes wonder why he wastes his time on us. Such a talented boy! Just listen to him!' I felt my eyes grow wide with a sadness that used up all my tears, a weariness so great it kept me from sleeping. I felt as though I had forever been walking in darkness to the rhythm of this harrowing unending music. Shadowy figures tugged at my lapels, pulling me in opposite directions, now calling me 'Lamballe', now 'Swing Troubadour', forcing me from Passy to Sèvres-Lecourbe, from Sèvres-Lecourbe to Passy, and still I did not know what it was all about. The world truly was full of sound and fury. No matter. I strode straight through the chaos, stilted as a sleepwalker. Eyes wide open. Things would calm down eventually. The languorous melody Philibert was playing would gradually pervade everyone and everything. Of that I was certain. Everyone had left the living room. On the console table was a note from the Khedive: 'Try to deliver Lamballe as quickly as possible. We need him.' The sound of the car engines grew faint. Then, standing in front of the Venetian mirror, clearly so distinctly, I said: I AM THE PRIN-CESS DE LAM-BALLE. I looked myself in the eye, pressed my forehead against the mirror: I am the Princess de Lamballe. Assassins track you in the darkness. They grope about, fumble, bump over the furni-ture. The seconds seem to last forever. You hold your breath. Will they find the light switch? Let it be over. I can't hold out much longer against this feverish madness, I'll walk up to the Khedive, eyes wide open, press my face to his: I AM THE PRIN-CESS DE LAM-BALLE, leader of the CKS. Or maybe Lieutenant Dominique will suddenly get to his feet and announce in a grave voice: 'We have an informant in our midst. Some man by the name of 'Swing Troubadour'. 'I AM Swing Troubadour, Lieutenant.' I looked up. A moth circled from one chandelier to the other, so to keep his wings from being singed I turned out the lights. No one would ever show me such kindness. I have to fend for myself. Maman was far away: Lausanne. Thankfully. My poor father, Alexander Stavisky, was dead. Lili Marlene had all but forgotten me. Alone. I did not belong anywhere. Not at the Rue Boisrobert nor at Cimarosa Square. On the Left Bank, among those brave boys of the CKS, I hid the fact that I was an informant; on the Right Bank, the title 'Princesse de Lamballe' meant I was in serious danger. Who exactly was I? My papers? A fake Nansen passport. Persona non grata everywhere. This parlous situation kept me from sleeping. No matter. In addition to my secondary job of 'recuperating' valuable objects, I acted as night watchman at No. 3 *bis*. Once Monsieur Philibert, the Khedive and their guests had left, I could have retired to Monsieur de Bel-Respiro's bedroom, but I stayed in the living room. The lamp under its mauve shade cast deep rings of shadow around me. I opened a book: *The Mysteries of the Chevalier d'Eon*. After a few minutes it slipped from my hands. I was stuck by a sudden realization: I would never get out of this alive. The doleful chords of the Adagio rang in my ears. The flowers in the living room were shedding their petals and I was growing old at an accelerated rate. Standing in front of the Venetian mirror one last time, I looked at my reflection and saw the face of Philippe Pétain. His eyes seemed to me too bright, his complexion too pink, and so I metamorphosed into King Lear. What could be more natural. Since childhood, I had stored up a great reservoir of tears. Crying, they say, brings relief but despite my daily efforts, it was a pleasure I had never experienced. So the tears ate away at me like acid, which explains my rapid aging. The doctor had warned me: by twenty, you'll be the spitting image of King Lear. I should have preferred to offer a more dashing portrait of myself. Is it my fault? I began life with perfect health and steadfast morals, but I've suffered great sorrows. Sorrows so intense I cannot sleep and, from years of staying open, my eyes became disproportionately large. They come down to my jaw. One more thing: I have only to touch something for it to crumble into dust. The flowers in the living room are withering. The champagne glasses scattered over the console table, the desk, the mantelpiece evoke some party that took place long ago. Perhaps the masked ball on 20 June, 1896, that Monsieur de Bel-Respiro gave in honour of Camille du Gast, the cakewalk dancer. The abandoned umbrella, the Turkish cigarette butts, the half-finished orangeade. Was Philibert playing the piano a moment ago? Or was it Mademoiselle Mylo d'Arcille, who died some sixty years before? The bloodstain brought me back to more pressing problems. I did not know the poor wretch who looked like Saint-Georges. While they were torturing him, he dropped a pen and a hand-kerchief monogrammed with the initials C.F.: the only traces of his sojourn here on earth . . .

I opened the window. A summer night so blue, so warm, that it could only be short-lived and immediately brought to mind phrases like 'give up the ghost' and 'breathe a last sigh'. The world was dying of consumption. A gentle, lingering agony. The sirens announcing an air raid sobbed. Then all I could hear was a muffled drum. It went on for two or three hours. Phosphorus bombs. By dawn Paris would be a mass of rubble. Too bad. Everything I loved about the city had long since ceased to exist:

the railway that once ran along the *petite ceinture*, the Ballon de Ternes, the Pompeian Villa, the Chinese Baths. Over time, it begins to seem natural that things disappear. The fighter squadrons would spare nothing. On the desk I lined up the mah-jongg tiles that had once belonged to the son of the house. The walls began to shudder. Any minute now, they might crumble. But I hadn't finished what I was saying. Something would be born of my old age, my loneliness, like a bubble on the tip of a straw. I waited. In an instant, it took shape: a red-headed giant, clearly blind, since he wore dark glasses. A little girl with a wizened face. I named them Coco Lacour and Esmeralda. Destitute. Sickly. Always silent. A single word, a gesture would be enough to break them. What would have become of them without me? At last I found a reason to go on living. I loved them, my poor monsters. I would watch over them . . . No one would harm them. The money I earned at Cimarosa Square for informing and looting assured them a comfortable life. Coco Lacour. Esmeralda. I chose the two most powerless creatures on earth, but there was nothing maudlin about my love. I would have broken the jaw of any man who dared to make a disparaging remark about them. The mere thought put me in a murderous rage. Red-hot sparks burned my eyes. I felt myself choking. No one would lay a finger on my children. My grief which I had suppressed until now burst forth in torrents, and my love took strength in it. No living thing could resist its erosive power. A love so devastating that kings, warlords, and 'great men' were transformed into sick children before my eyes. Attila, Napoleon, Tamburlaine, Genghis Khan, Harun al-Rashid, and others whose virtues I had heard extolled. How puny and pitiful they seemed, these so-called titans. Utterly harmless. So much that as I bent over Esmeralda's face, I wondered whether it was not Hitler I saw. A little girl, abandoned. She was blowing bubbles with a device I had bought for her. Coco Lacour was lighting a cigar. From the very first time I met them, they had never said a word. They must be mutes. Esmeralda stared open-mouthed at the bubbles as they burst against the chandelier. Coco Lacour was utterly absorbed blowing smoke rings. Simple pleasures. I loved them, my little weaklings. I enjoyed their company. Not that I found these two creatures more moving or more helpless than the majority of humankind. The ALL inspired in me a hopeless, maternal compassion. But Coco Lacour and Esmeralda alone remained silent. They never moved. Silence, stillness, after enduring so many useless screams and gestures. I felt no need to speak to them. What would be the purpose? They were deaf. And that was for the best. Were I to confide my grief to a fellow creature, he would immediately desert me. And I would understand. Besides, my physical appearance deters 'soul mates'. A bearded centenarian with eyes that seem to devour his face. Who could possibly comfort Lear? It hardly matters. What matters: Coco Lacour and Esmeralda. We lived together as a family on Cimarosa Square. I forgot the Khedive and the Lieutenant. Gangsters or heroes, those guys had worn me down. I had never managed to be interested in their stories. I was making plans for the future. Esmeralda would take piano lessons. Coco Lacour would play mah-jongg with me and learn to dance the swing. I wanted to spoil them, my two gazelles, my deaf-mutes. To give them the best education. I couldn't stop looking at them. My love was like my feeling for maman. But she was safe now: LAUSANNE. As for Coco Lacour and Esmeralda, I kept them safe. We lived in a comforting house. One that had always been mine. My papers?

My name was Maxime de Bel-Respiro. Before me hangs my father's self-portrait. And there is more:

Memories
At the back of every drawer
perfumes
in every wardrobe . . .

We really had nothing to fear. The turmoil and cruelty of the world died on the steps of No. 3 *bis*. The hours passed, silently. Coco Lacour and Esmeralda would go up to bed. They would quickly fall asleep. Of all the bubbles Esmeralda blew, one still floated in the air. It rose towards the ceiling, hesitantly. I held my breath. It burst against the chandelier. Now everything was over. Coco Lacour and Esmeralda had never existed. I was alone in the living room listening to the rain of phosphorus. I spared a last thought for the quays along the Seine, the Gare d'Orsay, the Petite Ceinture. Then I found myself at the edge of old age in a region of Siberia called Kamchatka. Its soil bears no life. A bleak and arid region. Nights so deep they are sleepless. It is impossible to live at such a latitude, and biologists have observed that here the human body shatters into a thousand shards of laughter: raucous, piercing like the slivers of broken bottles. This is why: in the midst of this polar wasteland you feel free of every tie that bound you to the world. All that remains is for you to die. Laughing. 5 a.m. Or perhaps it is dusk. A layer of ash covered the living-room furniture. I was looking down at the bandstand on the square, at the statue of Toussaint L'Ouverture. It felt as though I were looking at a daguerreotype. Then I wandered through the house, floor by floor. Suitcases lay strewn in every room. There had been no time to close them. One contained a hat from Kronstadt, a slate-gray woollen suit, a yellowed playbill from a show at the Théâtre Ventadour, an autographed photo of the ice-skaters Goodrich and Curtis, two keepsakes, a few old toys. I didn't have the courage to rummage through the others. All around, trunks multiplied: in steel, in wicker, in glass, in Russian leather. Several trunks lined the corridor. 3 *bis* was becoming a vast left-luggage department. Forgotten. No one cared about these suitcases. They held the ghosts of many things: two or three walks in Batignolles with Lili Marlene, a kaleidoscope given to me for my seventh birthday, a cup of verbena tea maman gave me one evening I don't recall how long ago . . . All the little details of a life. I would have liked to make an itemised list. But what good would it do?

Le temps passe très vite
et les années nous quittent . . .
un jour . . .

My name was Marcel Petiot. Alone amid these piles of suitcases. No point waiting. No train was coming. I was a young man without a future. What had I done with my youth? Day followed day followed day and I piled them up at random. Enough to fill some fifty suitcases. They give off a bittersweet smell that makes me nauseous. I'll leave them here. They will rot where they lie. Get out of this house as fast as possible. Already the walls are beginning to crack and the self-portrait of Monsieur de Bel-Respiro is starting to moulder. Industrious spiders are spinning webs among the chandeliers; smoke is rising from the cellar. Some human remains burning, probably. Who am I? Petiot?

Landru? In the hallway, an acrid green vapour clings to the trunks. Get away. I'll take the wheel of the Bentley I left in front of the entrance last night. One last look up at No. 3 *bis*. One of those houses you dream of settling down in. Unfortunately, I entered it illegally. There was no place there for me. No matter. I turn on the radio:

Pauvre Swing Troubadour . . .

Avenue de Malakoff. The engine is silent. I glide across a still ocean. Leaves rustle. For the first time in my life I feel absolutely weightless.

Ton destin, Swing Troubadour . . .

I stop on the corner of the Place Victor Hugo and the Rue Copernic. From my inside pocket I take the pistol with the ivory handle studded with emeralds that I found in Madame de Bel-Respiro's nightstand.

Plus de printemps, Swing Troubadour . . .

I set the gun down on the seat. I wait. The cafés around the square are closed. Not a soul in the streets. A black, Citroën Traction, then two, then three, then four more down the Avenue Victor Hugo. My heart begins to pound. As they approach, they slow to a crawl. The first car draws alongside the Bentley. The Khedive. His face, behind the car window, is a few centimetres from mine. He stares at me with soft eyes. Then I feel my lips curling into a horrible leer. My head starts to spin. Carefully, so they can read my lips, I mouth the words: I AM THE PRIN-CESS DE LAM-BALLE. I AM THE PRIN-CESS DE LAM-BALLE. I grab the pistol and roll down the window. The Khedive watches, smiling, as if he has always known. I pull the trigger. I've wounded his left shoulder. Now they're following me at a distance, but I know I cannot escape. Their cars are four abreast. In one of them, the henchmen of Cimarosa Square: Breton, Reocreux, Codebo, Robert le Pale, Danos, Gouari . . . Vital-Léca is driving the Khedive's Citroën Traction. I glimpsed Lionel de Zieff, Helder, and Rosenheim in the back seat. I am back on the Avenue de Malakoff and heading towards the Trocadéro. A blue-gray Talbot appears from the Rue Lauriston: Philibert. Then the Delahaye Labourdette that belongs to ex-Commandant Costantini. Now they are all here, the hunt can begin. I drive slowly. They match my speed. It must look like a funeral cortège. I have no illusions: double-agents die one day, after the endless postponements, the comings, the manoeuvres, the lies, the acrobatics. Exhaustion takes hold very quickly. There's nothing left to do but lie down on the ground, gasping for breath, and wait for the final reckoning. You cannot escape men. Avenue Henri-Martin. Boulevard Lannes. I am driving aimlessly. The others are fifty metres behind. How exactly will they finish me off? Will Breton give me the shock treatment? They consider me an important catch: the 'Princess de Lam-balle', leader of the CKS. What's more, I've just shot at the Khedive. My actions must strike them as strange: after all, did I not deliver the 'Knights of the Shadows' to them? This is something I will need to explain. Will I have the strength? Boulevard Pereire. Who knows? Maybe a few years from now some lunatic will take an interest in this story. He'll give a lot of weight to the 'troubled period' we lived through, he'll read over old newspapers. He'll have a hard time analysing my personality. What was my role at

Cimarosa Square, core of one of the most notorious arms of the French Gestapo? And at the Rue Boisrobert among the patriots of the CKS? I myself don't know. Avenue de Wagram.

La ville est comme un grand manège
dont chaque tour
nous vieillit un peu . . .

I was making the most of Paris one last time. Every street, every junction brought back memories. Graff, where I met Lili Marlene. The Claridge, where my father stayed before he fled to Chamonix. The Bal Mabille where I used to dance with Rosita Sergent. The others were letting me continue on my journey. When would they decide to kill me? Their cars kept a steady distance of fifty metres. We turn on to the *grands boulevards*. A summer evening such as I have never seen. Snatches of music drift from open windows. People are sitting at pavement cafes or strolling in groups. Street lights flicker on. A thousand paper lanterns glow amid the leaves. Laughter erupts from everywhere. Confetti and accordion waltzes. To the east, a firework sprays pink and blue streamers. I feel that I'm living these moments in the past. We are wandering along the quays of the Seine. The Left Bank, the apartment I lived in with my mother. The shutters are closed.

Elle est partie
changement d'adresse . . .

We cross the Place du Châtelet. I watch the Lieutenant and Saint-Georges being gunned down again on the corner of the Avenue

Victoria. Before the night is over, I will meet the same end. Everyone's turn comes eventually. Across the Seine, a dark hulking mass: the Gare d'Austerlitz. The trains have not run now for an age. Quai de la Rapée. Quai de Bercy. We turn into a deserted district. Why don't they make the most of it? Any of these warehouses would make an ideal place – it seems to me – for them to settle their scores. The full moon is so bright that, with one accord, we switch off our headlights. Charenton-le-Pont. We are leaving Paris behind. I shed a few tears. I loved the city. She was my stamping ground. My private hell. My aging, over made-up mistress. Champigny-sur-Marne. When will they do it? I want this to be over. The faces of those I love appear for the last time. Pernety: what became of his pipe and his black leather shoes? Corvisart: he moved me, that big meathead. Jasmin: one night as we were crossing the Place Adolphe Cherioux, and he pointed to a star: 'That's Betelgeuse.' He lent me a biography of Henri de Bournazel. Turning the pages I came across an old photo of him in a sailor suit. Obligado: his mournful face. He would often read me excerpts from his political journal. The pages are now rotting in some drawer. Picpus: his fiancée? Saint-Georges, Marbeuf, and Pelleport. Their firm handshakes and loyal eyes. The walks around Vaugirard. Our first meeting in front of the statue of Joan of Arc. The Lieutenant's commanding voice. We have just passed Villeneuve-le-Roi. Other faces loom: my father, Alexander Stavisky. He would be ashamed of me. He wanted me to apply to the academy at Saint-Cyr. Maman. She's in Lausanne, and I can join her. I could floor the accelerator, shake off my would-be assassins. I have plenty of cash on me. Enough for even the most diligent Swiss border guard to turn a blind eye. But I'm too exhausted. All I want is rest. Real rest. Lausanne would not be enough. Have they come to a decision? In the mirror I see the Khedive's 11 CV closing, closing. No. It slows down abruptly. They're playing cat and mouse. I was listening to the radio to pass the time.

Je suis seul
ce soir
avec ma peine . . .

Coco Lacour and Esmeralda did not exist. I had jilted Lili Marlene. Denounced the brave boys of the CKS. You lose a lot of people along the way. All those faces need to be remembered, all those meetings honoured, all the promises kept. Impossible. I quickly drove on. Fleeing the scene of a crime. In a game like this you can lose yourself. Not that I've never known who I was. I hereby authorise my biographer to refer to me simply as 'a man', and wish him luck. I've been unable to lengthen my stride, my breath, or my sentences. He won't understand the first thing about this story. Neither do I. We're even.

L'Hay-les-Roses. We've gone through other suburbs. Now and then the Khedive's 11 CV would overtake me. Ex-Commandant Costantini and Philibert drove alongside me for about a kilometre. I thought my time had come. Not yet. They let me gain ground again. My head bangs against the steering wheel. The road is lined with poplar trees. A single slip would be enough. I drive on, half asleep.

Ring Roads

for Rudy

for Dominique

'If only I had a past at some other point in
French history!
But no, nothing.'
Rimbaud

The heaviest of the three is my father, though he was so thin back then. Murraille is leaning towards him as if whispering something. Marcheret stands in the background with a half-smile, puffing out his chest a little, his hands gripping the lapels of his jacket. It's difficult to tell the colour of their clothes or their hair. It looks as though Marcheret is wearing a very loosely cut Prince-of-Wales check suit, and has fairish hair. Note the sharp expression on Murraille's face, and the worried one on my father's. Murraille seems tall and thin, but the lower half of his face is pudgy. Everything about my father expresses total dejection. Except his eyes, almost starting out of his head.

Wood panelling, a brick fireplace: the Clos-Foucré bar. Murraille has a glass in his hand. As has my father. Notice the cigarette drooping from Murraille's lips. My father has his wedged between his ring and little fingers. A jaded affectation. At the back of the room, in semi-profile, a female figure: Maud Gallas, the manageress of Le Clos-Foucré. The armchairs in which Murraille and my father are sitting are probably leather. There's a slight sheen on the back, just above the spot which Murraille's left hand is stubbing into. His arm curls around my father's neck in a gesture which could be hugely protective. Flagrant on his wrist is an expensive watch with a square face. Marcheret, given his position and athletic build, is half hiding Maud Gallas and the shelves of aperitif bottles. On the wall, behind the bar, you can see – without too much difficulty – a tear-off calendar. The number 14, clearly visible. It isn't possible to make out the month or year. But, looking closely at the three men, and at the blurred outline of Maud

Gallas, the casual observer would imagine the scene to be taking place in the distant past.

An old photograph, found by chance at the bottom of a drawer, from which you carefully wipe the dust. Night is drawing in. The ghosts file in as usual to the Clos-Foucré. Marcheret has perched on a stool. The other two have chosen armchairs by the fireplace. They ordered sickly and pointlessly elaborate cocktails which Maud Gallas mixed, with the help of Marcheret, who plied her with doubtful jokes, calling her 'my great big Maud' or 'my Tonkinese'. She didn't appear to take offence and when Marcheret slipped a hand into her blouse to paw a breast – a gesture which always causes him to make a sort of whinnying noise – she remained impassive, one cannot help wonder whether her smile reflects contempt or complicity. She's a woman of about forty, blonde and heavily built, with a deep voice. The brightness of her eyes – are they midnight blue or violet? – is surprising in such a coarse face. What did Maud Gallas do before taking over this *auberge*? The same sort of thing probably, but in Paris. She and Marcheret often refer to the Beaulieu, a nightclub in the Quartier des Ternes, that closed twenty years ago. They speak of it in hushed tones. Hostess? Ex-cabaret artiste? Marcheret has obviously known her a long time. She calls him Guy. While they are mixing the drinks and shaking with suppressed laughter, Grève, the maître d'hôtel, comes in and asks Marcheret: 'What would Monsieur le Comte like to eat later?' To which Marcheret invariably replies: 'Monsieur le Comte will eat shit', jutting his chin, crinkling his eyes and contorting his face in an expression of bored self-satisfaction. At such moments, my father always gives a little laugh to show Marcheret that he's enjoyed this witty banter exchange and thinks Marcheret's the funniest man he's ever met.

The latter, delighted at the effect he's having on my father, asks him: 'Isn't that right, Chalva?' And my father, hurriedly: 'Oh yes, Guy!' Murraille remains aloof from this repartee. One evening when Marcheret, in better form than usual, hiked up Maud Gallas's skirt and said: 'Ah, a bit of thigh!' Murraille put on a shrill society voice: 'You must excuse him, my dear, he thinks he's still in the Legion.' (This remark casts a new light on Marcheret.) Murraille himself affects the manners of a gentleman. He expresses himself in carefully chosen phrases and modulates his voice to make it as smooth as possible, adopting a kind of parliamentary eloquence. His words are accompanied by sweeping gestures, never failing to add some flourish of chin or eyebrow, and tends to flick his fingers as though opening a fan. He dresses elegantly: English tweeds, shirts and ties in subtle matching shades. So why the strong smell of Chypre which hangs around him? And the platinum signet-ring? Look at him again: his forehead is broad, his pale eyes express a joyful frankness. But, below that, the drooping cigarette emphasises the slackness of his lips. The craggy architecture of his face disintegrates at jaw level. His chin slides away. Listen to him: sometimes his voice grows harsh and cracks. In fact, one has a nasty suspicion that he's cut from exactly the same coarse cloth as Marcheret.

This impression is confirmed if you watch the two men after dinner. They're sitting side by side, facing my father – only the back of his head is visible. Marcheret is talking very loudly in a whip-like voice. Blood rushes to his face. Murraille has also raised his voice and his shrill cackling drowns Marcheret's more guttural laugh. They wink conspiratorially and slap each other on the back. A sort of complicity is established between them, one you can't quite pin down. You would have to be at their table, listen to every word. From a distance you can only hear confused – and meaningless – snatches of conversation. Now they're whispering together and their words are lost in the great empty dining-room. From the bronze ceiling fixture, a harsh light spills down on the tables, the panelling, the Normandy dresser, on the stag and roebuck heads on the wall. It weighs on them like cotton wool, muffling the sound of their voices. Not a single patch of shadow. Except my father's back. Strange how the light spares him. But the nape of his neck is clearly visible in the glare of the ceiling-light, you can even see a small pink scar in the middle. His neck is bent forward as though offered to an invisible executioner. He's drinking in their every word. He moves his head to within an inch of theirs. His forehead almost glued to those of Murraille and Marcheret. Whenever my father's face looms too close to his own, Marcheret pinches his cheek between his finger and thumb and twists it slowly. My father jerks back but Marcheret doesn't let go. He holds him like that for several minutes and the pressure of his fingers increases. He knows my father must be in considerable pain. When it's over, there's a red mark on his cheek. He strokes it furtively. Marcheret says: 'That'll teach you to be nosy, Chalva . . .' And my father: 'Oh yes, Guy . . . That's true, Guy . . .' He smiles.

Grève brings the liqueurs. His bearing and his ceremonious manner are in sharp contrast to the free-and-easy behaviour of the three men and the woman. Murraille, chin propped in his hand, eyes bleary, gives the impression of being more than relaxed. Marcheret has loosened his tie and is leaning his entire weight against the back of his chair, so that it's balanced on two legs. Any moment now, it's going to tip over. And my father is leaning towards them so intently that his chest is almost pressed against the table; a pat on the back and he'd be sprawled across his plate. The few words one can still catch are those grunted by Marcheret, thickly. A few moments later the only sound to be heard is his stomach gurgling. Is it the excessive meal (they always order dishes with rich sauces and various kinds of game) or the bad choice of wine (Marcheret always insists on heavy pre-war burgundies) which has stupefied them? Grève stands stiffly behind them. He asks Marcheret pointedly: 'Would Monsieur le Comte like anything else to drink?' stressing each syllable of 'Monsieur le Comte'. He says even more heavily: 'Thank you, Monsieur le Comte.' Is he trying to call Marcheret to order, and remind him that a gentleman shouldn't let himself go like that?

Above Grève's rigid form, a roebuck's head rears from the wall like a figurehead and the animal considers Marcheret, Murraille and my father with all the indifference of its glass eyes. The shadow from its horns traces a vast interlace on the ceiling. The light dims. A power-cut? They remain slumped and silent in the semi-darkness which gnaws at them. The same feeling again of looking at an old photograph until Marcheret gets up, so clumsily that he keeps knocking into the table. Then it all starts up again. The ceiling light and the sconces shine as strongly as ever. No shadows. No haziness. Each object is outlined with an almost unbearable precision. The movements which had grown torpid become brisk and imperious again. Even my father sits up as though to a command.

They are evidently heading into the bar. Where else? Murraille has laid a friendly hand on my father's shoulder and, cigarette dangling, is talking to him, trying to persuade him on some point they have been arguing about. They stop for a moment a few feet from the bar, where Marcheret is already installed. Murraille leans towards my father, adopting the confidential tone of one who is guaranteeing an irresistible offer. My father nods, his companion pats his shoulder as if they had at last reached agreement.

All three have sat down at the bar. Maud Gallas has the wireless playing low in the background, but when there's a song she likes, she twists the knob and turns it up loud. Murraille pays great attention to the eleven o'clock news which is hammered out by a reader in a brisk voice. Then there'll be the signature tune indicating the close of broadcasting. A sad and sinister little melody.

A long silence again before the memories and secrets start up. Marcheret says that, at thirty-six, he's washed up, and complains about his malaria. Maud Gallas reminds him of the night he came into the Beaulieu in full uniform and the gypsy band massacred the 'Hymne de la Légion' in his honour. One of our beautiful pre-war nights, she says ironically, grinding out her cigarette. Marcheret stares at her, gives her an odd look and says that he doesn't give a damn about the war. And that even if things get worse, he isn't worried. And that he, Count Guy, Francois, Arnaud de Marcheret d'Eu, doesn't need anyone to tell him what to do. He's only interested in 'the champagne sparkling in his glass', and he squirts an angry mouthful at Maud Gallas's bosom. Murraille says; 'Come, come . . .' No, not at all, his friend is far from washed up. And what does 'washed up' mean anyway? Hmm? Nothing! He insists that his dear friend has many more glorious years ahead. And he can count on the affection and support of 'Jean Murraille'. Besides, he, 'Jean Murraille', has every intention of giving his niece's hand to Count Guy de Marcheret. You see? Would he let his niece marry someone who was washed up? Would he? He turns towards the others as if daring them to challenge him. You see? What better proof could he give of his confidence and friendship? Washed up? What do you mean by 'washed up'? 'Washed up' means . . . But he trails off. He can't think of a definition, so he just shrugs. Marcheret observes him keenly. Then Murraille has an inspiration and says that if Guy has no objection, Chalva Deyckecaire can be his witness. And Murraille nods to my father, whose face immediately lights up in an expression of speechless gratitude. The wedding will be celebrated at the Clos-Foucré in a fortnight. Their friends will come from Paris. A small family party to cement the partnership. Murraille – Marcheret – Deyckecaire! The Three Musketeers. Besides, everything's going well! Marcheret needn't worry about anything. 'These are troubled times,' but 'the money's pouring in'. There are already all sorts of projects, 'some more interesting than others', afoot. Guy will get his share of the profits. 'To the last *sou*.' Cheers! The Count toasts the health of his 'future father-in-law' (odd, really: there isn't more than ten years between him and Murraille . . .), and, as he raises his glass, announces that he's proud and happy to be marrying Annie Murraille because she has the 'palest, hottest arse in Paris'.

Maud Gallas has pricked up her ears, and asks what he's giving his future wife as a wedding present. A silver mink, two heavy bracelets in solid gold for which he paid 'six million cash'.

He has just brought an attaché case bulging with foreign currency from Paris. And some quinine. For his filthy malaria.

'It's filthy all right,' Maud says.

Where did he meet Annie Murraille. Who? Annie Murraille? Oh! Where did he meet her? Chez Langers, you know, a restaurant on the Champs-Élysées. In fact, he really got to know Murraille through his daughter! (He laughs uproariously.) It was love at first sight and they spent the rest of the evening together at the Poisson d'Or. He goes into great detail, gets muddled, picks up the thread of his story. Murraille, who had been amused to begin with, has now returned to the conversation he started with my father after dinner. Maud listens patiently to Marcheret, whose story trails off in a drunken mumble.

My father's head nods. The bags under his eyes are puffy, which makes him look immensely tired. What is he playing at, exactly, with Murraille and Marcheret?

It's getting late. Maud Gallas turns out the big lamp, by the fireplace. Probably a signal to tell them it's time to go. The room is only lit by the two sconces with red shades on the far wall, and my father, Murraille and Marcheret are once more plunged into semi-darkness.

Behind the bar, there is still a small patch of light, in the centre of which Maud Gallas stands motionless. The sound of Murraille whispering. Marcheret's voice, growing more and more halting. He falls heavily from his perch on the stool, catches himself just in time and leans on Murraille's shoulder to steady himself. They stagger towards the door. Maud Gallas sees them off. The fresh air revives Marcheret. He tells Maud that if she gets lonely, his big Maud, she must telephone him; that Murraille's daughter has the prettiest arse in Paris, but that her thighs, Maud Gallas's, are 'the most mysterious in Seine-et-Marne'. He puts his arm round her waist and starts pawing her, at which Murraille intervenes with 'Tut-tut . . .' She goes in and shuts the door.

The three of them were in the main street of the village. On either side, great, sleeping houses. Murraille and my father led the way. Their companion sang 'Le Chaland qui passe' in a raucous voice. Shutters opened and a head looked out. Marcheret vituperated the peeping-tom and Murraille tried to calm down his future 'nephew'.

The villa 'Mektoub' is the last house on the left, right at the edge of the forest. To look at, it is a mixture between a bungalow and a hunting-lodge. A veranda along the front of the house. It was Marcheret who christened the villa 'Mektoub' – 'Fate' – in memory of the Legion. The gateway is whitewashed. On one side of the double gate, a copper plate with 'Villa Mektoub' engraved in gothic script. Marcheret has had a teak fence erected around the grounds.

They part in front of the gateway. Murraille thumps my father on the back and says: 'See you tomorrow, Deyckecaire.' And Marcheret barks: 'See you tomorrow, Chalva!', pushing the gate open with his shoulder. They walk up the driveway. And my father remains standing there. He has often stroked the name-plate reverently, tracing the outline of the gothic characters with his finger. The gravel crunches as the others walk away. For a moment Marcheret's shadow is visible in the middle of the veranda. He shouts: 'Sweet dreams, Chalva!' and roars with laughter. There is the sound of French windows shutting. Silence. My father wanders along the main road and turns left onto the Chemin du Bornage, a narrow country lane that slopes gently uphill. All along it, expensive properties with extensive grounds. He stops now and then and looks up at the sky, as if contemplating the moon and stars; or, nose pressed against the railings, he peers at the dark mass of a house. Then he continues on his way, but meandering, as though headed nowhere in particular. This is the moment when we ought to approach him.

He stops, pushes open the gate of the 'Priory', a strange villa in the neo-Romanesque style. Before going in, he hesitates for a moment. Does the house belong to him? Since when? He shuts the gate behind him, slowly crosses the lawn to the steps leading to the house. His back is bowed. He looks so sad, this overweight man shuffling through the darkness . . .

Certainly one of the prettiest and most idyllically situated villages in Seine-et-Marne. On the outskirts of the Forest of Fontainebleau. A few Parisians have country houses here, but they are no longer around, probably 'because of the worrying turn of events'.

Monsieur and Madame Beausire, the owners of the Clos-Foucré inn, left last year. They said they were going for a change of air to their cousins' place in Loire-Atlantique, but everyone realised that if they were taking a holiday, it was because regular customers were increasingly scarce. Which makes it difficult to understand why a woman from Paris has taken charge of the Clos-Foucré. Two men – also from Paris – have bought Mme Lamiroux's house at the edge of the forest. (It has stood empty for nearly ten years.) The younger of the two – apparently – had served in the Foreign Legion. The other was the editor of a Paris newspaper. One of their friends had moved into the 'Priory', the Guyots' country-house. Is he renting it? Or is he taking advantage of the family's absence? (The Guyots have settled in Switzerland for an indefinite period.) He's a chubby rather oriental looking man. He and his two friends obviously have very large incomes but they seem to have acquired their money fairly recently. They spend the week-end here, as middle-class families did in happier times. On Friday evening, they come down from Paris. The one who was in the Legion roars down the High Street behind the wheel of a beige Talbot and screeches to a halt in front of the Clos-Foucré. A few minutes later, the other's saloon is also parked up at the *auberge*. They usually have guests with them. The red-haired woman who always wears jodhpurs, for instance. On Saturday mornings, she goes riding in the forest and when she gets back to the stables, the grooms hover round her and take particular care of her horse. In the afternoon, she walks along the main road followed by an Irish setter whose russet coat (is it deliberate?) matches her tan boots and her red hair. Very often she is accompanied by a young woman with blonde hair – the daughter, apparently, of the magazine editor. This one always wears a fur coat. The two women call in for a minute at Mme Blairiaux's antique shop and choose some jewellery. The red-haired woman once bought a large Louis XV lacquer cabinet that Mme Blairiaux had despaired of selling because it was so expensive. When she realized her customer was offering her two million francs in cash, she looked scared. The red-haired woman put the wad of banknotes on a whatnot. Later a van collected the cabinet and delivered it to Mme Lamiroux's house (since they have been occupying it, the magazine editor and the ex-Legionary have christened it the 'Villa Mektoub'.) This same van has been seen taking *objets d'art* and paintings, the red-haired woman's haul from local auctions, regularly up to the 'Villa Mektoub'; on Saturday evenings, she arrives back from Melun or Fontainebleau in the car with the magazine editor. The van follows, loaded with every kind of bric-a-brac: rustic furniture, china, chandeliers, silver, which are all cached at the villa. Gossip among the villagers is rife. They would dearly like to know more about the red-haired woman. She is staying at the Clos-Foucré, not at the 'Villa Mektoub'. But you can tell that there's a close relationship between her and the editor. Is she his mistress? A friend? There are rumours the ex-Legionary is a count. And that the heavyset gentleman at the 'Priory' calls himself 'Baron' Deyckecaire. Are their titles genuine? Neither is exactly what one thinks of as a genuine aristocrat. There's something odd about them. Perhaps they are foreign noblemen? Wasn't 'Baron' Deyckecaire overheard one day saying to the editor in a loud voice: 'That doesn't matter, I'm a Turkish citizen!' And the 'Count' speaks French with a slight working-class accent. Picked up in the Legion? The red-haired woman seems to be something of an exhibitionist, why else does she wear so much jewellery, which is so out of keeping with her riding clothes? As for the young blonde woman, it's odd that she wraps herself up in a fur coat in June. The country air must be too much for her. She had her photograph in *Ciné-Miroir*. The caption read: 'Annie Murraille, 26, star of *Nights of Plunder*.' Is she still an actress? She often goes walking arm in arm with the ex-Legionary, with her head on his shoulder. They must be engaged.

Other people arrive on Saturdays and Sundays. The editor often invites as many as twenty guests. You get to know most of them in due course, but it's difficult to put a name to each face. Bizarre rumours are widespread in the village. That the editor organizes a 'special' kind of party at the 'Villa Mektoub' which was why 'all these strange characters' come down from Paris. The woman running the Clos-Foucré while the Beausires once ran a bordello. In fact, the Clos-Foucré was beginning to seem more like a brothel, given the curious clientele now staying there. People wondered, what underhand means had 'Baron' Deyckecaire used to get his hands on the 'Priory'? The man looked like a spy. The 'Count' had probably joined the Foreign Legion to avoid being prosecuted for some crime. The editor and the red-haired woman were engaged in nefarious trafficking of some sort. There were orgies being held up at the 'Villa Mektoub', and the editor even got his niece to take part. He was more than happy to push her into the arms of the 'Count' and anyone else whose silence he wanted to buy. In short, the locals ended up convinced that their village had been 'overrun by a mob of gangsters'. A reliable witness, as they say in novels and police reports, looking at the editor and his entourage, would immediately think of the 'crowd' who frequent certain bars on the Champs-Élysées. Here, they are completely out of place. On evenings when there is a crowd of them, they have dinner at the Clos-Foucré, then straggle up to the 'Villa Mektoub' in small groups. The women are all red-heads or platinum blondes, the men all wear brash suits. The 'Count' leads the way, his arm wound in a white silk scarf as if he had just been wounded in action. To remind him of his days in the Legion? They clearly play their music loud since blasts of rumba, hot jazz and snatches of song can be heard from the main road. If you stop near the villa, you can see them dancing behind the French windows.

One night, at about 2 a.m., a shrill voice screamed 'Bastard!'. The red-haired woman came running out of the villa with her breasts spilling out of her décolleté. Someone rushed after her. 'Bastard!' she shrieked again, then she burst out laughing. In the early days, the villagers would open their shutters. Then they got used to the racket the newcomers made. Now, no-one is surprised by anything.

The magazine was obviously launched recently, since the current issue is number 57. The name – *C'est la vie* – is emblazoned in black-and-white letters. On the cover, a woman in a suggestive pose. You would think it was a pin-up magazine were it not that the slogan – 'A political and society weekly' – claimed more high-flying aspirations.

On the title page, the name of the editor: Jean Murraille. Then, under the heading: features, the list of about a dozen contributors, all unknown. Try as you might, you can't remember seeing their names anywhere. At a pinch, two names vaguely ring a bell, Jean Drault and Mouly de Melun: the former, a pre-war columnist, the author of *Soldat Chapuʒot*; the latter a starving writer for *Illustration*. But the others? What to the mysterious Jo-Germain, the author of the cover story about 'Spring and Renewal'? Written in fancy French, and ending with the injunction: 'Be joyful!' The article is illustrated by several photographs of young people in extremely informal dress.

On the second page, the 'Rumour & Innuendo' column. Paragraphs with suggestive titles. One Robert Lestandi makes scabrous comments about public figures in politics, the arts and the entertainment world and makes oblique remarks that are tantamount to blackmail. Some 'humorous' cartoons, in a sinister style, are signed by a certain 'Mr Tempestuous'. There are more surprises to come. The 'editorial', and 'news' items, not to mention the readers' letters. The 'editorial' of number 57, a torrent of invective and threats penned by François Gerbère, contains such phrases as: 'It is only one short step from flunkey to thief.' Or 'Someone should pay for this. And pay they shall!' Pay for what? 'François Gerbère' is none too precise. As for the various 'reporters', they favour the most unsavoury subjects. Issue 51, for instance, offers: 'The true-life odyssey of a coloured girl through the world of dance and pleasure. Paris, Marseilles, Berlin.' The same deplorable tone continues in the 'readers' letters' where one reader asks whether 'Spanish fly added to food or drink will cause instant surrender in a person of the weaker sex'. Jo-Germain answers these questions in fragrant prose.

In the last two pages, entitled 'What's New?', an anonymous 'Monsieur Tout-Paris' gives a detailed account of the murky goings-on in society. Society? Which 'society' are we talking about? The re-opening of the Jane Stick cabaret club, in the Rue de Ponthieu (the most 'Parisian' event of the month according to the columnist), 'we spotted Osvaldo Valenti and Monique Joyce'. Among the other 'celebrities listed by 'Monsieur Tout-Paris': Countess Tchernicheff, Mag Fontanges, Violette Morris; 'Boissel, the author of *Croix de Sang*, Costantini, the crack pilot; Darquier de Pellepoix, the well-known lawyer; Montandon, the professor of anthropology; Malou Guérin; Delvale and Lionel de Wiet, theatre directors; the journalists Suaraize, Maulaz and Alin-Laubreaux'. But, according to our correspondent, 'the liveliest table was that of M. Jean Murraille'. To illustrate the point, there is a photograph showing Murraille, Marcheret, the red-haired woman in jodhpurs (her name is Sylviane Quimphe), and my father, whose name is given as 'Baron Deyckecaire'. 'All of them' – says the writer – 'bring the warmth and spirituality of sophisticated Paris nightlife to Jane Stick.' Two other photographs give a panoramic view of the evening. Soft lighting, tables occupied by a hundred or so men in dinner-jackets and women with plunging dresses. The first photograph is captioned: 'The stage is set, the curtains part, the floor vanishes and a staircase, decked with dancers, appears . . . The revue *Dans notre miroir* begins', the second is captioned 'Sophistication! Rhythm! Light! Now, that's Paris!' No. There's something suspicious about the whole thing. Who are these people? Where have they sprung from? The fat-faced 'Baron' Deyckecaire, in the background there, for example, slumped behind a champagne bucket?

'You find it interesting?'

In the faded photograph, a middle-aged man stands opposite a young man whose features are indistinct. I looked up. He was standing in front of me: I hadn't heard him emerge from the depths of those 'troubled' years long ago. He glanced down at the 'What's New?' section to see what I was reading. It was true he had caught me poring over the magazine as though inspecting a rare stamp.

'Are you interested in society goings-on?'

'Not particularly, monsieur,' I mumbled.

He held out his hand.

'Jean Murraille!'

I got to my feet and made a show of being surprised.

'So, you're the editor of . . .'

'The very same.'

'Delighted to meet you!' I said, off the top of my head. Then, with an effort – 'I like your magazine very much.'

'Really?'

He was smiling. I said:

'It's cool.'

He seemed surprised by this slangy term I had deliberately used to establish a complicity between us.

'Your magazine, it's cool,' I repeated pensively.

'Are you in the trade?'

'No.'

He waited for me to elaborate, but I said nothing.

'Cigarette?'

He took a platinum lighter from his pocket and opened it with a curt flick. His cigarette drooped from the corner of his mouth, as it droops there for all eternity.

Hesitantly:

'You read Gerbère's editorial? Perhaps you don't agree with the . . . political . . . views of the magazine?'

'Politics are not my game,' I replied.

'I ask . . .' he smiled ' . . . because I would be curious to know the opinion of a young man . . .'

'Thank you.'

'I had no difficulty in finding contributors . . . we work as a close team. Journalists came running from all sides . . . Lestandi, Jo-Germain, Alin-Laubreaux, Gerbère, Georges-Anquetil . . . I don't much care for politics myself. They're a bore!' A quick laugh. 'What the public wants is gossip and topical pieces. And photographs! Particularly photographs! I chose a formula that would be . . . joyful!'

'People need to loosen up "in these troubled times",' I said.

'Absolutely!'

I took a deep breath. In a clipped voice:

'What I like best in your magazine, is Lestandi's "Rumour & Innuendo" column. Excellent! Very acerbic!'

'Lestandi is a remarkable fellow. We worked together in the past, on Dubarry's *La Volontei*. An excellent training ground! What do you do?'

The question caught me off guard. He stared at me with his pale blue eyes and I understood that I had to answer quickly to avoid an unbearably awkward moment for us both.

'Me? Believe it or not I'm a novelist in my spare time.'

The ease with which the phrase came startled me.

'That's very, very interesting! Published?'

'Two stories in a Belgian magazine, last year.'

'Are you on holiday here?'

He asked the question abruptly, as if suddenly suspicious.

'Yes.'

I was about to add that we had already seen each other in the bar and in the dining-room.

'Quiet, isn't it?' He pulled nervously on his cigarette. 'I've bought a house on the edge of the forest. Do you live in Paris?'

'Yes.'

'So, apart from your literary activities . . .' he stressed the word 'literary', and I detected a note of irony – ' . . . do you have a regular job?'

'No. It's a little difficult just now.'

'Strange times. I wonder how it will all end. What do you think?'

'We must make the most of life while we can.'

This remark pleased him. He roared with laughter.

'Make hay while the sun shines!' He patted me on the shoulder, 'Look here, you must have dinner with me tonight!'

We had walked a little way into the garden. To keep the conversation going, I remarked that it had been very mild these last few afternoons, and that I had one of the pleasantest rooms in the inn, one of the ones that opened directly on to the veranda.

I mentioned that the Clos-Foucré reminded me of my childhood, that I often went there with my father. I asked him if he liked his house. He would have liked to spend more time here, but the magazine monopolized his time. But he liked to keep at it. And Paris could be very pleasant too. With these fascinating remarks, we sat down at one of the tables. Seen from the garden, the inn had a rustic, opulent air, and I didn't miss the opportunity of telling him so. The manageress (he called her Maud) was a very old friend, he told me. It was she who advised him to buy the house. I would have liked to ask more about her, but I was afraid my curiosity might arouse his suspicion.

For some time now I had been thinking of various ways I might get in touch with them. First I thought of the red-haired woman. Our eyes had met more than once. It would have been easy to get into conversation with Marcheret by sitting next to him at the bar; conversely, impossible to confront my father directly because of his mistrustful nature. And Murraille scared me. How to approach him tactfully? Now he solved the problem himself, after all. An idea occurred to me. Suppose he had made the first move to find out what I was up to? Perhaps he'd noticed the keen interest I had taken in his little group these past three weeks, the way I was intent on their every movement, on every word they spoke in the bar or the dining-room? I remembered the derisive way I'd been told, when I wanted to become a policeman: 'You'll never make a good cop, son. Whenever you're watching or eavesdropping, you give yourself away. You're a complete innocent.'

Grève steered a trolley loaded with aperitifs towards us. We drank vermouth. Murraille told me that I could read a 'sensational' article by Alin-Laubreaux in his magazine the following week. His voice took on a confidential tone, as if he had known me ages. Twilight was drawing in. We both agreed that this was the most pleasant time of the day.

The hulking form of Marcheret's back. Standing behind the bar, Maud Gallas waved to Murraille as we came in. Marcheret turned.

'How are things, Jean-Jean?'

'Good,' Murraille answered. 'I brought a guest. Actually . . .' he looked at me, frowning ' . . . I don't even know your name.'

'Serge Alexandre.'

This was the name I had signed in the hotel register.

'Well, Monsieur . . . Alexandre,' Marcheret announced in a drawling voice, 'I suggest you have a porto-flip.'

'I don't really drink' – the vermouth we had had was making me feel queasy.

'That's a mistake,' Marcheret said.

'This is a friend of mine,' Murraille said. 'Guy de Marcheret.'

'Comte Guy de Marcheret d'Eu,' corrected the other. Then he turned to me: 'He has a horror of aristocratic titles! Monsieur likes to think he's a republican!'

'And you? A journalist?'

'No,' said Murraille, 'he's a novelist.'

'Are you indeed! I should have guessed. With a name like yours! Alexandre . . . Alexandre Dumas! But you look miserable, I'm sure a little drink would do you good!'

He held out his glass, almost pushing it under my nose, laughing for no apparent reason.

'Have no fear,' Murraille said. 'Guy is always the life and soul of the party.'

'Is Monsieur Alexandre dining with us? I'll tell him stories he can put in his novels. Maud, tell our young friend about the stir I created when I walked into the Beaulieu in my uniform. A very dashing entrance, don't you think, Maud?'

She didn't answer. He glared at her sourly, but she didn't look away. He snorted:

'Oh well, that's all in the past, eh, Jean-Jean? Are we eating up at the villa?'

'Yes,' Murraille said curtly.

'With the Fat Man?'

'With the Fat Man.'

So this is what they called my father?

Marcheret got up. To Maud Gallas: 'If you feel like a drink later on up at the house, *ma chère*, don't hesitate.'

She smiled and shot me a brief glance. We were still very much at the politeness stage. Once I managed to get her alone, I wanted to ask her about Murraille, about Marcheret, about my father. Start by chatting to her about the weather. Then gradually inch towards the true heart of the matter. But I was worried about seeming too obvious. Had she noticed me prowling round them? In the dining-room, I always chose the table next to theirs. Whenever they were in the bar, I would sit in one of the leather armchairs and pretend to be asleep. I kept my back to them so as not to attract their attention, but, after a minute or two, I worried they were pointing at me.

'Goodnight, Maud,' Murraille said.

I gave her a deep bow, and said:

'Goodnight, madame.'

My heart begins to pound as we reach the main road. It's deserted.

'I do hope you will like the "Villa Mektoub",' Murraille says to me.

'It's the finest historic building in the area,' pronounces Marcheret. 'We got it dirt cheap.'

They stroll at a leisurely pace. I have the sudden feeling that I am walking into a trap. There is still time to run, to shake them off. I keep my eyes fixed on the trees at the edge of the forest, a hundred yards ahead. If I make a dash for it I can reach them.

'After you,' Murraille says, half-ironic, half-obsequious.

I glimpse a familiar figure standing in the middle of the veranda.

'Well, well!' says Marcheret. 'The Fat Man is here already.'

He was leaning idly against the balustrade. She, lounging in one of the whitewashed wooden chairs, was wearing jodhpurs.

Murraille introduced us.

'Madame Sylviane Quimphe . . . Serge Alexandre . . . Baron Deyckecaire.'

He offered me a limp hand and I looked him straight in the eye. No, he didn't recognize me.

She told us she had just been for a long ride in the forest and hadn't had the energy to change for dinner.

'No matter, my dear,' said Marcheret. 'I find women much more attractive in riding gear!'

The conversation immediately turned to horse riding. She couldn't speak too highly of the local stable master, a former jockey named Dédé Wildmer.

I'd already met the man at the bar of the Clos-Foucré; bulldog face, crimson complexion, checked cap, suede jacket and an evident fondness for Dubonnet.

'We must invite him to dinner. Remind me, Sylviane,' Murraille said.

Turning to me:

'You should meet him, he's a real character!'

'Yes, a real character,' my father repeated nervously.

She talked about her horse. She had put it through some jumps on her afternoon ride, something she had found 'an eye-opener'.

'You mustn't go easy on him,' Marcheret said, with the air of an expert. 'A horse only responds to the whip and the spurs!'

He reminisced about his childhood: an elderly Basque uncle had forced him to ride in the rain for seven hours at a stretch. 'If you fall,' he had said, 'you'll get nothing to eat for three days!'

'And I didn't fall.' His voice was grave suddenly '. . . That's how you train a horseman!'

My father let out a little whistle of admiration. The conversation returned to Dédé Wildmer.

'I don't understand how that little runt has such success with women,' Marcheret said.

'Oh I do,' Sylviane Quimphe smirked, 'I find him *very* attractive!'

'I could tell you a thing or two,' Marcheret replied nastily. 'It appears Wildmer's developed a taste for "coke" . . .'

A banal conversation. Wasted words. Lifeless characters. Yet there I stood with my ghosts, and, if I closed my eyes, I can still picture the old woman in a white apron who came to tell us that dinner was served.

'Why don't we eat out on the veranda,' suggested Sylviane Quimphe. 'It's such a lovely evening . . .'

Marcheret would have preferred to dine by candlelight, himself, but eventually accepted that 'the purple glow of twilight has its charm'. Murraille poured the drinks. I gathered it was a distinguished vintage.

'First-rate!' exclaimed Marcheret, smacking his lips, a gesture my father echoed.

I had been seated between Murraille and Sylviane Quimphe, who asked whether I was on holiday.

'I've seen you at the Clos-Foucré.'

'I've seen you there, too.'

'In fact I think we have adjoining rooms.'

And she gave me a curious look.

'M. Alexandre is very impressed by my magazine,' Murraille said.

'You don't say!' Marcheret was amazed. 'Well, you're the only one. If you saw the anonymous letters Jean-Jean gets . . . The most recent one accuses him of being a pornographer and gangster!'

'I don't give a damn,' said Murraille. 'You know,' he went on, lowering his voice, 'the press have slandered me. I was even accused of taking bribes, before the war! Small men have always been jealous of me!'

He snarled the words, his face turning puce. Dessert was being served.

'And what do you do with yourself?' Sylviane Quimphe asked.

'Novelist,' I said briefly.

I was regretting introducing myself to Murraille in this curious guise.

'You write novels?'

'You write novels?' echoed my father.

It was the first time he had spoken to me since we sat down to dinner.

'Yes. So what do you do?'

He stared at me wide-eyed.

'Me?'

'Are you here . . . on holiday?' I asked politely.

He looked at me like a hunted animal.

'Monsieur Deyckecaire,' Murraille said, wagging a finger at my father, 'lives in a charming property close by. It's called "The Priory".'

'Yes . . . "The Priory",' said my father.

'Much more imposing than the "Villa Mektoub". Can you believe, there's even a chapel in the grounds?'

'Chalva is a god-fearing man!' Marcheret said.

My father spluttered with laughter.

'Isn't that so, Chalva?' Marcheret insisted. 'When are we going to see you in a cassock?'

'Unfortunately,' Murraille told me, 'our friend Deyckecaire is like us. His business keeps him in Paris.'

'What line of business?' I ventured.

'Nothing of interest,' said my father.

'Come, come!' said Marcheret, 'I'm sure M. Alexandre would love to hear all about your shady financial dealings! Did you know that Chalva . . .' his tone was mocking now ' . . . is a really sharp operator. He could teach Sir Basil Zaharoff a thing or two!'

'Don't believe a word he says,' muttered my father.

'I find you too, *too* mysterious, Chalva,' said Sylviane Quimphe, clapping her hands together.

He took out a large handkerchief and mopped his forehead, and I suddenly remember that this is one of his favourite tics. He falls silent. As do I. The light is failing. Over there the other three are talking in hushed voices. I think Marcheret is saying to Murraille:

'I had a phone call from your daughter. What the fuck is she doing in Paris?'

Murraille is shocked by such coarse language. A Marcheret, a d'Eu, talking like that!

'If this carries on,' the other says, 'I shall break off the engagement!'

'Tut-tut . . .' Murraille says, 'that would be a grave error.'

Sylviane breaks the ensuing silence to tell me about a man name Eddy Pagnon, about how, when they were in a night-club together, he had waved a revolver at the terrified guests. Eddy Pagnon . . . Another name that seems naggingly familiar. A celebrity? I don't know, but I like the idea of this man who draws his revolver to threaten shadows.

My father had wandered over and was leaning on the balustrade of the veranda railing and I went up to him. He had lit a cigar, which he smoked distractedly. After a few minutes, he began blowing smoke rings. Behind us, the others went on whispering, they seemed to have forgotten us. He, too, ignored my presence despite the fact that several times I cleared my throat, and so we stood there for a long time, my father crafting smoke rings and I admiring their perfection.

We retired to the drawing-room, taking the French windows that led off the veranda. It was a large room furnished in colonial style. On the far wall, a wallpaper in delicate shades showed (Murraille explained to me later) a scene from *Paul et Virginie*. A rocking-chair, small tables, and cane armchairs. Pouffes here and there. (Marcheret, I learned, had brought them back from Bouss-Bir when he left the Legion.) Three Chinese lanterns hanging from the ceiling spread a wavering light. On a whatnot, I saw some opium pipes . . . The whole weird and faded collection was reminiscent of Tonkin, of the plantations of South Carolina, the French concession of Shanghai or Lyautey's Morocco, and I clearly failed to conceal my surprise because Murraille, in an embarrassed voice, said: 'Guy chose the furnishings.' I sat down, keeping in the background. Sitting around a tray of liqueurs, they were talking in low voices. The uneasiness I had felt since the beginning of the evening increased and I wondered whether it might be better if I left at once. But I was completely unable to move, as in a nightmare when you try to run from a looming danger and your legs refuse to function. All through dinner, the half-light had given their words, gestures, faces a hazy, unreal character; and now, in the mean glow cast by the drawing-room lamps, everything became even more indistinct. I thought my uneasiness was that of a man groping in the dark, fumbling vainly for a light-switch. Suddenly I shook with nervous laughter, which the others – luckily – didn't notice. They continued their whispered conversation, of which I couldn't hear a word. They were dressed in the normal outfits of well-heeled Parisians down for a few days in the country. Murraille wore a tweed jacket; Marcheret a sweater – cashmere, no doubt – in a choice shade of brown; my father a grey-flannel suit. Their collars were open to reveal immaculately knotted silk cravats. Sylviane Quimphe's riding-breeches added a note of sporting elegance to the whole.

But it was all glaringly at odds with this room where one expected to see people in linen suits and pith helmets.

'You're all alone?' Murraille asked me. 'It's my fault. I'm a terrible host.'

'My dear Monsieur Alexandre, you haven't tried this excellent brandy yet.' And Marcheret handed me a glass with a peremptory gesture. 'Drink up!'

I forced it down, my stomach heaving.

'Do you like the room?' he asked. 'Exotic, isn't it? I'll show you my bedroom. I had a mosquito net installed.'

'Guy suffers from a nostalgia for the colonies,' Murraille said.

'Vile places,' said Marcheret. Dreamily: 'But if I was asked to, I'd re-enlist.'

He was silent, as though no one could possibly understand all that he'd like to say on the subject. My father nodded. There was a long, pregnant pause. Sylviane Quimphe stroked her boots absent-mindedly. Murraille followed with his eyes the flight of a butterfly which had alighted on one of the Chinese lanterns. My father had fallen into a state of prostration that worried me. His chin was almost on his chest, drops of sweat beaded on his fore-head. I wished that a 'boy' could come with shuffling steps to clear the table and extinguish the lights.

Marcheret put a record on the gramophone. A sweet melody. I think it was called 'Soir de septembre'.

'Do you dance?' Sylviane Quimphe asked me.

She didn't wait for an answer, and in an instant we're dancing. My head is spinning. Every time I wheel and turn, I see my father.

'You ought to ride,' she says. 'If you like, I'll take you to the stables tomorrow.'

Had he dozed off? I hadn't forgotten that he often closed his eyes, but that it was only pretence.

'You'll see, it's so wonderful, taking long rides in the forest!'

He had put on a lot of weight in ten years. I'd never seen his complexion so livid.

'Are you a friend of Jean's?' she asked me.

'Not yet, but I hope to be.'

She seemed surprised by this reply.

'And I hope that we'll be friends, you and I,' I added.

'Of course. You're so charming.'

'Do you know this . . . Baron Deyckecaire?'

'Not very well.'

'What does he do, exactly?'

'I don't know; you really should ask Jean.'

'I find him rather odd, myself.'

'Oh, he's probably a black marketeer . . .'

At midnight, Murraille wanted to hear the last news bulletin. The newsreader's voice was even more strident than usual. After announcing the news briefly, he gave forth a kind of commentary on a hysterical note. I imagined him behind his mike: sickly, in black tie and shirtsleeves. He finished with: 'Goodnight to you all.'

'Thanks,' said Marcheret.

Murraille led me aside. He rubbed the side of his nose, put his hand on my shoulder.

'Look, what do you think . . . I've just had an idea . . . How would you like to contribute to the magazine?'

'Really?'

I had stuttered a little and the result was ridiculous: Re-re-really? . . .

'Yes, I'd very much like to have a boy like you working on *C'est la vie*. Assuming you don't think journalism beneath you?'

'Not at all!'

He hesitated, then in a more friendly tone:

'I don't want to make things awkward for you, in view of the rather . . . *singular* . . . nature of my magazine . . .'

'I'm not afraid to get my hands dirty.'

'That's very courageous of you.'

'But what would you want me to write?'

'Oh, whatever you like: a story, a topical piece, an article of the "Seen & Heard" variety. Take your time.'

These last few words he spoke with a curious insistence, looking me straight in the eye.

'All right?' He smiled. 'So you're willing to get your hands dirty?'

'Why not?'

We rejoined the others. Marcheret and Sylviane Quimphe were talking about a night-club which had opened in the Rue Jean-Mermoz. My father, who had joined in the conversation, said he liked the American bar in the Avenue de Wagram, the one run by a former racing cyclist.

'You mean the Rayon d'Or?' Marcheret asked.

'No, it's called the Fairyland,' said my father.

'You're wrong, Fat Man! The Fairyland is in Rue Fontaine!'

'I don't think so . . .' said my father.

'47 Rue Fontaine. Shall we go and check?'

'You're right, Guy,' sighed my father. 'You're right . . .'

'Do you know the Château-Bagatelle?' Sylviane Quimphe asked. 'I hear it's very amusing.'

'Rue de Clichy?' my father wanted to know.

'No, no!' Marcheret cried. 'Rue Magellan! You're confusing it with Marcel Dieu-donné. You always get everything mixed up! Last time we were supposed to meet at L'Écrin on the Rue Joubert, Monsieur here waited for us until midnight at Cesare Leone on the Rue de Hanovre. Isn't that right, Jean?'

'It was hardly the end of the world,' grunted Murraille.

For a quarter of an hour, they reeled off the names of bars and cabaret clubs as though Paris, France, the universe itself, were a red-light district, a vast al fresco brothel.

'What about you, Monsieur Alexandre, do you go out a lot?'

'No.'

'Well then, my boy, we shall introduce you to the "heady pleasures of Parisian nightlife".'

They went on drinking, talking of other clubs some of whose names dazzled me: L'Armorial, Czardas, Honolulu, Schubert, Gipsy's, Monico, L'Athénien, Melody's, Badinage. They were all talking volubly as though they would never stop. Sylviane Quimphe unbuttoned her blouse, and the faces of my father, Marcheret and Murraille flushed an unsettling crimson hue. I dimly recognised a few more names: Le Triolet, Monte-Cristo, Capurro's, Valencia. My mind was reeling. In the colonies – I thought – the evenings must drag on interminably like this. Neurasthenic settlers mulling over their memories and trying to fight back the fear that suddenly grips them, that they will die at the next monsoon.

My father got up. He said he was tired and had some work to finish that night.

'Are you planning to become a counterfeiter, Chalva?' asked Marcheret, his voice slurred. 'Don't you think, Monsieur Alexandre, that he's got the face of a forger?'

'Don't listen to him,' my father said. He shook hands with Murraille.

'Don't worry,' he murmured to him. 'I'll take care of all that.'

'I'm relying on you, Chalva.'

When he came up to say goodbye to me, I said:

'I must go, too. We could walk part of the way together.'

'I'd be delighted.'

'Must you go so soon?' Sylviane Quimphe asked me.

'If I were you,' Marcheret quipped, wagging a finger to my father, 'I wouldn't trust him!'

Murraille walked us out on to the veranda.

'I look forward to your article,' he said. 'Be bold!'

We walked in silence. He seemed surprised when I turned up the Chemin du Bornage with him rather than going straight on, to the *auberge*. He gave me a furtive glance. Did he recognize me? I wanted to ask him outright, but I remembered how skilled he was at dodging awkward questions. Hadn't he told me himself one day: 'I could make a dozen prosecutors throw in the towel'? We passed beneath a street lamp. A few metres farther on, we found ourselves once more in darkness. The only houses I could see looked derelict. The wind rustled in the leaves. Perhaps in the intervening decade he had forgotten that I ever existed. All the plotting and scheming I had done just so that I could walk next to this man . . . I thought of the drawing-room of the 'Villa Mektoub', of the faces of Murraille, Marcheret, and Sylviane

Quimphe, of Maud Gallas behind the bar, and Grève crossing the garden . . . Every gesture, every word, the moments of panic, the long vigils, the worry during these interminable days. I felt an urge to throw up . . . I had to stop to catch my breath. He turned to me. To his left, another streetlight shrouded him in pale light. He stood motionless, petrified, and I had to stop myself reaching out to touch him, to reassure myself that this was not a dream. As I walked on and I thought back to the walks we used to take in Paris long ago. We would stroll side by side, as we were tonight. In fact in the time we had known each other, this was all we had ever done. Walked, without either of us breaking the silence. It was no different now. After a bend in the path, we came to the gate of the 'Priory'. I said softly: 'Beautiful night, isn't it?' He replied abstractedly: 'Yes, a lovely night.' We were a few yards from the gate and I was waiting for the moment when he would shake hands and take his leave. Then I would watch him disappear into the darkness and stand there, in the middle of the road, in the bewildered state of a man who may just have let slip the chance of a lifetime.

'Well,' he said, 'this is where I live.'

He nodded shyly towards the house which was just visible at the end of the drive. The roof shimmered softly with moonlight.

'Oh? So this is it?'

'Yes.'

An awkwardness between us. He had probably been trying to hint that we should say goodnight, but saw that I was hesitant.

'It looks like a beautiful house,' I said, in a confident tone.

'A lovely house, yes.'

I detected a slight edginess in his voice.

'Did you buy it recently?'

'Yes. I mean no!' He stammered. He was leaning against the gate and didn't move.

'So you're renting the place?'

He tried to catch my eye, which I noticed with surprise. He never looked directly at people.

'Yes, I'm renting it.'

The words were barely audible.

'You probably think I'm being terribly nosy?'

'Not at all, monsieur.'

He gave a faint smile, more a tremor of the lips, as though afraid of being hit, and I pitied him. This feeling I had always experienced with regard to him, which caused a burning pain in my gut.

'Your friends seem charming,' I said. 'I had a lovely evening.'

'I'm glad.'

This time, he held out his hand.

'I must go in and work.'

'What at?'

'Nothing very interesting. Accounting.'

'Good luck,' I murmured. 'I hope I'll run into you again soon.'

'It would be a pleasure.'

As he opened the gate, I felt a sudden panic: should I tap him on the shoulder, and tell him every detail of the pains I had taken to find him? What good would it do? He trudged up the driveway slowly as though completely exhausted. For a long moment, he stood at the top of the steps. From a distance, his figure looked indistinct. Did it belong to a man or to one of those monstrous creatures who loom over you in feverish dreams?

Did he wonder what I was doing there, standing on the other side of the gate?

Eventually, thanks to dogged persistence, I got to know them better. It being July, work didn't keep them in Paris and they 'made the most' of the country (as Murraille put it). All the time I spent with them, I listened to them talking, ever meek and attentive. On scraps of paper, I jotted down the information I gleaned. I know the life stories of these shadows is of no great interest to anyone, but if I didn't write it down, no one else would do it. It is my duty, since I knew them, to drag them – if only for an instant – from the darkness. It is a duty, but for me it is also a necessary thing.

Murraille. At a young age, he started hanging out at the café Brabant with a group of journalists from *Le Matin*. They persuaded him to get into the business. Which he did. At twenty, general dogsbody, then secretary to a man who published a scandal sheet he used to blackmail victims. His motto was: 'Never threaten; only coerce.' Murraille was sent to the victims' homes to collect the envelopes. He remembered the frosty welcome. But there were some who greeted him with obsequious politeness, begging him to intercede with his editor, to ask him to be less demanding. These were the ones who had 'every reason to feel guilty'. After a while, he was promoted to sub-editor, but the articles he was called on to write were of a terrifying monotony, and they all began with: 'We hear from a reliable source, that Monsieur X . . .' or: 'How is it that Monsieur Y . . .' or 'Can it be true that Monsieur Z . . .' There followed 'revelations' that, at first, Murraille felt ashamed to be spreading. His editor suggested he always end with a little moral maxim such as: 'The wicked must be punished', or by what he called 'a hopeful note': 'We hold out hope that Monsieur X . . . (or Monsieur Y . . .) will find his way back to the straight and narrow. We feel sure that he will, because, as the evangelist says "each man in his darkness goes towards the light",' or some such. Murraille felt a brief twinge of conscience every month when he collected his salary. Besides, the offices of 30 *bis* Rue de Gramont – the peeling wallpaper, the dilapidated furniture, the meagre lighting – were conducive to depression. It was all far from cheering for a young man his age. If he spent three years there, it was only because the perks were excellent. His *patron* was generous and gave Murraille a quarter of the proceeds. The same editor (apparently, a dead ringer for Raymond Poincaré) was not without a sensitive streak. He had bouts of black depression when he would confide to Murraille that he had become a blackmailer because he was disillusioned by his fellow man. He had thought they were good – but had quickly realised his mistake; so he had decided to tirelessly condemn their vile deeds. And to make them pay. One evening, in a restaurant, he died of a heart attack. His last words were: 'If you only knew . . . !' Murraille was twenty-five. These were difficult times for him. He worked as film and music-hall critic for several second-rate papers.

He quickly developed an appalling reputation in the news-paper world, where he was currently regarded as a 'rotten apple'. Though this saddened him, his laziness and his taste for easy living made it impossible for him to change. He had a permanent fear of being short of money, the very prospect threw him into a state of panic. At times like this, he was capable of anything, like an addict desperate for a fix.

When I met him, his star was on the rise. He was editor of his own magazine. 'Troubled times' had made it possible for him to realise his dream. He had exploited the chaos and the murk. He felt perfectly at home in this world which seemed hell bent on destruction. I often wondered how a man who looked so distin-guished (everyone who met him will tell you about his unaffected elegance, his frankness) could be so utterly devoid of scruples. There was one thing I liked a lot about him: he never deluded himself. A friend from his old regiment had once accidentally shot him while cleaning his gun; the bullet had missed his heart by inches. I often heard him say: 'When I'm condemned to death and they order a firing squad to put twelve bullets in me, they can save a bullet.'

Marcheret was originally from the Quartier des Ternes. His mother, a colonel's widow, had done her best to bring him up correctly. She felt old before her time, and threatened by the outside world. She had hoped her son would go into the church. There, at least, he might be safe. But Marcheret, from the age of fifteen, had only one idea: to get away from their dingy apartment on the Rue Saussier-le-Roi, where the photograph of Maréchal Lyautey on the wall gently watched over him. (The photograph even bore an inscription: 'To Colonel de Marcheret. With fond wishes, Lyautey.') All too soon, his mother had genuine cause for concern: he was lazy and neglected his studies. He was expelled from the Lycée Chaptal for fracturing another pupil's skull. Frequented the cafés and the fleshpots of Paris. Played billiards and poker into the early hours. Needed money constantly. She never reproached him. Her son was not to blame, but the others, the bad boys, the communists, the Jews. How she longed for him to stay safely in his room . . . One night, Marcheret was strolling along the Avenue de Wagram. He felt the familiar surge of frustration twenty-year-olds feel when they don't know what to do with their life. The guilt he felt at causing his mother grief was mingled with anger at the fact he had only fifty francs in his pocket . . . Things could not carry on like this. He wandered into a cinema showing *Le Grand Jeu* with Pierre-Richard Willm. The story of a young man who sets off to join the Foreign Legion. It was as though Marcheret was seeing himself up on the screen. He sat through two screenings, enthralled by the desert, the Arabic town, the uniforms. At 6 p.m. he walked into the nearest café as Legionnaire Guy de Marcheret and ordered a *blanc-cassis*. Then a second. He signed up the next day.

In Morocco, two years later, he heard about his mother's death. She had never recovered from his leaving. Hardly had he confided his grief to one of his barrack-room mates, a Georgian by the name of Odicharvi, than the man dragged him off to a Bouss-Bir establishment that was part brothel, part cafe. At the end of the evening, his friend had the marvellous idea of raising a glass, pointing towards Marcheret and shouting: 'Let's drink to the orphan!' He was right. Marcheret had always been an orphan. And in enlisting in the Legion, he had hoped to find his father. But he had found only loneliness, sand and the mirages of the desert.

He returned to France with a parrot and a dose of malaria. 'What pisses me off about things like that,' he told me, 'is that no one comes to meet you at the station.' He felt out of place. He was no longer accustomed to the bright lights and the bustle. He was terrified of crossing the street, and in a blind panic on the Place de l'Opéra, asked a policeman to take his hand and lead him across. Eventually he was lucky enough to meet another former Legionnaire who ran a bar on the Rue d'Armaille. They swapped stories. The bar owner took him in, fed him, adopted the parrot, and in time Marcheret began to enjoy life again. Women found him attractive. This was in an era – so distant now – when being a Legionnaire made women's hearts flutter. A Hungarian countess, the widow of a wealthy industrialist, a dancer at the Tabarin –

in fact 'blondes' as Marcheret put it — fell for the charms of this sentimental soldier, who turned a healthy profit from the swooning sighs. Sometimes he would show up in night clubs in his old uniform. He was the life and soul of the party.

Maud Gallas. I don't have much information on her. She tried her hand as a singer — short-lived. Marcheret told me she had managed a nightclub near the Plaine Monceau that catered exclusively to female clients. Murraille even claimed that having been charged with receiving stolen goods, she had become persona non grata in *Département de la Seine*. One of her friends had bought the Clos-Foucré from the Beausires and, thanks to her wealthy patron, she now managed the *auberge*.

Annie Murraille was twenty-two. A diaphanous blonde. Was she really Jean Murraille's niece? This was something I was never able to confirm. She wanted to be a great movie actress, she dreamed of seeing 'her name in lights'. Having landed a few minor roles, she played the lead in *Nuit de rafles*, a film completely forgotten these days. I assumed she got engaged to Marcheret because he was Murraille's best friend. She had an enormous affection for her uncle (was he really her uncle?). If there are those who still remember Annie Murraille, they think of her as an unfortunate but poignant young actress . . . She wanted to make the most of her life . . .

Sylviane Quimphe I knew rather better. She came from a humble background. Her father worked as nightwatchman at the old Samson factory. She spent her whole adolescence in an area bounded to the north by the Avenue Daumesnil, to the south by the

Quai de la Rapée and the Quai de Bercy. It was not the sort of area that attracted tourists. At times, it feels as though you are in the countryside, and walking along the Seine, you feel you have discovering a disused port. The elevated métro line that crosses the Pont de Bercy and the crumbling morgue buildings add to the terrible desolation of the place. But there is one magical spot in this bleak landscape that inexorably attracts dreamers: the Gare de Lyon. It was here that Sylviane Quimphe's wanderings always took her. At sixteen, she would explore every nook and corner. Especially the main-line departure platforms. The words '*Compagnie internationale des wagons-lits*' brought colour to her cheeks.

She trudged home to the Rue Corbineau, reciting the names of towns she would never see. Bordighera-Rimini-Vienna-Istanbul. Outside her house was a little park, where, as the dark drew in, all the tedium and desolate charm of the 12th *arrondissement* was distilled. She would sit on a bench. Why had she not simply boarded some train, any train? She decided not to go home. Her father was working all night. The coast was clear.

From the Avenue Daumesnil, she glided towards the labyrinth of streets called the 'Chinese Quarter' (does it still exist today? A colony of Asians had set up shabby bars, small restaurants and even – it was said – a number of opium dens). The human dreck who prowl around train stations tramped through this seedy area as through a swamp. Here, she found what she had been looking for: a former employee of Thomas Cook with a silver tongue and a handsome body, living from hand to mouth doing shady deals. He immediately saw possibilities for a young girl like Sylviane. She longed to travel? That could be arranged. As it happened, his cousin worked as a ticket inspector aboard *les Wagons-lits*. The two men presented Sylviane a Paris–Milan return ticket. But just as the train pulled out, they also introduced her to a fat red-faced musician whose various whims she had to satisfy on the outward trip. The return journey, she made in the company of a Belgian industrialist. This peripatetic prostitution proved very lucrative since the cousins played their role as pimps magnificently. The fact that one of them was employed by the *Wagons-Lits* made matters easier: he could seek out 'clients' during the journey and Sylviane Quimphe remembered a Paris–Zurich trip during which she entertained eight men in succession in her single sleeper carriage. She had not yet turned twenty. But clearly miracles can happen. In the corridor of a train, between Basle and La Chaux-de-Fonds, she met Jean-Roger Hatmer. This sad-faced young man belonged to a family which had made its fortunes in the sugar and the textile trade. He had just come into a large inheritance and did not know what to do with it. Or with his life, for that matter. Sylviane Quimphe became his *raison d'etre* and he smothered her with polite passion. Not once during the four months of their life together did he take a liberty with her. Every Sunday, he gave her a briefcase stuffed full of jewels and banknotes, saying in hushed tones: 'Just to tide you over.' He hoped that, later, she would 'want for nothing'. Hatmer, who dressed in black and wore steel-rimmed glasses, had the discretion, modesty and benevolence that one sometimes encounters in elderly secretaries. He was very keen on butterflies and tried to share his passion with Sylviane Quimphe, but quickly realised the subject bored her. One day, he left her a note: 'THEY are going to make me appear before a board of guardians and probably have me confined to an asylum. We can't see each other anymore. There is still a small Tintoretto hanging on the left-hand wall of the living room. Take it. And sell it. *Just to tide you over.*' She never heard from him again. Thanks to this far-sighted young man, she had been freed of all financial worries for the rest of her life. She had many other adventures, but suddenly I find I haven't got the heart.

Murraille, Marcheret, Maud Gallas, Sylviane Quimphe . . . I take no pleasure in setting down their life stories. Nor am I doing it for the sake of the story, having no imagination. I focus on these misfits, these outsiders, so that, through them, I can catch the fleeting image of my father. About him, I know almost nothing. But I will think something up.

I met him for the first time when I was seventeen. The vice-principal of the Collège Sainte-Antoine in Bordeaux came to tell me that someone was waiting for me in the visitor's room. When he saw me, this stranger with swarthy skin wearing a dark-grey flannel suit, got to his feet.

'I'm your *papa* . . .'

We met again outside, on a July afternoon at the end of the school year.

'I hear you passed your baccalauréat.'

He was smiling at me. I gave a last look at the yellow walls of the school, where I had mouldered for the past eight years.

If I delve farther back into my memories, what do I see? A grey-haired old woman to whom he had entrusted me. She had been a coat-check girl before the war at Frolic's (a bar on the Rue de Grammont) before retiring to Libourne. It was there, in her house, that I grew up.

Then boarding school, in Bordeaux.

It is raining. My father and I are walking side by side, without speaking, as far as the Quai des Chartrons to the family I stayed with outside term time, the Pessacs. (One of those patrician families in the wine and cognac trade I fondly hope will soon be ruined.) The afternoons spent at their house were among the bleakest in my life, so the less said about them the better.

We climb the monumental steps. The maid opens the front door. I rush to the box-room where I had asked permission to leave a suitcase stuffed with books (novels by Bourget, Marcel Prevost, and Duvernois, strictly forbidden at school). Suddenly I hear Monsieur Pessac's peremptory voice: 'What are you doing here?' He is talking to my father. Seeing me with the suitcase in hand, he scowls: 'You're leaving? But who is this gentleman?' I hesitate, then manage to blurt out: 'MY FATHER!' Obviously, he doesn't believe me. Suspiciously: 'Unless my eyes deceive me, you were sneaking away like a thief?' This sentence is burned into my memory, because it was true that we looked just like a couple of thieves caught red-handed. Confronted by this little man with his moustache and his brown smoking jacket, my father remained silent and chewed his cigar to give the impression he was calm. For my part, I myself think of only one thing: how to get out of there as soon as possible. Monsieur Pessac had turned to my father and was studying him curiously. At that moment, his wife appeared. Followed by his daughter and his eldest son. They stood, staring at us in silence leaving me feeling as though we had broken into this bourgeois mansion. When my father let ash from his cigar fall on the carpet, I noticed their expressions of amused contempt. The girl exploded with laughter. Her brother, a spotty youth who adopted 'English style' (much in vogue in Bordeaux), piped up in a shrill voice: 'Perhaps Monsieur might like an ashtray? . . .' 'Really, Francois-Marie,' murmured Mme Pessac. 'Don't be so uncouth.' As she said this last word she looked point-edly at my father, as if to make it clear that the adjective applied to him. M. Pessac maintained a disdainful equanimity. I think what had made them so unfriendly was my father's pale green shirt. Faced with the blatant hostility of these four people, my father looked like a butterfly caught in a net. He fumbled with his cigar, not knowing where to stub it out. He backed towards the door. The others did not move, shamelessly revelling in his embarrassment. I suddenly felt a kind of tenderness for this man I barely knew, and went over to him and said in a loud voice: 'Let me give you a hug, monsieur.' And, having done so, I took the cigar from his hand and painstakingly crushed it on the inlaid hall table Mme Pessac so loved. I tugged my father's sleeve.

'That's enough, now,' I said. 'Let's go.'

We went to the Hôtel Splendid to collect his bags. A taxi took us to the Gare Saint-Jean. In the train, we struck up a conversation of sorts. He explained that 'business' had made it impossible for him to get in touch, but that from now on we would live together in Paris and would never be apart again. I stammered a few words of thanks. 'I suppose . . . ,' he said point-blank, 'I suppose you must have been very unhappy . . .' He suggested that I not call him 'monsieur'. An hour passed in utter silence and I declined his invitation to go with him to the restaurant-car. I made the most of his absence to rummage through the black briefcase he had left on the seat. There was nothing in it but a Nansen passport. At least he and I shared the same surname. He had two Christian names: Chalva, Henri. He had been born in Alexandria, at a time – I imagine – when the city still shimmered with its own particular radiance.

When he came back to the compartment, he handed me an almond cake – a gesture which I found touching – and asked if I was really a *'bachelier'* (he pronounced *'bachelier'* in a rather affected way, as though the very idea of passing the baccalauréat inspired in him a fearful respect). When I told him I was, he nodded gravely. I ventured to ask a few questions: why had he come to Bordeaux to fetch me? How had he tracked me down? His only answers were dismissive gestures and formulaic phrases: 'I'll explain later . . .', 'You'll see . . .', 'Well, you know, life . . .' After which he sighed and looked thoughtful.

Paris–Austerlitz. He hesitated a moment before giving the taxi driver his address. (Later we would find ourselves being driven along Quai de Grenelle when in fact we were living on the Boulevard Kellermann. We moved so often that we got confused and only belatedly noticed our mistake.) At the time, his address was: Square Villaret-de-Joyeuse. I imagined the square to be a little park where birdsong mingled with the murmur of fountains. No. A cul-de-sac, with opulent houses on either side. His apartment was on the top floor and the windows overlooking the street had curious, small circular windows. Three low-ceilinged rooms. A large table and two shabby leather armchairs made up the furniture in the 'living room'. The walls were papered in a pink, imitation 'Toile de Jouy' pattern. A large bronze ceiling light (I am not entirely sure of this description: I tend to confuse the apartment on the Square Villaret-de-Joyeuse with the one on the Avenue Félix-Faure, which we sublet from a retired couple. Both had the same musty smell). My father nodded to the smallest room. A mattress on a bare floor. 'Sorry about the lack of comfort,' he said. 'But don't worry, we won't be staying here long. Sleep well.' I heard him pacing the floor for hours. So began our life together.

To begin with, he treated me with a politeness, a deference that a son rarely expects from his father. Whenever he spoke to me, I felt as though he was carefully choosing his words, but the result was terrible. He resorted to increasingly convoluted phrases and circumlocutions, and seemed to be constantly apologising or anticipating some reproach. He brought me breakfast in bed with a ceremonious manner which jarred with our surroundings: the wallpaper in my room was peeling in places, a bare bulb hung from the ceiling, and when he pulled the curtains, the curtain rail would fall down. One day, he accidently referred to me by my Christian name and was mortally embarrassed. What had I done to earn such respect? I discovered it was the fact I was a '*bachelier*', when he personally wrote to the school in Bordeaux to ask them to send the certificate proving I had got my baccalauréat. When it arrived, he had it framed, and hung it between the two 'windows' in the 'living room'. I noticed that he kept a copy in his wallet. Once, on one of our nightly wanderings, he presented the document to two policemen who had asked for our identity papers, and seeing they were puzzled by his Nansen passport, he told them five or six times that 'his son was a *bachelier* . . .' After supper (my father often prepared something he called rice *à l'égyptienne*), he would light a cigar, give an occasional, worried, glance at my diploma, then slowly sink into despair. His 'business', he told me, was causing him a lot of trouble. Having always been a fight, having known the 'harsh realities of life' at a very early age, he now felt 'tired', and the way he said: 'I've lost heart . . .' moved me deeply. Then, he would look up: 'But you've got your whole life ahead of you!' I would nod, politely . . . 'Especially now you've got your BACCA-LAURÉAT . . . If only I'd had the chance . . .' the words died in his throat, 'the baccalauréat is really something . . .' I can still hear this little phrase. And it still moves me, like a forgotten melody.

At least a week passed without my knowing anything about his 'business'. I would hear him leave early in the morning, and he only got back in time to prepare supper. From a black oilcloth bag, he would unpack the provisions – peppers, rice, spices, mutton, lard, dried fruit, semolina – tie an apron round his waist and, having taken off his rings, he would fry up the contents of the bag in a pan. Then he would sit facing the diploma, call me to dinner and we would eat.

Finally, one Thursday afternoon, he invited me to go with him. He was going to sell a 'very rare' stamp, and the prospect made him agitated. We walked along the Avenue de la Grande-Armée. Then down the Champs-Élysées. Several times he showed me the stamp (which he kept wrapped in cellophane). It was, according to him, a 'unique' example from Kuwait, depicting 'the Emir Rachid and divers views'. We arrived at the Carré Marigny. The stamp market was held in the space between the théâtre de Marigny and the Avenue Gabriel. (Does it still exist today?) People huddled in little groups, speaking in low voices, opening cases, poring over their contents, leafing through catalogues, brandishing magnifying glasses and tweezers. This furtive flurry of activity, these men who looked like surgeons or conspirators made me feel anxious. My father quickly found himself surrounded by a dense crowd. A dozen men were haranguing him. Arguing over whether the stamp was authentic. My father, taken aback by the questions fired from all sides, could not get a word in edgeways. How was it that his 'Emir Rachid' was olive-coloured and not carmine? Was it really thirteen and one quarter perforation? Did it have an 'overprint'? Fragments of silk thread? Did it not belong to a series known as 'assorted views'? Had he checked for a 'thin'? Their tone grew acrimonious. My father was called a 'swindler' and 'crook'. He was accused of trying to 'flog some piece of rubbish that wasn't even documented in the Champion catalogue'. One of the lunatics grabbed him by the collar and slapped him hard across the face. Another punched him. They seemed about to lynch him for the sake of a stamp (which speaks volumes about the human soul), and so, unable to bear it any longer, I stepped in. Luckily, I had an umbrella. I distributed several blows at random, and making the most of the element of surprise, dragged father from this baying mob of philatelists. We ran as far as the Faubourg Saint-Honoré.

In the days which followed, my father, believing I had saved his life, explained in detail the kind of work he did, and suggested that I help him. His clients were twenty or so oddballs scattered over the whole of France whom he had contacted through various specialist magazines. They were fanatical collectors, obsessed by the most varied objects: old telephone directories, corsets, hookahs, postcards, chastity belts, phonographs, oxy-acetylene torches, Iowa Indian moccasins, ballroom slippers . . . He scoured Paris in search of such things, packed them up and sent them off to his contacts, having extorted vast sums from them in advance that bore no relation to the actual value of the goods. One of his clients would pay 100,000 francs apiece for pre-war Chaix railway timetables. Another had given him 300,000 francs on account, on condition that he had first refusal on all busts and effigies of Waldeck-Rousseau he might find . . . My father, eager to amass an even greater clientele among these lunatics, planned to persuade them to join a society – the 'League of French Collectors' – of which he would be appointed president and treasurer and would charge exorbitant subscription fees. The philatelists had bitterly disappointed him. He realized he couldn't use them. As collectors, they were cold-blooded, cunning, cynical, ruthless (it is hard to imagine the Machiavellianism, the viciousness of these apparently fastidious creatures). What crimes have been committed for a 'Sierra Leone, yellow-brown with overprint' or a 'Japan, horizontal perforations'. He was not about to repeat his unfortunate expedition to the Carré Marigny, an episode that had left his pride deeply wounded. At first he used me as a messenger. I tried to show some initiative by suggesting a market which he hadn't yet considered: bibliophiles. He liked the idea and gave me a free hand. Though I knew nothing about life yet, I had memorized Lanson's French Literature at school in Bordeaux. I knew every French writer, from the most trivial to the most obscure. What was the point of such recondite erudition if not to launch me into the book trade? I quickly discovered that it was very difficult to buy rare editions cheaply. What bargains I found were of poor quality: 'original editions' of Vautel, Fernand Gregh and Eugene Demolder . . . On a trip to the Passage Jouffroy, I bought a copy of *Matière et mémoire* for 3,50 francs. On the flyleaf, was a curious dedication from Bergson to Jean Jaurès: 'When will you stop calling me Miss?' Two experts formally identified the master's handwriting, and I sold on this curio to a collector for 100,000 francs.

Heartened by my initial success, I decided to pen a few spurious dedications myself, each highlighting some unexpected facet of the author. Those whose handwriting I could most easily copy, Charles Maurras and Maurice Barrès. I sold a Maurras for 500,000 francs, courtesy of this little sentence: 'For Léon Blum, as a token of my admiration. Why don't we have lunch? Life is so short . . . Maurras.' A copy of Barres's *Déracinés* fetched 700,000 francs. It was dedicated to Captain Dreyfus: 'Be brave, Alfred. Affectionately, Maurice.' But I soon discovered that what really fascinated my customers was the private lives of writers.

So my dedications became more salacious and prices rose accordingly. I favoured contemporary authors. As some of them are still alive, I will say no more for fear of litigation. All I can say is that they made me a lot of money.

Such was the nature of our shady deals. Business flourished because we were exploiting people who were not entirely sane. When I think back over our little schemes, I feel very bitter. I would have preferred to start my life in a less dubious fashion. But what else could you expect of a teenager left to his own devices in Paris? What else could the poor bastard do?

Though my father spent some of our capital buying shirts and ties of questionable taste, he also tried to increase it by dabbling in the stock market. I frequently saw him slump into an armchair with armfuls of share certificates . . . He would stack them in the halls of our successive apartments, check them, sort them, make an inventory. I eventually realized that the certificates had been issued by companies that were either bankrupt or had long since ceased to trade. He was convinced he could still use them, put them back on the market . . . 'When we're quoted on the Stock Exchange . . .' he would say with a mischievous look.

And I remember we bought a second-hand car, an old Talbot, in which we took night-time jaunts through Paris. Before setting out, we had a ritual of drawing lots. Twenty slips of paper were scattered over the rickety drawing-room table. We would choose one at random, and this would be our itinerary for the evening. Batignolles-Grenelle. Auteuil-Picpus. Passy-La Villette. Otherwise, we would cast off and set sail for one of those *quartiers* with mysterious names: Les Épinettes, la Maison-Blanche, Bel-Air, l'Amérique, la Glacière, Plaisance, la Petite-Pologne . . . I have only to set foot in certain secret parts of Paris for memories to erupt like sparks from a fire. The Place d'Italie, for example, was a favourite port of call on our trips . . . There was a café there, the Claire de Lune. Towards 1 a.m., all the flotsam from the music-hall would gather there: pre-war accordionists, white-haired tango dancers trying to recapture the languorous agility of their youth on that tiny stage, haggard old crones with too much make-up singing songs by Fréhel or Suzy Solidor. Desolate street entertainers entertained during the 'intermissions'. The orchestra consisted of Brylcreemed men in dinner jackets. It was one of my father's favourite places; he took great pleasure in watching these ghostly figures. I never understood why.

And let's not forget the illicit brothel at 73 Avenue Reille, on the edge of the Parc Montsouris. My father would gossip endlessly with the Madame, a blonde woman with a doll-like face. Like him, she was from Alexandria, and they would reminisce about the nights there, about Sidi Bishr, the Pastroudis Bar and various other places that have long since ceased to exist . . . We would often linger until dawn in this Egyptian enclave in the 14th *arrondissement*. But there were other places that called to us on our odysseys (or our escapes?). An all-night restaurant on the Boulevard Murat lost among blocks of flats. The place was always empty and, for some mysterious reason, a large photograph of Daniel-Rops hung on one of the walls. A pseudo 'American' bar, between Maillot and Champerret, the gathering point for a gang of bookies. And when we ventured as far as the extreme north of Paris – the region of docks and slaughterhouses – we would stop off at the Boeuf-Bleu, on the Place de Joinville, by the Canal de l'Ourcq. My father particularly liked this spot because it reminded him of the Saint-Andre district, in Antwerp, where he had lived long ago. We would go south-east to where the tree-lined streets lead to the Bois de Vincennes. We would stop by Chez Raimo on the Place Daumesnil, invariably open at this late hour. A gloomy 'patissier-glacier', of the sort you can still find in spa towns that no one – except us – seemed to know about. Other places come back to me, in waves. Our various addresses: 65 Boulevard Kellermann, with its view of the Gentilly cemetery; the apartment on the Rue du Regard where the previous tenant had left behind a musical-box that I sold for 30,000 francs. The bourgeois apartment building on the Avenue Félix-Faure where the concierge would always greet us with: 'Here come the Jews!' Or an evening spent in the run-down three-room flat on the Quai de Grenelle, near the Vélodrome d'Hiver. The electricity had been cut off. Leaning on the window-sill, we watched the comings and goings of the elevated métro. My father was wearing a tattered, patched smoking jacket. He point to the Citadelle de Passy, on the far bank of the Seine. In a tone that brooked no argument, he announced: 'One day we'll have a *hôtel particulier* near the Trocadéro!' In the meantime, he would arrange to meet me in the lobbies of grand hotels. He felt more important there, more likely to succeed in his great financial coups. He would sit there the whole afternoon. I don't know how many times I met him at the Majestic, the Continental, the Claridge, the Astoria. These places where people were constantly coming and going suited a restless and unstable spirit such as his.

Every morning, he would greet me in his 'office' on the Rue des Jardins-Saint-Paul. A vast room whose only furnishings were a wickerwork chair and an Empire desk. The parcels we had to send that day would be piled up round the walls. After logging them in an account book with the names and addresses of the addressees, we would have a 'work conference'. I would tell him about the book I intended to purchase, and the technical details of the dedications I planned to forge. The different inks, pens or fountain pens used for each author. We would check the accounts, study the *Courrier des collectionneurs*. Then we would take the parcels down to the Talbot and pack them on the back seat as best we could. This drudge work exhausted me.

My father would then make the rounds of the railway stations to dispatch the cargo. In the afternoon, he would visit his warehouse in the Quartier de Javel and from among the bric-a-brac, choose twenty or so pieces that might be of interest to our clients, ferry them to the Rue des Jardins-Saint-Paul and begin to parcel them up. After which he would restock with merchandise. We had to satisfy the demands of our clients as attentively as possible. These lunatics were not prepared to wait.

I would take a suitcase and head off on my own, to scout around until evening, in an area bounded by the Bastille, the Place de la République, the *grands boulevards*, the Avenue de l'Opéra and the Seine. These districts each have a particular peculiar charm. Saint-Paul, where I have dreamed of spending my old age. All I would need was a little shop, some small business. The Rue Pavée or the Rue du Roi-de-Sicile, that ghetto to which I would be inevitably drawn back one day. In the Temple district, I felt my bargain-hunting instincts come to the fore. In the Sentier, that exotic principality formed by the Place du Caire, the Rue du Nil, the Passage Ben-Aiad and the Rue d'Aboukir, I thought about my poor father. The first four *arrondissements* sub-divide into a tangled multitude of provinces whose unseen borders I eventually came to know. Beaubourg, Greneta, le Mail, la Pointe Sainte-Eustache, les Victoires . . . My last port of call was a bookshop called Le Petit-Mirioux in the Galerie Vivienne. I got there just as it was getting dark. I scoured the shelves, convinced that I would find what I was looking for. Mme Petit-Mirioux stocked literary works of the past hundred years. So many unjustly forgotten books and authors, we agreed regretfully. They had taken so much trouble for nothing . . . We consoled each other, she and I, reassuring ourselves there were still fans of Pierre Hamp or Jean-José Frappa and that sooner or later, the Fischer brothers would be rescued from oblivion and, on that comforting note, took leave of each other. The rest of the shops in the Galerie Vivienne seemed to have been closed for centuries. In the window of a music bookshop, three yellowing Offenbach scores. I sat down on my suitcase. Not a sound. Time had stood still at some point between the July Monarchy and the Second Empire. From the far end of the Galerie came the faint glow of the bookshop, and I could just make out the shadow of Mme Petit-Mirioux. How long would she remain at her post? Poor old sentinel.

Farther on, the deserted arcades of the Palais-Royal. People had played here, once. But no more. I walked through the gardens. A zone of silence and mellow half-light where the memories of dead years and broken promises tug at the heart. Place du Théâtre-Francais. The streetlights are dazzling. You are a diver coming up too quickly to the surface. I had arranged to meet 'papa' in a caravanserai on the Champs-Élysées. We would get into the Talbot, as we always did, and sail across Paris.

Before me was the Avenue de l'Opéra. It heralded other boulevards, other streets, that would later cast us to the four points of the compass. My heart beat a little faster. In the midst of so much uncertainty, my only landmarks, the only ground which did not shift beneath my feet, were the pavements and the junctions of this city where, in the end, I would probably find myself alone.

Now, though it grieves me, I must come to the 'distressing incident at the George V métro'. For several weeks my father had been fascinated by the Petite Ceinture, the disused railway-line that circles Paris. Was he planning to have it renovated by public subscription? Bank loans? Every Sunday, he would ask me to go with him to the outskirts of the city and we followed the path of the old railway-line on foot. The stations along the route were derelict or had been turned into warehouses. The tracks were overgrown with weeds. From time to time my father would stop to scribble a note or sketch something indecipherable in his notebook. What was he dreaming of? Was he waiting for a train that would never come?

On that Sunday, 17 June, we had followed the Petite Ceinture through the 12th *arrondissement*. Not without effort. Near the Rue de Montempoivre, the track joins those coming from Vincennes and we ended up getting confused. After three hours, emerging dazed from this labyrinth of metal, we decided to go home by métro. My father seemed disappointed with his afternoon. Usually when we returned from these expeditions, he was in excellent humour and would show me his notes. He was planning to compile a 'comprehensive' file on the Petite Ceinture – he explained – and offer it to the public authorities.

'We shall see what we shall see.'

What? I didn't dare ask. But, that Sunday evening, 17 June, his brash enthusiasm had melted away. Sitting in the carriage of the Vincennes-Neuilly métro, he ripped the pages from his notebook one by one, and tore them into minute scraps which he tossed like handfuls of confetti. He worked with the detachment of a sleepwalker and a painstaking fury I had never seen in him before. I tried to calm him. I told him that it was a great pity to destroy such an important work on a whim, that I had every confidence in his talents as an organizer. He fixed me with a glassy eye. We got out at the George V station. We were waiting on the platform. My father stood behind me, sulking. The station gradually filled, as if it were rush-hour. People were coming back from the cinema or from strolling along the Champs-Élysées. We were pressed against each other. I found myself at the front, on the edge of the platform. Impossible to draw back. I turned towards my father. His face was dripping with sweat. The roar of a train. Just as it came into sight, someone pushed me roughly in the back.

Next, I find myself lying on one of the station benches surrounded by a little group of busybodies. They are whispering. One bends down to tell me that I've had 'a narrow escape'. Another, in cap and uniform (a métro official perhaps) announces that he is going to 'call the police'. My father stands in the background. He coughs.

Two policemen help me to my feet. Holding me under the arms. We move through the station. People turn to stare. My father follows behind, diffidently. We get into the police van parked on the Avenue George V. The people on the terrace outside Fouquet's are enjoying the beautiful summer evening.

We sit next to each other. My father's head is bowed. The two policemen sit facing us but do not speak. We pull up outside the police station at 5 Rue Clement-Marot. Before going in, my father wavers. His lips nervously curl into a rictus smile.

The policemen exchange a few words with a tall thin man. The *commissaire*? He asks to see our papers. My father, with obvious reluctance, proffers his Nansen passport.

'Refugee?' asks the *commissaire* . . .

'I'm about to be naturalized,' my father mumbles. He must have prepared this reply in advance. 'But my son is French.' In a whisper: 'and a *bachelier* . . .'

The *commissaire* turns to me:

'So you nearly got run over by a train?' I say nothing. 'Lucky someone caught you or you'd be in a pretty state.'

Yes, someone had saved my life by catching me just in time, as I was about to fall. I have only a vague memory of those few seconds.

'So why is it,' the *commissaire* goes on, 'that you shouted out "MURDERER!" several times as you were carried to the bench?'

Then he turns to my father: 'Does your son suffer from persecution mania?'

He doesn't give him time to answer. He turns back to me and asks point-blank: 'Maybe someone behind pushed you? Think carefully . . . take all the time you need.'

A young man at the far end of the office was tapping away at a typewriter. The *commissaire* sat behind his desk and leafed through a file. My father and I sat waiting. I thought they had forgotten us, but at length the *commissaire* looked up and said to me:

'If you want to report the incident, don't hesitate. That's what I'm here for.'

From time to time the young man brought him a typewritten page which he corrected with a red pen. How long would they keep us there? The *commissaire* pointed towards my father.

'Political refugee or just refugee?'

'Just refugee.'

'Good,' said the *commissaire*.

Then he went back to his file.

Time passed. My father showed signs of nervousness. I think he was digging his nails into his palms. In fact he was at my mercy – and he knew it – otherwise why did he keep glancing at me worriedly? I had to face the facts: someone had pushed me so that I would fall on the tracks and be ripped to shreds by the train. And it was the man with the south-American appearance sitting beside me. The proof: I had felt his signet-ring pressing into my shoulder-blade.

As though he could read my mind, the *commissaire* asked casually:

'Do you get on well with your father?'

(Some policemen have the gift of clairvoyance. Like the inspector from the security branch of the police force who, when he retired, changed sex and offered 'psychic' readings under the name of 'Madame Dubail'.)

'We get on very well,' I replied.

'Are you sure?'

He asked the question wearily, and immediately began to yawn. I was convinced he already knew everything, but simply was not interested. A young man pushed under the métro by his father, he must have come across hundreds of similar cases. Routine work.

'I repeat, if you have something to say to me, say it now.'

But I knew that he was merely asking me out of politeness.

He turned on his desk lamp. The other officer continued to pound on his typewriter. He was probably rushing to finish the job. The tapping of the typewriter was lulling me to sleep, and I was finding it hard to keep my eyes open. To ward off sleep, I studied the police station carefully. A post-office calendar on the wall, and a photograph of the President of the Republic. Doumer? Mac-Mahon? Albert Lebrun? The typewriter was an old model. I decided that this Sunday 17 June would be an important day in my life and I turned imperceptibly towards my father. Great beads of sweat were running down his face. But he didn't look like a murderer.

The *commissaire* peers over the young man's shoulder to see where he's got to. He whispers some instructions. Three policemen suddenly appear. Perhaps they're going to take us to the cells. I couldn't care less. No. The *commissaire* looks me in the eye:

'Well? Nothing you want to say?'

My father gives a plaintive whimper.

'Very well, gentlemen, you may go . . .'

We walked blindly. I didn't dare ask him for an explanation. It was on the Place des Ternes, as I stared at the neon sign of the Brasserie Lorraine, that I said in as neutral a tone as possible:

'Basically, you tried to kill me . . .'

He didn't answer. I was afraid he would take fright, like a bird when you get too close.

'I don't hold it against you, you know.'

And nodding towards the terrace of the bar:

'Why don't we have a drink? This calls for a celebration!'

This last remark made him smile a little. When we reached the cafe table, he was careful not to sit facing me. His posture was the same as it had been in the police van: his shoulders hunched, his head bowed. I ordered a double bourbon for him, knowing how much he liked it, and a glass of champagne for myself. We raised our glasses. But our hearts weren't in it. After the unfortunate incident in the métro, I would have liked to set the record straight. It was impossible. He revisited with such inertia that I decided not to insist.

At the other tables, there were lively conversations. People were delighted at the mild weather. They felt relaxed. And happy to be alive. And I was seventeen years old, my father had tried to push me under a train, and no one cared.

We had a last drink on the Avenue Niel, in that strange bar, Petrissan's. An elderly man staggered in, sat down at our table and started talking to me about Wrangel's Fleet. From what I could gather, he had served with Wrangel. It must have brought back painful memories, because he started to sob. He didn't want us to leave. He clung to my arm. Maudlin and excitable, as Russians tend to be after midnight.

The three of us were walking down the street towards the Place des Ternes, my father a few yards ahead, as though ashamed to find himself in such miserable company. He quickened his pace and I saw him disappear into the métro. I thought that I would never see him again. In fact, I was convinced of it.

The old veteran gripped my arm, sobbed on my shoulder. We sat on a bench on the Avenue de Wagram. He was determined to recount in detail about the 'terrible ordeal' of the White Army, their flight towards Turkey. Eventually these heroes had washed up in Constantinople, in their ornate uniforms. What a terrible shame! General Baron Wrangel, apparently, was more than six foot six.

You haven't changed much. Just now, when you came into the Clos-Foucré, you shambled exactly as you did ten years ago. You sat down opposite me and I was about to order you a double bourbon, but I thought it would be out of place. Did you recognise me? It's impossible to tell with you. What would be the point of shaking your shoulders, bombarding you with questions? I don't know if you're worth the interest I take in you.

One day, I suddenly decided to come looking for you. I was in pretty low spirits. It has to be said that things were taking a worrying turn and that there was a stink of disaster in the air. We were living in 'strange times'. Nothing to hold on to. Then I remembered I had a father. Of course I often thought about 'the unfortunate incident in the George V métro', but I didn't harbour a grudge. There are some people you can forgive anything. Ten years had passed. What had become of you? Maybe you needed me.

I asked tea-room waitresses, barmen and hotel porters. It was Francois, at the Silver Ring, who put me on your trail. You went about – it appeared – with a merry band of night revellers whose leading lights were Messieurs Murraille and Marcheret. If the latter name meant nothing to me, I knew the former by reputation: a hack journalist given to blackmail and bribery. A week later, I watched you all go into a restaurant on the Avenue Kléber. I hope you'll forgive my curiosity, but I sat at the table next to yours. I was excited at having found you and intended to tap you on the shoulder, but gave up on the idea when I saw your friends. Murraille was sitting on your left and, at a glance, I found his sartorial elegance was suspect. You could see he was trying to 'cut a dash'. Marcheret was saying to all and sundry that 'the *foie gras* was inedible'. And I remember a red-haired woman and a curly-haired blonde, both oozing moral squalor from every pore. And, I am sorry to say, you didn't exactly look to be at your best. (Was it the Brylcreemed hair, that haunted look?) I felt slightly sick at the sight of you and your 'friends'. The curly-haired blonde was ostentatiously waving banknotes, the red-haired woman was rudely haranguing the head waiter and Marcheret was making his rude jokes. (I got used to them later.) Murraille spoke of his country house, where it was 'so pleasant to spend the weekend'. I eventually gathered that this little group went there every week. That you were one of them. I couldn't resist the idea of joining you in this charming rustic retreat.

And now that we are sitting face to face like china dogs and I can study your great Levantine head at leisure, I AM AFRAID. What are you doing in this village in the Seine-et-Marne with these people? And how exactly did you get to know them? I must really love you to follow you along this treacherous path. And without the slightest acknowledgement from you! Maybe I'm wrong, but your position seems to me to be very precarious. I assume you're still a stateless person, which is extremely awkward 'in the times we live in'. I've lost my identity papers too, everything except the 'diploma' to which you attached so much importance and which means so little today as we experience an unprecedented 'crisis of values'. Whatever it takes, I will try to stay calm.

Marcheret. He claps you on the back and calls you 'Chalva, old man'. And to me: 'Good evening, Monsieur Alexandre, will you have an Americano?' – and I'm forced to drink this sickly cocktail in case he takes offence. I'd like to know what your business is with this ex-Legionary. A currency racket? The sort of stock market scams you used to make? 'And two more Americanos!' he yells at Grève, the *maître d'hotel*. Then turning to me: 'Slips down like mother's milk, doesn't it?' I drink it down, terrified. Beneath his joviality, I suspect that he is particularly dangerous. It's a pity that our relationship, yours and mine, doesn't extend beyond strict politeness, because otherwise I'd warn you about this guy. And about Murraille. You're wrong to hang around with such people, 'papa'. They'll end up doing you a nasty turn. Will I have the strength to play my role as guardian angel to the bitter end? I don't get any encouragement from you. I scan your face for a friendly look or gesture (even if you don't recognize me, you might at least notice me), but nothing disturbs your Ottoman indifference. I ask myself what I'm doing here. All these drinks are ruining my health, for a start. And the pseudo-rustic décor depresses me terribly. Marcheret makes me promise to try a 'Pink Lady', whose subtle pleasures he introduced to 'all his Bouss-Bir friends'. I'm afraid he's going to start talking about the Legion and his malaria again. But no. He turns to you:

'Well, have you thought about it, Chalva?'

You answer in an almost inaudible voice:

'Yes, I've thought about it, Guy.'

'We'll split it fifty-fifty?'

'You can count on me, Guy.'

'I do a lot of business with the Baron,' Marcheret tells me. 'Don't I, Chalva? Let's drink to this! Grève, three vermouths please!'

We raise our glasses.

'Soon we'll be celebrating our first billion!'

He gives you a hearty slap on the back. We should get away from this place as quickly as possible. But where would we go? People like you and me are likely to be arrested on any street corner. Not a day goes by without police round-ups at train stations, cinemas and restaurants. Above all, avoid public places. Paris is like a great dark forest, filled with traps. We grope our way blindly. You have to admit it takes nerves of iron. And the heat doesn't make things easier. I've never known such a sweltering summer. This evening, the temperature is stifling. Deadly. Marcheret's collar is soaked with sweat. You've given up mopping your face and drops of sweat quiver for an instant at the end of your chin then drip steadily on to the table. The windows of the bar are closed. Not a breath of air. My clothes stick to my body as though I'd been caught in a downpour. Impossible to stand. Move an inch in this sauna and I would surely melt. But you don't seem unduly bothered: I suppose you often got heatwaves like this in

Egypt, huh? And Marcheret – he assures me that 'it's positively freezing compared with the desert' and suggests I have another drink. No, really, I can't drink any more. Oh come now, Monsieur Alexandre . . . a little Americano . . . I'm afraid of passing out. And now, through a misty haze, I see Murraille and Sylviane Quimphe coming towards us. Unless it is a mirage. (I'd like to ask Marcheret if mirages appear like that, through a mist, but I haven't got the strength.) Murraille holds out his hand to me.

'How are you, Serge?'

He calls me by my 'Christian name' for the first time; this familiarity makes me suspicious. As usual he's wearing a dark sweater with a scarf tied round his neck. Sylviane Quimphe's breasts are spilling out of her blouse and I notice that she isn't wearing a bra, because of the heat. But then why does she still wear her jodhpurs and boots?

'Shall we eat?' suggests Murraille. 'I'm starving.'

I manage to get to my feet. Murraille takes me by the arm:

'Have you given any thought to our idea? As I said, I'll give you a free hand. You can write whatever you like. The columns of my magazine are yours to command.'

Grève is waiting for us, in the dining-room. Our table is just underneath the centre light. All the windows are shut, naturally. It's even hotter than in the bar. I sit between Murraille and Sylviane Quimphe. You're placed opposite me, but I know in advance that you'll avoid looking at me. Marcheret orders. The dishes he chooses seem hardly appropriate in this heat: lobster bisque, richly sauced meats, and a soufflé. No one dares argue with him. Gastronomy, it appears, is his particular domain.

'We'll have a white Bordeaux to start with! Then a Château-Pétrus! Is that alright?'

He clicks his tongue.

'You didn't come to the stables this morning,' says Sylviane Quimphe. 'I was expecting you.'

For two days, she has been making more and more explicit advances. She's taken a fancy to me, and I don't know why. Is it my air of being a well-bred young man? My tubercular pallor? Or does she simply want to irritate Murraille? (But is she his mistress?) I thought for a while that she was going around with Dédé Wildmer, the apoplectic ex-jockey who runs the stables.

'Next time, you must keep your promise. You simply *have* to make it up to me . . .'

She puts on her little-girl voice and I'm worried the others will notice. No. Murraille and Marcheret are deep in private conversation. You are staring into the middle distance. The light overhead is as bright as a spotlight. It beats down on me like a weight. I'm sweating so much at the wrists that it feels as though my veins are slashed and my blood is leaking away. How can I swallow this scalding lobster which Grève has just set down? Suddenly Marcheret gets up:

'My friends, I want to make an important announcement: I'm getting married in three days! Chalva will be my witness! Honour to whom honour is due! Any objections, Chalva?'

You screw your face into a smile. You murmur:

'I'm delighted, Guy!'

'To the health of Jean Murraille, my future uncle-in-law,' roars Marcheret, throwing out his chest.

I raise my glass with the others, but immediately set it down again. If I drank a single drop of this white Bordeaux, I think I'd throw up. I have to reserve my strength for the lobster bisque.

'Jean, I'm very proud to be marrying your daughter,' declares Marcheret. 'She's got the most unsettling *derrière* in Paris.'

Murraille roars with laughter.

'Do you know Annie?' Sylviane Quimphe asks me. 'Who do you like best, her or me?'

I hesitate. And then I manage to say: 'You!' How much longer is this little farce going to last? She eyes me hungrily. Though I can't be a very pleasant sight . . . Sweat trickles from my sleeves. When will this nightmare end? The others are showing exceptional staying powers. Not a sign of perspiration on the faces of Murraille, Marcheret and Sylviane Quimphe. A few drops trickle down your forehead, but nothing much . . . And you tuck into your lobster bisque as if we were in an alpine chalet in mid-winter.

'You've given up, Monsieur Alexandre?' cries Marcheret. 'You shouldn't! The soup has a velvety creaminess!'

'Our friend is suffering from the heat,' Murraille says. 'I do hope, Serge, that it won't prevent your writing a good piece . . . I warn you that I must have it by next week. Have you thought of a subject?'

If I wasn't in such a critical condition, I would hit him. How can this mercenary traitor think I will blithely agree to contribute to his magazine, to get mixed up with this shower of informers, blackmailers and corrupt hacks who have flaunted themselves for the past two years on every page of *C'est la vie*? Ha, ha! They've got it coming to them. Bastards. Shits. Shysters. Vultures. They're living on borrowed time! Didn't Murraille himself show me the threatening letters they receive? He's afraid.

'I've just thought of something,' he says. 'Suppose you hatch me up a story?'

'All right!'

I tried to sound as enthusiastic as possible.

'Something *spicy*, if you catch my drift?'

'Absolutely!'

It's too hot to argue.

'Not pornographic exactly, but risqué . . . a little smutty . . . What do you think, Serge?'

'With pleasure.'

Whatever he wants! I'll write under my assumed name. But first I need to show willing. He's waiting for me to suggest something, so here I go!

'It's something I'd want you to run in instalments . . .'

'An excellent idea!'

'In the form of "confessions". That makes it a lot more titillating. How about: "The Confessions of a Society Chauffeur".'

I'd just remembered this title, which I'd seen in a pre-war magazine.

'Marvellous, Serge, marvellous! "The Confessions of a Society Chauffeur"! You're a genius!'

He seemed genuinely enthusiastic.

'When can I have the first instalment?'

'In three days,' I tell him.

'Will you let me read them before anyone else?' Sylviane Quimphe whispers.

'I simply adore filthy stories.' Marcheret declares pompously: 'You mustn't let us down, Monsieur Alexandre!'

Grève served the meat course. I don't know if it was the heat, the blaze of the ceiling light boring into my head, the sight of the rich food set in front of me, but I was suddenly seized by a fit of giggles which quickly gave way to a state of complete exhaustion. I tried to catch your eye. Without success. I didn't dare look at Murraille or Marcheret in case they spoke to me. In desperation, I focussed on the beauty spot at the corner of Sylviane Quimphe's lips. Then I simply waited, telling myself that the nightmare would surely end.

It was Murraille who called me to order.

'Are you thinking about your story? You mustn't let it spoil your appetite!'

'Inspiration comes while eating,' said Marcheret.

And you gave a little laugh; why did I expect anything else of you? You stood by these thugs and systematically ignored me, the one person in the world who wished you well.

'Try the soufflé,' Marcheret said to me. 'It melts in the mouth! Sensational, isn't it, Chalva?'

You agree in a sycophantic tone that breaks my heart. I should just leave here, you deserve no better, leave you with the malarial ex-Legionary, the hack journalist and the whore. There are moments, 'papa', when I'm sorely tempted to give up. I'm trying to help you. What would you be without me? Without my loyalty, my dogged vigilance? If I let you go, you would not make a sound as you fell. Shall we try? Be careful! I can already feel a comfortable listlessness creeping over me. Sylviane Quimphe has undone two buttons of her shirt, she turns and slyly flashes her breasts. Why not? Murraille languidly takes off his foulard, Marcheret props his chin pensively in his palm and lets out a string of belches. I hadn't noticed the greyish jowls that make you look like a bulldog. The conversation bores me. The voices of Murraille and Marcheret sound like a slowed-down record. Drawn out, droning on relentlessly, sinking into dark waters. Everything around me becomes hazy as drops of sweat fall into my eyes . . . The light grows dimmer, dimmer . . .

'I say, Monsieur Alexandre, you aren't going to pass out, are you . . .'

Marcheret wipes my forehead and temples with a damp napkin. The faintness passes. A fleeting malaise. I warned you 'papa'. What if next time I lose consciousness?

'Feeling better, Serge?' asks Murraille.

'We'll go for a little walk before going to bed,' Sylviane Quimphe whispers.

Marcheret, peremptorily:

'Cognac and Turkish coffee! Nothing better to buck you up! Believe me, Monsieur Alexandre.'

In fact, you were the only one who did not seem concerned about my health and this realisation simply added to my misery. Nevertheless, I managed to hold out until dinner was over. Marcheret ordered a 'digestive liqueur' and regaled us again about his wedding. One thing bothered him: who would be Annie's witness? He and Murraille mentioned the names of several people I didn't know. Then they began making a list of guests. They commented on each and I was afraid the task would take until dawn. Murraille made a weary gesture.

'Before then,' he said, 'we might all be shot.'

He glanced at his watch.

'Shall we go to bed? What do you think, Serge?'

In the bar, we surprised Maud Gallas with Dédé Wildmer. They were both sprawled in an armchair. He was pulling her to him and she was making a show of resistance. They had clearly had too much to drink. As we passed, Wildmer turned and gave me a curious look. We had not hit it off. In fact, I felt an instinctive dislike for the ex-jockey.

I was glad to be in the fresh air again.

'Will you come up to the villa with us?' Murraille asked me.

Sylviane Quimphe had taken my arm before I could make any objections. You walked along, shoulders hunched, between

Murraille and Marcheret. With the moon glinting on your brace-let watch, it looked like you were being led away in handcuffs by two policemen. You'd been taken in a roundup. You were being taken to the cells. This is what I dreamed about it. What could be more natural 'given the times we live in'.

'I look forward to "The Confessions of a Society Chauffeur",' Murraille said. 'I'm counting on you, Serge.'

'You'll write us a lovely smutty story,' added Marcheret. 'If you like, I can give you some advice. See you tomorrow, Monsieur Alexandre. Sweet dreams, Chalva.'

Sylviane Quimphe whispered a few words in Murraille's ear. (I may have been mistaken but I had a nasty feeling it was about me.) Murraille gave a barely perceptible nod. Opened the gate and tugged Marcheret by the sleeve. I watched them go into the villa.

We stood in silence for a moment, you, she and I, before turn-ing back towards the Clos-Foucré. You fell behind. She had taken my arm again and now rested her head on my shoulder. I was upset that you should see this, but didn't want to annoy her. In our situation, 'papa', it's best to keep people happy. At the cross-roads, you said 'good night' very politely, and turned up the Chemin du Bornage, leaving me with Sylviane.

She suggested we take a little walk, 'make the most of the moonlight'. We passed the 'Villa Mektoub' a second time. There was a light on in the drawing-room and the idea of Marcheret sitting alone, sipping a nightcap in that colonial mansion, sent a cold shiver down my spine. We took the bridle path at the edge of the forest. She unbuttoned her blouse. The rustling of the trees and the bluish twilight made me numb. After the ordeal of dinner, I was so exhausted that I was incapable of saying a word. I made a superhuman effort to open my mouth but no sound came. Luckily she began to talk about her complicated love life. She was, as I had suspected, Murraille's mistress – but they both had 'broad-minded' ideas. For instance, they both enjoyed orgies. She asked whether I was shocked. I said no, of course not. What about me, had I 'tried it'? Not yet, but if the opportunity arose, I was keen to. She promised I could 'join them' next time. Murraille had a twelve-room flat on the Avenue d'Iéna where these get-togethers were held. Maud Gallas joined in. And Marcheret. And Annie, Murraille's daughter. And Dédé Wildmer. And others, lots of them. It was crazy, the wild pleasures to be had in Paris at the moment. Murraille had explained to her that this was always the way on the eve of catastrophe. What did he mean? She had no interest in politics. Or the fate of the world. She thought only of coming. Hard and fast. After this statement of principle, she told me her secrets. She'd met a young man at the last party in the Avenue d'Iéna. Physically, he was a mixture between Max Schmeling and Henri Garat. Morally, he was resourceful. He belonged to one of the auxiliary police forces which had proliferated everywhere in recent months. He liked to fire his gun at random. Such exploits did not particularly surprise me. Were we not living through times when we had to thank God every minute for not being hit by a stray bullet? She had spent two days and two nights with him, and recounted all the details, but I was no longer listening. To our right, behind the high fence, I'd just recognized 'your' house, with its tower in the form of a minaret and its arched windows. You could see it better from this side than from the Chemin du Bornage. I even thought I saw you standing on one of the balconies. We were about fifty yards from each other and I had only to cross the overgrown garden to reach you. I hesitated a moment. I wanted to call or wave to you. No. My voice wouldn't carry and the creeping paralysis I had felt since the beginning of the evening made it impossible to raise my hand. Was it the moonlight? 'Your' villa was bathed in a bright northern glow. It looked like a papier mâché palace floating in the air, and you a fat sultan. Eyes glazed, mouth slack, leaning on a balustrade overlooking the forest. I thought of all the sacrifices I had made to be with you: bearing no grudge for the 'unfortunate incident in the George V métro'. Plunging into an atmosphere that sapped me mentally and physically; putting up with the company of these sickening people; lying in wait for days on end, never weakening. And all for the tawdry mirage I now saw before me. But I will hound you to the bitter end. You interest me, 'papa'. One is always curious to know one's family background.

It is darker now. We have taken a short-cut which leads to the village. She's still telling me about Murraille's apartment on the Avenue d'Iéna. On summer evenings, they go out on to the big terrace . . . She brings her face close to mine. I can feel her breath on my neck. We stumble blindly through the Clos-Foucré and I find myself in her room, as I expected. On the bedside table, a lamp with a red shade. Two chairs and a writing-desk. The walls are papered with yellow and green striped satin. She turns the dial of the wireless and I hear the distant voice of Andre Claveau through the static. She stretches out on the bed.

'Would you be kind and take off my boots?'

I obey, moving like a sleepwalker. She passes me a cigarette case. We smoke. Clearly all the bedrooms in the Clos-Foucré are exactly the same: Empire furniture and English hunting prints. Now she's toying with a little pistol with a mother-of-pearl handle and I wonder whether this is the first chapter of the 'Confessions of a Society Chauffeur' I promised Murraille. In the harsh light from the lamp, she looks older than I had thought. Her face is puffy with tiredness. There is a smear of lipstick across her chin. She says:

'Come here.'

I sit on the edge of the bed. She props herself on her elbows and gazes into my eyes. Just at that moment, there must have been an electricity cut. The room is framed in a yellow pall of the kind that glazes old photographs. Her face shifted out of focus, the outlines of the furniture indistinct, Claveau carried on singing faintly. Then I asked the question that I had been dying to ask from the beginning. Curtly:

'Tell me, what do you know about Baron Deyckecaire?'

'Deyckecaire?'

She sighed and turned towards the wall. Minutes passed. She had forgotten me but I returned to the attack.

'Strange guy, isn't he, Deyckecaire?'

I waited. She did not react. I repeated, articulating each syllable:

'Strange guy, Dey-cke-caire . . .!'

She didn't stir. I thought she had fallen asleep and I would never get an answer. I heard her mutter:

'You find Deyckecaire interesting?'

The flicker of a lighthouse in the darkness. Very faint. She went on in a drawl:

'What do you want with that creature?'

'Nothing . . . Have you known him long?'

'That creature?' She repeated the word 'creature' with that doggedness drunks have of repeating a word over and over.

'Am I right in thinking he's a friend of Murraille's?' I ventured.

'His crony!'

I planned to ask her what she meant by 'crony' but I needed to catch her off guard. She rambled on interminably, then trailed off, muttered a few confused phrases. I was used to this floundering around, to these exhausting games of blind-man's-buff when you stretch out your arms but catch only empty air. I tried – not without difficulty – to steer her back to the point. After an hour I had at least succeeded in coaxing some information from her. Yes, you were certainly Murraille's 'crony'. You served as a frontman and general factotum in certain shady deals. Contraband? Black marketeering? Touting? Finally she yawned and said: 'But it doesn't matter, Jean is planning to get rid of him as soon as possible!' That made things only too clear. We moved on to talk about other things. She fetched a little leather case from the desk and showed me the jewellery Murraille had given her. He liked it to be heavy and encrusted with stones, because, according to him, 'it would be easier to sell in an emergency'. I said I thought it was a very sensible idea 'given the times we're living in'. She asked if I went out much in Paris. There were lots of stunning shows: Roger Duchesne and Billy Bourbon were doing a cabaret at Le Club. Sessue Hayakawa was in a revival of *Forfaiture* at the Ambigu, and Michel Parme with the Skarjinsky orchestra were playing an early evening set at the Chapiteau. I was thinking about you, 'papa'. So you were a straw man to be liquidated when the time came. Your disappearance would create no more fuss than that of a fly. Who would remember you twenty years from now?

She drew the curtains. I could only see her face and her red hair. I went over the events of the evening again. The interminable dinner, the moonlight walk, Murraille and Marcheret going back to the 'Villa Mektoub'. And your shadow standing on the

Chemin du Bornage. All these vague impressions were part of the past. I had gone back in time to find your trail and track you down. What year were we living in? What era? What life? By what strange miracle had I known you when you were not yet my father? Why had I made so much effort, when a chansonnier was telling a 'Jewish joke', in a bar that smelled of shadows and leather, to an audience of strangers? Why, even then, had I wanted to be your son? She turned out the bedside light. The sound of voices from the next room. Maud Gallas and Dédé Wildmer. They swore at each other for a long time and then came the sighs, the moans. The wireless had stopped crackling. After a piece played by the Fred Adison orchestra, the last news bulletin was announced. And it was terrifying, listening to the frantic newsreader – still the same voice – in the darkness.

I needed all the patience I could muster. Marcheret took me aside and began to describe, house by house, the red-light district of Casablanca where he had spent – he told me – the best moments of his life. You never forget Africa! It leaves its mark! A pox-ridden continent. I let him go on for hours about 'that old whore Africa', showing a polite interest. He had one other topic of conversation. His royal lineage. He claimed to be descended from the Duc du Maine, the bastard son of Louis XIV. His title, 'Comte d'Eu' proved it. Every time, pen and paper at the ready, he insisted on showing me in detail. He would embark on a family tree and it would take him until dawn. He got confused, crossed out names, added others, his writing steadily becoming illegible. In the end, he ripped the page into little pieces, and gave me a withering look:

'You don't believe me, do you?'

On other evenings, his malaria and his impending marriage to Annie Murraille were the subjects of conversation. The malaria attacks were less frequent now, but he would never be cured. And Annie went her own way. He was only marrying her out of friendship for Murraille. It wouldn't last a week . . . These realisations made him bitter. Fuelled by alcohol, he would become aggressive, call me a 'greenhorn' and 'a snot-nosed brat'. Dédé Wildmer was a 'pimp', Murraille a 'sex maniac' and my father 'a Jew who had it coming to him'. Gradually he would calm down, apologize to me. What about one more vermouth? No better cure for the blues.

Murraille, on the other hand, talked about his magazine. He planned to expand *C'est la vie*, add a 36-page section with new columns in which the most diverse talents could express themselves. He would soon celebrate fifty years in journalism with a lunch at which most of his colleagues and friends would be reunited: Maulaz, Alin-Laubreaux, Gerbère, Le Houleux, Lestandi . . . and various celebrities. He would introduce me to them. He was delighted to be able to help me. If I needed money, I shouldn't hesitate to tell him: he would let me have advances against future stories. As time went on, his bluster and patronising tone gave way to a mounting nervousness. Every day – he told me – he received a hundred anonymous letters. People were baying for his blood, he had been forced to apply for a gun licence. Broadly, he was being accused of being part of an era when most people 'played a waiting game'. He at least made his position clear. In black and white. He had the upper hand at the moment, but the situation might turn out badly for him and his friends. If that happened, they would not get off lightly. In the meantime, he was not going to be bossed around by anyone.

I said I agreed absolutely. Strange thoughts ran through my mind: the man was not suspicious of me (at least I don't think he was) and it would have been easy to ruin him. It's not every day that you find yourself face to face with a 'traitor' and 'Judas'. You have to make the most of it. He smiled. Deep down, I rather liked him.

'None of this really matters . . .'

He liked living dangerously. He was going to 'go even further' in his next editorial.

Sylviane Quimphe took me to the stables every afternoon. During our rides, we often encountered a distinguished looking man of about sixty. I wouldn't have paid him any particular attention had I not been struck by the look of contempt he gave us. No doubt he thought it disgraceful that people could still go riding and think about enjoying themselves 'in these tragic times of ours'. We would not be fondly remembered in Seine-et-Marne . . . Sylviane Quimphe's behaviour was unlikely to add to our popularity. Trotting along the main street, she would talk in a loud voice, shriek with laughter.

In the rare moments I had to myself, I drafted the 'serial' for Murraille. He found 'Confessions of a Society Chauffeur' entirely satisfactory and commissioned three other stories. I had submitted 'Confidences of an Academic Photographer'. There remained 'Via Lesbos' and 'The Lady of the Studios' which I tried to write as diligently as possible. Such were the labours I set myself in the hope of developing a relationship with you. Pornographer, gigolo, confidant to an alcoholic and to a blackmailer – what else would you have me do? Would I have to sink even lower to drag you out of your cesspit?

Now, I realize what a hopeless enterprise it was. You become interested in a man who vanished long ago. You try to question the people who knew him, but their traces disappeared with his. Of his life, only vague, often contradictory rumours remain, one or two pointers. Hard evidence? A postage stamp and a fake *Légion d'honneur*. So all one can do is imagine. I close my eyes. The bar of the Clos-Foucré and the colonial drawing-room of the 'Villa Mektoub'. After all these years the furniture is covered with dust. A musty smell catches in my throat. Murraille, Marcheret, Sylviane Quimphe are standing motionless as waxworks. And you, you are slumped on a pouffe, your face frozen, your eyes staring.

It's a strange idea, really, to go stirring up all these dead things.

The wedding was to take place the following day, but there was no news of Annie. Murraille tried desperately to reach her by telephone. Sylviane Quimphe consulted her diary and gave him the numbers of nightclubs where 'that little fool' was likely to be found. Chez Tonton: Trinite 87.42, Au Bosphore: Richelieu 94.03, El Garron: Vintimille 30.54, L'Etincelle . . . Marcheret, silent, swallowed glass after glass of brandy. Between frantic calls, Murraille begged him to be patient. He had just been told that Annie had been at the Monte-Cristo at about eleven. With a bit of luck they'd 'corner' her at Djiguite or at L'Armorial. But Marcheret had lost heart. No, it was pointless. And you, on your pouffe, did your best to look devastated. Eventually you muttered:

'Try Poisson d'Or, Odeon 90.95 . . .'

Marcheret looked up:

'Nobody asked for your advice, Chalva . . .'

You held your breath so as not to attract attention. You wished the ground would swallow you. Murraille, increasingly frantic, went on telephoning: Le Doge: Opéra 95.78, Chez Carrère: Balzac 59.60, Les Trois Valses: Vernet 15.27, Au Grand Large . . .

You repeated timidly:

'What about the Poisson d'Or: Odeon 90.95 . . .'

Murraille roared:

'Just shut up, Chalva, will you?'

He was brandishing the telephone like a club, his knuckles white. Marcheret sipped his cognac slowly, then:

'If he makes another sound, I'll cut his tongue out with my razor . . . ! Yes, I mean you, Chalva . . .'

I seized the opportunity to slip out on to the veranda. I took a deep breath, filling my lungs. The silence, the cool of the night. Alone at last. I looked thoughtfully at Marcheret's Talbot, parked by the gate. The bodywork gleamed in the moonlight. He always left his keys on the dashboard. Neither he nor Murraille would have heard the sound of the engine. In twenty minutes, I could be in Paris. I would go back to my little room on the Boulevard Gouvion-Saint-Cyr. I would not set foot outside again, until times were better. I would stop sticking my nose into things that didn't concern me, stop taking unnecessary risks. You would have to fend for yourself. Every man for himself. But at the thought of leaving you alone with them I felt a painful spasm on the left-hand side of my chest. No, this was no time to desert you.

Behind me, someone pushed open the French window and came and sat on one of the veranda chairs. I turned and recognised your shadow in the half-light. I honestly hadn't expected you to join me out here. I walked over to you cautiously like a butterfly catcher stalking a rare specimen that might take wing at any minute. It was I who broke the silence:

'So, have they found Annie?'

'Not yet.'

You stifled a laugh. Through the window I saw Murraille standing there, the telephone receiver wedged between cheek and shoulder. Sylviane Quimphe was putting a record on the gramophone. Marcheret, like an automaton, was pouring another drink.

'They're strange, your friends,' I said.

'They're not my friends, they're . . . business acquaintances.'

You fumbled for something to light a cigarette and I found myself handing you the platinum lighter Sylviane Quimphe had given me.

'You're in business?' I asked.

'Have to do something.'

Again, a stifled laugh.

'You work with Murraille?'

After a moment's hesitation:

'Yes.'

'And it's going well?'

'Fair to middling.'

We had the whole night ahead of us to talk. The 'initial contact' I had long hoped for was finally about to happen. I was sure of it. From the drawing-room drifted the muted voice of a tango singer:

A la luz del candil . . .

'Shall we stretch our legs a little?'

'Why not?' you replied.

I gave a last glance towards the French window. The panes were misted and I could see only three large blots bathed in a yellowish fog. Perhaps they had fallen asleep . . .

That song, snatches of which still reached me on the breeze at the far end of the driveway, puzzled me. Were we really in Seine-et-Marne or in some tropical country? San Salvador? Bahia Blanca? I opened the gate, tapped the bonnet of the Talbot. We had no need of it. In one stride, one great bound, we could be back in Paris. We floated along the main road, weightless.

'Suppose they notice that you've given them the slip?'

'It doesn't matter.'

Coming from you, always so timid, so servile towards them, the remark astonished me . . . For the first time, you appeared relaxed. We had turned up the Chemin du Bornage. You were whistling and you even attempted a tango step; and I was fast succumbing to a suspicious state of euphoria. You said: 'Come and take a tour of my house,' as if it were the most natural thing in the world.

At this point, I realise I'm dreaming, and so I avoid any sudden gestures for fear of waking. We cross the overgrown garden, step into the hall and you double-lock the door. You nod towards various overcoats lying on the floor.

'Put one on, it's freezing here.'

It's true. My teeth are chattering. You still don't really know your way around because you have difficulty in finding the light-switch. A sofa, a few wing chairs, armchairs covered with dustsheets. There are several bulbs missing from the ceiling light. On a chest of drawers, between the two windows, a bunch of dried flowers. I presume that you usually avoid this room, but that tonight you wanted to honour me. We stand there, both of us embarrassed. Finally you say:

'Sit down, I'll go and make some tea.'

I sit on one of the armchairs. The problem with dust covers is that you have to balance carefully so as not to slip. In front of me, three engravings of pastoral scenes in the eighteenth-century style. I can't make out the details behind the dusty glass. I wait, and the faded décor reminds me of the dentist's living room on the Rue de Penthièvre where I once sought refuge to avoid an identity check. The furniture was covered with dustsheets, like this. From the window, I watched the police cordon off the street, the police van was parked a little farther on. Neither the dentist nor the old woman who had opened the door to me showed any sign of life. Towards eleven o'clock that night, I crept out on tiptoe, and ran down the deserted street.

Now, we are sitting facing each other, and you are pouring me a cup of tea.

'Earl Grey,' you whisper.

We look very strange in our overcoats. Mine is a sort of camel-hair caftan, much too big. On the lapel of yours, I notice the rosette of the *Légion d'honneur*. It must have belonged to the owner of the house.

'Perhaps you'd like some biscuits? I think there are some left.'

You open one of the dresser drawers.

'Here, have one of these . . .'

Cream wafers called 'Ploum-Plouvier'. You used to love these sickly pastries and we would buy them regularly at a baker's on the Rue Vivienne. Nothing has really changed. Remember. We used to spend long evenings together in places just as bleak as this. The 'living room' of 64 Avenue Félix-Faure with its cherry-wood furniture . . .

'A little more tea?'

'I'd love some.'

'I'm so sorry, I haven't got any lemon. Another Ploum?'

It's a pity that, wrapped in our enormous overcoats, we insist on making polite conversation. We have so much to say to each other! What have you been doing, 'papa', these last ten years? Life hasn't been easy for me, you know. I went on forging dedications for a little longer. Until the day the customer to whom I offered a love letter from Abel Bonnard to Henry Bordeaux realised it was a fake and tried to have me dragged off to court. Naturally I thought it better to disappear. A job as a monitor in a school in Sarthe. Greyness. The pettiness of colleagues. The classes of stubborn, sneering adolescents. The night wandering around the bars with the gym teacher, who tried to convert me to Hebert's 'natural method' of physical education and told me about the Olympic Games in Berlin . . .

What about you? Did you carry on sending parcels to French and foreign collectors? More than once, I wanted to write to you from my provincial bolt hole. But where would I write?

We look like a couple of burglars. I can imagine the surprise of the owners if they saw us drinking tea in their living room. I ask:

'Did you buy the house?'

'It was . . . deserted . . . ' You look sideways at me. 'The owners chose to leave because of . . . recent events.'

I thought so. They're waiting in Switzerland or Portugal until the situation improves, and, when they come back, we will, alas, no longer be there to greet them. Things will look just as usual. Will they notice we have been there? Unlikely. We are as careful as rats. A few crumbs perhaps, a dirty cup . . . You open the cocktail cabinet, nervous, as though afraid of being caught.

'A little glass of Poire Williams?'

Why not? Let's make the most of it. Tonight this house is ours. I stare at the rosette on your lapel but I have no need to feel jealous: I too have a little pink and gold ribbon pinned to the lapel of my coat, no doubt some military decoration. We'll talk about reassuring things, shall we? About the garden that needs weeding and this beautiful bronze by Barbedienne gleaming in the lamplight. You are a forestry manager and I, your son, a regular officer in the army. I spend my furloughs in our dear old home. I recognise the familiar smells. My room hasn't changed. At the back of the cupboard, my crystal radio, lead soldiers and Meccano, just as they used to be. Maman and Geneviève have gone to bed. We men remain in the living room. I love these moments. We sip our pear liqueur. Afterwards, our gestures mirroring each other, we fill our pipes. We are very alike, papa. Two peasants, two headstrong Bretons, as you would say. The curtains are drawn, the fire crackles cosily. Let's chat, my old partner in crime.

'Have you known Murraille and Marcheret long?'

'Since last year.'

'And you get along well with them?'

You pretended not to understand. You gave a little cough. I tried again.

'In my opinion, you shouldn't trust these people.'

You remained pokerfaced, your eyes screwed up. Perhaps you thought I was an agent provocateur. I shifted closer to you.

'Forgive my interfering in something that doesn't concern me, but I get the impression that they intend to harm you.'

'So do I,' you replied.

I think you suddenly felt you could trust me. Did you recognize me? You refilled our glasses.

'Perhaps we should drink a toast,' I said.

'Good idea!'

'Your health, Monsieur le Baron!'

'And yours, Monsieur . . . Alexandre! These are difficult times we're living in, Monsieur Alexandre.'

You repeated this sentence two or three times, as a kind of preamble, and then explained your situation to me. I could hardly hear you, as though you were talking to me on the telephone. A tinny voice, muffled by time and distance. From time to time, I caught a few words: 'Leaving . . .' 'Crossing borders . . .' 'Gold and hard currency . . .' And from them managed to piece together your story. Murraille, knowing your talents as a broker, had put you in charge of the self-styled 'Societé Française d'achats', whose mission was to stockpile a vast range of goods for resale later at a high price. He took three-quarters of the profits. To begin with, all went well, you were happy sitting in your large office on the Rue Lord-Byron, but recently, Murraille realised he no longer needed your services and considered you an embarrassment. Nothing could be easier, these days, than to get rid of someone like you. Stateless, with no social status, no fixed address, you had every disadvantage. It was enough to alert the ever-zealous *inspecteurs* of the *Brigades spéciales* . . . You had no one to turn to . . . except a night-club doorman by the name of 'Titiko'. He was willing to introduce you to one of his 'contacts' who could get you across the Belgian border. The meeting was to take place three days from now. The only assets you would take with you were 1,500 dollars in cash, a pink diamond and some thin sheets of gold cut to resemble visiting cards that would be easy to disguise.

I feel as though I'm writing a 'trashy adventure story', but I'm not making this up. No, this is not a fiction . . . There must surely be evidence, someone who knew you back then and who could corroborate these things. It doesn't matter. I am with you and I will stay here until the end of the book. You kept glancing nervously towards the door.

'Don't worry,' I said. 'They won't come.'

You relaxed a little. I tell you again that I'll stay with you until the end of this book, the last one dealing with my other life. Don't think I'm writing it out of pleasure; I had no choice.

'It's funny, Monsieur Alexandre, finding ourselves together in this room.'

The clock struck twelve times. A hulking object on the mantelpiece, with a bronze deer supporting the clock face.

'The owner must have liked clocks. There's one, on the first floor that chimes like Big Ben.'

And you burst out laughing. I was used to these outbursts of hilarity. Back when we were living on the Square Villaret-de-Joyeuse and everything was going badly, I would hear you at night, laughing in the next room. Or you would come home with a bundle of dusty share certificates under your arm. You would drop them and say in a lifeless voice: 'I'll never be quoted on the Stock Exchange.' You would stand, staring at your loot, scattered over the floor. And suddenly it would overwhelm you. A laugh that grew louder and louder until your shoulders shook. You couldn't stop.

'And you, Monsieur Alexandre, what do you do in life?'

What should I say? My life? As storm-tossed as yours, 'papa'. Eighteen months in Sarthe, as a school monitor, as I mentioned. School monitor again, in Rennes, Limoges and Clermont-Ferrand. I choose religious institutions. They afford more shelter. This domestic existence brings me inner peace. One of my colleagues, obsessed with Scouting, has just started up a troop for young people in the Forest of Seillon. He was looking for scout leaders and took me on. Here I am in my navy-blue plus fours and brown gaiters. We get up at six. Our days are divided between physical education and manual work. Communal sing-songs in the evening, round the campfire. A quaint idyll: Montcalm, Bayard, Lamoricière, 'Adieu, belle Françoise', planes, chisels and the scouting spirit. I stayed three years. A safe bolt-hole, just the place to be forgotten. Sadly, my baser instincts regained the upper hand. I fled this haven and found myself at the Gare de l'Est, without even taking the time to remove my beret and badges.

I scour Paris looking for a steady job. A futile search. The fog never lifts, the pavement slips away beneath me. More and more often I suffer dizzy spells. In my nightmares, I am crawling endlessly, trying to find my backbone. The garret I live in, on the Boulevard Magenta, was the studio of the artist Domergue before he was famous. I try to see this as a good omen.

Of what I did, at this time, I have only the vaguest memory. I think I was 'assistant' to a certain Doctor S. who recruited his patients from among drug addicts and gave them prescriptions for vast sums of money.

I had touted for him. I seem to remember that I also worked as 'secretary' to an English poetess, a passionate admirer of Dante Gabriel Rossetti. Such details seem irrelevant.

I remember only perambulations across Paris, and that centre of gravity, that magnet to which I was invariably drawn: the *préfecture de police*. Try as I might to stay away, within a few short hours my steps would lead me back. One night when I was more depressed than usual, I almost asked the sentries guarding the main door on the Boulevard du Palais, if I could go in. I could not understand the fascination the police exerted over me. At first I thought it was like the urge to jump you feel when you are leaning over the parapet of a bridge, but there was something else. To disoriented boys like me, policemen represented something solid and dignified. I dreamed of being an officer. I confided this to Sieffer, an inspector in the vice squad I was lucky enough to meet. He heard me out, a smile playing on his lips, but with paternal solicitude, and offered to let me work for him. For several months, I shadowed people on a voluntary basis. I had to tail a wide variety of people and note how they spent their time. In the course of these missions, I uncovered many poignant secrets . . . Such-and-such a lawyer from La Plaine Monceau, you encounter on the Place Pigalle wearing a blonde wig and satin dress. I witnessed insignificant people suddenly transformed into nightmarish figures or tragic heroes. By the end I thought I was going insane. I identified with all these strangers. It was *myself* that I was hunting down so relentlessly. I was the old man in the mackintosh or the woman in the beige suit. I talked about this to Sieffer.

'No point carrying on. You're an amateur, son.'

He walked me to the door of his office.

'Don't worry. We'll see each other again.'

He added in a gloomy voice:

'Sooner or later, unfortunately, everyone ends up in the cells . . .'

I had a genuine affection for this man and felt I could trust him. When I told him how I felt, he enveloped me with a sad, caring look. What became of him? Perhaps he could help us, now? This interlude working for the police did little to boost my morale. I no longer dared leave my room on the Boulevard Magenta. Menace loomed everywhere. I thought of you. I had the feeling that somewhere you were in danger. Every night between three and four in the morning, I would hear you calling to me for help. Little by little, an idea formed in my mind, I would set off in search of you.

I did not have very happy memories of you, but, after ten years, that sort of thing doesn't seem so important and I'd forgiven you for the 'unfortunate incident in the George V métro'. Let's deal with that subject once more, for the last time. There are two possibilities: 1) I wrongly suspected you. In which case, please forgive me and put the mistake down to my own madness. 2) If you did try to push me under the train, I freely admit there were extenuating circumstances. No, there's nothing unusual about your case. A father wanting to kill his son or to be rid of him seems to me to be symptomatic of the huge upheaval in our moral values today. Not long ago, the converse phenomenon could be observed: sons killed their father to prove their strength. But now, who is there for us to lash out at? Orphans that we are, we are doomed to track ghosts in our search for fatherhood. We never find it. It always slips away. It's exhausting, old man. Shall I tell you the feats of imagination I've accomplished? Tonight, you sit facing me, your eyes starting from your head. You look like a black market trafficker, and the title 'Baron' is unlikely to throw the hunters off the scent. You chose it, I imagine, in the hope that it would set you up, make you respectable. Such play-acting doesn't work on me. I've known you too long. Remember our Sunday walks, Baron? From the centre of Paris, we drifted on a mysterious current all the way to the ring roads. Here the city unloads its refuse and silt. Soult, Massena, Davout, Kellermann. Why did they give the names of conquering heroes to these murky places? But this was ours, this was our homeland.

Nothing has changed. Ten years later, here you are the same as ever: glancing at the living room door like a terrified rat. And here I am gripping the arm of the sofa for fear of slipping off the dustsheet. Try though we might, we will never know peace, the sweet stillness of things. We will walk on quicksand to the end. You're sweating with fear. Get a grip, old boy. I'm here beside you, holding your hand in the darkness. Whatever happens, I will share your fate. In the meantime, let's take a tour of this place. Through the door on the left, we come to a small room. The sort of leather armchairs I love. A mahogany desk. Have you ransacked the drawers yet? We'll comb though the owners' private life and gradually begin to feel as though we are part of the family: are there more drawers, more chests, more pockets upstairs that we can rifle through? We have a few hours to spare. This room is cosier than the living room. Smell of tweed and Dutch tobacco. On the shelves, neat rows of books: the complete works of Anatole France and crime novels published by Masque, recognizable by their yellow spines. Sit behind the desk. Sit up straight. There's no reason we can't dream about the course our lives might have taken in such a setting. Whole days spent reading or talking. A German shepherd on guard to deter visitors. In the evenings, my fiancée and I would play a few games of *manille*.

The telephone rings. You jump up, your face haggard. I must admit that this jingling, in the middle of the night, is not encouraging. They're making sure you're here so they can arrest you at dawn. The ringing will stop before you have time to answer. Sieffer often used such ruses. We take the stairs four at a time, tripping, falling over each other, pulling, scrabbling to our feet. There is a whole warren of rooms and you don't know where the light-switches are. I stumble against a piece of furniture, you feel around for the telephone. It's Marcheret. He and Murraille wondered why we had disappeared.

His voice echoes strangely in the darkness. They have just found Annie, at the Grand Ermitage moscovite, in the Rue Caumartin. She was drunk, but promised to be at the town-hall tomorrow, on the dot of three.

When it came to exchanging rings, she took hers and threw it in Marcheret's face. The mayor pretended not to notice. Guy tried to save the situation by roaring with laughter.

A rushed, impromptu wedding. Perhaps, a few brief references might be found in the newspapers of the day. I remember that Annie Murraille wore a fur coat and that her outfit, in mid-August, added to the uneasiness.

On the way back, they didn't say a word. She walked arm in arm with her witness, Lucien Remy, a 'variety artiste' (according to what I gathered from the marriage certificate); and you, Marcheret's witness, appeared there described as: 'Baron Chalva Henri Deyckecaire, industrialist.'

Murraille weaved between Marcheret and his niece, cracking jokes to lighten the mood. Without success. He eventually grew tired and didn't say another word. You and I brought up the rear of this strange cortège.

Lunch had been arranged at the Clos-Foucré. Towards five, some close friends, who had come down from Paris, gathered with their champagne glasses. Grève had set out the buffet in the garden.

We both hung back. And I observed. Many years have passed, but their faces, their gestures, their voices are seared on to my memory. There was Georges Lestandi, whose malicious 'gossip' and denunciations graced the front page of Murraille's magazine every week. Fat, stentorian voice, a faint Bordeaux accent. Robert Delvale, director of the théâtre de l'Avenue, silver haired, a well preserved sixty, priding himself on being a 'citizen' of Montmartre, whose mythology he cultivated. Francois Gerbère, another of Murraille's columnists, who specialized in frenzied editorials and calls for murder. Gerbère belonged to that school of hypersensitive boys who lisp and are happy to play the passionate militant or the brutal fascist. He had been bitten by the political bug shortly after graduating from the École Normale Supérieure. He had remained true to the – deeply provincial – spirit of his alma mater on the rue d'Ulm, indeed it was amazing that this thirty-eight-year-old student could be so savage.

Lucien Remy, the witness from the registry office. Physically, a charming thug, white teeth, hair gleaming with Bakerfix. He could sometimes be heard singing on Radio-Paris. He lived on the fringes of the underworld and the music-hall. And finally, Monique Joyce. Twenty-six, blonde, a deceptively innocent look. She had played a few roles on stage, but never made her mark. Murraille had a soft spot for her and her photograph often appeared on the cover of *C'est la vie*. There were articles about her. One such informed us she was 'The most elegant Parisienne on the Côte d'Azur'. Sylviane Quimphe, Maud Gallas and Wildmer were, of course, among the guests.

Surrounded by all these people, Annie Murraille's good-humour returned. She kissed Marcheret and said she was sorry and he slipped her wedding ring on her finger with a ceremonial air. Applause. The champagne glasses clinked. People called to each other and formed little groups. Lestandi, Delvale and Gerbère congratulated the bridegroom. In a corner, Murraille gossiped with Monique Joyce. Lucien Remy was a big hit with the women, if Sylviane Quimphe's reactions were anything to go by. But he reserved his smile for Annie Murraille, who pressed against him assiduously. It was obvious they were very close. As the hosts, Maud Gallas and Wildmer brought round the drinks and the *petits fours*. I've got all the photographs of the ceremony here, in a little wallet, and I've looked at them a million times, until my eyes glaze over with tiredness, or tears.

We had been forgotten. We lay low, standing a little way off, and no one paid us any attention. I felt as if we'd stumbled into this strange garden-party by mistake. You seemed as much at a loss as I was. We should have left as soon as possible and I still don't understand what came over me. I left you standing there and mechanically walked towards them.

Someone prodded me in the back. It was Murraille. He dragged me off and I found myself with Gerbère and Lestandi. Murraille introduced me as 'a talented young journalist he had just commissioned'. At which Lestandi, half-patronising, half-ironic, favoured me with an '*enchanté*, my dear colleague'.

'And what splendid things are you writing?' Gerbère asked me.

'Short stories.'

'Short stories are a fine idea,' put in Lestandi. 'One doesn't have to commit oneself. Neutral ground. What do you think, François?'

Murraille had slipped away. I would have liked to do the same.

'Between ourselves,' Gerbère said, 'do you think we're living at a time when one can still write short stories? I personally have no imagination.'

'But a caustic wit!' cried Lestandi.

'Because I'm not afraid of stating the obvious. I give it to them good and hard, that's all.'

'And it's terrific, François. Tell me, what are you cooking up for your next editorial?'

Gerbère took off his heavy horn-rimmed spectacles. He wiped the lenses, very slowly, with a handkerchief. Confident of the effect he was making.

'A delightful little piece. It's called: "Anyone for Jewish tennis?" I explain the rules of the game in three columns.'

'And what exactly is "Jewish tennis"?' asked Lestandi, grinning.

Gerbère gave the details. From what I gathered, it was a game for two players and could be played while strolling, or sitting outside a cafe. The first to spot a Jew, called out. Fifteen love. If his opponent should spot one, the score was fifteen-all. And so on. The winner was the one who notched up the most Jews. Points were calculated as they were in tennis. Nothing like it, according to Gerbère, for sharpening the reflexes of the French.

'Believe it or not,' he added dreamily, 'I don't even need to see THEIR faces. I can recognize THEM from behind! I swear!'

Other points were discussed. One thing nauseated him, Lestandi said: that those 'bastards' could still live it up on Côte d'Azur, sipping *apéritifs* in the Cintras of Cannes, Nice or Marseilles. He was preparing a series of 'Rumour & Innuendo' stories on the subject. He would name names. It was a civic duty to alert the relevant authorities. I turned round. You hadn't moved. I wanted to give you a friendly wave. But they might notice and ask me who the fat man was, over there, at the bottom of the garden.

'I've just come back from Nice,' Lestandi said. 'Not a single human face. Nothing but Blochs and Hirschfelds. It makes you sick . . .'

'Actually . . .' Gerbère suggested, 'You'd only have to give their room numbers to the Ruhl Hotel . . . It would make the work of the police easier . . .'

They grew animated. Heated. I listened politely. I have to say I found them tedious. Two utterly ordinary men, of middling height, like millions of others in the streets. Lestandi wore braces. Someone else would probably have told them to shut up. But I'm a coward.

We drank several glasses of champagne. Lestandi was now entertaining us with an account of a certain Schlossblau, a cinema producer, 'a frightful red-haired, purple-faced Jew', he had recognized on the Promenade des Anglais. There was one, he promised, that he would definitely get to. The light was failing. The celebrations drifted from the garden into the bar. You followed the rest and came and sat next to me . . . Then, as though hit with a jolt of electricity, the party came to life. A nervous jollity. At Marcheret's request, Delvale gave us his impersonation of Aristide Bruant. But Montmartre was not his only source of inspiration. He had played farce and light comedy and had us in stitches with his puns and witticisms. I can see his spaniel eyes, his thin moustache. The way he waited eagerly for the audience to laugh which nauseated me. When he scored a hit he would shrug as though he did not care.

Lucien Remy sang us a sweet little song, very popular that year: 'Je n'en connais pas la fin'. Annie Murraille and Sylviane Quimphe were eying him hungrily. And I was studying him carefully. The lower half of his face particularly frightened me. There was something strangely spineless about it. I sensed he was even more dangerous than the others. Never trust the Brylcreemed types who tend to appear in 'troubled times'. We were graced with a song from Lestandi, a cabaret song of the kind known back then as 'chansonnier'. Lestandi took great pride in showing us that he knew all the songs in *La Lune Rousse* and *Deux Anes* by heart. We all have our little weaknesses, our little hobbies.

Dédé Wildmer stood on a chair and toasted the health of the bride and groom. Annie Murraille pressed her cheek against Lucien Remy's shoulder and Marcheret didn't seem to mind. Sylviane Quimphe, however, was using all her wiles to attract the attention of the 'crooner', as was Maud Gallas. By the bar, Delvale was talking to Monique Joyce. He was getting more and more eager and was calling her his 'poppet'. She greeted his advances with throaty laughter, tossing her hair as if she were rehearsing a role in front of an invisible camera. Murraille, Gerbère and Lestandi were carrying on a conversation fuelled by alcohol. It was a case of organizing a meeting, in the Salle Wagram, at which the contributors to *C'est la vie* would speak. Murraille proposed his favourite theme: 'We're not pusillanimous'; but Lestandi wittily corrected him: 'We're not *Jew*sillanimous'.

It was a stormy afternoon and thunder rolled ominously in the distance. Today all these people have disappeared or have been shot. I suppose they're no longer of any interest to anyone. Is it my fault that I am still a prisoner of my memories?

But when Marcheret came towards us and flung the contents of a champagne glass in your face, I thought I'd lose control. You flinched. He said crisply:

'That'll freshen up your ideas, won't it, Chalva?'

He stood in front of us, his arms crossed. 'It's better than water,' stuttered Wildmer. 'It's sparkling!' You fumbled for a handkerchief to dry yourself with. Delvale and Lucien Remy made some cutting remarks about you which reduced the women to hysterics. Lestandi and Gerbère studied you curiously and suddenly realized they didn't like the look of your face.

'A sudden shower, eh, Chalva?' said Marcheret, patting the back of your head as though you were a dog. You gave a feeble smile. 'Yes, a nice shower . . .' you muttered.

The saddest thing was that you seemed to be apologizing. They went on with their conversations. Went on drinking. Laughing. How did it happen that, over the general hubbub, I overheard Lestandi say: 'Excuse me, I'm going for a short stroll'? Before he had left the bar, I was on the steps in front of the *auberge*. And there we ran into each other. When he mentioned that he was going to stretch his legs a little, I asked, as casually as possible, whether I could go with him.

We followed the bridle path. And then we moved into the undergrowth. A grove of beech trees, where the early evening sunlight spread a nostalgic glow as in the paintings of Claude Lorrain. He said it was sensible of us to be out in the open air. He was very fond of the Forest of Fontainebleau. We talked about this and that. About the deep hush, about the magnificent trees.

'Mature trees . . . They must be about 120 years old.' He laughed. 'I bet you I won't reach that age . . .'

'You never know . . .'

He pointed to a squirrel scampering across the path twenty yards ahead. My palms were sweaty. I told him I enjoyed reading his weekly 'gossip column' in *C'est la vie*, that, in my opinion, what he was doing was a public work. Oh, he could hardly take any credit, he replied, he simply hated Jews, and Murraille's magazine offered him the chance to express his views on the matter frankly. So different from the degenerate pre-war press. True, Murraille had a penchant for racketeering and easy money, and he was probably 'half-Jewish' but very soon Muraille would be 'eliminated' in favour of a 'pure' editorial team. People like Alin-Laubreaux,

Zeitschel, Sayzille, Darquier, himself. And particularly Gerbère, the most talented of them. Comrades in arms.

'What about you, are you interested in politics?'

I told him I was, and that I felt we needed a new broom.

'A new cosh would serve just as well!'

And, as an example, he told me again about Schlossblau defiling the Promenade des Anglais. Apparently Schlossblau was now back to Paris and holed up in an apartment, and he, Lestandi, knew the address. A little mention was all it would take for some armed thugs to come knocking. He was congratulating himself in advance on his good work.

It was getting dark. I decided to get on with it. I took a last look at Lestandi. He was chubby. A gourmet, certainly. I imagined him tucking into a plate of *brandade de morue*. And I thought of Gerbère too, with his schoolboy lisp and quivering buttocks. No, neither of them were firebrands and I mustn't let them scare me.

We were walking through dense thickets.

'Why bother going after Schlossblau?' I said. 'There are Jews all round you . . .'

He didn't understand and gave me a questioning look.

'That man who had a glass of champagne thrown in his face just now . . . you remember?'

He burst out laughing.

'Of course . . . We, Gerbère and I, thought he looked like a swindler.'

'A Jew! I'm surprised you didn't guess!'

'Then what the hell's he doing here with us?'

'That's what I'd like to know . . .'

'We'll ask the bastard to show us his papers!'

'No need.'

315

'You mean you know him?'

I took a deep breath.

'HE'S MY FATHER.'

I grabbed his throat until my thumbs hurt. I thought of you to give me strength. He stopped struggling.

It was silly, really, to have killed the fat slob.

I found them still at the bar at the auberge. As I went in, I bumped into Gerbère.

'Have you seen Lestandi?'

'No,' I answered absent-mindedly.

'Where can he have got to?'

He looked at me sharply and blocked my way.

'He'll be back,' I said in a falsetto voice, quickly clearing my throat to cover my nervousness. 'He probably went for a walk in the forest.'

'You think so?'

The others were gathered round the bar while you sat in an armchair by the fireplace. I couldn't see you very well in the dim light. There was only one light on, on the other side of the room.

'What do you think of Lestandi?'

'Great,' I said.

He remained glued to my side. I couldn't get away from his slimy presence.

'I'm very fond of Lestandi. He has the mind, the soul of a "young Turk", as we used to say at the École Normale.'

I nodded.

'He lacks subtlety, but I don't give a damn about that! We need brawlers right now!'

His words came in a torrent.

'There's been too much focus on niceties and hair-splitting! What we need, now, are young thugs to trample the flowerbeds!'

He was quivering from head to foot.

'The day of the assassins has come! And I say, welcome!'

He said this in a furiously aggressive voice.

His eyes bored into me. I sensed he wanted to say something but didn't dare. At last:

'It's extraordinary how much you look like Albert Préjean . . .' He seemed to be overcome with languor. 'Has no-one ever told you how like Albert Préjean you are?'

His voice cracked to become a poignant, almost inaudible whisper.

'You remind me of my best friend at ENA, a marvellous boy. He died in '36, fighting for Franco.'

I scarcely recognized him. He was getting more and more spineless. His head was about to drop on my shoulder.

'I'd liked to see you again in Paris. That would be nice, wouldn't it? Wouldn't it?'

He shrouded me in a misty gaze.

'I must go and write my column. You know . . . "Jewish tennis" . . . Tell Lestandi I couldn't wait any longer . . .'

I walked with him to his car. He clung to my arm, muttering unintelligibly. I was still mesmerized by the change which, in a few brief seconds, had seen him transformed into an old lady.

I helped him into the driving seat. He rolled down the window.

'You'll come and have dinner with me on the Rue Rataud . . .?' His puffy face was imploring.

'Don't forget, will you, *mon petit* . . . I'm so lonely . . .'

And he shot off at top speed.

Y ou were still in the same place. A black mass slumped against the back of the chair. In the dim light one might easily wonder whether it was a person or a pile of overcoats? Everyone was ignoring you. Afraid of drawing attention to you, I kept my distance and joined the others.

Maud Gallas was telling how she had had to put Wildmer to bed dead drunk. It happened at least three times a week. The man was ruining his health, Lucien Remy had known him back when he was winning all the big races. Once, at Auteuil, a crowd of regulars at the racetrack had carried him off in triumph. He was called 'The Centaur'. Back then, he only drank water.

'All sportsmen become depressives as soon as they stop competing,' observed Marcheret.

He quoted examples of retired sportsmen – Villaplane, Toto Grassin, Lou Brouillard . . . Murraille shrugged:

'We'll soon stop competing, ourselves, you know. A little matter of twelve bullets, pursuant to Article 57.'

They had just listened to the last radio bulletin and the news was 'even more alarming than usual'.

'As I understand it,' Delvale said, 'we should be preparing the speeches we'll make in front of the firing-squad . . .'

For nearly a quarter of an hour, they played this game. Delvale thought that *'Vive la France catholique, all the same!'* would have the best effect. Marcheret swore he'd shout 'Try not to ruin my face! Aim for my heart and try not to miss, it's broken!' Remy would sing 'Le Petit Souper aux chandelles', and if he had time, 'Lorsque tout est fini' . . . Murraille would refuse the blindfold, insisting he wanted to 'see the comedy through to the end'.

'I'm sorry,' he said finally, 'to be talking about such stupid things on Annie's wedding day . . . '

And, to lighten the atmosphere, Marcheret made his ritual joke, about 'Maud Gallas having the finest breasts in Seine-et-Marne'. He had already begun to unbutton her blouse. She did not resist, she went on leaning at the bar.

'Look . . . Take a look at these beauties!'

He pawed them, popped out of her brassiere.

'You've no need to be jealous,' Delvale whispered to Monique Joyce. 'Far from it, my child. Far from it!'

He tried to slip his hand into her blouse but she stopped him with a nervous little laugh. Annie Murraille, greatly excited, had subtly hiked up her skirt allowing Lucien Remy could stroke her thighs. Sylviane Quimphe was playing footsie with me. Murraille filled our glasses and said in a weary voice that we seemed in good spirits for men about to be shot.

'Have you seen this pair of tits!' Marcheret was saying again.

Moving across to join Maud Gallas behind the bar, he knocked over the lamp. Shouts. Sighs. People were taking advantage of darkness. Eventually someone – Murraille, if I remember rightly – suggested that they'd be much better off in the bedrooms.

I found a light-switch. The glare of the lights dazzled me. There was no one left except us. The heavy panelling, the club chairs and the glasses scattered across the bar filled me with despair. The wireless was playing softly.

Bei mir bist du schön . . .

And you had fallen asleep.

please let me explain . . .

With your head slumped forward, and your mouth open.

Bei mir bist du schön . . .

In your hand, a burnt-out cigar.

means that you're grand.

I tapped you gently on the shoulder.
'Shall we go?'

The Talbot was parked in front of the gates of the 'Villa Mektoub' and, as always, Marcheret had left the keys on the dashboard.

I took the Route Nationale. The speedometer read 130. You closed your eyes, because of the speed. You had always been scared in cars, so to cheer you up, I passed you a tin of sweets. We roared through deserted villages. Chailly-en-Biere, Perthes, Saint-Sauveur. You cowered on the passenger seat beside me. I tried to reassure you, but after Ponthierry, it struck me that we were in a decidedly precarious position: neither of us had papers, and we were driving a stolen car.

Corbeil, Ris-Orangis, L'Haÿ-les-Roses. Finally, the blacked-out lights of the Porte d'Italie.

Until that moment, we hadn't spoken a word. You turned to me and said we could telephone 'Titiko', the man who was going to get you across the Belgian border. He had given you a number, to be used in an emergency.

'Be careful,' I said in an even voice. 'The man's an informer.'
You didn't hear. I said it again, to no effect.

We pulled up by a café on the Boulevard Jourdan. I saw the woman behind the counter hand you a telephone token. There were some people still sitting at the tables outside. Beyond them the little métro station and the park. The Montsouris district reminded me of the evenings we used to spend in the brothel on the Avenue Reille. Was the Egyptian madame still there? Would she still remember you? Was she still swathed in clouds of perfume? When you came back, you were smiling contentedly: 'Titiko', true to his word, would be waiting for us at 11.30 p.m. precisely in the lobby of the Hôtel Tuileries-Wagram on the Rue des Pyramides. Clearly it was impossible to change the course of events.

Have you noticed, Baron, how quiet Paris is tonight? We glide along the empty boulevards. The trees shiver, their branches forming a protective vault above our heads. Here and there a lighted window. The owners have fled and have forgotten to turn off the lights. Later, I'll walk through this city and it will seem as empty to me as it does today. I will lose myself in the maze of streets, searching for your shadow. Until I become one with it.

Place du Châtelet. You're explaining to me that the dollars and the pink diamond are sewn into the lining of your jacket. No suit-cases, 'Titiko' insisted. It makes it easier to get across the border. We abandon the Talbot on the corner of the Rue de Rivoli and the Rue d'Alger. We're half an hour early and I ask you if you'd like to take a walk in the Tuileries. We were just coming to the fountain when we heard a burst of applause. There was an open-air theatre. A costume piece. Marivaux, I think. The actors were bowing in a blue glow. We mingled with the groups of people heading for the refreshment stand. Garlands were hung between the trees. At an upright piano, near the counter, a sleepy old man was playing 'Pedro'. You ordered coffee and lit a cigar. We both remained silent. On summer nights just like this, we used to sit outside cafés. We watched the faces round us, the passing cars on the boulevard, and I cannot remember a single word we said, except on the day you pushed me under the train . . . A father and son probably have little to say to each other.

The pianist launched into 'Manoir de mes rêves'. You fingered the lining of your jacket. It was time.

I can see you sitting on a plaid-upholstered armchair in the lobby of the Tuileries-Wagram. The night porter is reading a magazine. He did not even look up when we came in. You look at your wrist watch. A hotel just like those where we used to meet. Astoria, Majestic, Terminus. Do you remember, Baron? You had the same look of a traveller in transit, waiting for a boat or train that will never come.

You didn't hear them arrive. There are four of them. The tallest, wearing a gabardine, demands to see your papers.

'Monsieur was planning to go to Belgium without telling us?'

He rips the lining of your jacket, carefully counts the notes, pockets them. The pink diamond has rolled on to the carpet. He bends down and picks it up.

'Where d'you steal that?'

He slaps you.

You stand there, in your shirt. Ashen. *And I realise that in that moment you have aged thirty years.*

I'm at the back of the foyer, near the lift, and they haven't noticed me. I could press the button, go up. Wait. But I walk towards them and go up to the bleeder in the raincoat.

'HE'S MY FATHER.'

He studies us both and shrugs. Slaps me listlessly, as if it were a formality, and says casually to the others:

'Get this scum out of here.'

We stumble through the revolving doors which they push round at top speed.

The police van is parked a little way away on the Rue de Rivoli. We sit, side by side, on the wooden benches. It's so dark I can't tell where we're going. Rue des Saussaies? Drancy? Villa Triste? Whatever happens, I'll stay with you to the end.

As the van rounds corners, we're thrown against each other, but I can barely see you. Who are you? Though I've followed you for days on end, I know nothing about you. A shadow in the half-light.

Just now, as we were getting into the van, they gave us a bit of a beating. Our faces must look pretty comical. Like those two clowns that time at the *Cirque Medrano* . . .

Surely one of the prettiest and most idyllically situated villages in Seine-et-Marne: on the fringes of the Forest of Fontainebleau. In the last century, it was the refuge of a group of painters. These days, tourists regularly visit and a number of Parisians have country houses here.

At the end of the main street, l'auberge du Clos-Foucré, built in the Anglo-Norman style. An air of propriety and rustic simplicity. Distinguished clientele. Towards midnight, you may find yourself alone with the barman clearing away bottles and emptying ashtrays. His name is Grève. He has worked here for thirty years. He is a man of few words, but if he takes a shine to you and you offer him a plum brandy from Meuse, he is prepared to recall certain memories. Oh, yes, he knew the people I mentioned. But how can a young man like me have heard of these people? 'Oh, you know . . .' He empties the ashtrays into a square tin. Yes, that little gang used to come to the auberge a long time ago. Maud Gallas, Sylviane Quimphe . . . he wonders what became of them. With women like that, you never know. He even has a photo. Look, the tall thin one there is Murraille. A magazine editor. Firing squad. The other one, behind him, who's sticking out his chest and holding an orchid between his finger and thumb: Guy de Marcheret, known as Monsieur le Comte, used to be in the Legion. Maybe he went back to the colonies. Oh, that's right, they are not around any more . . . The fat one, sitting in the armchair, in front of them, he disappeared one day. 'Baron' something or other . . .

He has seen dozens like them, propped at the bar, dreaming, who vanished later. Impossible to remember all the faces. After all . . . sure . . . if I want the photo, I can have it. But I'm so young, he says, I'd be better off thinking about the future.

NOTES ON *LA PLACE DE L'ÉTOILE*

5   **Léon Rabatête:** a thinly-disguised parody of Lucien Rebatet (1903–1972), a French author, journalist, and intellectual; an exponent of fascism and virulent anti-Semite.

5   **Ferdinand Bardamu:** a character in Céline's *Voyage au bout de la Nuit*. Modiano calls him Doctor Louis-Ferdinand Bardamu, echoing Céline's title and first names. The first pages of the novel are a parody of the anti-Semitic tracts Céline wrote and published.

6   **Stay strong, Madelon:** a reference to the popular French WWI song 'La Madelon' (aka 'Quand Madelon') about an innkeeper's daughter who flirts with everyone but sleeps with no one.

6   **Cahen d'Anvers:** Louis Raphaël Cahen d'Anvers (1837–1922), French banker, scion of two wealthy Jewish banking families.

7   **I was compared to Barnabooth:** a reference to the title character in Valery Larbaud's novel *The Diary of A.O. Barnabooth* whose story mirrors that of our hero's 'Venezuelan inheritance'.

8   **'Laversine' … 'Porfirio Rubirosa':** all references to the polo. Porfirio Rubirosa was a famous Dominican polo player; Cibao-La Pampa, the team he founded; the Coupe Laversine is a celebrated tournament; Silver Leys is a polo club in the UK.

8   **three photos taken by Lipnitzki:** Boris Lipnitzky (1887–1971), famous Ukrainian–French photographer.

9   **Jean-François Des Essarts:** the name deliberately echoes that of Jean des Esseintes in Huysmans' novel *À Rebours*. Modiano's character is based on Roger Nimier, the founder of the literary movement 'les Hussards'.

11 **The Finaly Affair:** Robert and Gérald Finally, two Jewish children born in Vichy France, were taken in by a member of the Catholic network when their parents were arrested. After the war, the woman refused to return the orphaned children, whose parents had died in the camps and illicitly had the children baptised in 1948. A national scandal ensued, which involved Cardinal Pierre-Marie Gerlier and Abbé Roger

Etchegaray. The children were finally reunited with Jewish relatives in Israel in 1953.

11 *francisques*: 'double-bladed fasces' – the fascist emblem of the Vichy regime.

11 **PPF:** Parti Populaire Française, a French fascist and Nazi political party led by Jacques Doriot before and during the Second World War.

12 **'Saint Jacob X: Actor and Martyr':** a reference to Jean-Paul Sartre's *Saint Genet, Actor and Martyr*.

12 **'La Casquette du père Bugeaud':** a French military song.

13 **Maurice Sachs (1906–45):** (born Maurice Ettinghausen) French writer. The son of a Jewish family of jewellers, he converted to Catholicism in 1925. During the war, he extorted money from Jews to help them flee the Unoccupied Zone and may have been a Gestapo informer. He was later imprisoned and died during the long march from Fuhlsbüttel prison in 1945.

13 **Lola Montès:** the title of a Max Ophüls film which was based loosely on the life of the nineteenth-century dancer Lola Montez.

13 **Le Boeuf sur le Toit:** a famous Parisian nightclub.

14 **Drieu la Rochelle (1893–1945):** French novelist and essayist, la Rochelle was a leading proponent of French fascism in the 1930s, and a collaborationist during the Nazi occupation. After the liberation of Paris in 1944, he went into hiding and committed suicide later that year.

14 **Night and fog:** a reference to *Nuit et Brouillard*, the 1955 French holocaust documentary by Alain Resnais.

15 **Brasillach:** Robert Brasillach (1909–45), French journalist and editor of the fascist newspaper *Je suis partout*. He was executed as a collaborator in 1945.

16 **Hitler Youth Quex:** a 1932 Nazi propaganda novel (*Hitlerjunge Quex*) based on the life of Herbert 'Quex' Norkus.

16 **André Bellessort (1866–1942):** French writer and poet.

17 **This, then, was our youth … regained:** a quote from Claude Jamet's memoir of Brasillach before the war.

17 **Julien Benda: (1867–1956):** French philosopher and novelist, author of *The Betrayal of the Intellectuals*.

17 **Maurras:** Charles Maurras (1868–1952), a French author and poet, he was the principal thinker behind *Action Française*, a supporter of Vichy, he was arrested and sentenced to life imprisonment.

17 *Je suis partout:* (*I am everywhere*) a right wing anti-Semitic French newspaper founded by Jean Fayard in 1930. It supported the Nazis during the occupation and, during the war, was edited by Robert Brasillach.

17 **P.-A. Cousteau:** Pierre-Antoine Cousteau (1906–58), French far right journalist and contributor to *Je suis partout*.

18 **Pujo:** Maurice Pujo (1872–1955), French journalist and co-founder of the *Comité d'Action Française* which later became *Action française*.

18 **Maxime Real del Sarte (1888–1954):** French sculptor and political activist involved with the right-wing *Action française*.

18 **Jean Luchaire (1901–46):** French journalist and politician, later head of the French collaborationist press during the Nazi occupation. He was executed for collaborationism in 1946.

18 **Carlingue:** the informal name for the French Gestapo, which was headquartered on the Rue Lauriston.

18 **Brinon:** Fernand de Brinon (1884–1947), French lawyer and journalist, he was among the principal architects of French collaboration with the Nazis. He was found guilty of war crimes in 1947 and executed.

18 **Abetz:** Otto Abetz (1903–58), the German ambassador to Vichy France during the Second World War.

18 **General Commissariat for Jewish Affairs:** *Commissariat général aux questions juive*, the administrative committee tasked with enforcing the anti-Semitic policies of the Vichy Government.

18 **Stülpnagel:** Otto von Stülpnagel (1878–1948), head of the occupied forces and military governor of Paris. He committed suicide while awaiting trial after the war.

18 **Doriot:** Jacques Doriot (1898–1945), Communist turned fascist who, with Marcel Déat, founded the *Légion des Volontaires Français*.

18 **Déat:** Marcel Déat (1894–1955), founder of the *Rassemblement national populaire* (National Popular Rally), a political party in the Vichy Government; later appointed Minister of Labour and National Solidarity.

18 **Jo Darnand:** Joseph Darnand (1897–1945), a decorated French soldier during the First World War, Darnand went on to become a leading collaborator during the Second World War, founding the collaborationist militia *Service d'ordre legionnaire*, which later became the *Milice*.

18 **Franc-Garde:** armed wing of the *Milice*. In 1943–44, it fought alongside the German army against the *Maquis*.

20 **... beautiful lines by Spire:** André Spire (1868–1966), French poet, and writer.

25 **L'Aiglon:** Napoleon II 'the Eaglet' who died aged twenty-one.

25 **Süss the Jew:** the eponymous character in the 1940 Nazi propaganda film *Jud Süß* commissioned by Joseph Goebbels.

26 **The 'Horst-Wessel-Lied':** song penned by Horst Wessel in 1929, usually known as 'Die Fahne hoch' ('The Flag on High'), it was adopted as the Nazi Party anthem in 1930.

26 **Colonel de la Rocque:** François de La Rocque (1885–1946), leader of the French right-wing *Croix de Feu* during the 1930s and later the French nationalist *Parti Social Français*.

28 **Brocéliande:** in French literature, a mythical forest said to be the last resting place of Merlin the magician.

29 **Tante Léonie:** character in Proust's *In Search Of Lost Time* at whose house Marcel stays in Combray.

29 **Maurice Dekobra (1885–1973):** French writer of adventure novels.

29 **Stavinsky:** Alexandre Stavinsky (1888–1934), French 'financier' with considerable influence among government ministers and bankers. After his death in 1934, it was discovered that he had embezzled 200 million francs from the Crédit municipal de Bayonne, a scandal which rocked the French government.

29 **Novarro:** Ramón Novarro (1899–1968), Mexican actor, one of the great stars of the silent cinema.

29 **the anti-Jewish exhibition at the Palais Berlitz:** *Le Juif et la France*, a notorious anti-Semitic propaganda exhibition staged in Paris during the Nazi occupation.

30 *Bagatelles pour un massacre*: title of a collection of virulently anti-Semitic essays by Louis-Ferdinand Céline, translated as *Trifles for a Massacre*.

32 **Rue d'Ulm! Rue d'Ulm!:** the address of the prestigious École Normale Supérieure.

32 **Jallez and Jephanion:** the writer Jallez and the politician Jerphanion are the inseparable friends in Jules Romain's novel *Les Hommes de bonne volonté* (*The Men of Good Will*).

34 **to join the LVF:** *Légion des volontaires français (contre le bolchévisme)*, the Legion of French Volunteers (Against Bolshevism), a collaborationist French militia founded on July 8, 1941.

34 **Rastignac:** a character in Balzac's *La Comédie humaine*, Eugène de Rastignac is portrayed as a naïve but fervent social climber – he went by the name 'Rastignac de la butte Montmartre'.

35 **... to quote Péguy:** Charles Péguy (1873–1914) French poet and essayist, he coined the phrase 'les hussards noirs' in 1913 to refer to his teachers.

35 **He insisted that ... to notice him:** parodying the phrase 'if the Jew did not exist, the anti-Semite would invent him' in Sartre's *Anti-Semite and Jew*.

39 **my old friend Seingalt:** Casanova, who signed his *Memoirs* (as he did many other works) Jacques Casanova de Seingalt.

41 **Paul Chack (1876–1945):** French Naval officer and collaborationist writer.

41 **Monsignor Mayol de Lupé (1873–1955):** Catholic priest who served as chaplain for the *Légion des volontaires français* and later for the SS.

41 **Henri Béraud (1885–1958):** French novelist and journalist. Virulently Anglophobic and anti-Semitic, he supported the Vichy Government. After the liberation, he was sentenced to death for collaboration. The sentence was later commuted to life imprisonment.

41 **... attack on Mers-el-Kébir:** as a direct response to the signing of the French–German armistice, the British Navy bombarded the French Navy off the coast of Algeria in July 1940, resulting in the deaths of 1,297 French servicemen.

41 **'Maréchal, nous voilà':** a French song pledging loyalty to Maréchal Pétain.

42 *Romanciers du terroir*: a group of turn-of-the-century French novelists best known for their realistic depiction of rural life.

43 **Mistral:** Frédéric Mistral (1830–1914), French novelist awarded the Nobel Prize for Literature in 1904.

43 **Bichelonne:** Jean Bichelonne (1904–44), French businessman and civil servant, later head of the *Office central de repartition des produits industriels* in the Vichy government.

43 **Hérold-Paquis:** Jean Auguste Hérold aka Jean Hérold-Paquis (1912–45), a French journalist who fought for Franco during the Spanish Civil War and was later appointed Delegate for Propaganda to the Hautes-Alpes region by the Vichy Government. Executed for treason in 1945.

43 **admirals Esteva, Darlan and Platón:** three admirals who served in the Vichy regime.

45 **Joseph de Maistre (1753–1821):** Joseph-Marie, Comte de Maistre, philosopher and writer who famously defended the monarchy after the French Revolution.

49 **Maurice Barrès (1861–1923):** French symbolist writer, politician who popularised the notion of ethnic nationalism in France. An influential anti-Semite, he broke with the left wing to become a leading anti-Dreyfusard, writing: 'That Dreyfus is guilty, I deduce not from the facts themselves, but from his race'.

50 **Charles Martel (68?–741):** Frankish military leader who defeated Abdul Rahman's son, halting the advance of the Islamic caliphate circa 736.

50 **fleurs-de-lis on a field Azure:** the heraldic arms of 'France Ancienne'.

51 **I was secretary to Joanovici:** Joseph Joanovici (1905–65), a French Jewish iron supplier, who supplied both Nazi Germany and the French Resistance. After the war, he was found guilty of collaboration and sentenced to prison. In 1958 he escaped from France to Israel but was refused the right to request to naturalize and returned to France. He was released in 1962.

52 **Frison-Roche:** Roger Frison-Roche (1906–99) French mountaineer, explorer and novelist.

52 **Bordeaux:** Henry Bordeaux (1870–1963), French lawyer, essayist and writer. His novels reflect the values of traditional provincial Catholic communities.

54 **Capitaine Danrit:** penname of Émile Driant, (1855–1916), French writer, politician, and a decorated army officer. He died at the Battle of Verdun during the First World War.

57 **Édouard Drumont (1844–1917):** French journalist and writer who founded the Antisemitic League of France in 1889. He later founded and edited the French anti-Semitic political newspaper *La Libre Parole*.

58 **Each man in his darkness goes towards his Light:** a quotation from *Les Contemplations* by Victor Hugo.

61 **a new 'Curé d'Ars':** a reference to Saint John Vianney, a French parish priest, known as the Curé d'Ars.

61 *My heart, smile towards the future now* ...: from the poem 'La dure épreuve va finir' by Paul Verlaine

61 *The fireside, the lamplight's slender beam*: from the poem 'Le foyer, la lueur étroite de la lampe' by Paul Verlaine.

62 *furia francese*: the 'French fury' – attributed to the French by the Italians at the Battle of Fornovo.

64 **Giraudoux's girls love to travel:** Jean Giraudoux (1882–1944), French novelist, essayist, diplomat and playwright.

64 **Charles d'Orléans (1691–1744):** eighteenth-century French man of letters.

64 **Maurice Scève (c. 1501–64):** French Renaissance poet much obsessed with spiritual love.

64 **Rémy Belleau (1528–77):** sixteenth-century French poet known for his paradoxical poems of praise for simple things.

67 **even a thousand Jews ... Body of Our Lord:** an oblique reference to the line in Proust's *Sodom and Gomorrah*: 'A strange Jew who boiled the Host'.

68 **They strolled together ... spring waters:** alluding to a *Swann's Way*, the first volume of Proust's *In Search of Lost Time* where the narrator dreams that Mme de Guermantes will show him the grounds of her house.

68 **'The energy and charm ... eyes of rabbits':** paraphrasing a passage from Proust's *The Guermantes Way*.

68 *The Embarkation of Eleanor of Aquitaine for the Orient*: an allusion to Claude Lorrain's 1648 painting *The Embarkation of the Queen of Sheba*.

69 *The Fougeire-Jusquiames Way*: alluding to *Swann's Way* by Marcel Proust. The passage that Modiano follows offers a variation on the Proustian bedtime scenes of Combray.

69 **the Princesse des Ursins:** Marie Anne de La Trémoille, a lady at the Spanish Court during the reign of Philip V.

69 **Mlle de la Vallière:** Louise de La Vallière (1644–1710), mistress of Louis XIV.

69 **Mme Soubise:** Anne de Rohan-Chabot, a mistress of Louis XIV.

69 *La Belle aux cheveux d'or*: a story by Countess d'Aulnoy usually translated as *The Story of Pretty Goldilocks* or *The Beauty with Golden Hair*.

70 **'It was, this "Fougeire-Jusquiames," ... with heraldic details':** paraphrasing *The Guermantes Way* by Marcel Proust.

71 **Arno Breker (1900–91):** German sculptor, whose public works in Nazi Germany were praised as expressions of the 'mighty momentum and will power' ('Wucht und Willenhaftigkeit').

72 **The still pale moonlight, sad and fair:** from the poem 'Clair de Lune' by Paul Verlaine.

74 **Perhaps too, in these last days ... anti-Semitic propaganda had revived:** a quote from *Sodom and Gomorrah* by Marcel Proust.

75 **The Jew is the substance of God ... only a mare:** a parody of the nineteenth-century anti-Semitic text *Der Talmud Jüde*, by August Rohling, a professor at the German University of Prague.

77 **'Hitlerleute':** 'Hitler's people' – a fascist song using the same tunes as the official hymn of the Italian National Fascist Party.

78 **Baldur von Schirach (1907–74):** Nazi youth leader later convicted of crimes against humanity.

79 **Marizibill:** title of a poem by Guillaume Apollinaire about a prostitute in Cologne and her Jewish pimp.

81 **Zarah Leander (1907–81):** Swedish singer and actress whose greatest success was in Germany during the 1930s and 1940s.

81 **Skorzeny:** Otto Skorzeny (1908–75), served as SS-Standartenführer in the German Waffen-SS during the Second World War.

85 **the phosphorus of Hamburg:** the allied bombs dropped on Hamburg during the Second World War contained phosphorus.

86 **'Einheitsfrontlied':** 'The United Front Song', (by Bertolt Brecht and Hanns Eisler), one of the best-known songs of the German workers' movement.

86 **the anthem of the Thälmann-Kolonne:** the anti-fascist song, 'Die Thälmann-Kolonne', also known as 'Spaniens Himmel' ('Spanish skies'), was a communist anthem.

87 **Julius Streicher (1885–1946):** a prominent Nazi, the founder and publisher of the newspaper *Der Stürmer*. In 1946 he was convicted of crimes against humanity and executed.

87 **the traitorous Prince Laval:** Pierre Laval (1883–1945), prime minister of France during the Third Republic, later a member of the Vichy government. After the liberation he was convicted of high treason and executed.

89 **'I will not be home tonight … black and white':** alluding to the suicide note left by Gérard de Nerval for his aunt. 'Ne m'attends pas ce soir car la nuit sera noire et blanche.'

91 **Say, what have you done … with your youth?:** the last line of the poem 'Le Ciel est, par-dessus le toit' by Paul Verlaine.

94 **the roundup on 16 July 1942:** The Vel' d'Hiv Roundup was a Nazi ordered mass arrest of Parisian Jews by the French police.

97 **Émilienne d'Alençon (1869–1946):** French dancer and actress. She was famously a courtesan, and the lover of, among others, Leopold II of Belgium.

99 **'When I hear the word culture, I reach for my truncheon':** alluding to the line 'when I hear the word culture, I reach for my gun' often attributed to Hermann Göring. In fact, the line originally appears in Hanns Johst's play *Schlageter*: 'Whenever I hear the word Culture… I release the safety catch of my Browning!'

107 **'Du bist der Lenz nachdem ich verlangte':** 'You are the spring for which I longed' – Sieglinda's aria from Richard Wagner's opera *Die Walküre*.

108 **Radio Londres:** a BBC broadcast in French to occupied France during the Second World War.

114 *Moi, j'aime le music-hall … danseuses légères*: 'Moi j'aime le music hall' by Charles Trenet.

A NOTE ON THE AUTHOR

Patrick Modiano was born in Paris in 1945 in the immediate aftermath of World War Two and the Nazi occupation of France, a dark period which continues to haunt him. After passing his baccalauréat, he left fulltime education and dedicated himself to writing, encouraged by the French writer Raymond Queneau. From his very first book to his most recent, Modiano has pursued a quest for identity and some form of reconciliation with the past. His books have been published in forty languages and among the many prizes they have won are the Grand Prix du Roman de l'Académie française (1972), the Prix Goncourt (1978) and the Austrian State Prize for European Literature (2012). In 2014 he was awarded the Nobel Prize in Literature.

A NOTE ON THE TRANSLATOR

Frank Wynne has won three major prizes for his translations from the French, including the 2002 IMPAC for *Atomised* by Michel Houellebecq and the 2005 Independent Foreign Fiction Prize for *Windows on the World* by Frederic Beigbeder. He is also the translator from the Spanish of Tomás Eloy Martínez's *Purgatory*, Miguel Figueras's *Kamchatka* and Carlos Acosta's *Pig's Foot*. In 2014 he was awarded the Valle Inclán Prize for his translation of Alonso Cueto's *The Blue Hour*.

A NOTE ON THE TYPE

The text of this book is set in Fournier. Fournier is derived from the *romain du roi*, which was created towards the end of the seventeenth century from designs made by a committee of the Académie of Sciences for the exclusive use of the Imprimerie Royale. The original Fournier types were cut by the famous Paris founder Pierre Simon Fournier in about 1742. These types were some of the most influential designs of the eight and are counted among the earliest examples of the 'transitional' style of typeface. This Monotype version dates from 1924. Fournier is a light, clear face whose distinctive features are capital letters that are quite tall and bold in relation to the lower-case letters, and *decorative italics, which show the influence of the calligraphy of Fournier's time.*